DUBIOUS

A DARK MMM AGE GAP ROMANCE

BELLE ARGO ESCORTS
BOOK FOUR

BETH CHRISTOPHER

ISBN: 978-1-969810-21-3

This book was written by a human, one with a super twisted brain, but a human nonetheless.

Editing by Sydney Feron at Just Spicy Romance Edits

Proofreading by Lea Vickery PA and by Kate Wood Proofreading

Cover design by Babski Creative Studios

For questions/comments or to report typos, please contact bethchristopher romance@gmail.com

042026

About Dubious

AND CONTENT WARNING

A divorcé and two male escorts walk into a luxury hotel...

Wes

My life is falling apart.

At forty-two, my wife left me, my brother barely tolerates me, and my boss is sleeping with my ex.

On top of everything else, employees at the hotel I work for seem to be disappearing.

I don't know how much longer I can live like this.

A lifeline comes from the most unexpected place. Two of my brother's friends. Male escorts. I should stay away, but I don't.

To be honest, I thought I was straight. But they make me...feel things. Amazing things. Terrifying things.

Then disaster strikes. The three of us find ourselves involved in a situation I never imagined.

After, I'm not the same. And they're the only ones who understand.

Adam and Troy

Since our childhood, we have been each other's ride or die.

We helped each other run away from dangerous homes. Kept each other alive.

Lately there's something missing. Or maybe that's some*one*.

When we first meet Wes, we're only messing with him for fun.

Then the three of us need each other.

Which is when we realize.

He's the something we've been missing.

Dubious is a dark MMM late bi awakening, kink awakening, age gap romance. It contains a down on his luck divorcé, two chaos gremlins who teach him how to have fun, and a potentially haunted Bed and Breakfast.

***Possible triggers include:* on-page abduction, trauma bonding, patricide, homophobic slurs, consensual non con play, murder, a hero grappling with liking stuff he "shouldn't," and of course some dubious stuff**

Tropes: trauma bonding, queer awakening, throuple, age gap, enemies to lovers, dude in distress, forced proximity, power dynamics, repressed desires, strategic seduction, unhinged hero vs "innocent" hero, kink awakening, troubled pasts, found family, consensual non-monogamy

To everyone who's hung with this series and loved it, especially the ones shouting "Bring on the red flags!" in my DMs.

To anyone who's felt shame for wanting something they shouldn't.

To AJ Rose and Lee Savino for cheerleading this series idea when I first shared it.

And to my dog who looks at me like I'm the best person on earth no matter what the reviews say. <3

MUSICAL INSPIRATION

If you're like me and enjoy pairing your reading with music, the following songs helped to inspire Dubious:

- “Sleep” (Max Graham Remix) by Conjure One
- “Wanna Be Yours” by Arctic Monkeys
- “Run to the Water” by Live
- “Bite Into Desire” by Raster Dust
- “Seven” by Taylor Swift

NEWSLETTER

Want to keep in touch? Sign up for my newsletter to stay in the loop about future releases.
https://sendfox.com/BethChristopher

Want exclusive early access to upcoming releases? Check out https://www.patreon.com/cw/BethChristopherRomance

PROLOGUE

Prologue – Adam – 6 years ago

"It's bad this time." Troy's voice shakes. He's breathing in heavy pants through the phone. "He's getting worse." He sounds like he's been running.

From his dad.

When the anniversary of Troy's mom's death rolls around, his father changes from a regular abusive dick into a fucking nightmare.

"Can you get out of there? I'll come pick you up." I drop my backpack on the bed.

My camping stuff is already in the car. My diabetes kit is in my backpack along with water, snacks, and a change of clothes. I hate how it slows me down. If I hadn't had to get all this together I'd be out the door already.

I'm almost ready though. Soon as I grab my toothbrush.

"He took my car keys." There's thumping in the background on Troy's end. Is that yelling? "But if you can get here, I can try to get past him. Maybe he'll be passed out by then."

I zip my backpack closed. "What's that noise?"

"He's throwing shit again. Don't worry; I'm locked in my room. As soon as he passes out, I'll be able to leave."

I make a circle around my room. What am I forgetting?

My gaze lands on the pencil case sitting on my desk. I unzip it, check to make sure the emergency cash I've been saving is still inside, and then I shove it in my pack with everything else. Even though I'm the forgotten bastard, every once in a while my father decides to take an interest in my life. I don't trust him not to come in here and snoop while I'm gone.

"Hang tight," I tell Troy. "Soon as my father leaves to check his warehouses, I'll come and get you. We'll head to the campground, and we'll have a whole weekend of not dealing with our dads."

"Yeah." He's quiet for a minute. "Can't fucking wait until we can get out of here for good."

"One more year," I say.

"Two more."

"Troy." I go still. Are those footsteps I'm hearing out in the hall? "One year. When you go, I go."

"You leave before you're eighteen, your dad will report you missing, and you'll be back home in no time. Mine's threatened to do the same thing. As it is, we'll still have to worry about him sending his goons after you. We need to ride it out until it's safer for you."

We've already talked this to death. "You're not staying a day longer than necessary. You can't."

Yep, those are definitely footsteps. Not the quiet and unassuming steps of one of the staff, who are probably gone for the day anyway. Not my brother's quick thumps. These are a heavy thud, every other one followed by a quick scuffing noise, as if an old injury is affecting the smoothness of the person's gait.

My father is coming. "We'll talk about it this weekend," I say quietly. "We'll make a plan."

"Yeah. Definitely." But in spite of his words, Troy sounds so unsure.

The knob turns. "Gotta go."

If Troy replies, I don't hear him. I end the call and drop the phone into my backpack as the door opens. Last thing I need is my father asking who I'm talking to.

"Did I hear you talking to someone?" My father narrows his eyes.

"M-myself." Dammit. *Do not show weakness.* "It helps me think. Mr. Reynolds at school says I'm a verbal processor."

"So much bullshit they're teaching in school these days. It's past time to see about getting you transferred to St. Mark's Academy. Should've done it a long time ago. The nuns will straighten you out."

No. Absolutely not. If he moves me out of public school, I'll hardly ever see my best friend. My only friend.

"You said it was a waste of money."

What he actually said was that *I* wasn't worth the money. Which is fine. There are plenty of times when my father's lack of interest in me is to my benefit. This is one of them.

"You're sixteen, Adam. It's time to grow up. Time to stop spending time with that pansy-ass Ackerman kid. To prove yourself. Speaking of which, I need you to come with me."

"Uhm." Arguing with my father is a tricky thing. As in,

he's shot people for less. Still, I don't like how he's talking about me staying away from Troy.

"I'm getting ready to leave. I've got a study group." I indicate my backpack on the bed, hoping he doesn't notice it's way too stuffed to only contain books.

If I tell him I'm going camping with Troy, he won't let me leave. Our dads have some sort of business-related beef, and he never did like us hanging out. His dislike of Troy has only gotten worse lately.

"On a Friday night?"

"End-of-semester exams are coming up. They're worth a high percentage of our grade. It's important."

"This is more important."

He leads me down the polished stairs, through the marble entryway, and around to the kitchen. A small Christmas tree perches on the counter, most likely put there by the chef who cooks for us five days a week. My father has a general distaste for holiday decor, but he also doesn't come in here much.

"Where are we going?"

He doesn't answer, instead pushing open the windowed French doors that lead to the back terrace and heading across the grass through the yard. The *crunch* and *swish* of each of his steps echoes loudly in the quiet evening.

My breath puffs in front of me as I walk.

It's rare to see temperatures this cold in Miami. In history class our teacher mentioned we were seeing near-record lows. My khakis and threadbare T-shirt aren't made for this weather.

"If I'd known you wanted me to come outside, I would've grabbed my jacket."

"We're going to have to do something about all your sensitivity, Adam."

"I'm adjusted to the usual climate here. It's biology."

"You won't freeze walking across the yard, so shut that smart mouth of yours."

It's funny how him calling me smart is never a compliment.

We're heading for a large garage at the back of the property. The one where he keeps his boat. And where I'm usually told to stay the hell out of. "What are we doing out here?"

He steps inside and flips on the light. The smell hits me first; musty and moldy. Something nauseatingly coppery crawls down my throat and into my stomach. The boat is gone. In its place is a man who's been tied to the large racks where cleaning supplies and equipment are kept.

He's bleeding.

"What's going on?" I look around before turning to my father. "Where's Santi?"

My older brother usually handles situations like this alongside my father. He's the "real" son, after all.

"Your brother's handling something for me out of town." He gestures to the man. As if a switch has been flipped, the man goes from silent and wide-eyed to babbling.

"Sir, I'm sorry. I'm so sorry. She didn't do anything wrong, though. You don't want to make a name for killing innocent people, do you? That's not—I was protecting your interests."

"You were making a mess," my father replies. "I don't tolerate messes. I don't tolerate weakness."

I'm not sure what's going on here. Not entirely. Is this

guy one of my father's employees? Guess he didn't do whatever he was supposed to.

"She was innocent. You can't call me weak because I won't kill an innocent woman."

I'm too busy trying to keep my nerves under control to wonder who "she" is. Smart or not, I can tell where this is going. My stomach lurches.

"I gave you an order. One you didn't follow. That means I can no longer trust you." He pulls out a gun.

Wait. "You're going to kill him?"

Here? Now? He never involves me in this stuff.

"No." My father holds the gun out. "You are."

Already freezing, my body goes numb. "I—I can't." No. No, he won't accept me saying I can't. "I've never fired a gun."

"Point and pull the trigger. It's close range. You hardly need to aim. Even you can't mess this up. Just don't do it point blank. Might get his brain on your hands."

Jesus.

The man begs me with his eyes. We both know I don't want to kill him. We both know I won't have a choice.

I try to raise the gun, but my hand shakes. "Why are you making me do this?"

"Come on, Adam, you've got straight A's, and you can't figure this out? Trial by fire. Sink or swim."

"Why me? Why now?"

"You're old enough now to contribute to the business."

Okay. Now I get it. The "and if you don't, you're no use to me" is implied.

"Shoot him. Now."

The numbness has spread to my hands. My fingers. I can't make them tighten.

"Goddammit. You see? This is what happens when you spend too much time with that fag kid from school."

"Troy's not—"

My father huffs impatiently and grabs my wrist with a gloved hand. The one holding the gun. He raises it to aim at the man tied to the storage racks, puts his hand over mine, and squeezes the trigger.

The man slumps forward, unmoving.

"There," Father says calmly. "Not so difficult, was it?" He lets go and grabs some painting tarps from a different shelf.

Dizziness washes over me. My gaze keeps straying back to the man in front of me. A neat hole in the center of his forehead, blood oozing into his face. Sightless eyes looking at the floor.

There's a heavy hammering in my ears. It might be my pulse. Or the sound of a trap about to close on me.

"*Yes, it was fucking difficult,*" I want to yell. I don't think I'll ever get this out of my head. Instead I say nothing, because I don't want to be the next one my father shoots. I'm not stupid enough to think he cares for me as anything but another person he can control.

"Clean this up." He tosses the pile of cloth at me. "At least you can do that much."

You'd think so, wouldn't you? I'm still frozen. Still holding the damn gun. I can't even make my fingers let go.

"Adam." His sharp tone echoes around us, bringing me out of my fog. "Give me the damn gun before you shoot yourself with it."

Oh. Right. It's pointed practically at my feet. I lift it a little, still shaking.

"Jesus, I really am going to have to knock some sense into you. You're not even holding it right."

He pulls a handkerchief from his pocket, reaching out with the cloth spread over his fingers. "Come on. Hand it over."

Even though I haven't been involved much in my father's business, even though I'm barely able to calculate the gravity of what's just happened, something clicks when I see the cloth in his hand.

Somewhere in my head, a siren screams.

My father is wearing gloves. He's using the cloth to grip the muzzle of the gun.

His fingerprints won't be on this thing. Only mine.

He's done this before. I've overheard the threats spoken in low tones behind the door of his office. *Your prints are on the weapon now. If you want it back, you'll have to cooperate.*

I'm not my brother. My father didn't raise me to work alongside him. I was the maid's kid, and she fled town the second I was born. He sees me as weak—he always has. Even if I cooperate, how long before my father decides I'm too much trouble and I wind up like that man tied to the storage racks?

He's already threatening to take Troy away. Which can't happen. It can't.

My murmured "fuck you" sounds as if it's coming from someone else.

"I'm going to pretend I didn't hear that. Next time it's coming out of your fucking hide."

Fuck you. Fuck you, you fucking son of a bitch. Fuck you and your power-drunk controlling bullshit. Everything I've done to apologize for not being the son he wants, to stay off his radar, it's never been enough. It never will be.

The epiphany makes me lightheaded.

There's a tug on the gun. "Adam. Let go."

But I don't. I don't let go. I take a breath.

Finally, I'm able to squeeze the trigger.

The crack of the shot echoes, breaking my world open. The jerk of his body, still holding the muzzle, pulls me forward. But I hang on. Even when my ears ring and the recoil makes my arm feel like a noodle.

There's shock on his face as I squeeze the trigger again. And again. And I keep squeezing.

Until there are none left.

Until my father is nothing but a bloody heap on the floor.

My shaking hands feel heavy and dull, like they're not my own. Fuck.

What the fuck have I done?

Why didn't I see this coming? I should have known one day he'd turn me into a monster.

Get out of here.

Thanks to my father's paranoia even with his own staff, the only security we have here at night is the guy manning the front gate. Still, someone could have heard the shots. I use that stupid handkerchief to wipe off the gun. Wipe off my hands. Then I stuff it in my pocket, and I run.

I'm gasping from exertion by the time I get to my room, trying to catch my breath but trying to do it silently. The house is empty, I think. The staff is usually gone by now. But I don't *know*. I don't know anything right now, except that I have to go.

Until I'm in my car I don't take a full breath. With shaking hands, I dial Troy's number. The air rushing in and out of my lungs is too loud and choppy.

Troy answers on the first ring. "What's wrong?"

"My dad's dead," I tell him. "We have to go. Now. Tonight."

There's a long silence before he answers. "We don't have enough money saved."

Not nearly. None of this is what we planned. "We'll figure something out. Get your stuff. I'm on my way."

Then I hang up, and I hit the gas.

Wes – A few months ago

Faculty mixers are boring as hell. But the good part? Free drinks, free food.

Given the state of my finances right now, I need all the free shit I can get.

It's a brunch thing, but there's an open bar. Usually, I take my health too seriously to drink. When I've spent the morning fielding divorce demands from my ex, though? Let's say I've had a few too many vodka and sodas.

Gina: You make more than I do, Wes. It makes sense for you to keep covering the mortgage for the time being.

Wes: I make more because I'm working two jobs. You can't expect me to pay for a house I'm not living in.

As divorces go, mine has been pretty amicable. But the money stuff? With student loans, attorney fees, and bend-over-and-grab-your-ankles fees, I'm already stretched thin.

Gina: At least give me some time to figure out how I'm going to pay for it myself. Please?

We both know I'm going to give it to her. I always do. Dammit.

My wife and I have spent the better part of our marriage unhappy, and we both know that's mostly on me. For not being able to give Gina what she needed, for not trying enough. For not *being* enough.

What I keep wondering is, when am I going to be done making amends? How will I be able to fix things when my money runs out?

One thing at a time, though, because through my lightweight vodka haze and the ambient sounds of clinking utensils and old men congratulating themselves, I'm pretty sure my brother just told me he's about to flush his career down the toilet.

"Why the fuck would you go and do that? You said this job fucking saved you after Marina died."

Fallon lost his wife in a tragic accident a little over year ago. Never really got along with her, but I've had a ringside view of his grief. I wouldn't wish it on anyone. Now, he's in a relationship again with a damn college student. Wanting to quit his job.

He's talking about how his new boyfriend, PJ, has brought the spark back to his life. That in the contest between the job and PJ, he's choosing PJ. It's romantic. Sweet, even.

The trouble? I'm convinced PJ is scamming my brother. From what I can tell, the kid's flat broke. Also, he's a sex worker. I know, because I'm the one who hired PJ to go on a date with Fallon. I wanted to get my brother out of his funk. Get him to have a little fun.

Not...all of this.

"You know that kid is broke as fuck, right? He probably saw that sweet-ass beach house you live in and got dollar signs in his eyes. Probably thought he won the sugar daddy sweepstakes."

Speaking as someone who is also broke as fuck, I know desperation when I see it.

"We've been over this, Wes. You're insulting literally all of us right now—me the most. You're the one who wanted me to get out and start dating again. Now that I have, you want me to be alone again? You're the one who set us up. I don't care that you didn't know him that well. I like him, and I'm happy."

My empty drink cup crumples in my fist. The cracked plastic pinches my fingers. I'm so stunned by my brother's words I hardly notice.

"Look," Fallon continues, "I can't thank you enough for your support after Marina died. I needed it. I'm grateful. It's also time to get the hell out of my personal life. I've been staying at PJ's place recently, and we've gotten a lot closer. I'm not lonely and angry anymore. I've got a puppy to take care of. I appreciate that you helped me get this job, but I don't need it like I used to. If someone finds out about our relationship, I'll be fired. PJ could get expelled. There's too damn much at stake."

He runs a hand through his hair. "It's better to come clean now. Between PJ and the job, I'm choosing him."

"Fallon."

My brother's face gets red. "It's my decision. I know you don't trust him; I know you think he's too young. You didn't like Marina because you thought she was too controlling. Except I told you over and over that the control was something I consented to. So I don't expect you to understand my relationship with PJ, either. Lucky for you, you're not the one dating him."

He's right, I don't understand. Fallon and I both married women who weren't happy if they didn't get their way. Every passing year of my marriage, I felt myself disappear.

I heard how his late wife spoke to him. How his too-young boyfriend speaks to him. How could anyone be happy being treated that way?

"Fallon, wait." As he tries to leave, I catch him by the arm. "Don't do it, okay? Don't."

Even though I practically raised him, Fallon and I rarely fight. What I'm about to say might make him hate me, but I have to stop him before he makes a huge mistake.

My little brother deserves better.

"Wes. Stop. Were you not listening to everything I just said, or were you still distracted by that dead fly in your drink?"

What? Oh. Right. The dead fly that made me flinch and toss my drink all over Fallon. Given the sloshy way my stomach feels, it's for the best.

"I know, I know. But..." God, I really don't want to have to do this. I'm not proud of what I did, okay? I was *trying* to help.

"Okay, you know what? Tell me later." Fallon turns to walk away.

"He's a whore," I blurt out, way too loudly. "Did you know that? He bones other guys for money."

There. *There.* I said it.

Fallon doesn't seem as shocked as I expected. "Don't call him that. I know he's an escort. He told me. He takes lonely people to weddings and charity events and sometimes, in the case of a guy who says he has trouble dating because of his busy career, out for coffee and bagels one morning a week. He doesn't have sex with any of them."

"Y-you actually believe that?" There's no way it's true.

"Yes, Wes. I believe him. What's the alternative, spending the rest of my life not trusting anybody? If I think he's cheating on me, then I'll talk to him about that. Him, who I'm in a relationship with, not my interfering older brother who's manufacturing reasons to break us up."

"I'm not manufacturing shit, Fallon. He's lying." I suck in a breath, unable to hold back the final blow. "I know he's lying because he got paid to have sex with you."

Fallon freezes. The guy who was hell-bent on storming over to the dean to hand in his resignation a few minutes ago is now eerily silent. Shit, he's going to hate me.

I already hate myself, so I guess it's fine.

"What the hell do you mean he got paid to have sex with me?"

A waiter drops a bin of beer and ice with a loud crash, causing me to flinch. My chest is tight, and I'm already wishing I could take back what I said.

No, what I did.

"What the fuck are you talking about?" Fallon asks again.

"I didn't set you up on a blind date," I finally say. Quietly, because we're in a room full of people and I need to get my shit under control. "I called a guy. A pimp. Thought it would do you some good to get laid. It was only supposed to be one night."

Someone drops a fork. For a moment I'm focused on the metal clattering to the polished hardwood. Anything to avoid the way my baby brother is looking at me now.

"What do you mean you called a pimp?"

My collar's too tight. "Elliott, the events coordinator at the hotel, gave me a name and number. He had trouble getting back into the game after his wife died, and he said this nice young woman named Alexis helped him out. I thought..." Fuck me. "I thought it would be good for you. I didn't expect you to bring a damn moving van to your first date with the guy."

Shut up, Wes. The more I try to justify my actions, the worse it sounds. Alcohol has made my lips numb, yet I can't seem to stop running my mouth.

"I didn't—" With a hard swallow, Fallon looks away. "You know what? Fuck you, Wes. I have to go."

My stomach twists. Desperation has me reaching out again, silently begging my brother to stay and let me explain. Except I've already tried and every word from my mouth sounds stupider than the last.

Still, I have to try.

He shakes me off. "Don't. Don't you dare grab my arm again. Don't say another word. You've done enough."

My heart sinks as he storms out of the room. Once again, I've tried to fix a thing and made it worse. I'll be lucky if Fallon doesn't hate me now.

I suppose he can't hate me any more than I hate myself.

Troy – A few weeks ago

It's a spur-of-the-moment decision, like so many of mine are.

Adam and I are on the way back from the gym smoothie bar when this guy comes blowing into the locker room, looking frantic.

Wes.

He looks like the kind of man every boy who secretly jerked it to shirtless pictures of Tom Hardy in high school longs to wrap his legs around. Taller, though. Sharper cheekbones. Sad, tortured-looking blue eyes.

Zero tattoos, but I'd give him a pass for that if I didn't know the guy's actually a massive dick. Why are the hot ones always dicks?

Right now, though, Wes is frazzled and unsure, and damned if I'm not curious about what misfortune might have befallen him. Who wouldn't be?

Before I can wonder too much, my phone buzzes in my hand.

PJ: At the gym. Knocked off work early to meet you guys. Where is everyone? Did something happen with Adam's blood sugar or something? Also, have you seen Wes? Fallon's looking for him.

PJ is a friend and a male escort, like my best friend and me. Or he used to be one, before he fell in love with his client. Said client happens to be the brother of the frantic-looking dick in front of me.

Troy: Just had to handle a little something. We are allllll good. If I see Wes, I'll let you know.

Telling PJ I'm looking right at the guy can wait until Adam and I have had a chance to say hello. Or punch him in the mouth. TBD.

Sliding my phone into my pocket, I'm grinning as Wes strides toward us, clearly lost in thought and not looking where he's going. Oh, yeah. We're handling something, all right.

Among our small but mighty group of male escorts in the seaside town of Belle Argo, Florida, one thing we know how to do is look out for our friends.

Wes here is the reason PJ and Fallon got together. He's also the person who tried hardest to break them up. Some might argue it's not my job to get my friend payback, but I disagree.

Besides, I'm way beyond tired of people thinking we're all expendable and unfeeling because we're paid companions. I'm worn out in general, to be honest. Some days I manage to pull myself out of bed and feel okay in spite of the daily grind, but every day gets harder.

Unfortunately for Wes? Today I'm in the mood to let him walk right into me and see what happens.

Next to me, Adam slides to the side to avoid the collision. I don't.

"Sorry, I—" Wes stumbles back, mouth moving but nothing coming out.

"Hey, it's Brunch Daddy." I'm looking at Wes, but I'm talking to Adam. We've been calling him that since he busted into one of our weekly escort gatherings at a downtown breakfast spot to hassle PJ about dating his brother.

Super original, I know. "How's it going, Westy?"

"It's Wes." He's leaning away. Guarded. Figures. "Just Wes. My mom calls me Westlake. Nobody calls me Westy."

"Oh, yeah, Westham." Adam winks at me, taking a big drink of the smoothie in his hand.

Westy clearly doesn't appreciate that at all.

"I like Westy better," I say to poke the bear.

"It's Wes." The tall drink of water spits each word, jaw clenched so hard he's got a muscle twitching.

Easy as hell to rile, this guy. Fun.

He grips the gym bag in his hands tighter and tries to squeeze past us. Not today, bitch. Today I register the split second when he scans me up and down. The flare of curiosity in his eyes, followed by confusion. The red flush that crawls up his throat.

Today, I'm not in the mood to suffer hypocrites. I'm in the mood to create a little chaos.

"Look, never mind." Wes moves to push past us again. "I'm late meeting Fallon. We're supposed to be working out while his boyfriend is fixing up his little ice cream stand."

Ooh. Judgmental much? Wait until he finds out PJ's here at the gym after all.

"Oh, right," I say. "Is that why you're in a hurry? Don't wanna have to deal with PJ? We've noticed you seem to have a real beef with our friend."

He looks down at where I've got my hand wrapped around his wrist. I didn't realize I had even grabbed him until now. He doesn't pull away though, so I hang on.

"There's no beef."

What a filthy liar.

Every time Wes is around us, he's looking down his nose with some flavor of contempt or judgment. Like simply standing too close to a sex worker might give him an itchy rash.

Fuck this guy.

With a tug of his arm, he pulls out of my grip and heads for the bank of lockers in the back corner of the locker room. It's the farthest from the showers, and the cubbies here look older and more beaten up, so not many people use them.

Wes doesn't seem to notice we've followed him until Adam asks, "You homophobic or something?"

Which makes Wes jump. Heh. Nice.

"Hom—what? No. Of course not. I'm the one who set up PJ and Fallon on their first date. Would I do that if I were homophobic? What I am is control phobic."

His face reddens, every word spilling out faster than the last.

Ah. It's coming together now. Fallon is submissive. Apparently, Wes isn't comfortable with someone bossing his little brother around.

Which I guess is...nice-ish? Sort of. Also fucking ignorant.

"It's just that we remember the day you came storming into our weekly brunch spot looking ready to throw down with PJ." I wave my hand, gesturing between me and Adam.

Our weekly escort brunch is a little bit of connection and normalcy in an ocean of getting paid insane amounts of money so long as we're willing to overlook getting used and tossed out like red cups at a party. Plus, there are mimosas and French toast. It's a good time.

None of us like having our good time fucked with.

The one single time things got ugly? Wes's fault.

"Right," Adam agrees between sips of the green smoothie I bought him. Gotta keep that blood sugar happy. "And then there was the way you lost your shit at Fallon's birthday party last month."

Pretty sure I can smell Wes's brain catching fire. He's actually kind of sexy when he's frustrated. Full lips parted, eyebrows crouched low, clenched fists making those forearm veins pop out...

Bet the guy's got a great O face too.

"I walked in on them fucking when I went to ask if we had more ice," he whisper-yells. "Nobody wants to see their little brother getting choked by his twenty-year-old boyfriend."

Hmm. "Pretty sure PJ's, like, twenty-three. Twenty-four?" Adam's better with that stuff, so I give him a nudge.

"Twenty-four, I think," Adam agrees. "Or twenty-five?

No, I think he's about a year older than you, so that would be twenty-four."

Wes rubs a hand across his forehead. "Look, guys. This is pointless. I told you I don't have a problem with—"

I don't give him a chance to finish. Little does Wes realize, this entire time he's been arguing with us, he's also been stepping backward. Adam and I have matched him inch for inch until he's practically cornered in this way-back section of the locker room that hardly ever gets used.

There's a bench seat running between the lockers for people to sit on, put their shoes on, or whatever. He stumbles back and sort of awkwardly lands sideways.

"What the fuck are you...?" He doesn't finish. Instead, he glances around with wide eyes like he's only now realizing he's alone with us.

"Look, whatever this is—"

Adam, who almost always knows how to read me, puts a hand on Wes's shoulder. He's got a pretty strong grip for someone on the leaner side, and I sort of envy the way his fingers dig into the place where Wes's neck meets his shoulder.

Wes winces a little, but he doesn't protest. If anything, I could swear his shoulders relax under Adam's grip.

Iiiinteresting.

Encouraged, I straddle the bench in front of him, grabbing one of his legs to pull it over to the other side so we're mirroring each other. Then I scoot forward, hooking each of my legs over each of his, effectively putting us crotch to crotch.

Wes's eyes widen. I swear I can hear his breath catch.

It takes a lot to surprise me, but I'm surprised right now. I expected protesting on Wes's part, like an enhanced game of gay chicken where at some point he'd tell us to back the fuck off, maybe even threaten to throw hands. I most certainly figured that would happen before I got close enough to grind my dick against his.

But Wes isn't saying no. He's staring, lips parted and breathing shallow. I'd bet my classic convertible that the heat in his wide blue eyes is genuine.

There's no way I can resist kicking the tires on this situation a little. See how far he'll let things go before he asks us to knock it off. So I grab hold of his upper thigh. He coughs in surprise, but there's a groan underneath. It's not clear to me whether Wes knows what he wants, but I know. Adam and I get paid a lot of money to give men what they crave. We're damn good at it.

"Adam, keep a lookout."

"Got it," my best friend murmurs. With one hand he adjusts his grip on Wes, and with the other he takes a slurp of his smoothie.

We've basically broadcast to the man between us loud and clear that we're about to fuck with him, and yet? Every bit of him eases back against Adam. So, he hates that his brother is a sub but doesn't seem to realize he's basically got the same bent?

When I reach for his fly, he seems to wake up a little.

"What the hell are you—"

He cuts himself off. I'm already pulling him out, stroking him rough and dirty. My hands are callused from side jobs working construction, and I don't have any lube on me. Still, Wes is no wilting violet.

Imagine my excitement when a strained "Oh, God" comes out of his mouth. I do love being right.

For a second, he goes somewhere in his head. There's a

visible shift from a man in the moment feeling good to one who's caught up in something else. It happens right before he goes to cover his dick as if he's ashamed.

Nah. We're not doing that today. Besides, I've seen all kinds of bodies, and the dick is never the problem. If anything, it's the person the dick is attached to that's a problem.

"Chill, Westy. Sit back. Let me make you feel good."

"It's Wes," he groans. Does he press his head back against Adam, though? Do his eyes flutter closed for a second? Sweet hell, yes he does, and yes they do.

He bites his lips together as I touch him, only here and there making a quiet moan or a hiss. Whether he wants to admit it out loud or not, he likes this.

I keep half an ear out for the sounds of people elsewhere in the locker room, but everyone sounds far away right now.

Adam meets my eyes over the top of Wes's head. He raises an eyebrow, wondering what my plan is, but he's not exactly put out by it.

Giving him a grin, I say, "Got a live one here, Adam."

Behind Wes, Adam's leaning down to get a better look. He slides one hand across Wes's chest, stroking those hard nipples through the guy's shirt. My friend has the side of his face pressed against Wes's, and I could swear they're breathing in unison. Quiet moans. Short, heavy, heated pants.

Adam's long hair is pulled back, which lets him rub his perpetual stubble against Wes's face. I could swear Wes is rubbing back, like a needy kitten.

Our needy kitten. For now, at least.

"That's a pretty looking cock you've got there, Westy," Adam breathes.

"It's not—*oh God*." Wes cuts off his own protest.

Maybe because I'm spitting right on his cock.

Hey, man. Chafing is real, and we might want this guy to come back for seconds. This is already turning out to be far more interesting than expected.

"Somebody likes this," I sing-song softly. "Don't worry. We won't tell. You sit there and fuck my fist like a good boy, and we'll let you come."

The sound that comes out of his mouth is so filthy and sweet that I want to roll around in it. Maybe it hurts, maybe part of him doesn't think he should want what I'm giving him. Doesn't stop him from thrusting into the tunnel of my fingers like it's life or death.

By the time he comes, he's shaking all over. He forgets himself, letting a loud moan slip out before Adam clamps a hand over his mouth from behind.

Pretty sure Wes is biting Adam's fingers, because Adam gasps like he might get off himself. Hell. Fallon's brother is wound tighter than we thought.

Keeping one hand pressed on Wes's leg, I stare right into his hooded blue eyes while I lick him off of me. It's not something I usually do, but I'm making a point here. I want this guy to sit here and watch me and know exactly who made him come.

He tastes good, too. Probably eats lots of fresh fruit.

Then the post-nut clarity sets in. His fuck-drunk eyes go from sleepy to wide. Something worse than regret comes over him. Shame.

"What the fuck was that?" he whispers. His parted lips are wet and puffy from being bitten.

A locker slams in the next row, which must remind him of where we are, because he stiffens and jumps. It's the first time he flinches away from Adam's touch, causing my best friend to let go.

"That?" I tuck his cock away and zip his slacks. Never say I can't be a fucking gentleman. "Just showing you how letting someone control you can be sexy, babe. Fun even. It was fun, right?" I lean forward, letting my lips brush against his ear. "Imagine what we could do to you if you weren't so embarrassed by your own dick."

"It was—" We never get to hear the end of that sentence, though. In the end Wes only shakes his head, and Adam and I are disengaging before we wear out our welcome.

Gonna go ahead and assume his fried brain is a sign that we have a satisfied customer.

"Thought so. Kaybye, Westy."

I grab my best friend's hand and hustle for the door, though I kind of hope we'll be having fun with him again.

CHAPTER ONE

WES

THERE MUST BE something more infuriating and emasculating than your boss publicly shoving his tongue down your wife's throat. I'd rather not find out.

Whatever it is, I'd probably deserve it.

It's six in the evening, and I haven't even started my shift as the night manager of the Belle Argo Premiere hotel. Already, though, I'm at the end of my rope.

"Wes. Hold up."

As I'm nearing the employee entrance, my boss's voice stops me. My neck cracks as I turn around. "Something you need, Max?"

Something other than checking my wife's tonsils?

Over his shoulder, my ex, Gina, gives me a look of apology and then ducks into her car.

The car I paid for.

Max approaches me with long strides. It's not exactly

that I hate him. More like I daydream about holding his head underwater in the hotel pool until he stops kicking.

"You need to get your shit out of Gina's house."

Remember, Wes, he's your boss. You can't afford to lose a paycheck. You'd look like shit in prison orange.

"She may be riding your dick, Max, but it's my name on the title. It's still my house."

Max, who seems to enjoy looming over me with all two inches of his height advantage, finds this funny. "Still sounds like a you problem, Monroe. I don't give a shit who's paying the mortgage. I give a shit that my lease is up next month, and I'm planning to move in. You've got boxes clogging up the closets."

Awesome. My temples throb. I resist the urge to rub at them, then do it anyway.

"Yeah, well, I'm working on it, Max. I'm still looking for a place."

You can't punch him. You can't run him over with your car. You cannot—

But God, I want to.

"Work on it harder, will you? The hotel's new owner's got a bug up his ass about us giving you a reduced-rate room, so I've gone about as far as I can go with my generosity."

"Real fucking generous when the reason I'm staying here is you fucking my wife behind my back. You deserve a medal."

Max's grin is all teeth, and I do my best to hide the fact that I'm picturing taking them out one at a time with my knuckles.

"Christmas and New Year's are coming, Wes. It's one of our busiest times. You've got until the end of next week to vacate your room." He leans in. "And if you don't get your nasty old running shoes and shitty workout equipment out of that garage, I'll happily hire someone to haul it all away. Because that's what buddies do."

With another oily grin, he turns on his heel and gets into his douchey sports car. The engine is loud enough to wake the dead, and the exhaust trail slaps me in the face as he pulls out of the lot.

Asshole.

I'm fuming as he drives away. Where does this fucker get off telling me what to do? He has the power to make my living hell even shittier, though, and we both know it.

My trek toward the employee entrance is spent pulling myself together. Or trying to. I also text my brother, desperate for a lifeline even though he rarely answers these days.

Wes: Hey, man. Lunch soon?

No reply. Still. Again. As I approach the sprawling, mirrored, luxury beachfront hotel, I hear a familiar laugh.

Standing side by side when I turn around are two young men. In their early twenties, they have the bearing and ego of guys who make money from their looks. Because they do. Troy, with his short sandy hair, sculpted arms, and dimpled chin; Adam with his olive skin and his round-the-clock, too-sexy-to-shave stubble, and a man bun that should look stupid but infuriatingly does not.

Troy, on the left, looks especially amused. "Hey, Brunch Daddy. Rough night? "

Asshole. He's fucking with me. The last thing I want is to reward him with my reaction.

A reaction is hard to avoid, though, seeing as how the last time I saw these guys, one of them had a hand on my dick. After cornering me in a locker room, Troy jerked me off so aggressively he might as well have punched the orgasm out of me.

I want to land my fist between his eyes almost as much as I want him to do it again. Which *really* makes me want to punch him in the fucking face.

"Don't call me that. You enjoy on playing with your food or are you just bored?"

Where the hell do these guys get off making me question myself at the age of forty-two? I don't have enough fucks left for this. I left the last one back at the house Gina and I bought together, and it's stuck in the garbage disposal, which she had the nerve to ask me to fix before I moved out.

So, I give Adam and Troy an unprofessional middle finger as I push past them both, focused on getting inside.

"Is that finger an invitation?" That comes from Adam. He's closer to my height and leaner than Troy, with deep brown eyes. It makes my chest hurt to acknowledge, but I can see his lashes even from where I'm standing.

For a moment, I get lost staring at them.

What would happen? If I walked over there and inserted myself between them right now, and I told them they could manhandle me into the nearest corner or closet? If I let them throw me against a wall and do whatever they wanted to me like before?

Or, hell, if I took them upstairs to my temporary accommodations and told them that the day they shoved me into a corner of a gym locker room and held me down had me closer to losing it than my wife cheating on me. That I wanted to lose it again.

What would happen then?

When I turn to fully face them, Troy is right fucking

there. Close enough to punch him. Or spit in his face. Or... other things.

I'm *not* noticing how full his lips are. Or following the column of his throat as he swallows. The quirk at one corner of his mouth. I'm not remembering him spitting on my dick while stroking it.

I'm also not *not* doing those things.

"Someone looks like he needs a hug," he says in what must be the least sympathetic way possible.

Okay, I really can't handle this. I'm not letting some twenty-three-year-old menace screw with my head. I've got much bigger problems.

After glancing around, I lean in and lower my voice to counter with, "It's interesting to me that two known sex workers can get away with spending so much time loitering around this very expensive hotel without someone calling the authorities. Perhaps someone should."

"Ooh. That sounds like a threat." Troy fakes a shiver and steps into me. At six feet, two inches tall, I have a height advantage, but he has longer legs, while I have a longer torso. This means that I would only need to move forward a few measly molecules of space for our crotches to touch. Like they did before.

"It's an observation. The Belle Argo Premiere isn't a place for whores."

Far from seeming offended, he chuckles and presses forward. The dimple that pops on his cheek makes my eyelid twitch. He's one of those guys literally anyone would call good-looking. Razor-sharp nose and cheekbones. That jaw could break rocks. Lips any plastic surgeon would be proud to hang a photo of on their wall.

He smells like a thunderstorm. I want to roll around in that smell.

Not that I'm *trying* to smell him. It's oxygen and proximity, that's all.

He grabs onto my upper arm. My nostrils flare with the force of my exhale, but do I back away? I do not.

As a representative of the hotel, I tell myself it behooves me not to cause a scene. Outside an entrance used primarily by employees, where there are no security cameras and no guests aside from Troy's partner in hand job, Adam.

Right.

"This classy establishment you work for is exactly the sort of place we do business." Troy bats his blond lashes. He presses up on his toes, leaning so we're chest to chest as he murmurs into my ear. "Most of our customers stay on the VIP floor of this place, Kitten. Report us, and you'll be pissing off a whole lot of important people. That's before it even gets back to our pimp. And long before any of that happens, I'll have fucked you from here to Tallahassee."

He probably doesn't mean that the way it sounds. Not like... Right?

My cock twitches even as my jaw clenches. I hate this. I hate his threats. I hate that they're making me hard. "Why are you doing this?"

Troy laughs.

"So fucking glad I can amuse you," I growl.

"Eh." He pats my chest with his free hand.

My nipples tingle at his touch. Why the hell are my nipples tingling? "Why?"

"Who knows, Kitten? Maybe we like holding a mirror up to other people's hypocrisy. Maybe we just like fucking with you."

Hypocrite. The word smacks me across the face.

"I'm not..." But fuck, aren't I? Hating all the times my brother let his late wife boss him around, all the times I heard him refer to his boyfriend, PJ, as his "keeper" with affection rather than disdain. These things have elicited such an immediate and negative reaction from me, but what did I feel that day I accidentally walked in on my brother being dominated by his boyfriend?

Envy. In all my years of marriage I'd never felt the passion and abandon on my brother's face. And what did I do when Adam and Troy shoved me onto a bench and jerked me off? I let them. Without a single word of protest.

Because I didn't want them to stop.

"I'm not a hypocrite," I say with no conviction whatsoever. All these new thoughts have my stomach churning.

Troy shrugs. "I mean, I remember you giving your own brother all sorts of shit for being submissive and fucking around with a male escort. But, Kitten, look how easy you are every time I put my hands on you. Isn't that right, Adam?"

From his spot a few feet away, Adam grins and gives a thumbs-up.

Jesus. I tighten my right hand into a fist with no good outlet for my frustration.

Now's the time to back away. Instead I ask, "Kitten?"

Troy licks his lips. "You didn't like it when we called you Brunch Daddy. So I tried a bunch of nicknames out in my head and chose the one I thought would piss you off the most."

"Classy." Also, he's not wrong. The implied comparison makes me want to claw his eyes out.

Again, I tell myself to back away. To straighten my spine

and go inside. In my head, though, there's a whirling tornado of questions and emotions. I still don't understand why I responded to him the way I did. To both of them.

Fuck's sake. I'm broke, and my life is in the toilet. I can't think—what the hell am I supposed to do with two sex workers giving me an identity crisis?

Someone up above must have my back for a change, because as soon as I wonder, two things happen: a young woman with gorgeous curves, golden-tan skin, and pouty lips to rival Adam's lashes comes out of the building. Adam's gaze stays on me even as she takes hold of his hand, and I don't like the way I keep noticing their interlaced fingers.

Troy spares her the briefest glance before returning his predatory gaze to me. He's still got one hand on my arm. With the other, he's making jerk-off motions.

"Jesus." Turns out there *is* something more infuriating than seeing my wife kiss her boss. I run my hand over the front of my shirt, smoothing the tie and the buttons in a desperate attempt to beat back how goddamn messy I am inside.

My phone rings. I pull it from my pocket and see Belle Argo Oncology on the screen. Troy looks down at the display, frowning.

Fuck. *Fuck.* Dread squeezes everything inside me into a tiny, painful ball.

"Fuck off. I have to take this," I mumble, yanking out of his grip. I hustle past the two young men to get inside while trying to pretend that I don't know what it feels like to have one of them hold me down while the other one makes me come.

Once inside, I'm immediately bombarded.

"Wes. Good. I need to talk to you." Nancy, one of the

desk clerks, comes out of a nearby storage room. From the far hall, our maintenance guy, Glen, walks up, trying to flag me down. The phone stops ringing in my hand.

Dammit.

I give everyone a "wait a minute" gesture as I head to the front desk and duck into the manager's office. My desk is covered in notes that already need my attention. Either they were written by the daytime manager, or the little prick has been playing video games on the job. Again. That's what happens when Max hires some business associate's son instead of someone with actual experience.

I'm too flustered from my parking lot encounter to care much. Shaky enough that the first two times I try to unlock my phone, I fail.

Everything around me goes still as I finally manage to pull up my voicemail. A burning sensation in my chest tells me I've been holding my breath.

Please don't tell me I need to make an appointment.

They never want to give bad news over the phone.

"Mr. Monroe, this is Nurse Sheila at Belle Argo Oncology. We wanted to let you know that your blood work came back, and everything looks good..."

Ignoring the knocks at the door, I let my body sink against the wall. *Thank fuck.*

Well. I may be forced to see my ex tongue-fucking our boss every day, and I just ran into my latest source of shame, and my brother won't answer my texts, but at least I'm not dying.

Not today, anyway.

CHAPTER TWO

Adam

I'm in that foggy place between not quite awake and not quite asleep when someone slaps my naked ass.

"I'm hungry." A sharp acrylic nail pokes at my shoulder. Ruby.

When I don't do anything except groan and tuck my head under my pillow, her manicured finger scratches at my cheek. "Adam. Wake up. Feed me."

"You can suck my dick if you want," I mumble.

Ruby makes an impatient noise, followed by the flop of her landing on the pillow beside mine. "Your dick doesn't taste anything like French toast with strawberries."

My sleepy haze is popped by a splinter of disappointment. Ruby's funny and cute, but that line doesn't work on me like it would have in the past.

"You sure? Maybe you should check again." I know, it's a real head-scratcher that we've broken up so many times.

It doesn't help that she's engaged to someone else.

My eyes are still closed, so I can't see her rolling her eyes. Some things you just know.

Soft lips press against my shoulder blade. "Pretty please."

"We went out to eat last night. I'm tired."

She flings one leg over my hip. "My treat, yeah? And when we get back, I'll give you a bonus treat."

Oof. The spirit is willing, but the dick is soft. And the body is worn out. I already fucked her last night, and I hate to say it, but I'm not as into that as I used to be, either. Took me forever to nut.

We both know she's using me. There are no strings, so I don't even mind most of the time. But it's getting old.

"Adam." She sing-songs my name while she straddles my ass, fingers spider-walking across my back. I squirm against the sensation, wondering if I'd be a total dick to throw her off bucking bronco style.

Then my door bursts open, and with a mouse-like squeak, she rolls herself off.

"Breakfast!"

The sound of my best friend's voice gets me out from under my pillow. Troy's standing in the doorway holding two mason jars and two spoons.

Ooh. Overnight oats. I like it when he makes the PB&J kind.

That's the thing about Troy—he doesn't try to barter with food. He just feeds me.

Ruby scrambles to pull the covers up over her tits. "Troy, what the hell? I know you were raised by cave people, but haven't you learned to knock?"

He blows out a dismissive "pssht" noise. "Babe, I've seen

your tits before. I don't know why you're bothering to cover those things up."

There's a moment of silence while they stare each other down. Ruby doesn't really like Troy. Troy doesn't really like Ruby. They don't even get along when all three of us fuck, though it's better then. Mostly, they seem to tolerate each other because of me.

Troy tolerates her because I'm not great at breaking up with people, and Ruby tolerates Troy because she doesn't have a choice.

I have a short list of nonnegotiables: insulin and Troy. I'd do away with the first thing if I could. Never the second.

Troy sidesteps the discarded laundry on my floor while Ruby side-eyes the jars of oats in his hands. "Seriously? That stuff tastes like wallpaper paste."

He plunks one jar on my bedside table. "Lady, you haven't done a day's work in your life. What would you know about wallpaper paste?"

"I know it's disgusting, and I don't want to eat it. And besides, I do have a job." She crosses her arms over her impressive chest. Her dad got implants for her as a high school graduation gift, which is better than whatever I would've gotten from my father had I graduated. Had he been alive.

"Working ten hours a week at a fancy stationery store downtown hardly counts as gainful employment. Though I guess that doesn't matter when you've got Daddy paying your rent."

She surges forward, forgetting her modesty. "You know what—"

"Kids. Stop. Don't make me turn this bed around." I put

my hands over my ears, but then I go ahead and reach for the jar Troy put on the table.

There's a blissful few seconds of silence while I stir what's in the jar, until Troy says, "Eat, man. Your numbers are a little low."

Ruby huffs. "I'm going to take a shower."

She flounces up and into the next room, glancing backward once to see if I'll follow. I notice, but I pretend I don't. I'm already digging into my food.

"Mmm. The blueberries are a nice touch. Thanks, man."

Troy drops himself into the spot Ruby vacated, digging into his own portion. "Always."

"You could have offered her some," I say.

He shrugs. "You heard her. She doesn't even like them."

"You didn't know that."

"Sure I did. She doesn't like anything. I'm not even convinced she likes you."

This time I'm the one who shrugs. "She likes what I can do with my dick."

"That dick's like a city bus, babe."

"You're thinking of my ass."

He laughs, but he's avoiding my gaze. "Whatever."

Troy's been a little...off, lately. Feels like there's something missing. A distance between us that didn't used to be there. Not sure what to do about that.

He flicks his gaze over to the bathroom door, where a terrible screeching noise announces the starting of the shower. Our apartment building isn't the best, but it's in an okay neighborhood and conveniently located. The landlord lets us pay the rent in cash.

"Seriously though. Isn't she, like, engaged or something?"

"I think so?" I scratch an itch over my eye using the handle of my spoon. "Apparently the guy went through some crazy shit a while back. Kidnapped and taken to some island? One of those stories people were throwing around on the group chat. Pretty wild. He hardly speaks now, apparently. Not sure if they're still planning on walking down the aisle after all that."

Troy chuckles, setting his jar of oats down. "You think she's going to pick you instead?"

"Come on." I'm sort of laughing too, but his question sobers me up. "You know that wouldn't happen."

"Why not?" Troy's tone tries a little too hard to be casual. "She's rich. Killer body. Real catch."

"And you can't stand her," I murmur. Rolling toward him, I reach up and run my fingers across the top of his head. His short hair is soft in the mornings before he's styled it. I like it this way.

Troy scoots down until he's under the sheet, rolling onto his side to face me. "I don't like the way she treats you like a sentient dildo with a wallet. Her family's richer than God, and she keeps making you take her out to every expensive restaurant in town. At least when clients use us that way, we get paid."

My phone pings from inside one of my boots. I keep it there a lot of the time. Old habits from when we lived in places that weren't as safe. Troy's buzzes from his pocket at the same time, which means it's probably our fellow escorts' group chat. I ignore mine because I'm eating, but Troy checks his.

He reads the text out. "Dean needs a fake boyfriend for some event at his kid's school. Guess Michael's unavailable."

Dean and Michael are both escorts we work with.

They're not completely enmeshed like Troy and I are, but they're together an awful lot. Apparently they're related somehow? Sometimes it seems like they hate each other. Sometimes I'd swear they're fucking.

Every time I try to think about it too hard, my brain glitches.

"I'm not touching that one," I say. Much as I want to help a buddy in his time of need, I'm not going to risk accidentally getting into whatever drama those two have going on. Plus, Troy and I are both terrible with kids.

Troy puts the phone down. "No shit. Funny how our friends have some stupid pool going about when we're going to finally admit we're a couple, but nobody asks questions about those two."

We both laugh, and then we both go quiet. Probably because the topic of defining what we are to each other always gets a little sticky.

For the most part, we say we're best friends. It's true.

That we're best friends who sleep together both professionally and recreationally while I sometimes have a sort-of girlfriend who we sometimes share, but also we've only been apart for a handful of days in the last six years? Well, that's a mouthful. Not worth trying to explain.

We're not a couple. Couple is too simple. More like fated mates, if that concept actually existed.

"Ruby did offer to pay for breakfast," I say.

"After the three-hundred-dollar meal we had last night at the Premiere, that's sure fucking generous."

Anger creeps into his words, and they manage to find that soft spot in my chest. The one that hates to disappoint people. Especially Troy.

"It's not as if we can't afford it."

He doesn't say anything. Instead, he runs his fingers through my shoulder-length hair like I've been doing to him. Carefully, he untangles the snarls that have formed during sleep. Anyone watching us would think he's looking in my eyes, but he isn't really. The way his gaze is distant and unfocused, I know he's thinking hard.

For Troy, it could be about anything. He's a thinker. A worrier. Anytime his lips aren't moving, he's busy running through everything from our grocery list to nearby escape routes.

But he's been a little distant lately. Extra quiet. Especially since last night.

"Kind of fucked up, what we saw last night."

"Hmm?" For a second I almost buy that he doesn't remember what I'm talking about. Except he can never keep his mask on around me. "Westy's drama is none of our business."

"His name is Wes. And you immediately knew I meant him. Not that asshole yelling at his kid in the hotel lobby. Or that news article Ruby showed us about an increase in drug overdoses around Belle Argo."

"To be fair, I did almost punch out that dick yelling at his kid."

"Same." Abusive parents are an issue for both of us. Who knows why? "But Wes. Remember when you jerked him off that one time?" I know he remembers. It wasn't that long ago.

Troy gives me an impatient look. "Vaguely."

"You thought he was homophobic. Must not be, if he let you jerk him off."

"You're the one who asked him if he was homophobic. Besides, plenty of self-loathing closet cases out there, babe.

They're practically our bread and butter." Troy tugs my hair a little. "Wes messed with our friends. And he's a breeze to fuck with. You can't tell me it wasn't fun."

Troy's right. That look of utter confusion on Wes's face after he leaned his head back against my stomach, mouth parted when he came. At one point he'd looked right at me. Pupils wide, lips puffy from biting them together, caught between pleasure and panic.

I felt that way the first time a guy touched me, too. At least my first guy was Troy.

Well...now that I think of it, Wes's first guy was also Troy. Not sure that fact was as comforting for him.

"It was fun," I admit.

"I asked last time we were at the hotel. He's working the night shift these days. Six at night until six in the morning."

I put my hand over Troy's to stop him fussing with my hair. "And?"

"And..." He bounces his eyebrows. "Like I said. He's fun to fuck with."

Uh-oh. When Troy's fixated and he's got you in his tractor beam, there's no getting out. I know this because back in the ninth grade, I was the one caught in Troy's tractor beam.

"Why him?" I almost whisper the question.

How much do I need to worry about this?

"He's fun to fuck with," Troy repeats. I wait, because there has to be more.

"Is this about him trying to break up PJ and Fallon?"

We know Wes partly because we spend a lot of time at the hotel where he works. We got to know him better when our friend and former sex worker started dating a client.

That client was Wes's brother. And boy, did Wes have some big feelings about that shit.

Honestly, I can kind of see the whole thing from his perspective.

After a minute, Troy runs his fingers through my hair again. "He's fucked up."

"Everyone's fucked up."

Except, knowing Troy the way I do? I think I get what he means. He's always been good at seeing when a person has ghosts. He can pick out insecurities and traumas as if they were following a person around and holding up glittery signs.

Right now, I'm not sure I like it.

Troy and I became close because we realized that our baggage and fucked-up-ness vibrated at the same frequency. The second we met, it felt like we'd always known each other. Our fathers hating us and hating each other only sweetened the deal.

"You want to play with him?" I ask. "Or is this something else?"

A nervous tremor shimmies up my spine. Troy's fixations can be a problem, especially if the person on the receiving end doesn't feel the same, and I get the feeling Wes would rather forget the time we both got him off in the Belle Argo University locker room.

The shower shutting off barely registers with me. I can predict what will happen because we've been here before. Ruby will come out and get annoyed that Troy is still in here taking up my attention. She'll huff and put on her clothes and go home. It'll be a few weeks or even months before I hear from her again. That's how it goes with us.

She comes out in nothing but a towel, grabbing my boots from beside the bed as she passes.

"I need to borrow some cash." She pulls out my flip phone and a wad of bills. "It's super gross that you keep your money in your shoes, you know?"

Troy rolls his eyes, even though he agrees with her. When you live the way he and I have, you learn not to make it easy for people to steal your shit. Troy carries an actual wallet now. Me? The shoes may be nicer, but consistency and routine have kept me alive this long, so I'm not stopping now.

Troy narrows his eyes at Ruby. "Didn't I hear you offer to buy breakfast this morning?"

"I have a credit card, which my father monitors. Meals once in a while are fine. Anything else I have to buy with actual money or steal." She gives him a look. "And unlike some people, I'm not cut out for jail." Then she crawls across the bed, giving me an over-the-top, exaggerated kiss where she seems to be checking all my fillings with her tongue.

"I don't know if we'll be able to do this again," she says as she pulls on her clothes. "At least not for a while. Father's holding my engagement dinner tonight. Unless Cam starts talking and gets his parents to agree to call it off, the wedding is still on for next month."

There's nothing I can think of to say in response. It sucks that she's going to have to marry a guy she doesn't want and who it sounds like doesn't want her. Still, it's not as if I was ever going to be her alternative. Even if Troy had been cool about it, she'd have gotten tired of slumming with someone who gets paid to let other men fuck him.

Troy decides to shove the knife home, because he's that

kind of asshole. "Ooh. I love weddings. Can I be Adam's plus one?"

While I'm busy elbowing my friend in the ribs, the slamming bedroom door announces her exit.

It's like I said. This thing with Ruby was always temporary.

But Troy? Whatever his interest in Wes, I won't let him use it to leave me. All these years he's protected me. It might be my time to protect him in return.

Like Ruby, Wes isn't made for our kind of life. And Troy's stuck with me.

I'd kill him myself before I let him go.

It's not a threat or anything. Just the truth.

CHAPTER THREE

WES

WINTER IN BELLE ARGO, Florida, is the best time to run. When the weather is in the forties and fifties, there is finally enough chill in the air. Lower humidity so you don't feel like you're breathing water. I force myself to get out year-round, but running on the beach with this cool breeze? That's the sweet spot.

Which is why I want to fucking punch something when my phone rings.

"Mom?"

I slow to a walk, the tension that had bled out during my first few miles already returning. I love my mom. I do. She can be a lot, though.

Her shouty voice shatters the beauty of the sun rising over the water and the sand beneath my feet. It'll be a cold day in hell before she admits her hearing is going.

"Sweetheart, I've been worried. You haven't called."

Say it louder, Mom. Not everyone in the state heard you. I pull the phone away from my ear.

"I've been busy, Mom. Gina wanted me to move my stuff out." Which I haven't done. But in between living at my fucking job and trying to find a new place, it's been enough.

"I still don't like it that you left her. Gina's lovely, and the two of you have been together forever. Why can't you work things out?"

It's a bit late for that. "The papers get signed soon, Mom. We haven't gotten along in forever. We're roommates who annoy each other."

"You're what? Blue states?"

Big surprise, telling her to get her hearing checked didn't go over any better than news of my divorce. I've quit trying with her. On many fronts.

"Never mind. How's Philly? "

"Cold. I've been thinking maybe I should move closer to you and Fallon."

With clenched fingers, I use the phone beat myself in the forehead. "Ma. You love Philly."

"It's lonely here. I haven't seen Fallon in months, and it's been longer since I've seen you. You could visit more, you know."

Anyone who has ever felt jealous about not being the preferred sibling? They don't know how fucking good they have it. Fallon's the baby of the family, but I raised him more than Mom did, so they've never been close. He doesn't have the same baggage with her.

Me, on the other hand? I'd be grateful if she could go a single week without needing something from me. A favor, a visit, or advice she's only going to ignore.

One phone call without her asking me to visit when I can barely fucking afford gas.

"I'm working on it. Money's tight now."

She makes a noise that could either mean she's dismissing what I said, or she didn't hear me at all. Honestly, I'm worried about her living all the way up north on her own. At the same time, I don't want her to be *here.*

Which makes me an asshole. But if a parent was never there when you needed them, the expectation to be there for *them* in their old age is a burden. I'm already struggling under the weight of what everyone else wants from me.

I half listen as she prattles on about her church group and the fundraiser they're having, while I send a text to my brother.

Wes: Hey, can we meet up at the gym tomorrow? Or maybe get coffee? Need to talk about Mom.

Still no answer. Guess I can't blame him. He's prickly with me ever since I went meddling in his love life because I couldn't fix my own.

Karma's hitting me hard right now.

Down the beach I spot the objects of my recent... I don't know what to call Adam and Troy exactly. Obsession feels simple, too light a word. Fixation. Infuriation. Humiliation.

They must be staying at the hotel again. These two twenty-something escorts infuriate me even more than my brother's snotty new boyfriend. I also can't stop thinking about them. Until the day they got their hands on me in that locker room, I'd only been intimate with one person.

Nothing in my entire relationship with Gina felt as intense and charged as that one bold and dirty hand job.

That's got to be why I can't get them off my mind.

Maybe it was their brashness. Their rudeness. Their audacity.

Maybe it was how fucking hard I came.

The first person I was with after Gina was always likely to be memorable, I suppose. Probably more memorable since it was all so unexpected. Being with two men was never something I anticipated. If I'd had money to bet, I would have wagered it all on the assumption that the rest of my orgasms would be solo efforts. Maybe if I got lucky, a nice single mom who was looking for companionship without commitment.

The worst part? Even though I would bet all of my meager worldly possessions that they were only screwing with me, I felt more alive with those two young men surrounding me and jerking me off than I did in the past few years of my marriage.

As I walk through the employee entrance of the Premiere hotel, I'm sweaty and exhausted. If I run into Max, he'll probably hassle me for looking like shit in front of guests, but I'm not wearing my name badge and I'm sure as hell not the only person sweating in this place. The hotel has a gym and a heated pool, after all.

Passing through the brightly lit, multi-story lobby, I wave to our event coordinator, who's making notes at the front desk. "Hey, Eliott. How's your mom doing?"

"Better. Thanks. Getting her strength back after that hip surgery." He looks left and right, seeming nervous. "Hey, so, are you doing okay? I heard Max has been coming down hard on you lately. Sorry about that."

"Why? Is it your fault?" Immediately, I regret my tone. "Sorry. Tired." *I worked all night, and then I ran four miles and then had to dodge these two sex workers I keep thinking about*. As one does. "My brain's fried. I appreciate the concern."

He gives me a sympathetic smile. "Don't sweat it. I sure as hell was no fun to be around at first after Kiki passed. Why do you think I stuck with one-night stands and escorts for a while?"

Wait. "Didn't you move in with someone recently? "

Grinning, he pulls off his glasses to buff them on his shirt sleeve. "Alexis." He leans in. "The escort I was seeing, actually. So much for some no-strings fun, but she really gets me. So, yeah, she's moving into my place."

I take a quick look around to make sure nobody's close enough to hear us. "She's not still..." I can't think of a polite way to express my concern. It's not a polite thing to ask. I'm curious as hell, though. "Is she?"

"I mean...yeah. She is. For now, anyway." To my surprise, his grin widens. "Honestly, I kind of like it. All these rich assholes throwing money and clothes and jewelry at her, and I'm the one she comes home to? Makes me feel like I'm something special. Powerful. We accept each other for who we are. Throw in a smidgen of jealousy, and the sex is crazy explosive. Might sound strange, but we're happy. Everyone deserves that, right? "

On the one hand, I'm not sure how his woman fucking other men feels powerful. Not once did I feel that way when Gina cheated. On the other hand, I'm envious. Explosive sex? Acceptance? *Happy*?

Sounds nice.

"Of course. Yeah. Right. That's great. Congrats, man." I knock on the surface of the front desk, walking backward as a cue that I'm taking off.

"Don't knock it till you've tried it, is all I'm saying."

"Oh, I'm not. Not...knocking it. No judgment here." OK, there's a little judgment, mostly aimed at myself. If I stand here too long he might see all the buttons he's unknowingly pushing and call me out. "Glad you're happy. Really."

"Thanks. Oh, by the way, you should know Gina's been looking for you."

Lovely. "Appreciate the heads-up. I'll catch up with her in a bit."

My shift ended at six a.m. According to the giant clock on the lobby wall, it's nearly eight now. As the daytime restaurant manager, she's probably helping to get breakfast going. If I hustle, maybe I can get upstairs and into a shower before she spots me.

In a closet where we keep spare amenities, I grab a new tube of toothpaste. If I have to spend most of my waking hours in this place, the least they can do is give me some free stuff.

I'm at the elevators when high heels click behind me. "There you are."

So close. "Gina." Does my smile look as strained as it feels? "Heard you were looking for me."

"I need you to get the rest of your stuff out of the house."

For fuck's sake. "Yeah. I already talked to Max."

"He said you were a dick about it. I wanted to be sure this wasn't one of those times when you dragged your feet on something to be spiteful."

Oh, that's absolutely happening. "You don't think maybe I'm entitled to keep a few boxes of belongings in the house that I'm still paying the mortgage on while I find someplace to live other than a room with a double bed and a view of the hotel parking lot? "

She scowls. “You agreed I should be the one to stay in the house.”

I rub the back of my neck, which feels as if it’s strung with steel cables. “No, Gina, I didn’t agree. I had a lawyer with less fight in him than a baby bird, because that was all I could afford, and you had a lawyer that our boss, who you also happen to be fucking, helped you pay for.”

We weren’t always like this with each other. What we are now makes my chest hurt. There was a time when we clung to each other through the hard days and made each other laugh. Now, we’re practically strangers.

“You don’t think I deserve that place after everything I went through for you?”

I’ve pissed her off. I’m good at that lately.

Part of me is pleased to be able to strike a blow when she’s struck at me so many times. But there’s also pain making her voice tremble, so on top of the guilt I feel for blowing off my mother, now I feel guilty for attacking my wife.

Not wanting to fight, I take a step back from the elevator and turn toward the stairs. “Yeah, Gina. You deserve all the compensation for having to put up with me.”

She opens her mouth, but I don’t give her time to reply, slipping into the stairwell like an asshole. She won’t bother to follow. Not in those shoes.

The second I get up to my room, I strip off my sweaty workout clothes. Tossing them in a pile on the floor brings me a certain satisfaction. Nobody’s around anymore to insist I put them in their proper place.

Under a hot shower spray, I manage to wash my hair and my face before giving up the pretense that I’m not going to take advantage of the privacy to get myself off. I could use the release after this morning.

The truth is, I've struggled some with my libido in the last few years. Being a constant disappointment to your life partner can have that effect. After running into Adam and Troy before my shift last night, I've had trouble getting them out of my head.

That hand job in the gym locker room at Belle Argo University? It honestly haunts me.

I went there to meet my brother, hoping he could put me in contact with an investigator-type person he knows. There've been an unusually high number of hotel employees leaving work and never showing up again. Worse, leaving mid-shift.

Turnover is a regular thing in the hotel industry. Low pay. Hard work. The churn rate is steady, and by my math the Premiere loses an average of one or two employees a month. Last month it was seven. The month before it was four. Two so far this month, and we're not that far into December.

I mentioned it to Max, but like most of our conversations, it was a lot of him sneering and calling me an idiot. Somehow he thinks years of marriage to Gina made me an idiot, but after fucking her for six months he knows everything? Fine.

The conversation with my brother's friend never happened because I was stopped by Adam and Troy, full of fury on behalf of Fallon's boyfriend.

In my admittedly flimsy defense, after years of being ordered around by a woman with control issues, I didn't see how Fallon could be happy in that kind of relationship. I still don't.

"What the hell are you—"

With head-spinning efficiency Troy's pulled my cock out, and he's stroking me with his hand.

And I try to tell myself I don't want him to, until a strained "Oh, God," comes out of my mouth.

Nobody's touched me in so long.

They decided to show me a little something about control. A power play that at once pissed me off and piqued my curiosity.

No amount of anger or indignation stops me from bracing against the tile as I work my conditioner-covered hand over my cock. Hard, fast. Rough.

I didn't even know what to say when Troy inched down my zipper right there under the bright lights of the locker room.

In the end I said nothing. If pressed about it, I'd say it was because I'd been taken so off guard.

Also? If I'd asked them to stop, maybe they would have.

Ultimately, the pressure and heat of hands on my body were too much to resist. I hadn't been touched by another human in so long that I barely remembered what it felt like. The firmness and the confidence in every word and every stroke grounded me. For the first time in too long, it wasn't my job to handle anything or please anyone.

All I had to do was surrender. What a fucking relief.

I can't stop remembering how I ejaculated into Troy's hand in painful spurts, the way I'm shooting now into my own.

Then that twenty-three-year-old male escort looked me dead in the eye while he licked every drop of my cum from his hand.

As the water beats down on my shoulders, I experimentally lift my fingers and taste myself with the tip of my tongue.

What did Troy taste when he swallowed me? What did it feel like for him to know he'd owned me so thoroughly in that moment?

"Ech." I shudder at the strange, musky flavor. Then I try it again.

It's not terrible. A little bitter. Salty.

In all our years together, Gina never did anything like that. Not that I minded. I wouldn't have wanted her to do something she didn't enjoy. But watching Troy clean me off his hand? I become aroused almost every time I think about it. Or a strange warmth floods my chest, like it's doing now.

"Just showing you how letting someone control you can be sexy, babe. Fun, even. It was fun, right?" Troy leans forward, lips against my ear. "Imagine what we could do to you if you weren't so embarrassed by your own dick."

He was right. About everything. I still don't really understand how or why.

Throughout my entire life, I've felt dragged around by the whims of circumstance. After my father got sick and after he died, someone needed to take care of my mother and brother. Gina getting pregnant spurred us into getting married. Throughout our entire relationship, I felt as though I was paying for the pain caused by that mistake, and later the miscarriages that shattered us both.

It was only a couple of years after Gina and I married that I was diagnosed with leukemia, several years earlier than the age my dad was when the disease took him. Which still drives many of my decisions, even after so many years of remission.

"Chill, Westy. Sit back. Lemme make you feel good."

When was the last time I'd had no responsibility other than to feel?

Catching my breath against the shower tile, I squeeze my eyes shut tight when I get to the part of the memory where I managed to shake myself back to awareness, chasing the two men down so I could talk to them. Try and understand what happened.

The disappointment that struck me in the chest when I failed to find them still shakes me. What I'd wanted from them, I'm not sure.

I just...wanted. To touch them again? Talk to them? Even though it didn't make any sense. Even though I shouldn't have.

Unfortunately, closing my eyes causes a new movie to play in my head. The memory from last night, where Adam with his warm eyes and long lashes captivated me by asking if I was making them an offer. Troy pressing his crotch against mine right out in the open. His claiming grip on my arm.

I couldn't have possibly answered Adam's question in the affirmative for so many reasons. Not even if I'd wanted to.

And I didn't. I *didn't* want to.

"I really didn't," I whisper to myself.

CHAPTER FOUR

TROY

WE'RE LATE for our workout today. We meet with some friends a couple of mornings a week at the Belle Argo University gym, but today Adam had a doctor's appointment. Since he's got diabetes, his doc likes to check in with him every three to six months—a commitment I make sure he doesn't miss.

"It's the swimmer," I say as we approach the desk. "You go first. She seems to like you."

Neither of us is a BAU student. Usually it's a straightforward thing for one of us to flirt a little, and then we slide right through without anyone noticing we didn't scan a student ID.

There's this one adorable and stern little redheaded sophomore who always wears a BAU Swim tank top, and she does not play around.

While Adam's approaching the desk with maximum swagger, I check my notifications.

Prince: What does a person wear to a private school interview? I'm thinking suit and tie, like with a client

Dean: I already told you, just wear regular clothes

Prince: That means different things to different people

Michael: You might want to tell him to take all ten pounds of jewelry out of his face so he doesn't set off a metal detector. Or scare the admissions board.

Huh. Is something going down here? Michael's usually a lot nicer.

Ravi: Does someone know of a way I can realistically tie myself to a bed? Liam's out of town and I'm trying to plan a good welcome home surprise

I laugh as I type in my response.

Troy: Let us know if Adam and I can help

"ID?" When I look up, the young woman at the desk is inspecting us both with one eyebrow raised.

"Heidi, you look like you're glowing this morning. Still doing those cold plunges?" Adam practically drapes himself over the raised divider, fanning his award-winning eyelashes for all he's worth.

"I remember you. Did you both 'forget' your ID again?" Based on her air quotes around the word "forget," I don't think she's taking the bait.

We might have to offer to fuck her. When in doubt, it usually works.

She's got that fresh-faced look, like she isn't wearing makeup even though she actually is, and a bun on top of her head without a hair out of place. Bet I could bend her over that thing and muss her right up. Bang all that rule following right out of her.

"Came here to see you, actually." Adam's laying it on

thick, reaching over the divider as if he's about to brush his fingers over her knuckles.

It's a good move. High success rate. Five stars.

She's keeping her "don't fuck with me" face on, but when her freckled cheeks catch fire, I can see we've got her. Doesn't matter, though, because as we're about to get in, the subject of our recent amusement is on his way out.

Wes Monroe's tree-trunk thighs stride toward us alongside his brother, Fallon, though our buddy PJ is nowhere in sight. They're encased in a respectable pair of slacks that are making me think extremely disrespectful thoughts. Wes's thighs. Not... Well. Anyway.

The two men walking towards us seem wrapped up in a spicy debate of some kind, but it doesn't keep Wes from flashing some side-eye. First at me, and then at Adam, where he's flirting with the cute swimmer.

Interesting. The judgmental glare his brown eyes are broadcasting and the set of his jaw only make me want to fuck with him more.

I grab hold of Adam's shoulder, interrupting whatever he's saying. "Change of plans, babe. Gotta go."

He comes along after throwing the redhead a hasty wave. "You know you've only made sure it's going to be harder for us to get in the next time."

"Tomorrow's problem." I gesture up ahead to where Wes and Fallon are still bickering as they head down the path toward the university's staff parking lot. Apparently, they both teach part-time here.

"I don't get what the issue is," Fallon is saying. "You said you didn't have a problem with PJ. So why won't you come over for dinner?"

"Aside from there not being enough eye bleach in the

world to wipe out the last time I walked in on you two fucking? How about all the times PJ has put a knife to my throat?"

Has he? Heh.

"Neither of those things is going to happen at dinner. You're the one who keeps asking to hang out."

"For coffee. Maybe lunch. Right now, I don't have time to hang out all evening. I'm still trying to find an apartment that's available immediately in my price range and then I have to move my shit. This isn't about you."

"I didn't say it was, but, Wes—"

"You're the one who said you wanted me to butt out of your personal life. Now you want me to come over for dinner so I can sit across from your boyfriend, who multiple times now has threatened me with physical violence."

There's a hint of sullen teenager in Wes's tone, and honestly? I'm here for it. This guy sounds like he's on the edge of losing his shit and trying so hard not to. The idea of pressing all his buttons right now is like fucking catnip.

"Someone needs a hug," I say to Adam, who offers a noncommittal grunt.

"He's not seriously going to stab you," Fallon tells Wes. They both sound exasperated. "And you're still my brother."

"Right. Well, that's great, but I've got other shit to deal with. Like I said. Gina wants my stuff out of the house. I'm a few days from being homeless. Mom keeps hassling me about visiting, and I don't know what to do about that. She's not hearing me when I tell her I can't. And then the shit with the hotel..."

Oof. Why's the frustration in his voice so damn hot? Maybe Adam and I could help him out. We could offer to let him crash on our couch and also fuck him over it. Win-win, as one of our clients likes to say.

"You could always stay with me and PJ."

Wes runs a hand over the back of his neck, which looks flushed with red. "Thank you for the offer. I'm going to refer you back to my previous remark about you and PJ having sex."

Fallon rolls his eyes. "Be serious."

"I'm not mooching off my baby brother, okay? I practically raised you. I'm not taking your money."

Fallon's quiet for a minute. I'm thinking he'll make another argument. Instead, he says, "Hey, don't take this the wrong way, but have you considered maybe dating again?"

Pretty sure I see a twitch in Wes's eyelid. "What's the right way for me to take that, Fallon? Because it sounds an awful lot like you're telling me I need to get laid."

"Honestly, based on how tight his shoulders look, I'm inclined to agree," Adam says next to me.

"Shh." Sometimes Adam's not great at whispering. Inside my head, where Wes and Fallon can't hear me, however, I'm also inclined to agree.

"Do I need to remind you that you set me up with a male escort under the guise of a blind date, so I'd get laid?"

"Jesus. No, you do not. I'm reminded every time I see the two of you together. I've also apologized at least six hundred times."

"Look, Wes. It was a dick move, but you weren't entirely off base. You setting me up with PJ is one of the best things to happen to me."

"That's kind of sweet," Adam murmurs.

"Nice to see our friends happy," I agree.

Adam gives me a knowing look, which I avoid.

It isn't that I'm unhappy, exactly. Sometimes things just feel...a little empty. A little like something is missing. It doesn't help that I can still close my eyes and see my mother's lifeless body the day I found her in the garage.

The strange explanations that didn't make sense then or now. *She couldn't help it. She just couldn't stay, Troy.*

Is that going to happen to me someday? Is there going to be a moment when I just can't stay?

Wes takes a deep breath. His entire body swells and then deflates with the force of it. "You say that, but you still haven't forgiven me."

Fallon shakes his head. "You have to admit, your motives were less than pure. Never mind the fact that you kept trying to break us up after."

"I've apologized about that too. But, Fallon, you can understand why the whole situation concerned me."

"No, Wes. I can't."

Oooh, our Wes doesn't like that. He's shuffling his feet and crossing and uncrossing his arms, all while that red flush creeps higher up the back of his neck.

I'm dying to sink my teeth into that spot behind his ear.

It seems like he's about to continue the argument, but then he doesn't. "You know what? Fine. I have to go anyway. I have a class to teach."

They part ways. Fallon gets into his car, and Wes heads in the direction of the academic buildings, keeping to the sidewalks like a good boy in spite of all the students criss-crossing the grass.

He's temporarily waylaid by a pretty young student—bobbed black hair, nose ring, and perky tits—who smiles a little too widely when she stops him to let him know she won't be able to make it to class today on account of leaving town for her sister's wedding. She's doing that cute thing where she tugs a little at her own hair, tucking it behind one ear. Practically presents that cleavage on a platter.

Wes nods and says something I can't hear before moving on. But Manic Pixie Coed is glancing back and licking her lips like she's tempted to volunteer for any kind of extra credit that involves crawling under the teacher's desk.

Looking at the way those tan slacks hug Wes's bouncy ass, I'd be happy to do the same. Maybe Adam could suck him off while I fuck him over his own desk.

Wes Monroe would be so fun to ruin.

"Hey." Adam flags her down. I know what he's thinking because I'm thinking it too. "Where's, uh..."

"Mr. Monroe." I elbow him.

"Right." Adam gives the student a full-wattage grin. "Where's Mr. Monroe's next class? We kind of need to talk to him."

She points us in the right direction, and we head off.

I nudge Adam again. "You thinking what I'm thinking?"

He lifts one shoulder in a casual shrug, but his smile is pure menace. "You said you like to fuck with him. So let's fuck with him."

Hell yeah. This is going to be fun.

CHAPTER FIVE

WES

I'M ONLY a few minutes into my lecture when I hear the double doors open at the back of the classroom. I don't look up right away. Late arrivals happen, and I try not to let them distract me.

"Today we'll be discussing problems that are currently affecting or likely will affect the future of the hotel in...dus..." When I do look up, I wish I hadn't.

Panic seizes my insides as Adam and Troy slide into the nearly empty back row with mischief on both their faces. The only other person up there is a student who's barely passing the class. He's already fallen asleep.

I grope around on the lectern for the bottle of water I keep with me, forcing myself to take a swallow. Nothing seems to clear the heat and tension that's suddenly clogging my throat and squeezing my entire body.

After another drink I manage to get my bearings, and

that's when I realize I've got eighty freshman and sophomore students staring right at me.

Because I trailed off mid-sentence.

"Sorry about that. Dry throat." I clear it for good measure, as if anyone who actually cared would buy my performance.

My gaze is drawn to Adam and Troy again, sitting with studious expressions at the long tables that line the tiered room, pretending they're actually here to learn. Meanwhile. I've forgotten my entire lesson plan.

Looking down at my notes helps refresh my memory, but it doesn't alleviate the thrumming in my body. "S-uh. Wh-who wants to get us started? Problems in the hotel industry. Go."

I call on the first student to raise their hand, an eager-looking kid in the front row wearing a BAU basketball shirt. He says something about wage gaps and labor shortages, but I can barely make sense of his answer.

Because Adam and Troy are making out in the back row.

"Interesting. Who's next?" Did anyone else hear the way my voice went up an octave? I hope not.

That echo in my ears must be steam pouring out. How dare those two come in here and screw with my job, my livelihood, when I'm already forced to deal with them at the hotel where they fuck rich men while I pretend to look the other way?

I try another throat clear. This one because I can't seem to swallow. "Uh, okay. I think someone mentioned economic conditions. Someone say more about that." Did they? I have no idea who's saying what at this point, only that Adam is sinking his teeth into Troy's throat as if they're auditioning for one of those vampire shows Gina loves.

All the same, when Adam tips his head back and Troy runs his tongue from Adam's collarbones to his chin, my blood surges to my cock so suddenly I feel as if I might pass out.

What on earth is happening to me?

A brunette with Greek letters on her shirt says some things about sustainability that may or may not be correct. I make a show of shuffling the papers in front of me, attempting to make sense of my notes while I gather my thoughts.

Don't look. Do not play their game. If students notice I'm looking too hard in a certain direction, they might turn around to figure out why the hell I'm so fixated.

If they did, they would see what looks an awful lot like Troy's hand between Adam's legs. Given the design of the seating and the way each long desk has a front panel that hides most of the students' lower bodies, I can't say for sure. It's the angle of his arm and the smirk on his face when he looks my way as my cock betrays me—

Jesus fucking Christ. I'm hard. In front of an entire lecture hall. God forbid one person notices or turns around and sees what's happening in the back row. If they do, I'm done.

Another hand goes up. "Y-es, uh..." Where the hell did my seating chart go? "Did you have something to add?"

The young man in question asks a question about short-term vacation rentals. I'm trying to rein in my shallow breath—is Troy jerking Adam off back there?

Troy shoving me down onto a bench while Adam presses his hands to my shoulders. Troy unzipping my slacks and pulling out my cock. Adam telling me my cock is pretty.

The same cock Gina used to ridicule.

"Uh. Well." Fuck.

I chug more water. "That's a good question." What the hell did that kid ask me again?

Even from the front of the classroom, I can see Adam's lips parting. His head tilted back.

I should call them out. Call security. They're not students. They don't belong here. At the very least I need to stop fucking *watching*.

Think. I force myself to return my focus to the student who asked the last question. "The, uh, answer, uh..." *Dammit, Wes.* "It comes down in part to county laws. In the state of Florida..."

Whew. Thank fuck I've taught this class enough times that I manage a semi-coherent answer. I hope. The rest of the lecture passes in a blur where I desperately will my hard cock to go down and even more desperately try to not look a single student in the eye.

Getting through the lecture with an erection is bad enough. Watching the two men in the back row as if it's a private performance? So much worse.

I dismiss class early. Did we go over everything on today's agenda? Or even any of it? Probably not. There's supposed to be a quiz next class, and I couldn't begin to say if I covered the necessary material. More likely, I spent the entire lecture sounding as if I was having a stroke.

As soon as I escape into the hallway, I'm searching for someplace to hide. My office is two floors up. Right now that's way too far. I duck into a room with a "staff only" sign on the door, only to find myself in a custodial supply closet.

Well. At least it's quiet in here.

Hugging my notes to my chest, I press myself against a

metal shelving unit stocked full of paper products. I attempt to catch my breath, taking giant gulps of pine-scented air.

The throbbing in my pants is as enraging as it is unbearable. I can't jerk off in here. God help me if the actual custodian comes in. I'll never survive the shame if I've got my dick out when some poor employee shows up looking for a mop.

As if my thoughts have power, the door creaks open. No sooner have I straightened up and covered myself with my folder of lecture notes than I realize I'm not looking at someone wearing coveralls and a name tag. I'm looking at two someones who are amused as hell to find me. Again.

And once again, they've got me cornered.

"Hey there, Kitten," Troy practically croons.

"Kitten?" Adam raises one eyebrow at Troy.

"He likes it. Don't you, Kitten?"

"No, I do not fucking like it," I whisper-yell. "I sure as hell didn't like that shit you pulled in my classroom. Are you trying to get me fired?"

"Fired?" Adam looks confused. "Nobody even noticed."

"Yeah, teacher. Except for that one dude in the back sleeping off his hangover, all eyes were on you."

"Probably all hot for the teacher." Adam nods.

"Who wouldn't be?" Troy adds with a grin.

"Hot for—no. Stop fucking around." Nobody in my life has ever called me hot, not even the woman I married. I take a step, but they're blocking me in. "Let me out of here."

"You really want us to do that?" Troy's the one who speaks, but they share a look of genuine confusion.

Adam's the one who addresses the situation in my pants. I may not be the most well-endowed, but apparently these slacks don't hide much. Not exactly something I thought I'd need to worry about when I bought them.

"Looks like you could use some help," he says.

"I think you both have helped enough."

"Have we?" Once again Troy comes forward. It always seems to be Troy. Is he the ringleader? Is it still considered a "ring" if there are only two members?

He presses me against the shelf, sliding his palm over my chest and between the top two buttons of my shirt, popping them open. The gentle sensation of his nose running up the side of my neck gives me the shivers.

"Mm. You smell good. Freshly showered from the gym. Spicy. And are you saying if Adam were to get down on his knees right now and suck your cock into his mouth, you'd have an objection?"

I am absolutely supposed to be objecting right now. Aren't I?

"Y-y..."

Great. I've forgotten how to make words.

Tell them you object, goddammit. They're sex workers. I've got twenty years on each of them. For now at least, I'm still married. Oh, and we're in a goddamn janitorial closet with no lock on the door.

"Speak up, Kitten. Couldn't quite hear you."

"There's no lock on that door."

Nice one, Wes. Way to put your foot down.

Adam chuckles as he grabs a yellow floor sign that says "Cuidado! Piso mojado" and wedges it under the doorknob. Then he turns back to me and drops to his knees.

Just like the first time these two cornered me, my tongue thickens and refuses to work. This is completely unprofessional. If we're caught, I'll get fired.

And yet...

Instead of pushing away, I lean into the press of Troy's

palm against the side of my neck. My tongue slides over my lower lip as Adam's gaze finds mine.

Somehow, all I can do is stare with eyes that must be bulging out of my head as Adam slides down my zipper and reaches inside.

All the usual insecurities run through my head. *Too small. You don't know how to please anyone.* All the criticism sounds suspiciously like Gina, but this time I don't have time for the shame to take hold.

This time, when I try to cover myself with my folder again, I've got Adam looking up at me with dark, liquid eyes. When he gently pushes my hand away and closes his mouth around me, he moans as if he's actually fucking enjoying himself.

"Oh fuck, that feels good." The words come out without my permission, on a jagged, unsteady puff of air.

There's a man—*a man*—sliding his lips and tongue up and down my dick with sooty lashes fanned across the most perfect looking warm-toned cheekbones. His dark, wavy hair is pulled into a bun as it so often is. A few tendrils have escaped down the back of his neck. I realize this when the fingers of my left hand somehow grab hold, tangling with the loose strands.

No man has touched me this way. *Nobody* has touched me this way. Blow jobs went the way of the dodo after my first year of marriage. Even when Gina was willing, it was never with this level of enthusiasm.

This is how he makes money. He's probably pretending. Gina used to pretend, but with Adam I don't know how to tell.

Why would he, though, when I'm not paying him?

Voices and hundreds of footsteps echo in the halls outside, full of laughter and loud discussion as students are released from their classes and move on to wherever they're going next.

"Christ, we can't do this here." I barely manage the protest.

Troy pops open the rest of the buttons on my shirt. His palm caresses my chest, stimulating my nipples, which seem to have a direct line to my dick. Tiny shivers follow the path of his hand, over my sternum and down my stomach. Every muscle jumps under his touch, trying to get closer.

"God. This is—" I'm gasping for air, not that it helps. "We should stop."

Even as I say it, my fingers push farther into Adam's hair. Clenching. Pulling. Dragging him closer until the tip of his nose presses against my pubic hair.

Troy was right, I'm a filthy fucking hypocrite. A liar.

My cock glides across the ridges on the roof of his mouth, wrapping me up in a pleasure-pain that's brand new. Followed quickly by my tip getting squeezed in his throat. How is he doing that?

I don't know what the hell this is, only that I'm not supposed to want it. I also don't know what I'll do if he stops.

Even as I moan when Adam swallows around me, I hear Gina's comments the last time I tried to initiate sex. *I think it's time we stop pretending we please each other, don't you?*

I don't know what to do when tears press at the backs of my eyes. Especially when, at the same time, to my horror, my orgasm is bearing down on me. "You might want to... I-I'm going to..."

I try to pull my hips back, shocked when Adam's grips my ass, tugging me forward. Sucking me back into his mouth.

It's all over too soon. For a moment I forget myself and cry out when I come, only to have the sound stifled by Troy's lips on mine. As I'm coming, he pinches one of my nipples hard enough to make me cry out again, but he's there to swallow my pleasure and pain.

My shoulders press painfully into the shelf behind me as Adam drinks me down. I'm trying desperately to keep my footing. Fuck knows my sanity is long gone.

The back of my head smacks against a case of hand towel refills as I catch my breath. I can't bring myself to open my eyes. Not sure I can handle the way they're probably looking at me. Probably thinking it's funny as hell that they've once again manipulated me into a compromising position. That they've gotten a straight guy to—

Okay, that's too much right now. I'm going to have to think about that part later.

Much later. Alone.

Not sure it still makes sense to think of myself as straight after I came into Adam's mouth. Or after I looked Troy in the eye while he jerked me off. After I salivated watching him lick my cum off his hand.

I don't open my eyes until lips press against mine. A tongue pushes its way inside. This time it's Adam. I can taste myself on him.

"Later, Kitten." His expression is as grim as Troy's is gleeful. What am I supposed to make of that?

I'm still wondering as they move the sign away from the door, and they both leave me here.

All I can do is watch them go. What do I even say? Thanks for the blow job? What the hell are you two trying to pull?

A glance down reminds me I'm a fucking mess. Used and

spent. Shirt hanging half off of me, zipper undone, softening cock out. I'm burning with humiliation, but why am I still so fucking turned on?

For the first time since I was Adam and Troy's age, I'm not sure it would take much to get hard again.

I hurry to pull myself together, cleaning off with some stolen paper towels. God forbid I'm caught in here like this.

My phone buzzes in my pocket. Hoping for a text from my brother, I hurry and fish it out, only to see it's from the housekeeping manager at work:

Any chance you can swing by when you come in for your next shift? Need to run something by you.

Great. On the upside, I've been meaning to talk to him. Downside? Well, I'm kind of busy having an identity crisis.

Are drive-by orgasms a thing? Because I think this is the second time I've gotten one.

CHAPTER SIX

WES

For most of my life I've felt completely out of place. Never as out of place as I feel right now, standing inside the entrance of Dance!, Belle Argo's only gay club.

I'm wearing my only pair of jeans and one of the few T-shirts I haven't worked out in. Granted, I don't wear the shirt to work out because it's too tight. I should get rid of it. It's uncomfortable, the way it digs in under my arms.

The place seems crowded for a weeknight. The dance floor is fairly full. I've got no plan here. It's my night off, and the decision to come was spur of the moment. Probably should've turned around in the parking lot.

Making my way to the bar, I nearly trip over my own feet. "Bottle of Dogfish Head if you have it."

The bartender, a pretty, petite young woman wearing light-up fairy wings, nods and disappears. She's back a few minutes later to pop the bottle and hand it to me, and I settle against the scarred wood with nothing better to do than observe.

The place is filled with a mix of pretty people, most of them looking young enough to make me feel like a criminal. On one side of the room, what appears to be a bridal party has taken up most of the tables. Or sorority girls? They're all wearing tiaras and sashes. There's a sign for the bathrooms across from me, under which two young men are making out.

A couple of go-go boys dance under flashing lights on a side stage, wearing nothing but leopard-print shorts. I could do my laundry on either of their abs, but I don't feel turned on so much as envious. Even as much as I work out, my days of looking that good in shorts are probably behind me.

Thanks to my complete lack of social skills, the only person I ever even dated was my roommate's sister after college. Then I got her pregnant, and I married her. Aside from Gina, I've got no other sexual experience unless I count Adam and Troy.

Well... I guess I do have to count them. They've both put their hands or mouths on my dick. They've both kissed me. I'm blaming Troy for the fact that I needed to pinch my nipple to come the last time I jerked it in the shower.

I scan the dance floor, looking for...what? Someone I find attractive, I guess? It's not a matter of wanting to hook up. I wouldn't know where to begin.

It would be nice if I could see something, anything, that would give me a definitive answer. *Yes, you're definitely into men, or no, you're really not.* Ideally, something that explains why I keep letting these two guys, who are nearly young enough to be my students, back me into corners.

"This is stupid," I tell myself halfway into my beer.

It's just, well, I'm forty-two. How have I made it this far in life not realizing I might be attracted to men? The only explanation I can think of is that I never considered it a possibility. At all.

Gina got pregnant the second time we had sex. We got married. That was supposed to be the end of my sexual exploration.

Even after I suspected her of cheating, I never considered doing the same. Holding two jobs and trying to mind my health after cancer treatments kept me plenty busy.

Someone bumps me from the right. A strange, sweaty chest swipes against my shoulder as I'm busy mopping beer off my shirt.

"Sorry, man." The perpetrator of the hit-and-run is already disappearing into the crowd as he tosses his apology over his shoulder.

The muscles in his back are retreating, leaving me uncertain whether I'm experiencing physical attraction or simple appreciation. They're nicely defined muscles. The jaw I caught a glimpse of was a little big.

Which reminds me that Troy's nose hooks a little to the left. Has he broken it at some point? It's not a stretch to imagine him getting into a fight. His mouth could easily start one.

Is there something about Adam and Troy specifically? Is it men in general? So far, I don't see anyone in here who really gets my motor going. I guess the two guys kissing under the restroom sign are nice to watch.

I'd check out porn, but that's challenging in Florida. Due to current state laws, most of the major streamers no longer allow people here to access their sites. Not that I've checked everywhere. Something about endlessly searching the internet for porn access feels too sad even for me.

Mostly I've stuck to watching the stuff already downloaded to my computer, and most of that was your standard rough fucking boy/girl shit. A few gang bangs. Nothing that tells me anything deep about myself, aside from an obvious interest in sex that's maybe...not so polite?

"My, aren't you a big one. I'd love to climb you like a tree."

My brain stutters as I look down to find a man who appears even younger than Troy and Adam staring up at me. Even seated on a barstool, he isn't tall enough to look at me eye to eye. He's cute, I guess. Highlighted blond hair, glittery face. Crop top.

Twink, my brain supplies.

Is that right? I'd have to ask my brother. Or look it up. Neither of which I'm going to do right now. Nor am I about to ask.

Hey, not to be rude, but I'm trying to determine where I lie on the Kinsey scale. Also, would you refer to yourself as a twink?

The young man sidles up next to me. "You must be new here. Buy me a drink?"

I glance around. If I buy him a drink, he might think I'm interested. If I don't, I'll feel like I'm being rude. Ultimately, I signal the bartender. Luckily, it's too loud in this place to hear the sobbing coming from my credit card.

"Thanks," the kid says after he orders. He turns to me with his elbow propped on the bar and his cheek on his fist. "So. New in town? Tourist?"

I swig my beer. "Neither. Been in town for eight years. Just never came in here before."

"Ah." His expression turns knowledgeable. "Divorced?"

"How'd you guess?"

He thanks the bartender for handing over something bright red and garnished with pineapple. "Aside from your complete discomfort and the way you keep looking around as if you're expecting to get caught?" He taps one of his fingers on one of mine. "Wedding ring tan line."

"Right." I'm sure I'm making a face right now. "Stopped wearing it a couple of months ago, but the line is taking forever to go away. Guess I need to spend more time outside."

Just like that, I think I might be flirting with a guy who wasn't even born yet when I graduated college.

"Poor guy." He pouts sympathetically, then thrusts his hand out. "I'm Bryce."

All at once I'm overly concerned about the salad I had before I came here. What if there's spinach stuck between my teeth?

"Wes." I shake back. "Nice to meet you." For no real reason, I run my tongue over my teeth.

Look, Mom, I'm making friends.

Fuck my mom right now. Fuck Gina.

"So tell me about this ex of yours, Wes. What's his name? Is he crying himself to sleep over losing you?"

Another drink. A long one. "Her name is Gina, and I don't think so. She's moving in with our boss."

Bryce shakes his head, biting his pineapple wedge while plunking his empty glass on the counter. "That's absolutely fucking tragic, Wes."

Here I'd always thought it was somewhat depressing, but Bryce is upping the ante. Not sure if I feel seen or embarrassed.

He slaps his hand on the bar top. "Come on. I know what you need."

Before I can make heads or tails of the situation, he's dragging me toward the dance floor.

"Oh, no, no, no." I dig in my heels. "Sorry. I don't dance."

I absolutely cannot dance. Accidentally stepping on Gina's dress and tearing the train at our wedding dissuaded me from ever trying again. The closest I get these days is swaying side to side a little when Rihanna's "SOS" plays. Which is still embarrassing. But how can you not dance to Rihanna?

Except as I close my eyes and let the music wrap around me, I can feel Adam's tongue sliding over my lip. Troy's mouth hot against mine. His fingers brushing and then bruising my nipples. I blink and then close them again, letting the drumbeats and sense memories wash over me.

Am I addicted to them, is that it? Or is it more like a bruise I can't stop prodding?

Bryce puts his hands on my hips. "Come. On. I'll do all the work. All you gotta do is stand there and look handsome."

For the first time in a while, I laugh. "My ex said that about our wedding, and then I was forced to participate in 'The Time Warp.'"

Bryce either doesn't hear me or doesn't care. He gives me a goofy grin and drags me farther onto the polished wood floor. Before long, he's dancing around me, looking as shiny as the lights above us, while I awkwardly sway to the music. In a weird way I wish he did something for me, because he seems nice. And fun.

Self-consciousness aside, I'm almost enjoying myself. There's a song playing I haven't heard before. Something with heavy drums and lyrics about being addicted to someone's touch.

Tingles skate over the tops of my bare arms, and I try not to think about how I've been chasing the dragon ever since the day Troy touched me in that locker room.

My cock begins to fill, which it always seems to do when I revisit those memories. Whether I want it to or not.

Slim hips press against mine. Hands brush up my arms, teasing gently at the hair at the base of my skull and then moving downward. I may not be particularly attracted to this guy, but I can't deny it feels nice. It feels like someone wants me.

Maybe if he were a little bigger. Stronger. Rougher. Longer hair and darker lashes, or bluer eyes and shorter hair. Both.

Both.

Still, it's impossible not to respond to the way he's grinding against me. My skin heats and my balls ache. There's a certain rush in the way this young man is looking up at me as if he might actually find me attractive.

Am I turned on by this particular person in front of me? Or am I simply touch starved and liking the friction?

Relaxing into the dance some, I try to let my body go loose and my hips move a little. Bryce smiles up at me, and I sort-of manage to smile back. People bump into us from all sides. Which is probably why I don't realize someone has grabbed my arm until they yank me right off the dance floor.

"What the fuck do we have here, Adam?" Out of nowhere I'm sandwiched between two familiar bodies. Troy narrows his eyes, pushing one long finger into the center of my chest. "Did you come out here to hook up, Kitten?"

Bryce seems to have disappeared into the crowd again. Any chance I can do the same?

"No!" Okay, that sounded like way too much protesting. In my defense, all my blood seems to be pooling at my feet. I clear my throat and try again. "No. I wanted to see..."

Am I really into men, or did you guys short-circuit my motherboard?

Frustration pricks at the back of my neck. "What the hell are you two doing here? Did you follow me?"

"Not this time."

Not this time. *This time??*

Adam scoffs and points across the room. Through the hazy play of light and shadow, I spot a large booth filled with guys who only sort of look familiar. I've met most of them at Fallon's house, I think. Or the gym or something.

Or possibly that one ill-advised time I followed PJ to a weekly brunch gathering the escorts all have and nearly had my throat cut. Which means everyone over there has seen me at one of my lowest points. Jesus, what if my brother and PJ show up?

One of them, the one with a lot of piercings on his face, waves at me. That recognition is ice water down my spine.

"I have to go."

"Wes, baby, what's the rush? If that sparkly twink got to dance with you, then we want a turn, yeah?" Troy tugs on my hand.

"Is he your type?" Adam's eyebrows rise expectantly.

Their questions *sound* like simple curiosity, so why do I feel more like a baby penguin being circled by leopard seals?

"No. I don't even—I don't have a type. Coming here was a mistake. I do not have the fucking time for this." I throw them off and shove through the crowd, hoping they don't follow.

I can't handle running into my brother and him asking questions I don't know how to answer. And I definitely don't need any more of Adam and Troy's stupid games. Going in circles with them will only confuse me more.

As I make it to the door, just when I can smell and taste fresh air and freedom, a hand wraps around my arm. Troy's grin stretches ear-to-ear. He looks far too pleased with himself.

"Not so fast, Kitten."

CHAPTER SEVEN

TROY

"WHAT THE HELL are we doing here?" Wes, who's between me and Adam looking like the six-foot-something muscly filling in a particularly juicy sandwich, looks around at the beach-side arcade we've dragged him to.

The Belle Argo Boardwalk is one of our favorite places to screw around. It smells like churros and popcorn and the kind of childhoods Adam and I never got to have.

Especially this time of year. Christmas is coming, so everything from the balloon game and the shooting gallery to the Ferris wheel to the mini golf course is decked out in red and white poinsettia flowers and twinkle lights. Hot cocoa wafts to us on the breeze.

Fucking heaven.

"Seriously. What the hell am I doing here?" Wes looks around again as we approach the mini golf course, seeming to be asking himself more than anyone else.

Still, Adam answers with, "Troy tugged on your arm and

told you to come with us, and you did. For some reason. Apparently nobody taught you about getting into cars with strange men."

"Not that I recall." Wes's gaze is distant. "My dad was too busy dying. My mom was busy taking pills and not getting out of bed." He shakes himself and blinks. "You dragged me out of a gay bar because you wanted to play mini golf?"

"You were leaving anyway," Adam points out.

"You were," I agree.

Wes glances side to side, anxiously rubbing his hand over the leg of his tight-as-fuck jeans. "Those guys you came in with. I think I've seen them at my brother's house. I didn't want..." He shakes his head again. "Couldn't deal with that right now."

"They're not gossips. They wouldn't tell your brother you were in a gay bar."

Adam rolls his eyes. "Yes, they are."

"Okay," I concede. "We're gossipy as fuck. Still. They're not going to tell your brother they saw you in a gay bar."

"Probably," Adam adds.

I give him a look that says, *What the fuck are you doing?* He answers with the same grin he wears when he's about to cannonball next to me in the swimming pool.

Big surprise, Wes doesn't look at all comforted. He keeps looking around as if he's done something illegal and he's afraid of getting caught. Still wondering how we got here? Worried about seeing someone he knows?

Truth be told, I'm waiting for it. Just let one of his employees or a member of his church congregation walk by. I won't shove my tongue down his throat right in front of them, but I'm not above dragging him into a shadowy corner so he can marinate in shame while I make him hard.

Wait. "Do you go to church, Kitten?"

"What? No. Why?"

Heh.

Adam's pocket starts pinging at the same time mine emits a series of buzzes. Text messages. From the group chat, I'm betting.

Sure enough:

Michael: Where did you guys go?

Dean: The manager keeps asking me where you two are.

Nico: So did some guy in leather pants. Seemed like he was REALLY looking forward to seeing you, if you know what I mean.

Christian: He means he was looking forward to seeing your dicks

Troy: Had to see a horse about a man. Have fun without us.

Honestly, if we'd known Wes was at that club getting hit on by a pretty boy in a crop top? We'd have grabbed our guy and gotten out of there a whole lot faster.

Adam checks his phone, raises an eyebrow at me, and then shoves it back into his pocket. I silence my notifications and do the same.

"Come on, Kitten." I grab hold of Wes's shoulder. "Who doesn't love mini golf?"

"I still don't understand why we're here." Is he glitching? Should we try to reboot him?

Adam nudges me not-so-gently with his elbow. "Yeah, Troy, why *are* we here?"

"Because Wes is a guy who clearly needs to relax.

Getting him off didn't work. Drinking at a bar didn't work. Time to try something else."

Funny how Adam and Wes are both wearing the same dubious expression. Neither of them understands why I'm making this my problem.

It's a valid question. The truth is that the answer keeps changing. At first it was about knocking a smug SOB off his high horse. All these rich fucks Adam and I deal with—we're nothing to them. I've had guys hammer out business deals and discuss shit about their families they probably don't want anyone knowing while I'm lying naked in their bed a few feet away. If I were their peer, they might watch what they say, but to them we're nothing more than window dressing.

So, yeah. At first, screwing with Wes was a way to get a little revenge for all the bastard's righteous judgment. It was a chance to fuck with someone we could actually get away with.

"Come on. Who doesn't like mini golf?" I lead the way to pay for some balls, avoiding looking at either of them.

The reason now? Well, there was that look on his face as we left him in that closet. He had the same look as he was leaving the bar.

It wasn't confusion, and it wasn't questioning. It wasn't even fear, which I might have taken some perverse pleasure from.

It was the same look I see on my own face sometimes in the mirror. The one Adam gets whenever he thinks about his biological family.

It was agony.

Which made me damn curious. Does our new kitten have so much pain inside him that he struggles to receive pleasure? Why does this man, who's built as fuck, a legit fucking adult, teaches college, and helps to manage an entire luxury hotel, look the way Adam and I look when we each think the other one isn't watching?

"I should probably get home." Wes might be finally grasping that he's at a mini golf course with two male escorts. No weirder than seeing him at Dance! with a twink hanging off him.

"Not so fast, Kitten." I hook his arm with mine. "One game. Then we'll drop you back at your rusty minivan before you turn into a pumpkin. Deal?"

Not that it bothered me to see him dancing with that kid, but, well, okay, it bothered me some. Fucking with Wes is like getting a hot stock tip. You don't want other people catching on to how good it is.

"Fine. One game." Wes reaches for his wallet.

I slap his arm down. "Relax, Kitten. We got this."

His jaw goes slack as I pull out my wallet. Adam may still insist on keeping cash in his boots, but I don't let it worry me so much. We have actual bank accounts now. *Plural.*

Like it always does, this place teleports me to a childhood that never was. Adam seems to relax, even though he looks like he's not yet a hundred percent on board with the Wes thing. He plucks a green ball from the giant bucket near the entrance and grabs one of those dinky clubs.

"Extra fun route," he says.

Wes pauses, still pondering all the balls. "Extra fun?"

"They've got two courses." I point to my club. "One's easier, more of a kiddie course. They call it the fun route. Then there's a harder one; more challenging but more cool shit where the ball goes inside a waterfall and comes out on another level, that sort of thing."

"Extra fun route." Wes nods. "Got it."

He's stiff as we play the first few holes, but polite and patient with all the families around us. He's kind to the kids, even when one little gremlin accidentally whacks him in the shin with their club. Maybe it's all that customer service shit he does at the hotel, but when he laughs good-naturedly and tells the apologetic mom not to sweat it, I realize something.

All the times we've seen him, from dropping by our weekly brunch to beef with PJ, to meeting his brother at the gym to work out, to running into him at that hotel where he works...

This is the first time I've seen him smile.

Lights up his whole damn face. Makes his eyes glow. Even Adam's paying attention.

We're about halfway through when we reach a hole Wes can't get his ball into to save himself. The surface around the hole itself is full of turf-covered bumps that make it nearly impossible. Except Adam and I have played this course enough to have it down.

After Wes's tenth try, I step forward. "Here. Let me educate you, Kitten." When I wrap my arms around his middle, he stiffens but doesn't make any effort to get out of my grasp.

It's a super fucking cliché move, right? I press my chest against his back to guide him through the situation. I might as well be one of those d-bags at a bar drinking hard seltzer and hitting on a chick by "helping" her with her pool shot. Except, also, I can suddenly see the appeal.

His body feels good in my arms. Sturdy. Solid. Does he even realize how he's always relaxing a little when one of us touches him?

Adam definitely notices. He's shifting his attention back and forth between us both with curiosity. How does Adam not see what I'm seeing? We're usually so on the same page with these things. Wes may not have our background, but he's like us more than he realizes.

Shitty parents. Trying to survive. He may be a dick, but I'm beginning to think he doesn't even know himself. He's been too busy trying to keep his head above water. Adam should understand that better than anyone.

Besides, how fucking fun will it be when Wes here figures out who he really is, and we're there to catch him?

"What are you doing, exactly?" my best friend asks while Wes retrieves his ball. "Thought you just wanted to mess around with him a little. This isn't that."

Here we go. "I also told you he's fucked up the way we're fucked up."

"So he's, what? A project?"

"Call it a hobby."

Adam scoffs. There's anger on his face I'm not used to seeing. Generally, he's a pretty laid-back guy.

"Hey." I slap his chest with the back of my hand. "You good?"

"I'm great. So long as you remember, you do not get to fucking leave me. If you ever try to leave me, I'll cut you open from nose to balls and leave you on the nearest fire ant hill." His flat stare falters, showing me a flicker of vulnerability.

Sort of laid back.

"Wait." As he turns to walk away, I grab his arm and spin him back to face me. We're standing in the middle of the little golf green, with Wes's curious eyes on us, along with at least one family of four. Fuck all that. My lips brush his ear as I whisper, "Only in death, babe. You know that."

"Good. Fucking asshole." He leaves me to walk over to Wes. In a strange and sudden one-eighty, he links their fingers together. "Come on. You'll like the next one. You gotta jump the ball over an octopus."

Wes stumbles along behind Adam like a toddler who just woke up from their nap—confused, but also like he has no other destination in mind.

By the time we finish the last hole, all of us are laughing. Because being sad while playing mini golf at the beach is fucking wrong.

For a little while, Wes seems to have forgotten he kind of hates us, busy making self-effacing jokes about the hole where he tried to give the ball some juice and ended up popping himself in the forehead. Adam's got his fingers hooked in Wes's back pocket.

My best friend responds to my raised eyebrow with a subtle shrug. Okay.

Should have realized all Adam needed was some reassurance. Occasionally—a lot of the time—I assume Adam knows he's stuck with me for however long I have left on this earth. Even if I worry sometimes that it won't be as much time as I'd like.

I won't deny wanting to get Wes to unfurl his freak flag, but I'd never willingly leave Adam. We're flip slides of the same coin. A bonded pair of shelter dogs.

When we drive Wes back to where he left his car, I drop the top on the Mustang and crank up a remix of Conjure One's "Sleep." This song always gets me thrilled and sort of horny. It was playing the night Adam and I made our escape. It also makes me want to touch Wes.

Adam climbs into the narrow back seat and doesn't even give me shit when I speed too fast down Oceanside.

In spite of the fact that we sort of kidnapped him, Wes gives me a slight smile before sprawling tiredly in the passenger seat with a sigh. The wind and the music make it too loud for words, but I decide to take a chance on another form of communication.

Reaching across the gear shift, I slide my hand over his thigh. Though I stop short of full-on groping his package, my message is pretty damn clear. At first he moves to cover himself, something he seems to do every time. Seems to come more from self-consciousness than from actually not wanting us to touch him.

Wes wants us to touch him. He's afraid to admit it, but he does.

Then, to my surprise, he looks over at me and shakes his head. And I guess he decides to let me in some. This time when he smiles, it's a little bit shy.

And it's aimed right at me as he widens his legs.

CHAPTER EIGHT

Wes

My day off left me more exhausted than a full workweek. Whether it was the mini golf or the emotional leakage, I can't be sure. What I do know is I'm twisted into a damn pretzel by the time I make it to the hotel to start my shift the next evening.

My afternoon was spent in my closet-sized office on campus, trying to call around for apartments in my price range while doing a shit job of processing what happened in an actual closet on campus.

Never mind the gay bar, which left me with more questions than answers. Or after, when I didn't simply let Troy and Adam back me into a corner. This time I followed them willingly.

I don't think I've ever been a bigger fucking mess.

Christ, when I finally caught Gina cheating, I didn't lose it the way I feel like I'm losing it now.

On my way into work, I check my phone to see if my brother has followed up to his last text:

Fallon: Ravi said Liam's out of town but he'll have him get in touch as soon as he's back. Not sure when that'll be.

Nothing new from him, but I also have another message from the premier's head of housekeeping:

Murray: Hey man, can you swing by my office on your way into work this evening?

Fuck, I was supposed to do that last shift, wasn't I? It's not like me to forget these things, and I hate how foggy my brain has been. Worse, I know exactly why.

I swing by the management office for a bottle of water before trekking down the long hallway that leads to the kitchens and laundry. An older woman pushing a laundry cart limps past me. She's got her head down, tapping at her phone as she goes.

"Emmy. Hey."

She shoves the phone inside her smock. "Mr. Monroe. Sorry, sir. I was checking in on my granddaughter."

"It's fine." I nod toward her foot. "Thought you were supposed to get surgery on that thing."

"Oh." She clears her throat as she glances down. "Sure. I need to accrue some more leave time first. I missed a week of work when my granddaughter was sick, and they say I'll need a few weeks of rehab before I can return to the job. Big Boss has been threatening to let people go for missing too many days. Not sure if that's why we're short-staffed lately, but it's not making things easier."

By the big boss, she means Max. There's nobody in the world I want to have a conversation with less, but that isn't her fault. She's clearly struggling to walk. "Let me have a talk with him. Maybe we can reach a compromise on the time off, or you can take on something less strenuous for a while." I gesture to the cart, piled high with sheets and towels. "I know how heavy those things are."

She gives a light laugh. "Do you, sir?"

"Hey. I'll have you know, I've done literally every job in this hotel." When Gina and I first moved here to be closer to my brother, I had to work my way up.

Also, the glamour of this place requires flexibility. When we're short-staffed, it's on me or the daytime manager to ensure those gaps get filled.

"You think working housekeeping is bad? I once had a maintenance call on a clogged toilet on the VIP floor. Someone had tried to flush an entire wad of latex gloves and razor blades. To this day I don't know what went on in that room."

Yes, I wondered. Who wouldn't? But whatever fucked-up thing the guest in that room had been part of, I was happier not knowing.

She chuckles again and shakes her head. "Probably something kinky. Back before you came to work here? I had to clean a room where this couple had absolutely destroyed the place. Blood smeared on the sheets. Champagne everywhere. We even had to repaint the walls."

Suddenly the protein bar I wolfed down on my way in is tumbling like rocks in my stomach. "Well, as much as I'm enjoying this game of who's had to deal with the weirdest hotel problems. And trust me, I could play all day." She gives me a look that suggests she could match me detail for detail. "I need to go talk to Murray. And I'm betting you're about ready to clock out."

She nods. "As soon as I get this last load down to the laundry." She points toward the storage room where we keep cleaning supplies and equipment. "Last I saw Murray, he was in there. Doing inventory. Probably wants to talk to you about Nadia."

"Great. Thanks. And leave that." I point to the cart. "I'll take it down when I'm done."

I turn to look in the direction she pointed. The last fucking thing I need is to walk into another custodial closet.

I've spent all afternoon pushing away the mental images of Adam with his lips wrapped around me, his eyes wide and full of lust, his mouth stretched wide while he looked right at me. The way Troy pinched my nipple, causing me to orgasm harder than I can remember in my entire fucking life.

My nipple is still sore. I resist the urge to reach up and rub at the tender flesh. It's bad enough that every bend and twist makes the cotton of my dress shirt brush the swollen and sensitive skin. I'll be in a world of trouble if I get hard standing here in front of a kind lady who's been working at the Premiere since its grand opening twenty years ago.

Wait. "What about Nadia? Is something wrong?"

Nadia's a new employee. Young and eager, a single mom. Housekeeping isn't directly my domain to oversee, but since moving out of the house Gina and I shared, I'm at the hotel more often. I've seen nothing from Nadia but stellar work.

Emmy gestures with both hands up, a nonverbal "Who knows?"

"She didn't come into work today," she says. "Or yesterday."

Dread settles in my stomach. This is sounding way too familiar. “Maybe the baby’s sick. Did she call in?”

It could be nothing. We can always hope, anyway.

Another shrug. “Don’t think so.”

I shake my head, waving her off. “I’ll let you get on with your evening.” At the last second I lean in, lowering my voice. “Hey, but do me a favor. Tell me if you hear anything, would you? I know sometimes issues with daytime folks don’t make it to me on the night shift.”

It was around the time I first suspected something was going on with Gina and Max that I got moved to nights. Coincidence? When the move allowed Gina and Max plenty of time to be in contact with each other while I was busy sleeping off the previous night’s work, I highly fucking doubt it.

As Emmy limps down the hall, however, I realize I’ve got to fucking deal with Max whether I like it or not. I’m honestly concerned Emmy won’t make it through the holidays if something doesn’t change.

The ever-present two-way radio that I keep clipped to my belt when I’m on shift crackles to life. “Room service delivery needed. VIP floor.”

Shit. Mentally, I cross my fingers while I head to the custodial storage room. If someone else doesn’t grab that delivery soon, it’ll be on me to take it upstairs. As the manager, one of my priorities is to keep the VIPs happy and spending money.

A knock on the door when I reach the closet brings Murray’s head around. He’s unpacking boxes of disinfectant and clicking a counter as he places them on a shelf.

While I do my damnedest to focus on the housekeeping

manager, a bespectacled older redhead who's a bit stooped over from years of working in the industry, the first whiff of cleaning products brings back memories from my time with Adam and Troy.

The ghost sensation of Troy's nose on my neck, and the way he whispered to me that he liked my smell, forces me to suppress a shiver.

What the hell is wrong with me?

Too many things.

"You wanted to talk to me?" I ask Murray, pushing the memory down again.

After my first encounter with Adam and Troy at the gym, I did my best to dismiss it as a one-time occurrence. But now?

After the run-in at the gay bar, after that moment when my sanity left me and I went with them on what felt oddly like a date? And then the teasing touches when they drove me back to where I'd parked my car...

Now, I don't know what to think or do. Logic tells me these guys are fucking around, giving me a hard time because I tried to get my brother to dump their friend. It's a lot of damn trouble to go to, though, simply because they think I'm an asshole.

Isn't it?

Maybe I'm making too much out of everything? Maybe they've had their fun and now they'll lose interest in whatever game they're playing.

Murray finishes emptying the box in his hands and straightens. "Nadia didn't show up for work yesterday or today."

"I heard. She's got a kid at home. Maybe—" Even as I

repeat the same explanation I gave to Emmy, the rocks in my belly tumble again.

The explanation sounds so hollow. For a while now I've worried that the unusual turnover is a sign of a bigger problem.

Murray nods, clearly having already considered my explanation. "I called the number on her paperwork. No response."

"That doesn't necessarily mean anything."

"No. It doesn't. It's a lot lately, though. Don't you think?"

Glad someone else is finally thinking what I'm thinking, I nod. "Have you talked to anyone else about this?"

"Sure. I wanted to have information before I ran it up the flagpole. At first, I thought maybe it was working conditions. Someone causing a hostile environment, perhaps. I worked at a boutique resort in Orlando that deteriorated significantly after the owner's son took over. Had a bad habit of cornering the women on staff in closets and unoccupied rooms and pressuring them into a non-traditional sort of performance review, if you get my meaning."

"That's disgusting." Even as I say it, I'm back on campus in that custodial closet. I'm in that gym on campus, holding my breath while Troy spits on my cock to lube it up.

Aaand now I'm repositioning myself behind a floor polisher to hide my body's response. Disgusted isn't exactly how I felt at the time, even if I should have been. Unless you count disgusted with myself.

"Umm. Uh-huh." Fuck. Pulling a cough drop from my pocket, I clear my throat. "Sorry. Allergies."

Get yourself together, Wes.

But I like the lie. It soothes my jagged edges a little to

pretend my problems are simpler and less cliché than a midlife identity crisis.

"What did you find out with the staff?"

"Nothing much aside from Max..." He glances out into the hallway. So do I, but nobody's around. "Max has been an even bigger dick than usual. Not in a harassing way, though. Just a regular dick way."

"Yeah. I'm well aware of his...dick." Not even going to go there right now. "Anything else?"

"Nothing definitive. I did try informing Max."

"Better you than me," I mumble. I tried to bring my concerns to him as well. Would've been better off putting pictures of the absent staff on milk cartons.

Murray laughs. "Right. Well. He clearly isn't concerned. Suggested maybe it's the time of year. Holidays are coming. People visiting family. Ghosting the job altogether if they don't have enough leave time."

I think back to my conversation with Emmy and make a mental note to have a talk with the dick in question.

"I suppose it's possible. As far as I recall, though, this time last year wasn't this bad."

My radio crackles to life again. "Still waiting on room service for fourteen twenty-four."

"Shit." I pull the radio off my belt and press the button. "On my way."

To Murray I say, "Gotta take care of this. Let me know if you hear anything else. My brother's boyfriend knows a guy who knows a guy who does some sort of security work. It's a long shot, but I'm trying to get in touch to get another perspective. He's supposed to contact me when he gets back from out of town."

God knows, Max is too busy screwing me over to give a shit.

Murray gives a tight smile. "What else can you do, right? I wondered about going to the police, but what if we're making too much out of nothing?"

"Right." I've thought the same thing.

Nodding, I hustle out of the supply closet and down to the kitchen. The only good thing that came out of that conversation is that it made my erection go down.

CHAPTER NINE

ADAM

I'M GRABBING water in the suite's bathroom when there's a knock at the door.

Snacks must be here. "Thank God," I murmur as I go to answer the door.

Troy almost always gets the client to order some food for us. He's good like that.

I glance into the bedroom on my way to get the door. My best friend's already got our client tied and blindfolded, slurping on the man's cock like he's winning a prize.

He's good at that, too.

Padding across the patterned carpet, I pull open the heavy door, focused more on the cart and the food than the person wheeling it in. When I finally look, I'm pleasantly surprised to see a familiar face. "Westy. Fancy meeting you here."

"I work here," he grumbles as he wheels in a tray. "And for the last fucking time, it's Wes. Christ, I don't know what it is with you guys and nicknames. My name is Wes. Not Westy. That's worse than calling me Kitten."

He sets the food out on the dining table with frustrated, jerky movements. The tips of his ears are pink, which is honestly sort of cute. My stance on him has warmed up a little since Troy's reassurance at the mini golf place. Now my approach is to take a page from his book, which is what I do most of the time anyway.

For example. "Got it. Kitten it is, then."

Like I suspected might happen, that little bit of blush on the tops of his ears spreads down to his lobes. Then his cheeks. The back of his neck.

He freezes in the middle of setting a fruit and nut plate down on the table. Much to my delight. His bent position stretches the slacks he's wearing across his ass. I've seen this guy in short shorts at the gym. Wes keeps himself in shape. That ass could crack walnuts.

"I'm not your fucking ki—"

Moans from the next room bring his head around. I don't need to look to know what he's seeing. A pair of hairy legs spread wide on the fancy bed cover, tied down with ankle straps. Troy in between those legs, ass in the air, naked.

That ass looks especially tasty right now. I helped him wax a couple of days ago.

"You might want to mention to, uh, whoever that is, housekeeping doesn't wash those coverlets after every guest." Wes tries to swallow and ends up coughing. "Not the cleanest surface around here."

"Not sure they care. Like what you see, Wes?"

"I..." He straightens, sort of half dropping the plate in his hand onto the table with a loud plink. Not that anyone in the next room notices.

The more I pay attention to Wes, the more I can tell why Troy's into him. The world we come from is jaded and ugly. Kitten here may be older, but every time we touch or flirt with him, he's got the wide-eyed gaze of someone who's just discovered an ancient treasure.

Don't think Troy and I were ever that kind of innocent. Not the way we grew up.

If only poor Wes here could fully admit he wants the treasure.

I use my thumb to point toward the other room. "'Bout to go in there and fuck him in a minute. You want to stay and watch? Client won't notice. We've got him blindfolded."

Does Wes realize the way he's licking his lips?

"N-no. I—I'm working." He turns to look at the scene in the bedroom. "You're going to fuck Troy? He doesn't seem like..."

It's almost as if he's too distracted looking at Troy's ass to finish his thought.

Taking a step closer, I can't help but chuckle at the look on this guy's face. Half wonder, half anger. I'd almost say he's jealous, but I can't imagine that's true. Not after a couple of quickies. Not with whores. Nobody's ever been jealous over us. Not even my sort-of not-really girlfriend.

"You're wondering if Troy's a bottom?" Taking a page from Troy's book, I crowd into Wes's space more. All I'm wearing right now is one of those free cushy hotel robes, but he doesn't seem to notice.

Wes's not much taller, but I like that he's got a couple of inches on me. When I lean in, there's a subtle whiff of cologne.

"Here's a secret, Kitten. Most of the time, we're whatever we get paid to be." Slowly, deeply, I breathe in through my nose, filling my nostrils with canned hotel air and one skittish night manager.

"Troy's right," I murmur into his ear. "You *do* smell good."

"If... Uhm..." Now that I'm so close to Wes, I can hear each shallow breath. The wet swallows. The rustling of his pants as he shifts his weight from one foot to the other.

Kitten's nervous. And a little horned up, methinks.

"If?" I slide my fingers over the back of one hand. He doesn't react.

For the first time since I sucked him off in that closet, he meets my eyes. "If you're whatever you get paid to be, what the hell are you two doing with me?"

The question is a gut punch I don't expect. Not that I blame Wes for his mistrust. We're in a business built on lies. How can I expect him to see things the way we do?

I'm still breathing through the sting when he continues. "You guys give me shit because I tried to get Fallon to dump PJ. I can admit that I was wrong, but when it came to my lonely, wealthy, widowed brother dating a broke twenty-something sex worker, I stand by my concerns."

Honestly, it's hard to hate him with that look on his face. A fierce protector, our kitten.

"That first time when we fucked with you at the gym, it was different. That was to get under your skin. You may not realize it, but you used to look at all of us like we were gum under your shoe. We don't tolerate haters. But the thing is, Kitten, Troy's been feeling you out. Turns out, you're sooo fun to fuck with."

"Oh. Well. Great." He scoffs. "As long as you've got a good reason."

"You really don't get it." My fingers slide up to his right wrist, tracing the tendons just under the cuff of his dress shirt. "Do you see that in there?" I gesture to where my friend is going for a solid gold medal at sucking dick.

My friend even pulls off long enough to give our client, Mr. Rigby, a smooth line about how his dick "tastes so fucking good."

"Fake as hell." I lean in, lowering my voice. "Boring. Routine. Slobber on one wealthy asshole's knob, you've slobbered on them all. Trust me."

Wes runs his free hand down the side of his face. "I don't even know how to respond to that. I don't even know what it means." He's so flustered right now.

"Let me give you a demonstration, Kitten." I tug on my robe sash with one hand and his wrist with the other. He follows easily when I bring his fingertips to my abs. Only a sharp intake of his breath and parted lips. He tries to suppress a shiver, but he can't.

"The way you're reacting to me right now? That's real."

I'm taking a risk when I guide Wes's hand downward. sliding it over my abdomen, my happy trail, and down to my cock. My heavy breath is full of desire and relief when he wraps his fingers around me and begins to pump with slow, steady strokes. It also doesn't take much to get me hard, the way he's looking at my dick like it's got him in a trance.

Heh.

I put my lips to his ear. "You have no idea how fucking sexy it is to see you flustered and fascinated when one of us touches you, Kitten. The way you look with your hand on me now? Eyes all wide? You're like a wild animal raised in captivity, and you're finally discovering the colorful expanse of the outside world, yeah? A little terrified. A lot excited. Super fucking horny."

"Wild animals get horny?" He barely breathes the words, still focused on jacking my dick. My hand rests lightly over his. He could pull away if he wanted, but he doesn't.

"Someone needs to watch a nature documentary."

"I don't..." He shakes his head, like he doesn't even know what he was about to say.

Wes's fingers brush under my head, where it's sensitive. We both moan, and at that moment what's got me captivated isn't his hand but his face. When he looks at me, it's with hooded lids and his tongue tracing over his lips.

As I'm locked here in the world's hottest staring contest, I'm not sure anymore who's in control. I thought it was me, but Wes's gaze has me trapped.

Seeing this hot-as-fuck older man in his respectable khakis and navy tie, jacking me in the middle of doing his job?

I get it now, what Troy was saying. It scrambles my brain a little bit.

"You get what I'm talking about now? The way I respond to you, the way you respond to me? That's different. Troy and I get paid to be a fantasy. We're expensive performance art. You know that much, because you hired a male escort to lay your brother. But we're still people. You? This? That's real."

His sharp inhale? The nervous working of his throat? Fucking delicious.

"Of course we like fucking with you," I murmur. "Of course we want to do it again and again. How could we not?"

There's a little walkie-talkie deal clipped to his belt. It makes some noise before a tinny voice asks, "Mr. Monroe, could you come to the front desk, please?"

The trance is broken. Wes pulls his hand away from my dick so fast you'd think it bit him.

"What the fuck am I doing?" He stumbles backward toward the door. There's a moment when his arm twitches, like he might be about to reach for me again, but in the end he shakes it off. "Jesus. I need to go."

My hand goes to my chest, to the sudden soreness in its center. "Too bad. Maybe next time you can stay and watch."

Then I drop my robe to the floor right in front of him. The heavy fabric hits the floor with a quiet thump. With a grin, I turn to join Troy and Mr. Rigby in the bedroom.

A strained groan follows me out of the room. I don't see Wes's eyes on my ass as I walk away, but I know they're there.

CHAPTER TEN

WES

I JERKED off in an electrical service closet after leaving the room where Adam and Troy were...working. In the last several hours I've ducked into a private bathroom or my temporary hotel room on the second floor more than once to do the same thing all over again.

Now it's seven in the morning, and I'm spent physically and emotionally, too keyed up and too exhausted at the same time.

Thank goodness it was a slow night at the Premiere. My mind has been going in circles, even before my run-in with Adam up in one of the VIP suites. But more so ever since.

Why didn't I stop him? The question has tumbled in my head until it's shiny and smooth. Until all the angles look the same. Every inch of me burns with an exquisite mix of arousal and shame.

Why *the hell* didn't I pull my hand away when Adam guided me to touch him? Why didn't I *want* to?

In theory, I don't have a problem with being something other than straight. My brother has had relationships with both men and women. In actual practice, though? I was with Gina for so many years. I never considered the possibility of other people, period.

Feels like I'm way too old to become someone new.

This is less spiritual rebirth and more like I'm standing on quicksand.

My stomach grumbles, and I put my mental roller coaster to the side. Everything will look better after I get some nutrients into my body.

"Morning, Cheyenne." I approach the lobby smoothie bar as it's opening, needing an energy boost. "Berry smoothie with a shot of green tea, please."

Most mornings I try to go out for a run after my shift, but an earlier text from my brother said his security friend was going to stop by. I need to make sure my brain is still online for that conversation.

Cheyenne winces, looking apologetic. "I'm sorry, Mr. Monroe. Max—I mean, Mr. Walker—said he'd have my job if I gave you any more free drinks."

Fucking Max.

"That's fine. I can charge it to my room."

Another apologetic look. "He also said not to charge things to your room. Said you're not supposed to be here much longer? He, uh, went around telling everybody."

Great. Fantastic. Fuck it. I'm too tired to deal with this shit right now.

"Not a big deal." Even in my own ears, my cheerfulness sounds false. "My wallet's up in my room. I'll drop by later." Despite my frustration, I manage a smile.

Except I probably won't stop by later, because I've

recently locked all my credit cards in a hidden tool compartment in my car to keep from using them. I'm not entirely certain about the current state of my checking account, so my debit card is out too.

I'm at the front office pilfering cough drops as well as a packet of chalky tablets for my stomach when a familiar young man comes in, followed by a guy whose hard jaw and narrowed eyes make him look as if he'd put your head through a table simply for looking at him funny.

"Hey, Mr. Monroe's brother!" Ravi, that's who the younger one is. He's at the university gym some days when I go to meet my brother for a workout. Also, he stayed here at the hotel not too long ago. On the VIP level. His bill was covered by the owner of a private sex dungeon or something a couple of towns over, which means he's yet another sex worker.

Or at least, he used to be.

The man behind him, the one in tactical pants with a chip on his shoulder, steps up to me, reaching an arm across the check-in desk to shake. "Westlake Monroe? Liam Masters. Your brother said you wished to speak with me."

"Well, actually, Mr. Monroe told PJ, who told me, who told Liam, but I guess the end result is the same." Ravi puts his finger to his chin dimple, clearly giving the communication chain serious thought.

Liam looks at the young man fondly. "Nobody likes it when people 'well actually,' baby. Especially not when the end result is the same."

Ravi responds with a "Sorry, Daddy" that doesn't sound at all sorry, followed by a satisfied smile and an obvious roll of his eyes. The way Liam's looking back at him? I'm not sure I should be here right now.

My awkward foot shuffling must break the spell. Liam clears his throat and gestures to me. "Someplace we can talk privately?"

There are so many questions on the tip of my tongue about the relationship these two appear to have. None of them are at all appropriate.

Working in a luxury hotel, I've learned to be the opposite of interested in people's personal business. Whatever goes on in the VIP suites stays in the VIP suites. My job is to keep things running smoothly and make their lives easier while they're guests here.

Basically, I'm a talking microwave. Microwaves don't ask questions or have opinions. They beep. They overheat.

They short-circuit when nobody's looking.

Suddenly, though, this man who looks awfully close to my age walks in with someone I know is in college because I've seen him swipe his student ID at the gym. He's calling him baby. Ravi's calling him Daddy. There's so much heat between them I fear for the safety of the potted banana trees lining the shiny marble lobby.

So, yes. I definitely have some questions. For a friend. For...science.

Ignoring the curious looks from the morning desk clerk, I lead the two into a small conference room we rent out for meetings.

Once inside with the door closed, I get right down to business. "We've had several employees fail to show up recently. Some even disappeared in the middle of their shifts. No trace, no email, no phone call, no responses when I tried to reach out."

Liam's brow furrows. "Isn't that fairly common in the hotel industry? High turnover?"

"Sure," I concede. "Typically we see an average loss of one to two people per month here. Maybe more, depending on the time of year, but the numbers year over year have been fairly steady. I went back through some of our employment records to confirm. Lately, it's closer to one or two a week."

The man rubs his forehead, and like everyone else I've spoken to about this, I can see he's already dismissing it. "There could be so many reasons for people not showing up to work at a high-traffic hotel. It's not necessarily anything awful."

Urgency pushes my pulse higher. "The housekeeping manager has polled the housekeeping staff about the work environment. Nothing unusual has been reported." Like the hotel GM being a dick. Annoying, but typical. I keep that one to myself.

Liam nods, considering. Then he shakes his head. "It's the holidays. People could simply want time off. Workers at minimum wage are notoriously unreliable."

Dammit. I'm tired of having this conversation over and over, tired of wondering if I'm the one who's wrong. Rubbing my hand across my jaw does little to ease the ache from clenching. I used to be one of those "unreliable" employees. This isn't an easy town to find work in, and nobody can convince me that that many people would simply walk away from reliable income.

"The most recent employee to not show up is a single mom with an infant. I know she needs the job, and she's mentioned not having much in the way of family. It doesn't seem like her to simply not show up." I step forward. "Maybe I'm crazy, but we've had some good people simply disappear, most of whom I've known to be responsible employees. The general manager's already blown me off, but I really don't think I'm wrong here."

"People have all sorts of things going on we don't always know about, Mr. Monroe. This single mother of yours could have been ill, or maybe she couldn't get childcare. Maybe she got a better offer."

"She would have called." No, I'm not certain. I'm grasping at straws.

"Daddy." Ravi slides an arm around Liam's waist. "Can't you at least look into it a little? The downside of Mr. Monroe's brother being right is much worse than if he's wrong."

Hell. His eyes are so wide and liquid even I'm dying to give the young man whatever he wants. I don't even care that he keeps referring to me as Fallon's brother instead of by name.

Never thought I'd see the day when I was grateful to my brother's boyfriend or one of his buddies for anything, but here I am. Thanks to Ravi, Liam might reconsider.

Sure enough, after a brief stare-off, Liam gives me a nod. "If you can, get me the names of the people you're concerned about. I can't do a whole lot to investigate in the hotel if the general manager isn't on board, but I can try to find out what the employees might be up to. Until you know more, though, assume they're fine. The chances are good that they are."

"Thank you." I take down his email address so I can send him the information.

"By the way." He stops on our way back out to the lobby. "Do you happen to know a Joseph Rigby? I believe he's a guest here."

"Name doesn't ring a bell."

Liam nods, looking for a moment as if there's more he wants to say.

I'm not supposed to share guest information, but... "Do you need me to—"

"Nah. It's nothing I can back up yet. I'll let you know." He puts his hand on Ravi's shoulder, who's busy chattering about the butternut squash ravioli he had while he stayed here at the hotel.

"Can we get some before we leave, Daddy?"

Liam catches my curious stare. "The more he thinks I'm likely to be embarrassed by it, the more he calls me that." Then he grins. "It's fine, because I'll punish him for it later."

"I..." What am I supposed to say here? "Okay."

"Guys!" Ravi calls to someone, frantically waving his arms to catch their attention.

There's an abrupt shift in the air as two men and a child approach.

One is several inches taller than me, lean, with blond hair and blue eyes. The other is a handsome Black man, a bit shorter than I am, with the kind of muscles that mean his clothing has to work extra hard. Between them is a young girl. I'm not great at guessing age but I've seen enough kids come through with their families to estimate she's somewhere in elementary school.

The Pokémon shirt she's wearing does some of the heavy lifting for me.

"What are you two doing here?" Ravi asks as they get closer.

The blond points up toward the ceiling. "Adam and Troy are staying here—"

The mere mention of their names causes something hot to unfurl in my belly. Jesus.

"That's right." Ravi nods. "They mentioned they had an appointment with—" He meets my horrified gaze and snaps his mouth shut. "Never mind."

Oh, I'm well aware. Though I try to make my face more neutral, I'm not sure I succeed. Not when thinking about them too much simultaneously makes me feel as if someone has stroked my dick and punched me in the stomach.

"Anyway, they invited us to have breakfast with them," the tall one says. "Also, Ella wants to hit the pool. Slide down the slide."

My insides tumble. It's not simply that Adam and Troy are men; it's that they're, well, them. If my sexual orientation was going to veer off course this late in life, wouldn't it be with someone who made more sense?

Or any sense?

That's it. That's the problem. I have no sense.

Ravi and the others chat among themselves while Liam's at the desk writing some additional contact information on his business card.

Before I can extract myself, Gina comes by and snags my arm. "Wes. I need to speak with you."

"Is it urgent?" I nod to the group in front of me.

She hesitates. She manages the restaurant and not the hotel proper, so she wouldn't know if they're guests or not. Even if they aren't, she knows better than to be rude.

"I guess it can wait—"

"Westy! There you are, Kitten."

What the actual fuck is happening? I'd give my left testicle to be able to set myself on fire right now. I don't need to turn around to see who's behind me, and even if I did, Ravi calling out to greet Adam and Troy clears up any mystery.

Gina's eyes are narrowed as if she's trying to calculate something. I need to get her away from here before she finishes the math.

"Gina." I gesture to Ravi. "This gentleman would like to be able to take some butternut squash ravioli home with him. He was recently a guest here in one of the Oceanview suites and can't stop talking about it."

Not only does this get Ravi chattering at her so she's not focused on me, but mentioning the Oceanview suite should head her off before she tells him the ravioli isn't available this early in the morning. The golden rule here is to keep the VIP guests happy, and Ravi was recently one of them.

"Oh." Her eyes widen. "I'll...stop in at the kitchen and see what I can do."

Great. Good.

Just when I think I'm home free, an arm slides around my waist and a large cup with a straw is thrust in my face. "Here, babe. Got you a smoothie. Berries and green tea. I know how you love your antioxidants."

How the hell did he know? "Have you been watching me?" I breathe into Troy's ear.

He gives me an exaggerated wink.

There's too much happening at once. My brain can't catch up. The hand holding the smoothie cup isn't attached to the same person who has a possessive arm around my waist.

While I'm processing that, while I take the smoothie from Troy's hand with a quiet "thank you" because I actually do appreciate it, it hits me that everyone around us has gone silent.

With the exception of the little girl, who's busy squealing over a fluffy goldendoodle getting walked across the opposite end of the brightly lit lobby, everyone else is staring.

Even a man standing near the concierge desk across the lobby seems to be observing with far too much curiosity. He's about my age, maybe a little older, wearing clothes that probably cost a year of my salary. All cream colors and finely woven material. Something about him is familiar. Probably a VIP guest, so I'm sure this moment isn't making me look great.

Even Gina is staring. Especially Gina.

Ravi has his hand over his mouth. To think, minutes ago, I was ready to ride into battle for him. Whatever he's holding in, he's probably seconds from blurting it out.

"Gina." My tone is too sharp. "Weren't you going to check with the chef about that ravioli?"

Her gaze bounces from Adam's hand on my waist to Troy's smug smile with increasing confusion.

While I'm trying to formulate another way to make her leave, dammit, the worst possible thing happens. Troy reaches out to shake her hand.

"Hey there, sweetness. Troy. Professional homewrecker. How you doing?"

A chuckle comes from somewhere. I don't look to see who. I'm busy begging Troy to shut up with my eyes.

"Pleasure." Gina's demeanor shifts. Her shoulders straighten and her smile brightens. It's the one she uses with customers. "I'm going to see about that ravioli. Wes, can you come with me, please?"

My first impulse is to say no. I'm talking to guests, and whatever else she may think of the situation, that's my priority. The fact that one of those guests has just put his hand on my ass doesn't do much for my credibility.

I disengage from Adam and avoid eye contact with anyone until Gina and I are out of earshot. "Gina. Look—"

"What in God's name is going on, Wes?"

"Nothing."

"Nothing is not a man calling you 'Kitten' in the lobby while another one puts his arm around you and shoots daggers at me."

Oh. Hadn't noticed that part.

Is it wrong that between the smoothie and whatever look Adam gave Gina, likely on my behalf, I'm oddly touched?

"It's not—"

"They're sex workers, Wes. I've seen them all here before. And the two who were touching you?"

"They weren't both touching me." Yeah, I hear it as soon as I say it out loud.

"That's not the quality argument you seem to think it is. The two who were feeding and groping you, then."

Every word out of her mouth tightens the muscles in my back. "Do you have a point?"

She runs her tongue over her teeth. "I don't know what on earth is going on with you. Whatever it is, it's going to get you in trouble."

I make the mistake of turning my head to look in the direction we came from. Troy sees me and gives an obnoxious (and obvious) finger wave. There's a split second when his tongue makes an appearance between his lips, and I'm taken back to that moment in the closet. To the feel of his tongue in my mouth.

My skin turns blistering hot. When I look back at Gina, my neck cracks.

"Whatever I'm doing, it's none of your business."

She opens her mouth, but I cut her off.

"No. I kept my mouth shut all the times I suspected about you and Max. I've taken my ration of shit from the fact that your new boyfriend is my boss, and he seems to get off on making my life difficult. I agreed to cover the mortgage on our house until the divorce paperwork shakes out. Although if Max is moving in, you can bet your ass I'm not paying for it any longer. We won't be married anymore in a matter of days, and then it'll be even less your concern than it is now. I'm not discussing this with you."

I turn on my heel, satisfied to leave her with her mouth hanging open. Stopping briefly to collect Liam's business card and let him know I'll be in touch, I escape out the door to the employee parking lot.

I've got an appointment to look at an apartment this morning anyway. Moving out of here can't come soon enough.

At this point I'll take any shithole, as long as the walls don't listen or talk back.

CHAPTER ELEVEN

TROY

Brennan (pimp daddy): So, remember when my guys burned down the old peach canning factory? The one where those pills were being produced?

Ravi: You mean the time I got a face full of some nasty drug powder stuff that almost killed me? Sort of.

Brennan (pimp daddy): Right. Turns out, we didn't kill the supply, so you fuckers be careful out there.

Troy: Not to be a dick, but Brennan, are you warning us for safety reasons or because whoever's supplying this shit is competition?

Brennan (pimp daddy): Do what you want I'm not your mother. But you can bet your ass I'm not out there using some cut rate chemist to cook up shit that will kill people and then flooding the streets with it. This shit is bad news.

Michael: Kind of you to warn us, Brennan.

Dean: Kiss ass.

"Uh-oh. Mom and Dad are fighting again," I tell Adam as he pulls the Mustang up to our apartment building. The exterior paint is peeling, and the hallways smell like onions, but it's not the worst. It's on the outskirts of downtown, where the nice part of town starts to get a little less nice.

We've talked about moving, but this place is familiar. It was the first place we found when we were finally able to afford something real. The landlord's kind of shady, but he also doesn't ask questions. It's convenient.

"Huh?"

"Dean and Michael. They must be in the off-again phase of their...whatever it is."

Adam huffs a laugh. "I don't know what's up with those two."

"They're destined to either ride off into the sunset or murder each other. Let's get your insulin and get back to the hotel. Next time you should pack more."

"How did I know Rigby was going to want an extra night with us?"

"There's never a downside to making sure you have extra insulin. It's better than running out."

"Except for the times I've ended up accidentally leaving hundreds of dollars' worth in a hotel mini fridge," Adam grumbles.

Eh. "That's fair. It's worse, though, if you run out."

"Hey." Adam puts his hand on mine. "It's not like it used to be. I'm fine. We're fine."

We're long past the days when I begged, borrowed, stole, and fucked—sometimes all at once—to keep Adam healthy and alive. Are we fine, though? Are we safe? I don't know. In the same way Adam still hides valuables in his boots, I'm not sure I'll ever stop worrying about him having what he really needs.

We're not on the streets anymore, which was terrifying. The things we did—the things *I* did—to keep Adam safe back then? Well, the worst part was not always knowing if they'd work. The times he got hospitalized and I couldn't get in to see him, those almost killed me. The worst was the time, shortly before he turned eighteen, when a social worker wanted to send him back to his family, and we had to run again.

Which is how we ended up in Belle Argo, working for Brennan.

A lot of people don't trust Brennan, but as pimps go, we've definitely seen worse. It's good we found him when we did. The guy may be a snake, but we grew up around vipers, and Brennan is more of a python. He'll at least give you a hug and make you feel good about yourself while he's killing you.

"Shit. Check this shit out."

Adam's still in his seat, staring at the front of our building. "Is that...?"

Yeah. Our kitten is here. "What the hell is this about, you think?"

Wes is coming out of the front door of our building, still wearing the same tired-ass business casual he had on when he walked out of the hotel earlier. Poor guy's got dark circles under his eyes, and he carries himself with an unusual stiffness.

Adam hustles out of the car. I follow.

"Kitten, you look lost," I call out to him.

Given the adorable way his ears turn red every time I call him Kitten? It's what I'm calling him forever and ever.

When he sees us, he practically flattens himself against the cement wall by the entrance. "Jesus Christ, are you guys following me now?"

If he didn't look ready to pass out, I might actually laugh. We're the ones who live here. I'm too caught up by how his clothing is rumpled and his dark hair is a little shaggy, like he hasn't had time to give it a good brush, let alone get it trimmed into something befitting a manager in a pricey hotel.

Digging the overgrown stubble, though. Makes me want to rub up against him.

"We live here," Adam says. Then he points to the Mustang, which is parked in a space marked Resident.

"How is that supposed to tell me anything? In my limited experience with the two of you, you're not exactly concerned with following the rules." That angry scowl of his is just precious. Kitten's trying to act all big and bad.

"Is this about us jerking you off at the gym?" I ask. "Or when Adam blew you in that closet? No rules against any of that."

"There are all sorts of rules against *all of that.*" Poor man looks exasperated. Guess we haven't helped him relax enough yet. "By the way, the gym specifically has posters up in the locker room telling people not to masturbate."

"That's only in the showers though. Because of the plumbing," Adam points out.

"Right. The jizz gums up the pipes." I nod along with my best friend.

"That is not the only—" Wes shakes his head. "You know what? Never mind. I'm not going to stand here and do this with you. And now I'm definitely not taking the apartment. No offense, but I cannot live in the same building as the two of you."

"Wait." I catch his arm as he tries to pass me. "The building's full."

Wes frowns. "I just looked at a place on the third floor. I filled out an application."

That fucking scum-sucking, cock-smoking landlord. "Was the place furnished?"

A crease divides Wes's forehead. "Yeah. Gina kept the house and the furniture, so it was ideal."

"Did you pay an application fee?" Adam adds.

Wes's frown deepens. "For the credit and background check."

I cut my gaze to Adam, who's already starting for the door. "Go take care of it."

"Way ahead of you," he announces, taking the steps two at a time.

"What is happening right now?" Wes looks down at where my fingers are gripping the crook of his arm, as if he's seeing me touch him for the first time. That's all he does, though. Stares.

Every time one of us touches him, I think that'll be the time he tells us to take our hands off. Surely at some point he'll storm away and freeze us out. Instead, he's like this feral cat my mom fed in the backyard when I was a kid. He'd snarl at anyone, but all I had to do was scratch him under the chin, and he'd purr.

So Kitten really is a fitting name for Wes. Wonder what would happen if I tried to pet him? Would this kitten bring his claws out? I'm half-hard at the thought.

"The building is full," I tell Wes again. "And our landlord

is a sack of shit. What you probably looked at was Jalen's place. Third floor? Works for our pimp. He's a neat freak, and he's not home too often, so it would be easy to make it look like the place is vacant."

Wes sags back against the wall. I'm not exactly caging him in, but I'm right there, up close and personal. Enough that if either of us took a deep breath our bodies would press together.

Which means I can see the little signs that I'm getting to him. The bob of his Adam's apple when he swallows. A twitch at the corner of his eye. The pulsing blood vessel in his neck. Little splotches of color on his throat and face and ears that are way cuter than they have a right to be on a grown-ass man.

This is a guy gripping the windowsill with white knuckles, but his fingertips are slipping. What are the chances he'll let us catch him?

"So he took my deposit knowing there's no apartment available. Great."

"Yeah. He does shady shit like this all the time. Fuck knows how many poor saps he's had through here that he's collected some 'non-refundable application fee' from for a supposed background check on an apartment that isn't available."

"And I'm another poor sap. Of course I am." Kitten looks like someone cut all his strings.

This close, I can make out the flecks of silver in his hair. The subtle lines fanning out from his eyes. His chin lifts and his lips turn down simultaneously, as if he is trying to keep his head up but losing the battle.

Kitten's gonna drown if he isn't careful. Maybe that's why this guy intrigues me so much. Something deep inside me recognizes its own kind. Someone trying to keep his head above water, sometimes not sure if he's winning or losing.

I slide my hand along his stubbled jaw, forcing him to look down into my eyes. "Don't give up on me now, Kitten. It'll all work out."

"I don't see how." Those four words are so achingly honest I wonder if he's forgotten who he's talking to.

"You'll figure it out. You will because you have to. Because you've come too far to give up now. This is a detour, that's all."

When he puts his hand over mine, I'm not sure which of us is more surprised. "I don't know why you're being nice to me."

Excuse me? "I don't know what the fuck you're talking about. We've been nothing but nice to you."

His eyes go wide. Like a tall, sexy deer in headlights. "Is that really what you think? You shoved me into a corner of the gym locker room and jerked me off—"

"I swallowed you down and everything," I remind him.

"Because you thought I was homophobic."

"Misunderstanding. Still, we both know you loved it."

He drops his chin to his chest and rubs his forehead a little. "You put on a fucking porn show in the back of my classroom while I was teaching."

Can't keep the grin off my face. "You looked so fucking hot up there, by the way. About to blow a gasket and trying to play it cool."

"You sucked me off in a goddamn closet!" He's whisper-yelling now. Glancing around in all directions to make sure nobody heard him. As if anyone around here even cares.

"That was Adam. Still, I'm failing to see how any of this is bad, Kitten."

"You cockblocked me at a gay bar."

"You didn't want that guy anyway. He couldn't give you what you need."

"How the hell would you even know what I need?"

"Hey. Settle down there, babe. You're going off like our elderly neighbor's tea kettle." My hand finds its way to his waist. It's such an easy thing to tug his belt a little, to bring his body flush against mine. It's not a hug exactly—his head is still flopped against the stone wall—but he's surprisingly willing to let himself melt against me. He eases farther forward when my free hand finds his, one thumb making circles on the webbing between his thumb and forefinger.

And he thinks I don't know what he needs. "Kitten, I know exactly what you need. I think you do, too. Only you're afraid to admit you need it."

"I'm too fucking tired right now to play your games, Troy. I am drowning in debt, I am exhausted, and I've got days to be out of the hotel room I've been living in since I caught my wife and our boss naked in our upstairs bathroom. I'm too old to be learning new things about myself, too fucking wrung out to even process what any of it means. Whatever you're trying to do here, you need to stop. Okay?"

His lower lip juts out some. A slight pout that I can't keep myself from kissing off him.

When I brush my lips over his, he sighs. It's a deep thing that seems to come from down in his core. "You really want us to stop, Kitten?"

"I'm nothing but a game to you," he mumbles against my lips. "Adam told me you guys like that I'm easy to fuck with. I don't have time for games. And I'm too damn old for fucking around."

"Not a game at all, Kitten." Maybe it was, but it's something different now.

I grip his chin between my thumb and forefinger, pushing it upward. Taking a big inhale of his spicy scent, I press the flat of my tongue to the base of his throat and lick upward, stopping with a bite to his chin. He's salty and a little bit bitter. The way he gasps and then his breath stills is music to my ears.

"What..." His heart is racing. I can feel it pounding against mine. When he exhales, eucalyptus and menthol puffs against my lips. "What is it, then?"

"You know that old saying, 'I licked it, so it's mine?' Well, I licked you. You're mine now. Since I share everything with my best friend, that makes you his, too. Ours."

Oh, shit, I love the look on his face right now. If I didn't know better, I'd think he was drunk.

The door beside us swings open, and out comes Adam with one of his backup diabetes kits under his arm. "Got the insulin. Good to go." Then he stops and looks at us both. "Everything okay?"

My best friend's single eyebrow raise loudly asks what the hell I'm up to out here. As if he doesn't already know.

I slide my nose along Wes's neck again, drinking in his spicy scent. His swallow rings in my ears, wet and loud. "Peachy."

Adam grins and blows a kiss as he heads to the car.

I fucking knew it.

Once Adam got over his issues, I knew he'd be into this like I am. I know him better than I know myself.

As I'm backing away, our landlord, Eddie, comes out,

cradling a swollen jaw. He thrusts a sort of damp-looking crumpled-up check into Wes's hand. Damn. I'm betting Adam tried to shove the thing down his throat.

Which, I mean, gross. But also, hell yeah.

Wes takes the nasty thing, still looking a little shell-shocked after that kiss, if I can blow my own damn horn for a minute.

"Place is taken. Should've told you." Eddie glances at Adam, who's giving him the stink eye and crossing his arms over his chest. He tacks on a hasty "Sorry" before hustling back inside.

"That look like fucking around to you?" I ask Wes.

His lips part on a stuttered exhale. "I don't know what that was."

The way Wes is little lost and confused, I don't want him hanging around here after we leave. I'd hate for Eddie or anyone else to get any bright ideas. This isn't the worst neighborhood, but it also isn't the best. Only a couple of blocks over I know guys who sling the sort of cut-rate pills Brennan's been warning us about, and where that shit goes, tragedy follows.

"Change of plans," I announce. "Give us a ride back to the hotel, eh, Westy? You're living there now anyway. No sense in us wasting gas. Gotta protect the environment and all."

The way his fingers curl and uncurl into fists, I wonder if I've pushed him too far. The shock on his face firms into annoyance, and then something a whole lot like anger. Adam, who knows damn well my tendency to push until something breaks, is trying not to laugh and failing. Badly.

Our kitten looks like he's about to take a swipe with his

claws out. Fuck knows he's shooting laser beams with his eyes.

Right about when I think he's about to tell us to piss off, he pulls out his keys and shoves the check into his pocket. "Call me Westy again and I'll leave you by the side of the road."

Adam gives me a subtle fist bump behind Wes's back.

CHAPTER TWELVE

WES

GINA and I gave up on having kids when the effort started to break us both down, and not just physically. But riding with Adam and Troy in my car is what I imagine it's like to have toddlers. The sexy and in-command men who cornered me in a closet and guided me into jerking them off have turned into, well...

"Punch buggy!" Adam slugs Troy from his spot in the back seat when we pass someone driving a vintage yellow VW Beetle.

Troy turns around and growls, "Just for that? Wait until it's your turn to bottom again. I'll tear your asshole's asshole a new asshole."

So, they're lewd toddlers. Still.

The wild part? I'm trying like hell not to laugh at them. I can't count how many times during the drive from their apartment I've nearly cracked.

The crinkle of a wrapper raises my hackles, though. "Hey. Whatever that is, save it for after you're out of my car."

"But I'm hungry." Without even looking, Troy's garbled complaint tells me the ship has sailed, and whatever he unwrapped is already in his mouth.

"Fuck. Just...please try not to drop crumbs."

He waves a dismissive hand. "That's what vacuums are for."

Okay, no. "Look, asshole. I am about five minutes away from being homeless. I'm paying a mortgage on a house I don't even get to live in. So fuck you and your damn granola bar."

My hands tighten on the steering wheel. When I open my mouth next, the anger that flies out shocks even me. "This car may be ancient and rusty, but it's the one thing I have that's mine. It is *all* I have. So if you drop crumbs, you'd better fucking pick them up."

Silence. Stopping at the red light nearest to the Premiere's main entrance, I rub my gritty eyes.

"Something wrong, Kitten?" Troy turns to look at me, and his expression fucks me up, because all of a sudden he seems so earnest and sincere. Even as he finishes chewing the bite in his mouth and swallows.

Too bad neither of them can actually fix any of my problems.

Would I ask them for help if I thought they could?

That thought creates a fizzy sensation inside me that I can't afford to feel. I can't lean on people or hope for help. It only makes things shittier when people disappear and let you down. That goes double for two young men who are at best passing through my life, leaving chaos in their wake.

Troy bought you a smoothie when you weren't able to get one for yourself.

I still don't know for sure how he knew about that. I've tried not to dwell. That fizzy sensation is addictive and dangerous. It's worse than hope. If I didn't know better I'd be tempted to call it something like affection.

It's best if I keep myself officially closed off to all floaty, hopeful, fizzy feelings. To all sensations having to do with two men in their early twenties, for God's sake, who alternate between acting as if they're older and wiser than me and acting as if they're children.

Never actually wanted kids, anyway.

Except Troy is still looking at me as the light turns green, and it feels rude not to answer. "The two of you are so fucking immature; I'm trying to figure out how I keep letting you both have your way with me."

Out of the corner of my eye, Troy's smile is impossibly bright. "I'll address the second thing first." He does something akin to jazz hands. Spirit fingers? "You've got a secret desire to be dominated, and we've got magic hands."

A secret desire to...

My stomach flips.

Oh. No. No, no, no. I most certainly do not.

Do I?

Chills race up my spine. "I don't even know where to begin unpacking that statement."

As if he senses it's a new hot spot, Adam reaches from the back seat and tickles the hair at the base of my skull. "The other thing is on account of our fucked-up childhoods," he says. "Troy grew up with an abusive and homophobic piece of shit, and I grew up in organized crime...with an abusive and homophobic piece of shit."

"Jesus," I breathe. My eyelids suddenly weigh an awful lot.

Now I feel like an asshole. Nobody knows better than I do about shitty childhoods, and mine wasn't nearly as bad as what these two probably dealt with.

"Tell us about your childhood, Westy." Troy nudges my side.

"For the last fucking time, it's Wes."

"Or Kitten," Adam supplies.

The Premiere's employee lot is always full of cars. For obvious reasons, the hotel prefers to reserve most of the parking areas for paying guests. Still, they really need to expand enough to cover their staffing needs. Currently we're short on housekeepers and kitchen staff, yet I'm still having to park in the grass way in the back because there's nothing else open at this time of day.

When I'm finally in what can only be loosely called a parking space, I turn off the car and face them both. "My childhood was nothing special."

"Hey. We're trying to get to know you, Kitten. It's what you do on dates." Troy bats his eyelashes. They're shorter and lighter than Adam's, but still nice, I guess. Curly, if you're into that sort of thing.

Stop pretending you aren't.

"You can't call a fifteen-minute car ride where the two of you spent most of it acting like unruly children a date."

"He's right." Adam nods. "We should all go out to a movie sometime."

Troy perks up. "There's an old horror film coming to that taphouse theater in the north end. The one where an old house is haunted by the ghosts of murdered children. What are you into, Kitten?"

The thing is, I'd actually planned on seeing that one. But...

"I'm sorry." I twist farther around in the seat. "When did this change from you guys humiliating me via orgasm to the three of us dating? You both sound ridiculous. For at least a little while, I'm still married. I'm nearly twice your age. Let's not forget you're both regularly fucking other people. You rode with me back to the hotel because you're *on the way to fuck someone else right now.*"

I wince at the volume of my voice. Glancing around, I'm grateful to see the rest of the lot appears to be empty right now. There's a flash of alarm when I think I hear footsteps, but it must be paranoia because I don't see anyone.

Good. The last thing I need is someone who works under me hearing my unhinged rant about dating two sex workers.

As I exit the car and speed-walk toward the door, Adam and Troy's footsteps hustle behind me. It's a good thing I've got longer legs, although possibly not enough. They're getting closer.

"Is that a deal-breaker for you, Kitten?" Troy asks. "Because it's something we can have a conversation about."

"Yeah, when we're getting to know each other," Adam adds.

"For God's sake, both of you, stop. Stop with the teasing and the taunting and the trying to get to know me. I spent a decade and a half in a marriage with someone who actively hated me almost as much as I hated myself and I cannot handle—"

Something lurches in my chest. The second I realize I've strayed into actual getting-to-know-you territory, I snap my mouth shut.

"Don't you remember the conversation we had back at our place? What I hear you saying is you need to have fun as much as we do, Westy." Troy's obviously trying to get a rise out of me. I refuse to take their bait again.

When I glance back over my shoulder, though, he looks achingly sincere. I try to shake off the unsettling wobble in my center as I turn back toward the hotel.

"Troy's right, Kitten," Adam adds. "Maybe you even need it more than—"

Someone grunts. The footsteps behind me stop.

It takes me a second to notice. I'm too busy speed-walking away from them. When I turn around, Troy is laid out flat on the ground. Adam is down too, but he's groaning and trying to push himself off the pavement.

When I hurry over to see if they're okay, there's a shuffling noise behind me. I look over my shoulder in time to see a gloved fist coming at my face.

It's the last thing I see before things go dark.

CHAPTER THIRTEEN

WES

When I wake up from what I can only assume was an assault, my first thought is that my hip and jaw are sore. But at least I got to take a nap.

Until I get a better feel for my surroundings. I'm sandwiched in between two bodies. My hands are zip-tied in front of me. Something smells like foot funk.

"You were only supposed to get the one," someone says. The voice is gruff and deep. Gravelly.

"Well, we didn't have much choice, did we? Bet we'll get a little something for the extra ones, yeah?" Am I imagining things, or does the other guy sound British?

A careful glance to either side tells me the bodies I'm sandwiched between are Adam and Troy, which is when the memory of what happened in the parking lot returns.

Troy's jaw looks puffy. There's blood trickling from Adam's temple. All three of us are lying in this musty van like so many rolled-up area rugs, and at least two of us are injured. Looking at them both makes my stomach roil.

Thank God they both seem like they're breathing.

"They were too close to him. You know how it goes. You got witnesses; you either have to bring them or end them. Couldn't end them in a parking lot. It's broad daylight."

Until this moment I was overly warm in the back of the van, pressed in between two people. After that comment, I'm freezing cold.

Maybe he didn't mean what I'm thinking. My mother and Gina both used to call me overdramatic.

There's this need in me to keep my eyes on Adam and Troy. Aside from the blood and bruising, they might as well be asleep. My feelings about them may be complicated and confusing, but I sure as hell don't want them to die.

Except I have no idea what to do. Why were we taken? Where are we going, and what are they going to do to us once we get there?

It's too tight in here to move much. Seeing the faces of the drivers up front is a no-go.

Adam's fingers twitch and flex, indicating he's either about to wake up or having a really intense dream. Troy seems to be breathing more heavily, but I can't tell for sure. So, I start nudging at him as best as I can with my bound hands.

Not that I have the first clue what I'm doing. It just seems as if we're all better off if we're awake.

"If you're going to try to get to know my cock better, less poking and more stroking, Kitten."

My breath rushes out. *Thank fuck.*

For once, I don't care what he calls me. He can call me anything he wants. "Are you okay?"

Again, I try to glance up. Did anyone in front hear us? Right now they seem to be fighting over the radio.

"Feels like someone took a hammer to my face," Troy mumbles. "How's Adam?"

"Not awake yet. Bleeding."

"Fuck." His eyes fly open. "He's got diabetes. Prone to infections. He needs—"

"I know," I whisper too harshly. Troy's panic is rising over our need to keep quiet. "Not much we can do about it right now."

"Any idea where the hell they're taking us?" Troy's wrists are bound like mine, but he manages to roll more toward me, so our faces are almost touching.

"You joked about kidnapping me, but this is a bit much." God, why am I trying to make jokes? I guess I don't know what else to do.

He rolls his eyes. "Kitten, we would have taken you someplace with a much better view."

In spite of the situation, I almost manage to laugh a little. "I'd take a do-over of mini golf over this."

The three of us can't be anything but a distraction, even though I can admit I'm curious. I'm discovering a world I never even thought I wanted to visit. If I were in their position, I might also find myself entertaining.

But right now, this isn't about what we are to each other. We need to be a team, because we're in this together.

Next to me, Adam makes a noise. His hands come up toward his face, trying to wipe at the blood, perhaps. Which is when his eyes open, and he realizes he's tied up.

"Fuck. Who did you piss off?" He seems to be talking over my head, to Troy.

"Me? This is probably about the rich girl who's fucking

arranged to be married you keep sticking it to. Bet her daddy found out and decided to get you out of the picture."

Okay, I definitely have questions about this. Let's hope we're alive later for me to ask.

"I don't think they were after one of you," I say quietly. "They were talking earlier about meaning to get one of us and accidentally getting all three."

"This is going to come out sounding wrong," Adam says slowly, "but why would they want you?" He tugs uselessly at the zip tie on his wrists. "What I mean is, Troy and I are more likely to have enemies."

"Maybe. I don't know." I don't know anything right now. "What the hell are we going to do?"

"Easy." Troy's voice is low and raspy. "Soon as they open the back of this thing to let us out, I kill them."

My shock is there and gone in a split second. I don't know what these guys want with us, but I'm not convinced killing us is off the table. If it's us or them, I'm choosing us.

"With what?" I glance around. There are some rectangular containers lining the side of the van, gas cans or something, but they're huge and I don't know how we'd even pick one up with our hands smashed into prayer position. "None of us have a weapon. Dammit, I don't even have my phone."

Its conspicuous weight is missing from my left pocket. The guys who clocked us must have taken it.

"Shit. I do." Adam glances up. "You guys create a distraction, okay?"

"What—how? What do we do?"

Troy whispers, "I have an idea." Without warning he shrugs his arms up and loops them around my neck. Then he tosses one of his legs over both of mine. Then he kisses me.

It isn't a chaste kiss. It's like the kiss from the closet, only dirtier. More desperate. There are teeth clicking and tongues tangling. And moaning. Loud moaning. More from Troy than from me, which I assume is intentional, but mine is less theatrical and more "Oh holy shit, I had no idea."

I can't catch my breath. I'm not sure I want to. For a second, I think I want to keep kissing him more than I want out of this van.

I'm hard. In a van. With my hands tied.

Over the years, Gina and I wound down from newlyweds making an effort, to the more perfunctory intimacy of trying to make a baby, to chaste pecks, to nothing. The only kiss in my life that's come close was from this same man.

Holy shit.

I'm only realizing it now, but I hadn't truly felt desired until these two came along. Ever.

Even if I'm only fun for them, they see my desires and don't laugh at them. They *want* me. They make me feel things I've never felt.

Shit, I really am starting to like them.

After a few years of marriage, I began to feel bad for stud horses. Right now, in the back of a van with my tied hands crushed between my chest and Troy's, his erection grinding against mine, I don't think I've felt more turned-on. If this is only a performance for him, it's a damn good one.

Unfortunately, the van stops as we're catching up with each other.

There's a muttered "Jesus Christ, what the fuck are they doing?" and then seconds later the back door being thrown open.

Then yelling.

“Get that fucking thing away from him.”

Adam is dragged out, kicking and fighting the whole way. Troy and I are literally tangled together. Before we can get disconnected, there’s a sickening thud. When I can finally turn my head, my heart stops. Adam’s slumped over again, still conscious but looking rough.

“You motherfucker—” The second Troy sees Adam, he’s struggling to his feet.

The one guy, who I’d guess is in charge, raises the gun in his hand. “You wanna end up worse off than your friend here? If not, I suggest you shut your mouth.”

The man is larger than me, with unkempt hair and a beard. To me, the scariest thing about him is that his left hand is missing two fingers. This is someone who’s probably seen some shit and isn’t playing pretend with the weapon he’s pointing.

Troy’s shaking against me. I know what he’s thinking. He said it earlier, and that was before they hurt Adam again. He wants to kill these guys. Something tells me he’d do it in a second if he had the chance.

Fear clogs my throat. Even I know we’ve got no chance against someone holding a gun. At best, he’d knock Troy over the head like he did Adam. At worst...

“You can’t kill anyone if you’re unconscious,” I manage to say into Troy’s ear before they drag him out.

They have the most trouble with me, even though I don’t fight.

“This one’s fucking heavy,” the younger one with the accent complains.

“I’ve been doing a lot of squats,” I say dryly. Nobody appreciates the joke.

Not even me.

Adam's confiscated phone is crushed under the big guy's booted heel. Dammit. Did he manage to get word to anyone? We're all herded through a rusted door. Trying to get some idea of our location, I swivel my head as they drag us inside.

There's not much to go on. We seem to be in one of those strips of industrial buildings, except every bit of it looks completely abandoned. Grass and weeds push up between cracks in the paved parking lot.

We're guided through a large room that's full of some type of equipment. There's a lumpy mattress on the floor. As soon as they get us inside, a steel bay door is rolled down and closed with a padlock. Which doesn't bode well for any possible escape plans.

We pass what looks like photography stuff—a tripod and what I think is a boom mic. I've seen them used for high-profile wedding videos at the Premiere. I'm still trying to look around when we're shoved into what looks like an industrial refrigerator. A big one. It's the door that gives it away. The solid metal looks a lot like the one in the Premiere's kitchen.

Thank God this one isn't cold inside, but it smells awful. Sickening, in a way that reminds me of a busted freezer at one of my first jobs. Blood from a pack of steaks had gone everywhere. Jesus, is it blood I'm smelling?

Please tell me it's not from people.

The far wall has a couple more huddled bodies, who are also zip-tied at the wrists. All of them have a mix of exhaustion and fear on their faces.

As I'm shoved from behind, I realize one of them is familiar. Oh hell.

A door slams. I squint into the darkness.

"Nadia? Is that you?"

"Mr. Monroe?"

"You know her?" Troy whispers next to me.

"Nadia. From work. One of the employees I talked to Liam about. One of the ones I thought might be missing."

I was worried something had happened to her, but this? "Nadia, how did you end up here?"

For that matter, where is here, and what do we do now?

CHAPTER FOURTEEN

ADAM

HOURS after they dropped us in here and slammed the door, my head's killing me. My stomach's upset. Maybe because I was hit in the head, but...

This has happened before. More than once. The worst was weeks after Troy and I left home, after we'd sold my car and the money had run out. Finding food had become an issue. That was the day Troy starting tricking, to make sure we'd never be hungry again.

If we're stuck here for too long? I'm in trouble.

I have no insulin, and I need to eat something. Fuck knows what happened to the kit I was carrying on the way into the Premiere, but it isn't with me now.

It's too soon to say anything. No point, anyway. Troy will figure it out before too long. The bigger issue is if we're stuck in this room for too many hours, things will only get worse. Whatever these guys' plans are, they're not good.

"Nadia? What happened? How did you get here?" Wes is

shuffling around, trying to get closer to her. It's dark since they shut the door on us, and the poor girl has been barely responsive since then.

"Hey, it's okay," he says gently. Sounds like he's next to her now. "I don't know what's going to happen, but right at this moment we're okay. Right now *you're* okay."

It's the soothing tone of his voice that raises the hairs on my arms.

"Damn," Troy whispers as he presses his arm against mine. "He's good. Now I want to tell him all my secrets."

I press back against Troy's arm in acknowledgment.

This Wes we're seeing? This isn't the controlling dick we first met, the one who meddled in his brother's love life and looked down his nose in judgment at us. This version is soft-spoken and kind. If words had fingers, his would be giving Nadia a gentle back rub about now.

Maybe this is how he bagged that pretty blonde he married. A few soothing sentences, and I'm practically drooling.

Thanks to Wes's coaxing, Nadia finally finds her voice. "A couple of days ago, I went out on my break to get my sweater from my car." Her voice shakes. "I think it was a couple of days ago? It feels like it's been so long. Someone grabbed me near my car. Two men. One clamped his hand over my mouth, and the other grabbed my legs so I couldn't kick at them. Next thing I knew, they'd injected me with something and stuck me in a van. When I woke up I was here."

Did we get drugged? Must have. That might partly explain why I feel so fucked up.

"Any idea what's going on here?" Troy's tense next to me.

The other guy pipes up. "I got a better look last time they let us go to the bathroom. It's porn, I think. Except not the cheesy 'secretary fucks her boss at the office' kind. They're getting people to do things. Fucked-up things. Sounds like they're selling it to sick fucks who get their jollies on that sort of thing."

"How do you know?" Wes asks.

"I got here a day before she did." He must mean Nadia. "They come in here, drug two or three people at a time, and after the drugs've kicked in they take them out to that other room. It's hard to hear, but one of the girls..." The hiss of his breath suggests he's gathering himself. Or maybe he's pissed. "Even with the pills, she... There was a lot of yelling." His breath hitches. "The one guy, he laughed. Said they'd love the show."

Someone makes a quiet whine. Maybe Nadia. Maybe the other guy. I know the sound of someone who knows they're about to die. Some guys react loudly, fighting and begging.

Some don't.

Shit. This is bad. Troy and I can handle it. Fucking someone, or getting fucked, to stay alive is old news for us. For most people it would be awful.

How do we get out of this? Can we? The pounding in my head is making my thoughts cloudy.

"Do you know what drugs?" I ask.

"Gotta be something illegal. It's not as if we can see much of anything in here. When they come in the light is so bright you're basically blind," the guy says.

Troy scoots close to me and whispers, "Do you think your message got through to anybody?"

"I sent something to the group chat. Someone will see."

Hopefully Brennan. Or Ravi will tell his boyfriend.

"They still have to find us," Troy says.

And they have to do it soon. We might have a couple of days. We might have a couple of hours. "I know."

"Okay. We need to buy time if we can. We've got help coming," Troy says a little louder. He wants the whole room to hear, but we don't know how well the sound carries outside. The other guy said he could hear yelling from the outer room, so how loud is it safe to raise our voices?

"Does anyone know how long whatever drugs they give you take to wear off?" Troy asks.

"Nobody comes back," Nadine says, less shaky than before. "They drug you, they take you out, and then who knows?"

I have a pretty good idea. "If nobody came back, they're probably either dead, or they've been shipped somewhere."

It's what my dad would have done. What my brother would probably do. Holding a person takes resources. Why not send them someplace else to make money again?

Wes pipes up. "What are you guys thinking? What can we do?"

It's the first time he's spoken to us as if we're all on the same team. We're going to need each other to have any chance of getting out of this.

Troy says, "They probably untie you first before they make you do whatever they make you do. There might be a window when we can fight back, if the drugs don't have us too fucked up."

"At least one of those guys had a gun, though," Wes points out.

"More than one," the other guy says. "At least a couple."

"Probably all of them." Not to bring down the mood, but we need to be realistic. "How many people total?"

"They seem to come and go," Nadia says sadly. "Fewer than you'd think, honestly. There are a couple of guys who seem to be in charge of transporting people, and a few who are here all the time. One who seems to oversee everything."

"I don't think he's calling the shots, though. He keeps taking calls from someone," the guy across from us adds.

Troy shuffles next to me. "They're keeping it small to keep it controlled. The more people you have involved in an operation, the riskier it gets. My father shipped guns overseas under the cover of a legitimate art export business. Only a few trusted employees knew."

"Nadia," Wes says her name softly. "Is Caitlyn okay?"

"I-I think so." Her voice breaks. I think she's trying not to cry. "My neighbor watches her. I can only hope she's still got her."

"She does. I'm sure of it." Wes is kind, but firm. Not the sexy, awkward stammering we get when we touch him, but someone who's confident and in charge. Who the hell knows if that woman's neighbor is still looking after her baby, but Wes must realize that giving her another thing to fear will only make matters worse.

There's rustling, like he's moving closer to her. Comforting her, maybe.

Of course he is. I'm beginning to see he's that kind of guy.

I agree with Troy that how Wes meddled with Fallon and PJ's relationship was shitty, but he's not a total dick.

Wes Monroe is more like Troy than maybe either of them realize. They're helpers. Misguided ones, but still. They're both the type of guys who come up with fucked-up ways to solve a problem and think they're helping.

Wes attempted to help by setting his brother up on a

date with a sex worker. Troy went out and gave blow jobs when I landed in the hospital.

"Look alive," someone shouts from the outer room.

The heavy door is wrenched open on screaming hinges. Light floods from the other room. Some dude walks in with a gun in one hand and a flashlight in the other. Another follows behind him, holding something. I can't tell what.

"You." The big guy points both his gun and his high-beam light straight at Nadia, who's back to shaking like a leaf. His grin isn't only cruel, it's also excited. He knows he's scaring her. He likes it.

The second guy crouches down in front of her. "Open up, sweetheart. This all goes easier if you cooperate."

So that's what the other guy has. Pills. Suddenly, I'm remembering those drugs Brennan warned us about.

"No." Wes shoves Nadia aside to get in front of the gun, almost knocking the dude with the pills off his feet.

My heart's hovering somewhere near my collarbones. Wes is going to get himself killed.

Sure enough, the bro with the gun pushes the muzzle up against Wes's temple. "The fuck do you think you're doing, buddy?"

"I think..." Wes clears his throat. I can make out his ragged breath from over here. "No, I know. You-you're making a mistake. You're in the business of depravity, right? That's what this is all about. What about..."

I could swear for a second he looks our way. The mix of light and shadow make it tough to tell. "What about a six-foot-two straight guy who's never been fucked getting split open on camera, huh? What if s-someone had to hold me down while I fought b-back? Or...or tied me down? Shoved their cock in my throat? Wrecked my asshole? Bet your sicko viewers would really get off on that shit."

Oh, Wes. No.

I get what he's doing. We need to stall to give Brennan or whoever time to find us. Letting that shaky wisp of a girl across the way get thrown to the wolves is no good. Hell, my sicko dick even likes what he's suggesting. But the way he's putting ideas in their head?

Fucking disastrous.

Sure as hell not a good idea to have these people tie him up. If we are to have any chance of fighting our way out of here, we'll need our hands free.

Unless he's offering himself up as some kind of sacrifice.

He's got that haunted look on his face all the time. I could almost see it. Like he thinks he has things to atone for. Just like me. Just like Troy.

"Fuck no." Troy pushes his back against the wall, struggling to his feet. "You don't want him. You want someone who can take a dick like a pro."

"No. I'm the one you want." I push to stand, too. "Bet your audience would love a stellar DP. I'm looser than your mom after a few drinks, and I'm a great fucking actor. I don't even need drugs to make people think I'm absolutely dying while a couple of guys fuck me."

It's not my thing. From experience, I know if you don't prep enough, things don't feel great. But I can do it if I have to.

Also? I'm not letting Wes offer himself up when I'm the one least likely to get out of here alive.

A lot of things would have to align for us to be found before I'm too far gone. I'm not giving up, but I'm also not super hopeful.

The two men stand there for a moment, staring. The gun's still on Wes, but it's clear they're having trouble deciding what to do. Not the sort of situation where people usually volunteer.

Now that my eyes are adjusting to the bright light in the room, I can make out the rapid rise and fall of Wes's chest. He's got to be coursing with adrenaline right now.

Finally, the one with the gun presses it harder into Wes's temple. "This one."

Shit.

Before anyone else can say anything, the other guy is shoving two pills into Wes's mouth. They stick a bottle between his lips and upend it, making him sputter. Forcing him to swallow.

"Let me fuck him, then," Troy growls. "Let me tear up that pretentious middle management dick's asshole. I've been dying to."

The best lie has a hint of truth, right? Troy's eagerness is a hundred percent believable. His smile is unhinged.

"Me too." This isn't how we wanted it with Wes. But better us than a stranger.

"Fine." The guy approaches and quickly shoves pills into Troy's mouth too.

Huh.

I get a better look at the party favors when he pulls the baggie out of his pocket. They're round, a chalky green color with a leaf stamped on the top.

They call it Spark. It's the same stuff that's been circulating on the streets recently. The stuff Brennan warned us all against because it's killed some people.

Troy's taken it, though. One of our clients paid extra. At least we know what it does.

I'm busy looking between Wes and Troy when the guy with the gun grabs me by the hair. I usually keep it pulled back, but my hair tie got lost somewhere in the scuffle. He's got a big fistful and he's tilting my head up to the ceiling.

"No, he can't take that shit." Troy pushes toward me, but I try to give him a warning with my eyes.

They can't know. If they have any idea I'm sick, I'm dead. My father dealt in trafficking. If I'm a liability, I'm done.

Troy's dad was into shady shit too, so he's not stupid. He settles down pretty fast.

When they pour the water into my mouth, I get lucky. The pills get caught in the crease where my lip meets my gum. The taste while I hold them in there is bitter and nasty as hell, but who cares? If I'm less fucked up it'll be a good thing.

With the way I'm already feeling, I'm not even sure it'll be hard to fake.

I don't breathe again until the two men are gone. Thank fuck.

As soon as the door closes, I spit them out and crush them under my shoe. Then we wait.

It feels like a while passes before they come back. Wes is definitely getting hit the hardest. The light's gone again, so I can't see him well, but he's sort of moaning and lolling his head against the wall.

By the time they come back my butt's fallen asleep from sitting on the hard floor. One at a time, they drag us out. They drop Wes face up on a mattress in the middle of the room. His hands are free, but it doesn't seem to matter. He's loose-limbed and half out of it, his eyes hooded.

"Shit, we need more time." Troy says next to me. He doesn't elaborate, but he doesn't need to.

Between the two of us, we can maybe manage taking down these guys. But at least one has a gun. There might also be guards if we try to leave. We need Wes able to stand on his own two feet. Otherwise, he's a liability. Which means we're going to need to do the thing.

This is going to be an absolute mess.

"Get the fuck over there." Someone shoves me between the shoulder blades, making me stumble toward where Wes is lying.

"W-what do you want us to do?" As if I can't guess.

"Spit roast." He looks at Troy. "Make him scream."

Wes groans, and so do I. Because we're going to have to hurt him to save him.

CHAPTER FIFTEEN

WES

I THOUGHT they were going to shove pills down our throats and drag us out, but no. More waiting. Hours of waiting.

At first I didn't notice much. A sense of relaxation, which a still-lucid part of my brain told me was odd given the circumstances. Some sleepiness.

Then the tingles and the shivers on my skin. The horniness. Did they mix ED meds into whatever they gave me?

All I know is I've been desperately, painfully hard for a while now. This must be how they do it.

When I offered myself, I did so hoping either Adam or Troy would step in. If getting fucked bought us time, at least it could be with someone who, for better or worse, also turned me on.

It made sense in the moment.

Also, this is the worst idea I've ever had.

Without question.

Proposing to Gina the second I found out she was pregnant, that was stupid. Staying married when I found out she was cheating might have been worse. Setting my brother up with a male escort because I thought it would break him out of his grief funk if he got laid? Downright awful.

Offering myself up to get drugged and have my asshole torn open? Stupid. Stupid, stupid, stupid.

How can I be so proficient at solving problems at work and so terrible at it in my personal life?

Still, I'd do it again. What was the alternative? Sitting in here while they drugged Nadia? Listening to her scream, or even worse, having to participate?

The thought of it turns my stomach.

Or maybe that's the drugs.

Stuff is going on around me, but I can't manage to open my eyes. Every time I try, things look warped and blurry. All the dark shadows swirl and morph into monsters.

Someone, or a couple of someones, hooks their arms through mine and hauls me out of the room into one so bright I still can't see.

"Spit roast," someone says. "Make him scream."

Ohhh no.

Are they talking about me? Because I think...

Yeah. I think I oversold it when I pitched them my virgin asshole.

Or Troy did, when he acted way too excited about ripping me to shreds. That was an unnecessary level of enthusiasm.

Psst! Wes. Remember when you were diagnosed with leukemia and you thought you were going to die? Is this better or worse?

This is next-level ridiculous.

I'm thrown onto a mattress, and someone starts

giggling. There's nothing funny about this situation. Also, I think that person is me.

The mattress dips and moves. There's pain and pressure as someone cuts my hands free. Someone's blowing air on my face. They're pulling at the buttons on my shirt. I try to brush them off.

I'm horny, but also my limbs don't want to cooperate.

"Fucking hell, Wes. Let us do this." Is that Adam? I pry open my eyes to see warm brown ones staring back at me.

"Adam," I murmur. Some of the worry eases from his face. "They want you to make me scream."

I think. I'm not sure, but I think I heard that somewhere?

Is there really any chance of someone finding us here before we're killed or carted off to parts unknown? Shit, I hope so. The possibility seems so far away now.

We don't know where we are. In a fair fight, the three of us might be able to take on the three guys who seem to be running things. Except right now I don't know if I can touch my nose to my finger.

Wait. I give it a try, but I can't tell if it's working.

"Get his clothes off faster," someone insists. Someone with a deep, gravel-filled voice.

Footsteps approach. There's clicking noise.

"Christ, let me do it." Troy sounds like an impatient dick. An even bigger dick than usual.

"You're going to tear up my asshole," I mumble.

Troy appears in my line of vision, blue eyes sharp and icy. "Dammit, he's gone around the bend."

He sounds awfully sober. How is that possible when I saw them give the pills to both of them right after me?

"You look like you did the day you ate my cum." I'm pretty sure I'm babbling.

Usually I've got a decent filter. You have to, working around rich folks. But now it's all dribbling out, isn't it?

I feel like I can think clearly. I can *hear* myself. But my inside thoughts are all on the outside now.

Troy leans down, gripping either side of my shirt and ripping it the rest of the way open. He must've taken his own off already because his bare chest touches mine. His lips brush my ear.

"No way around it, Kitten. This is going to hurt. Do us both a favor and act like I'm killing you. The more you react, the less I'll have to make you."

"Make me." My lips feel funny. "Make me. Make me. Make. Me." It's like that thing where you say something over until it sounds weird.

"So, he's really fucked up," Adam whispers.

"Not..." Oooh. The place where their skin touches mine? It's like little prickles of static electricity. I think I like it. "Not *really* fucked up." I insist. "Only sort of."

See? My brain is working fine.

Really, though, what do I know about being fucked up? Once in high school my friend's cousin got me to take a hit off a joint. My mom was at home needing her medication, and my brother needed someone to make him go to bed. Actually getting high would've been irresponsible.

The only other drugs I've ever taken were the legal kind. When I was going through treatment I took, like, half the number of painkillers they gave me. Gina grew up in West Virginia, and her stories about the rampant opioid addiction in her hometown scared me into white-knuckling it more often than not.

"Hey, muscle dude," Troy's shouting to someone. "Hit me with some lube."

More laughter. “No lube. You’ll have to make do.”

“These people make my family look like pushovers.” That’s Adam, I think. If today is anything to go by, he’s quieter when he’s stressed. Troy gets loud.

“Fuckers.” Troy’s growling again.

“Uh-oh, Daddy’s mad.” Why does that seem so funny right now?

Someone’s laughing again. Is that me?

Someone pulls off my pants. Someone’s crawling up my body. Straddling me. Straddling my torso.

“Fucking open your eyes, Kitten.” Troy looks weird. Sort of tortured and distorted but also pissed.

Is he mad at me again?

“Is this about my brother? I swear I’m not homo... homo...phobic.”

Anyway. I volunteered to get fucked, didn’t I?

“Whatever. Listen to me,” Troy growls in my ear. “You better get my dick so wet fucking gators try to move in on it. I don’t want to hurt you if I don’t have to. You got me?”

“Got you.” Wait, what did he say?

His hand brushes my balls, reminding me I’m not wearing any pants. Or anything.

Which means everyone in here can see my dick.

“Uugh.” Who’s making that annoying whining noise? “My penis is small, and now everyone can see.”

“Shut up, Kitten,” Troy snaps.

“Your dick is pretty, babe,” Adam whispers. “Perfectly average.”

Oh. *Oh.* That’s nice.

Troy shoves his fingers into my mouth, gagging me. “Get ’em wet, baby.”

I gag against the intrusion, but I swirl my tongue around anyway. Trying to follow directions. Trying to please him.

Which I really want to do, I realize in a bright burst of clarity. "Oh, this must be why people take drugs."

But if I'd known I was getting fucked today I might have done more research.

One night I searched for "Is it weird to suddenly like men in your forties?" and then ended up on an extremely depressing Reddit thread. It's where my research stopped.

Someone pushes my knees up. And then "Hey! That fucking hurts."

Hell of a time to remember I tweaked my hamstring last time I went for a run. When was that? Feels like forever ago.

Adam leans over me, pressing his lips to mine and then whispering, "Good. That's good. Scream, babe. We want to make it good for you, but you need to give them a show. Just don't hate us later, okay?"

Troy's pushing a finger—is it multiple fingers?—into my asshole. The pressure and the burning sensation send heat throughout my body. This must be the drugs, at least partly. What starts out as minor discomfort builds and spreads until it's impossible to stay still.

Isn't there usually some more foreplay involved in this sort of thing? Drinks or conversation? Maybe not. But, like, can you get fucked without feeling like your asshole is on fire?

Is there a word for *not* setting someone's asshole on fire?

Adam told me to scream, I remember. So, I fucking scream. I writhe. I call Troy names like savage and bully and sadistic cunt, all while he fucks his fingers in and out of me.

"You're a goddamn asshol—" *Oh God.* Pleasure zings

through me. Like the burning sensation before, it builds and spreads until I'm a giant ball of need. "What the *fuck?*"

My prostate. He must have touched my prostate. I'm familiar with the concept. I get annual checkups, after all. But this is very different. It must be, since I never had the urge to beg my doctor to do it more.

This is... "Holy shit. Holy...oh God," I whine. "What is this? How does it feel good when it also feels like you're tearing me in half? Oh my fucking Goddd."

Waves of pleasure roll through me, centered around that magic spot he's stroking and spreading through every nerve in my body. I can't look. My head is too heavy. But I swear my dick is weeping. Every drop welling up is magnified like I'm a broken faucet.

"Hehe, yeah, someone's starting to like having his ass destroyed." This from a voice off to the side. I can't see them, but it's not Adam or Troy. This one is raspy and smug. One of those pieces of shit is watching us.

Do you really think you wouldn't do this if you were sober?

Another moment of clarity. Maybe I was scared to want it, but I did. I wanted this. I wanted them.

I probably even would have begged. "Please. Please."

Well, I'd like to think I would've at least demanded nicer conditions for getting fucked. Fewer audience members.

I hiss in pain as Adam bites down around my nipple. It hurts more because he's getting the sensitive tip and not the muscley part like Troy did. And that weird thing where the sensation builds and spreads.

Someone's yelling now. Yelling again?

"There you go, Kitten," Adam murmurs. "Fucking scream for us."

He's biting me all over. Some of those spots make me

laugh, like at the top of my rib cage. Some of them make me yell.

All the while, Troy's working his fingers in and out of me with such intensity I'm honestly frightened by how much I like it.

"Oh God," I moan again. "Please. Please. Don't."

Don't stop.

Whatever I do, whether it's to moan or beg, I do it as loud as I can. As long as I can. Whoever might be watching, I want to make it so good they don't even consider killing us.

Killing us. Fuck.

Don't think about that.

So, when Troy straddles my chest and shoves his cock into my mouth, I open up and let him. I yell. I gag. I kick my feet, or at least I try to.

I even try to pull away from the velvety length nudging at my tonsils, because some part of my brain tells me I'm supposed to.

"There you go, Kitten. There you go. Good boy. Get me so fucking wet. Swallow that cock. Squeeze it with your fucking throat. I'm gonna jam this thing so far up your ass you'll be able to taste me all over again."

I don't... What?

Things get fuzzy when he pushes hard into my throat. "Bite me and I'll fucking strangle you."

Right now, Troy sounds like a different person. Angry. Lethal.

Why is that hot?

A hazy memory floats through me. The time I accidentally walked in on my brother getting fucked by his boyfriend. PJ had his hand wrapped around Fallon's throat as if controlling his breath was his only mission.

Not that I'm into seeing my brother get fucked, but now I wonder: am I into the other thing? I might be.

Someone mumbles something that sounds a lot like "Choke me, Daddy." Now why am I giggling again?

Gina only ever wanted me to get her pregnant again. Maybe it could've been fun, but it wasn't. I think I felt more pressured then than I do right now.

Huh.

I'm drooling so much I can't keep it in. All I can do is hold on.

As abruptly as Troy shoved his dick down my throat, he pulls it out again. I'm still gasping and trying to catch my breath when the blunt head presses at my asshole. Slow but steady, he pushes in.

If I thought his fingers were intense, this is so much more. The burning. The pressure. If I can handle getting a million IVs, I can handle this.

You wanted this, my brain supplies. *Some part of you wanted this.*

"Aaah!" After a few pumps, it starts to feel good. Those waves of pleasure when he hits my prostate layer on top of each other, each more consuming than the next. I can't even keep my hips on the mattress.

You're supposed to hate this. You're supposed to protest.

"Jesus. Fuck. No. Stop!" Through my haze, there's a moment where everything comes to a halt. When Troy pauses for a painful second. He's pressed deep inside me, his gaze burning into mine. The crease deepens in the center of his forehead. Like for a second he really might stop because I yelled for him to.

I try to give a subtle shake with my head. To tell him with my eyes to keep going.

He asked me to react. He told me to yell, so I did.

The weird part? This is oddly freeing.

There can't be any guilt or worry for wanting something I'm not supposed to want, can there? Not now.

Fuck, I see why people take these drugs now. Every thought in my head is like a light bulb exploding. Every touch does the same to my nerves. My body. It's a shower of sparks, lighting me up.

"Yeah. You're okay. You're okay," Troy murmurs as he starts going again. Is he assuring me, or himself?

Doesn't matter. I'm damn near euphoric. My nerve endings have been plugged into a light socket. My eyes flutter closed as sensation envelops me.

A minute later when Troy gives my face a series of hard slaps and then demands "Hey. Look at me when I'm fucking you" I'm even more awake. More alive.

In that fraction of a second when his icy gaze melts into something almost tender, I don't know what to do with the way that look seeps into my chest.

Is *all* of this the drugs or would I feel like this anyway? With every passing moment my fuzzy thoughts come into sharper focus. Perhaps it wouldn't be too different. I don't think so.

Right now there's no confusion. No agonizing over why I want this. Why I want *them.* There's no telling myself all the reasons I shouldn't. All I have to do is lie here and take it.

And scream.

"Fuck! You're fucking killing me. What—mmmph!"

Adam straddles my face and shoves his dick into my open mouth. It's oddly frustrating not to be able to yell at Troy anymore.

I can growl, though. Rage from the back of my throat. Grunt and groan and scream until I'm raw.

"Oh yeah, babe," Adam groans. "That mouth is so fucking hot. Suck me, baby. Suck me so fucking hard. I want to feel my brains blow out through my cock and go down your throat. That's so good. Such a good fucking boy."

His words send a surge of desire through me. All at once I'm on the verge of coming.

Ooh. Interesting.

Prickles dance over my skin. It's as if my entire body has been asleep and it's waking up now. Maybe it has been. Maybe I've been sleepwalking through my entire fucking life.

Going along. Doing what was expected of me. Holy fuck.

Now I'm screaming around a cock jammed into my throat while a twenty-two-year-old man is telling me what a good boy I am, and I've never felt more alive.

Adam's dick swells in my mouth. I'm drooling everywhere. His words turn to nonsense, getting louder and louder, his movements jerkier, until he erupts into my mouth with a yell.

When I sputter and struggle to swallow, I'm not acting. It's overwhelming, and for a second I think I might drown.

Drowning in cum. What a way to go.

It doesn't taste like mine, but it's not the worst thing I've ever swallowed. That trophy belongs to the time Gina tried to cook curried deer meat.

Which was a mistake to think about. Now I really am gagging. My impending orgasm retreats a little.

I'm distantly aware of Adam's hand on my cock. Of his encouraging words, the "Come on, babe" and the "Yeah, you want it, don't you?" The "He's owning your asshole so fucking good, isn't he?"

Owning my asshole. Why does that sound so...right?

I'm so close to the edge I barely have time to care.

Someone yells about not wasting the money shot. For a blissful moment, I'd forgotten again there are people here. Filming. *Watching.*

Adam's mouth engulfs my cock in heat, and I'm back in that closet. Back when Adam was sucking me off and Troy was kissing me, pinching me, sinking his teeth into my pecs. When wanting them to touch me, needing to cum mattered more in the moment than any possible consequences.

"Oh God, please," I babble. "Hurt me. Hurt me. Fuck me. Hurt me, oh God, fuck me..."

Every sensation in my body builds on the last one. My tongue's lost its off switch. The closer I get to coming, the more the words tumble out.

Then, with a shout, I'm spilling onto Adam's hand and onto my stomach.

Troy, apparently taking my words seriously, is pounding into me so hard I think he might loosen my fillings.

Teeth sink into the upper thigh of one leg, which is draped over his shoulder. Then he lets out an eardrum-rattling bellow, before pulling out to paint my cock and my thighs with his release. Each drop makes my skin sizzle.

There's a shadowy figure hovering over us. A bright light. A camera? Right. The money shot.

Somewhere in the distance a phone rings. "Gotta take this. Clean them up and then get ready for transport."

I'm catching my breath. Blinking at the ceiling. Trying to make sense of everything through my brain fog.

That was...something.

My asshole twinges. The rough fucking is making itself known. I think later I'm going to have a lot of questions.

"Only two now. Here's our shot. Time to go," Adam whispers.

"What?" Fuck, they said something about transporting us somewhere. Icy fear sobers me up, pulling me out of my orgasm haze.

Without warning, Adam's weight lifts from my body. Naked feet slapping on concrete. Adam and Troy, running.

Shouting.

I stumble to my feet, trying to make my eyes focus.

Something hits a wall and shatters. There's a symphony of dull thuds of punches being thrown. Troy's hoisting what looks like camera equipment over his head.

"Troy. Adam." I feel around for my clothes.

I have to help them.

CHAPTER SIXTEEN

TROY

HELL OF A TIME TO realize this, but our Wes doesn't seem exactly nimble in a crisis.

Then again, Adam and I have had more practice with this stuff. And my high wore down before we even got in front of the cameras. Probably because I've taken this shit before.

When I look up from where I've beaten the cameraman with his own tripod, Wes is standing in the middle of the mattress where we both fucked him. Sticky and naked. Eyes the size of dinner plates.

He's sort of grabbing at the air, for some reason.

Adam's entered the danger zone. His skin is pale, and he looks shaky, but maybe that's adrenaline. He's whaling on the dude who force-fed us those pills, so I'm not sure. In spite of how he was raised, my oldest friend doesn't like to get violent. When he does, it's a thing of beauty. Total and efficient.

Little fuckface's features are a swollen, pulpy mass.

"Troy. Adam." They're the only words Wes has spoken since I shot cum all over his dick.

Footsteps force me to look away from Wes. That big guy in charge storms back into the room. Phone in one hand, gun in the other. With the camera tripod still in my grip, I don't give him a chance to aim. I just swing.

His head jerks back, his body crumpling to the floor at Wes's feet. Wes, who's still standing there naked. Staring.

So I grab his pants from the floor and shove them into his hand. "Wes. Hey. You in there?"

"Yeah." Blinking, he shakes himself all over like a dog covered in water. Finally, there's someone home behind his eyes again.

He takes in the scene around us. "What the fuck do we do now?"

His lips are wet and puffy. I've got adrenaline coursing through me like the world's best hit of coke. Grabbing Wes behind the neck, I crush his lips to mine, pushing my tongue inside.

He kisses me back, and it's deliberate. Right now, in the middle of chaos, it feels like he's choosing us.

It's painful to pull away from him, but we have bigger worries.

"Can't fucking believe you let us spit roast you like that."

"Spit roast?"

Hell. "I'll explain later. Get your pants on. Let those other people out." I glance over at Adam. Pretty sure the dude he's still hitting is dead, but Adam's sort of in the zone. Physically, he doesn't look great.

We've been here for hours at this point, I think. All night maybe. Too long.

"Wes." I shove the pants at him again. "Now."

Finally, he pulls them on one leg at a time. He's moving less like we need to flee the scene at any moment and more like he's getting dressed for a leisurely Sunday brunch.

Shit, I don't even know what day it is. We're going to have some wild stories the next time we sit down for a meal with our fellow escorts.

Adam gives up hitting the dead guy and collapses on the floor. He is sort of curled in on himself, looking like he might be ill. He probably is. I'm not an expert on these things, but over the years I've learned a few things. They took my phone, but I'll bet his blood sugar is dangerously low.

The last night we ever slept on a sidewalk was the one before Adam was first hospitalized. After that, I swore I'd do literally anything to keep a roof over our head before I'd let anything bad happen to him again. And I did.

I can't even count the number of times I was afraid I was going to accidentally kill my best friend over the years. On the inside, I'm probably as old as Wes.

"Hey, buddy. Hang tight, okay? We're going to get out of here."

"Guards," Adam mumbles. "Might be guards coming."

"I didn't see any."

He pushes himself up to a sitting position. "If I were a criminal doing criminal things, I'd have someone keeping an eye out. If my dad had had more guards, I wouldn't have been able to kill him."

My gaze swings to Wes, who must have heard every word, going by how his mouth's hanging open.

A screeching noise sets my teeth on edge. Wes fumbles to button his shirt with one hand as he wrenches open the heavy door where the other people are.

He's murmuring something quietly, maybe comforting the woman he knew when we came in. An employee, I think. He's tripping over his own feet a little, but at least he looks like he's got his wits about him now.

Adam blinks at me. "I'm feeling a little better. We need to get out of here before the wrong people find us."

I'm helping him up when I hear Wes yell again. Someone grabs me from behind. I'm spun around with a fist driving into my face before I can figure out what's up.

Fucking big man, again. Guess I didn't knock him out hard enough.

I duck a little too late. My world turns white when the fist connects with my eye. My head snaps back.

I'm bracing for another one when the dude makes a gurgling noise. A silent gasp. Then he slumps over.

Behind him is a petite young thing holding a knife in her hands. A bloody knife. Her mouth is open on a silent scream, with tears running down her face. Shit.

I mean, she might have saved my life. But she also looks like she's about thirty seconds from melting down.

It's Wes who comes to the rescue. He takes the knife out of her hand. Wipes the knife and her with a discarded rag he finds in the corner. Whatever he whispers in her ear, I can't make out. Something soothing. She nods, looking relieved.

Even with Wes's comfort, she's shaking all over. Nothing surprising, considering.

Whatever it is, we've got a bigger issue right now. "Adam needs a hospital," I tell him.

Wes swallows, turning to the woman...Nadine? No, Nadia. "Where's the other guy?"

"I think...he ran." She's almost whispering. "Down that way." She points in the direction the big guy went before. A quick check tells me it leads to a hallway of some sort, but I'm not sure it's wise right now to go exploring.

"Fucking pussy." Using the rag Wes had, I clean the blood from Adam's hands. Then I haul him off the floor. He's helping me, but his movements are sluggish. "Keep your eyeballs peeled. Adam thinks there might be guards."

"There are definitely guards," Adam mumbles.

"I really feel like now's not the time to argue with me, Cupcake."

Wes snorts.

"Something funny, Kitten?"

He lazily gestures with his middle finger at me before heading to the nearest door. Which is still padlocked.

"Keys are probably on one of those guys," I say. "If someone can hang onto Adam I'll go look."

"I've got it," Wes says. Then he proceeds to take a deep breath and hold it while he rummages through the pockets of every dead guy on the floor.

Right here is what makes Wes a puzzle to me. The version of him we see when he's working at the Premiere is different from the one he shows in his classroom, is different from the version we see when he's hanging out with his brother.

This is another side of him still. One that freezes when the fists start flying but then comforts the chick who stabbed a guy to death and searches the pockets of dead bodies.

Somewhere along the way, Wes got dropped on a hard surface and splintered into a hundred different shards. Which piece are we seeing now?

Sure, when Adam and I started messing around with him, we figured he was a shallow, judgmental, homophobic prick. At the very least, one of those guys who just can't help getting into other people's business.

But that's not who he is at all, is it?

Wes's brother thinks he's straight. The guy told us so. He married the girl he got pregnant and, from what I can tell, stayed with her forever. Yet he's willingly let us push him into corners and put our hands and mouths on him over and over.

When someone with a gun tried to shove drugs at one of his employees and threatened to do horrific things to her on camera, he insisted on going in her place.

It'd be easy to think anybody would make that kind of decision. Except personal experience tells me most people aren't so noble when shit gets real.

"Found the keys." Wes stands from the boss man's body as a pool of blood creeps toward his feet.

Pounding at the door makes us all jump back. I use my free hand to grab the tripod again. It's unwieldy, though, trying to lift it while I'm holding on to Adam.

Wes grips the knife and stares at the door. "Get behind me," he says to Nadia.

Not sure our guy can fight his way out of a paper bag, but he's going to try to save that girl anyway, isn't he?

"I'm going to come in there and tear you motherfuckers apart for doing business in my territory, I swear to fucking God."

I relax back onto my heels. "You can put the knife away, Wes. It's our pimp."

He blinks. Some sort of shiver seems to go through him, but he wipes the knife off again and tosses it into a corner. It's a big one. Too big for a pocket.

"Hang the fuck on, we've got a key." I turn to Wes. "Get the door for them, Kitten."

He scowls. But he does what I ask.

On the other side are Brennan and Liam, our friend Ravi's boyfriend. Behind them both is a guy I've only met briefly. Daniel Corvus. He owns a kink club in the area, and he's insisting to Brennan that this is actually his territory. Which really seems like an argument for another time.

There are a handful of other armed men. Some I recognize, like Jalen, Brennan's right hand. Some I don't. One of them has his arm clamped around a dude in camo, whose face is bleeding.

"Good news: we took care of the guards," a guy I don't recognize says.

Adam mumbles, "I told you there would be guards." Then he doubles over and pukes on the floor.

"Hey. Stay with us. Don't do this now." I shake him gently, trying to keep him conscious.

Brennan looks around. "Everything cool in here?"

I point to the bodies on the floor. "Gonna need some cleanup. Also..." I gesture to Adam.

"Yeah. Fuck." He turns to Jalen. "We need to get these idiots to the hospital in Beacon Hill."

"Is that where we are?" Beacon Hill is technically a couple of towns over from Belle Argo, if you count all the unincorporated miles of mostly farmland in between.

Jalen pulls out his phone. "On it."

"On the far end, yeah. Didn't know this place was here. Did you?" Brennan's asking Liam and Corvus.

They both shake their heads.

Liam looks around, appraising the room as if he were evaluating a house he wants to buy, rather than an old, dilapidated building full of blood and bodies. "Could come in handy. We'll have to figure out who owns it." He raises his eyebrows, looking at Corvus. "If that's okay with you?"

Whatever Corvus says, I don't hear. I don't care.

"There was somebody in charge." Wes stumbles forward. "Someone who wasn't here. The guy kept taking phone calls."

Liam nods. "We'll look into it."

"You got our text?" I ask Brennan.

"Tracked the last known location of Adam's phone. Lucky for me and for you, the best hackers in town happen to also be criminally affiliated."

Wes barges into the conversation, shoving the still-crying girl forward. "Nadia needs to get home. She's got a baby she's been away from for days."

Brennan's jaw firms. For a second I'm not sure what he'll do. Brennan's an interesting guy. He can be good, or he can be bad, but he's never really on anyone's side except his own. His affiliations change faster than the Florida weather.

"Ambulance is on the way," Jalen says as he approaches.

Brennan motions him forward. "Good. Get this young lady wherever she needs to go."

She shakes her head violently. "I don't know you."

Brennan sighs. "Miss, we are here to save you, not kidnap you again."

Turning, she grabs Wes's hand. "Come with us? Please?"

Wes's eyes search mine. Honestly, I thought he'd come with us to the hospital. After what happened between us all, I feel like there's a conversation we need to have. Many conversations.

But I'm not a big enough dick to tell him he can't escort a terrified coworker home.

"Go," I tell him. "I'm sure we'll talk later." Who knows when.

Two guys I don't recognize drag in a body. The guy who ran off in the midst of all the fighting. "What happened to him?"

"Guards probably shot him." One guy shrugs. Probably nothing to him. He doesn't know them.

"Karma." I should probably feel worse than I do. Mostly, I'm relieved it wasn't us.

Inside, though, my core goes cold and dark. Years ago, Adam and I were the ones who ran, while Adam's dad lay dead and mine was passed out at the bottom of a bourbon bottle. That could have been us. Easily.

"Wes," I call to him as he starts to follow Jalen out the door. Nadia's still clutching his hand as if it's a lifeline.

He stops and turns. Once he does, I'm not sure what to say. Anything I can think of isn't something I want to air out in front of all these people.

After the silence has stretched between us for a while, he turns to Brennan. "I'm the one who stabbed the guy." He points to the man who almost knocked my head off. "He attacked Troy, so I killed him."

Fuck, I want to kiss him again so badly right now.

He sounds so sure I almost believe him, and I'm one of the only people who saw Blondie with the knife in her hand.

Brennan shrugs again. "Doubt it'll be an issue. We've got a good working relationship with the local PD."

By "good working relationship," he means bribes. Lots of bribes.

Wes nods and walks out the door, glancing for a second over his shoulder.

My tongue won't cooperate, and Wes is already getting into one of the cars that are haphazardly stopped out front.

A few minutes later, the ambulance pulls in.

I slap Adam's cheek again. "Cavalry's here, babe. Don't die on me now."

He lifts his head. "Where's Wes?"

"We'll find him later."

I hope.

CHAPTER SEVENTEEN

WES

I'M NOT sure what time it is when that Jalen guy drops me back at the hotel. The sky is still dark, but I smell coffee as I trudge across the shiny tiles toward the elevators. Probably morning, then. My head's fuzzy, so I'm not sure.

I'm not sure about anything.

He gave me back my phone—found in a trash can where we were being held, with the screen shattered. The battery was dead anyway. I'm too busy spinning in circles to care.

I head straight to my room on the second floor of the Premiere. Muffled voices surround me. If anyone speaks directly to me, I don't know and I don't care.

A few minutes after I get inside and plug my phone in, it sets off a series of rapid text message pings.

My brother, trying to find out if I'm okay.

What a difference a kidnapping makes. A few days ago he was barely speaking to me.

Even though I can read the messages through the cracks

in the screen, typing is another matter. I manage to voice dictate a simple "I'm okay" message to respond and then plunk the broken thing down to go take a shower.

I don't get far. Attempting to undo the buttons on my shirt reminds me that some of them popped off during... Well.

All of a sudden I'm shivering. Uncontrollable body spasms like I haven't had since the last time I had a bad flu. I try to chafe my arms with my hands, but the chills have that bone-deep feeling like I may never get warm again.

The kind another person's body heat would help chase away.

Since I'm probably not supposed to be wishing Adam and Troy were here, I do my best to push any thoughts of them away.

I'm on my way to the shower when the phone rings. My brother calling.

"Hey, man." My voice sounds flat. It's all I've got at the moment.

"Wes, Jesus Christ. Thank God. Adam sent a message to PJ's group chat saying you guys had been kidnapped. Nobody knew what the hell was going on. Are you okay?"

"I sent you a text that said I'm okay."

With one hand holding the phone, I unplug it again and pry my shoes off. Maybe the barely charged battery will die again, and I won't have to continue this conversation with Fallon right now. As much as I want to make amends, I'm too raw to get into it all now.

I amble toward the bathroom to turn the shower on. I crank it almost to the hottest setting. There's still sort of, I don't know, this odd sensation inside me. Everything's a little off and I can't put my finger on why.

Am I still high? Is it because I got kidnapped, like, a day ago and now I'm back in my hotel room as if nothing happened?

Is it because I'm still processing how I feel about getting fucked at both ends by two men half my age while people watched? And filmed the whole thing?

Is this about the fact that I didn't hate it, but I know I was supposed to?

The shivers ramp up in intensity.

It's at least partly that last thing.

I shake my head, realizing my brother's still been talking while my brain wandered off.

"...told them they should call the police, but PJ said Brennan could probably get there faster."

"He's right. Besides, it's better the police didn't come." I'm not sure I even sound like myself. Never thought I'd see the day when I'd agree with Fallon's asshole boyfriend, but I guess it's a day for firsts all around.

First blow job given. First time getting hate-fucked. First time admitting to killing someone I didn't actually kill.

First time wishing the men who sort of hate-fucked me could get into bed with me and cuddle until I'm not cold anymore.

"What the hell do you mean it's better the police didn't come?" Honestly, I've never heard my younger brother sound this much like our mom. Anxious and frantic. I'm the controlling one. Fallon's the more laid-back one.

The order of the universe has been disturbed.

"Uh..." I study myself in the mirror. Right now you could put my picture next to the definition of "hot mess." My hair's standing out all over. My cheek is swollen. My shirt is in tatters. I'm covered in so many scrapes and bruises I'm a walking cautionary tale.

It's probably for the best I can't see my own asshole right now. It's sore as hell.

My skin is itchy where Troy's cum dried on me.

"Wes?"

"Oh. Sorry." I don't really know how to answer my brother's question, but I'm too worn out to make up excuses. "There were, uh...bodies."

"Whose bodies? What happened?"

"The people who took us. And it's a long story." I'm hit by another round of shaking. "Look, we probably shouldn't be talking about this over the phone. I need a shower anyway. I need..." So many things.

"Yeah, okay." Fallon's voice is quiet. "You're sure you're okay?"

"I'll be fine." I think?

"Hey, Wes. Before you go."

"Hmm?" I drop my pants to the floor. I don't know where my shorts went after Troy took them off of me.

Did I really announce my anal virginity to a room full of strangers? I still can't believe those words came out of my mouth.

My brother huffs through the phone. "Look, I know you've been going through a lot. And I know I haven't helped. I've been kind of a dick to you lately, and I apologize. I want you to know I'm here if you need anything."

There's pressure behind my eyes. Honestly, my little brother is one of the best people I know and I don't deserve him.

"You had every reason to be a dick to me, Fallon. I hired a male escort to get you laid and then accused him of being a gold digger when you fell in love. I tried to split you up, repeatedly. If I were you, I wouldn't be speaking to me."

"You didn't get my relationship with him. Or with Marina. I shouldn't have expected you to understand."

Fallon's submissive. Both his current boyfriend and his late wife were dominants. He's right. I didn't understand. Not really. I didn't want to.

After what happened in that building with Adam and Troy, and the way it made me feel, I think I understand better. Every one of my thoughts keeps circling back to them.

"You've got a secret desire to be dominated, and we've got magic hands."

Where are they? Is Adam okay?

When will I see them again?

Is it completely and utterly wrong that I want them here right now?

"Most of the years Gina and I were together she was controlling," I admit to my brother. "Not like Marina or PJ, but... She was in so much pain after those miscarriages. Hurt. Angry. When I got sick, and the treatments left me sterile, things got worse between us. Every time I looked at you and your relationships, I couldn't help but draw parallels. I was miserable, so I assumed you were too and just afraid to say anything."

Fallon makes a sympathetic *hmm* noise. "It's not the same. But I get it. I'm sorry you had to deal with that. I didn't realize how bad things were between you."

"It's okay. I think... No, I know. I shouldn't have judged."

"You've got a secret desire to be dominated..."

I close my eyes against a rapid assault of mental images, going back in time from Troy slapping me and demanding I look at him while he fucked me to Adam holding my shoulders in the BAU locker room while Troy reached into my slacks and pulled my cock out.

Astonishingly, the last one makes my cock twitch.

"I just wanted to show you how giving up control can sometimes be a lot of fun."

Troy's words make my skin tingle.

"I get that you were trying to help," Fallon says.

Shit, I'd forgotten we were talking again. "Hey, I don't want to be rude, but I really have to go, man. I'm exhausted and honestly not feeling great. I need to get some rest."

I'm lying, sort of. It's true that I'm fucking exhausted. I'm also so wired I may never sleep again.

"Yeah, okay. Call me if you need anything."

"Sure, little brother."

As the older sibling, I've never called Fallon for help in my life. I doubt that's going to change now. Not when I can't see how he'd understand what I'm dealing with.

One of the benefits of living in a hotel is unlimited hot water. When you have hundreds of guests all showering at a time, you need to be sure you can keep it going. So I step under, grateful for the heat beating on my sore muscles. I'm trying not to replay the last few days, few weeks, but doing it anyway.

At some point I manage to work shampoo into my hair. I lather up, scrub the dried cum from my skin. Then I rinse and squeeze a dollop of conditioner from the wall-mounted dispenser.

With the sensation of choking on Adam's cock fresh in my head, I find my hand wandering down to my erection. My initial light strokes do nothing but frustrate me. I find myself getting faster and more aggressive. Wiping off some of the conditioner, because it makes the glide too smooth. Scraping with my short nails.

My breath comes faster and more ragged as my hand squeezes tighter. I touch myself with long, firm strokes. I move faster, thrusting into my own fist. It's good, pleasurable enough, but not what I'm looking for.

I'm struggling to recreate the way they touched me. It's not really possible on my own.

Behind my closed eyes I see Troy's sharp gaze, full of malice the first time he wrapped his hand around me. The obscene way he spat on my cock. I feel the even filthier way he ran his tongue up my throat outside of his apartment building.

Before I can overthink it, I'm resting one foot on the corner of the tub. One conditioner-slicked finger is working its way behind me. Prodding at my hole.

It's sore. Really fucking sore. I push my finger in anyway, searching for that magic spot Troy found.

The sound that comes out of me this time isn't a scream. It's not a performance required to please someone watching us fuck. It's a low, quiet moan that's for nobody but me.

Now I understand what Adam meant when he said sex is different when it's not a performance. But is it also different when you're performing with someone who legitimately turns you on?

I wish I could talk to them about this. Who else would I ask?

A coworker? My brother? Hell no.

There's nothing I can fill my mouth with to make myself feel like I'm tasting Adam's cock. Anyway, I don't have enough hands. Maybe it's messed up that I'd want to recreate what happened, but the strange thing is, it wasn't awful.

I hate the *reason.* If I let myself think that we all could've been killed, or about where those missing employees may have ended up, I'll lose it. But I also had one of the most explosive orgasms of my life when Troy was inside me.

It would probably take a lifetime of therapy to sort through the tangle of my emotions.

The insistent ringing of my phone interrupts my exploration, pulling me back out of the shower. Fuck.

Don't people know I'm busy having a mental breakdown right now?

It's not my brother this time; it's Max.

"Where the hell are you?"

All of my fucks must be back in that illegal porn studio, because I don't have any now. Especially not for Max.

"I can't work tonight, Max. I had an emergency."

"You missed your last shift. You can't miss work without arranging a replacement."

Entitled prick. "Perhaps you don't understand what emergency means."

Ignoring his rant, I put the phone down while I slide into my robe. I'm still cold, but the hot water helped. When I pick it up again, he's still going.

"...right now. I would rather not have to fire you, Monroe."

"You didn't seem to mind taking my wife and my place to live. I'm sure you wouldn't mind taking my job." I don't wait for him to respond before I plow forward. "Look, Max, I've had the world's shittiest day. I feel like hell. I'm going to bed. Fire me if you want. Good fucking luck replacing me on short notice."

He's still sputtering when I hang up.

I add an extra blanket to the bed and climb in. Then I close my eyes and relive the moment when I woke up in that van, sandwiched between Troy and Adam.

Honestly, if I hadn't been terrified, it might have been nice. I didn't expect to have getting smooshed between two men on my "life after forty" bingo card, but remembering the heat and pressure of their solid bodies eases the chill inside me.

For a while I try to sleep, but all I do is stare at the ceiling. A siren going past the hotel has me freezing in place, heart racing with the certainty that someone will come for me after my fake murder confession. But nothing happens. At some point, I lose track of time.

Along with everything else I've been stewing on, I can't stop worrying about how Adam looked when I last saw him. I'd like to know he's okay.

If I had his number, I could send a text, but I'd have to ask someone for that. My brother or, God forbid, PJ. That's a no. Given what they did to Adam's phone, it might not have been salvageable anyway. I'd be replacing mine right now if I thought I could afford to.

Brennan said they were taking Adam to the hospital in Beacon Hill.

I pull my phone off the charger and dig my spare car key out of my suitcase, heading down to the employee lot to get my car.

The sun makes me wince when I step out. The shock of it starts my head pounding. I get in the car anyway. As I pass through, I'm studying bumper stickers and license plates. Anything to ignore what happened here before.

Once I can be sure Adam and Troy are all right, I'll feel better.

CHAPTER EIGHTEEN

ADAM

WHEN THE KNOCK comes after a shitty hospital meal, I'm expecting the doctor, who said he'd check back with me later. Or Mary, the overly cheerful nurse who has a bright smile and bottle-dyed flame-red hair.

"You think he's okay?" Troy asks as the knock comes.

Could be one of the guys, since the group text has been active and some of them did ask which hospital I was in so they could stop by. Which is nice.

"I'm sure he's fine. PJ and Fallon probably checked on him."

As Troy goes to open the door, I concede he's not the only one wondering about Wes. Before the three of us got thrown into that van, Troy and I were playing around. Teasing, testing, bit by bit raising the stakes to see what Wes could handle.

Getting kidnapped and having your anal virginity pounded out of you on camera? That's beyond getting tossed into the deep end. More like getting dumped overboard and bleeding into shark-infested waters.

So, when Wes walks through the door, I think Troy and I are both shocked. Troy surges forward when he sees the guy, probably without even thinking. Troy's always been the caretaker between us. The one who fixes things. I don't think he knows how to fix Wes.

"How you holding up, Kitten?"

Wes's face pretty much tells Troy to fuck off with his fake cheer.

"That's a good question, Sugar Pie." Wes sags against the closed door. "I don't think I've decided yet."

"You look like shit," I tell him.

Troy comes over and whacks me on the shoulder.

"What? We all look like shit right now." Wes really does, though. His eyes are rimmed with red, and the dark circles underneath have only gotten darker. His hair is sticking up in all directions. It looks like he's at least showered, but his slacks look like they came out of the laundry pile, and his shirt is buttoned all wrong.

"I'd offer to help you fix that shirt, but I'm kind of hooked up to an IV right now." I raise my arm slightly to show him.

Wes looks down at himself and sighs. "Good thing I didn't come here for help getting dressed."

"What did you come for, then?" Troy's failing so badly at sounding casual. His jaw is firm, and his arms are crossed over his chest.

Right now my best friend looks and sounds exactly the way he did the first and last time I took on a client without letting him know where I'd be. We'd had too many friends and acquaintances meet a bad end back in the day. At the time we needed the money, and I hadn't been able to get word to him.

This one isn't on Wes, though. If anything, it's on us. We should've kept a better eye out.

Wes takes a few steps into the room. He presses his lips together, rolling his gaze to the ceiling as if he's thinking. Or maybe the answer is something he doesn't want to say out loud.

"To be honest, I'm not sure..." Wes shakes his head. "My boss called earlier. Gave me a dressing down about missing my shift without calling in. I don't know how to do that right now. To respond rationally or... I don't know how to talk to anyone or just...go back to 'normal' yet. We weren't even gone that long, but it feels like the rest of my life happened forever ago. You know?"

Troy catches my gaze, and my stomach clenches. I can relate. We both can.

Except Troy decides to be an extra-large dick and says, "After I wrecked your ass? Course not. Nobody's the same after that."

Mindful of the IV in my arm, I reach over and pinch the back of Troy's hand.

"Ow." He yanks his arm away. "What the hell was that for?"

I answer him with my eyes. He fucking knows.

To Wes I say, "We get it."

"Yeah. I thought you would." He sighs and sinks into a chair. I don't miss the subtle way he winces and shifts before finding a place to settle. From the mix of concern and satisfaction on Troy's face, he doesn't either.

"Look, Troy and I both ran away from shitty situations. Didn't take long to burn through our money, and we learned quick that having diabetes and living on the streets are not compatible. We did things that were dangerous, illegal, and downright fucking appalling. You're entitled to be fucked up about what happened in that building. We all survived, though, and that's what matters."

"I don't know how to stop replaying it all in my head." Wes rubs an exhausted hand over his face. Then he looks up, giving me a hard stare. "And I don't know what to do about how glad I am that you were both there."

Wes's bold statement shoots a tremor through me, almost like the first time Troy and I kissed. The sound of Troy's sharp inhale slaps me across the face.

The three of us look back and forth at each other as the bomb in the room slowly detonates. As Wes presses his fingers to his mouth.

Troy breaks the silence. "I still don't get what happened. What were those guys doing lurking in the damn employee lot in the middle of the day?"

Mood broken, Wes tips his head back, eyes drifting shut. Remembering. "That's one of the things I keep thinking about. Nadia said she was taken the same way. Went out to her car on her break, and someone grabbed her. I can't help but wonder if all the employees missing recently had the same thing happen."

"Pretty bold, snatching people in the middle of the day," I point out.

"Unlike the guest lots, that one is really only active at shift change," Wes says. "There are no cameras back there. So, maybe risky, but obviously it worked. Jesus, if we hadn't been taken, how long would they have kept it going? Nobody has been especially concerned about the situation. Even I wasn't sure it was a real problem."

"So, if we hadn't gotten snatched, you'd probably still have housekeepers and bellboys dropping like flies. There's a silver lining you gotta really want to see." Troy nudges Wes's leg with his foot. "You really are looking wrecked, Kitten. How about some coffee?"

Troy being Troy, he doesn't wait for an answer, just pats me on the arm to let me know he'll be right back and disappears.

Wes has barely gotten out a tired sounding "Oh. Thanks, I—" when he realizes Troy is gone.

"It's easier to let him do his thing," I say. "He kind of needs to take care of people."

People he considers family, but I don't say that part out loud. It's something I'm not a hundred percent ready to acknowledge myself.

While I can't deny feeling a connection with Wes, especially after what we all went through, Wes isn't exactly all in. He's here right now because he's floundering. What happens when he's not anymore?

We can't count on him. Not yet. I feel for what he's dealing with, but I'm hesitant about getting attached. But here's Troy bringing him smoothies and coffee like Wes is one of his responsibilities.

Over in his chair, Wes looks like he's staring into the great beyond.

"Wes. Get over here."

He rises and approaches slowly, in a shuffling, almost zombie-like fashion.

"Lean over," I tell him.

Ignoring the discomfort in my arm, I reach up and unbutton the top half of his shirt to redo them properly. I don't bother getting adorable with him this time by flirting or touching, though it's impossible not brush his chest a little.

"You know, it's easy to miss it, but you're pretty ripped under these business-casual clothes you always wear. I noticed it before."

Before. When we were kidnapped. When he was naked. When I fucked his face while Troy destroyed his ass.

What are you even saying right now? Shut up.

He huffs an almost-laugh. "I had cancer back in my early thirties. Since then I've tried to look after my health."

"Oh yeah? That must have sucked."

It's more of a real laugh this time. "I wouldn't call it fun." He gives me a curious look. "Most people look sympathetic and change the subject."

I shrug. "I'm not most people. Besides, I know what it's like to have to stay vigilant about your health."

"I can imagine."

Can't say a whole lot for the way my father raised me, but one thing I learned was how not to look away when things are uncomfortable. In his house, it wasn't a choice. There's a naked vulnerability on Wes's face that he probably doesn't show many people.

Troy's right. He's fucked up like we are.

"It did suck." Wes shrugs like he's not even sure what he means by that. He scoots his chair over, closer to the bed. "It also didn't. It was hell, and at the same time it also made me change things I think I needed to change. Slowly, but I did."

"Like your divorce?"

"That's something I really should have done sooner. We got married because I got her pregnant. She miscarried. We kept trying. After I got sick, it was no longer an option. In trying to soothe her heartbreak, I ignored the fact that I didn't actually want kids, and we'd both have been happier if we hadn't let the tide drag us along. So. Yeah. For the best."

He's got his hand resting on the bed rail. Since I'm not sure what to say right now, I put my hand over his and leave it there, surprised when he laces his fingers with mine.

When the door opens again, I'm expecting Troy back with coffee. Instead, a group of our fellow escorts pile into the room.

Simon, a former escort, walks in with his boyfriend, who seems nice but looks scary as fuck because he's got a wicked scar on his face. Behind them are Christian, who took a break from escorting but recently came back, Dean and Michael, and then—"Oh shit." —PJ.

Before I can think of how to handle this, PJ steps up to Wes. "What the hell are you doing here?"

Wes's face freezes in surprise before he can rearrange it into something more neutral.

The last thing we need is a blowup here in my room. "PJ, leave him the fuck alone. He came to visit me."

Wes glances at me, looking grateful. Belatedly, we both realize we're still holding hands when PJ glances downward and does a double take. With an apologetic expression, Wes pulls his hand into his lap.

Then he looks back at PJ with an almost hopeful expression. "Is my brother here?"

PJ shakes his head. "He's upset about you blowing him off earlier, and obviously we weren't thinking you'd be here. He was planning to swing by the hotel later to check on you." He looks Wes up and down. "Guess you're fine."

"For fuck's sake, PJ, put your dick away." Troy shoves his way back into the room, holding two to-go cups. "We all fucking got kidnapped, remember? Wes was nice enough to make sure Adam was doing okay. You're acting like he wasn't in the mood to talk for no good reason. Stop making this all about your baby bitch boyfriend."

"Hey. Stop." Wes, suddenly alert, issues a sharp whistle. "Both of you." He looks at Troy. He's pissed, but there's a heavy dose of guilt on his face. They might be on the outs, but of course he's going to defend his brother.

There's a second where guilt splashes across PJ's face, but then he puts it away. Arms crossed over his chest, he stations himself against the far wall and glares at Wes silently. Which, I guess, is an improvement?

Still. This is my room, and Wes is ours. Our guest, I mean. Can't let PJ's attitude stand. My father would've shot him in the kneecap by now.

"He's right, PJ. It's been a shit time for everyone. You can stop being an ass to Wes, or you can leave."

PJ's eyebrows rise slowly as he seems to put the pieces together. He turns his head to take in Troy standing next to Wes, handing him a coffee cup. Troy's leaning into Wes's space. All other eyes in the room follow suit. The only people who don't seem to realize how this looks are Wes and Troy.

After another stretch of staring, PJ shrugs at Wes and mutters a halfhearted apology.

"It's okay, I get it. I should go anyway." Wes stands and toward the door.

"Wes." Troy grabs for his arm, but misses.

"You don't have to leave," I tell Wes.

"No, I really should." He holds up the cup. "Thank you for the coffee, Troy. PJ, good to see you again."

The door closes behind him, and everything is silent. For

several long, tense seconds it's nothing but open mouths and bugged-out eyes.

PJ's mouth works open and closed a few times before a halting "What the...?" comes out.

Someone chuckles. Michael, I think?

Then the room erupts in a flurry of questions.

CHAPTER NINETEEN

WES

I'M TRYING to pack my things as evening falls outside my temporary room at the Premiere. It's slow going, partly because I don't know where I'll end up yet.

A bone-deep exhaustion weighs me down. Still, I haven't been able to sleep. Or eat. On the table there's a half-finished bowl of miso soup and some rice that the chef downstairs was kind enough to make for me, but even that tasted like ash.

At first, I ignore the knock at the door. There's nobody here I want to talk to. But I keep expecting law enforcement to have questions for me about what happened, so maybe that's finally them.

When I swing open the door, I wish I hadn't. "Gina."

Next time check the peep hole first, idiot.

She gives me a familiar look of worry before bustling inside. She's got her purse and a cooler bag slung over her shoulder. Heading home for the night, then.

"Max said you called out sick for the rest of the week. I wanted to be sure you were okay."

My brain's been on a delay since this morning. Her words take a moment to catch up with me. "What?"

"God. You don't have a fever do you?" She puts the back of her hand to my cheek. My forehead. Something she's done a thousand times over the years and now my nerve endings can't handle her soft touch.

I flinch away. "Gina, what are you doing here?"

"Max said you were sick. I was worried." The weird thing is, she looks sincere. Her eyes are wide and watery, her brow furrowed. She hasn't looked concerned about me that way in a long while. I don't know why she is now.

Unless she thinks sick means the cancer came back. Even so, my health is no longer her problem.

"I'm not sick. I was fucking kidnapped."

She rears back, gripping her cooler bag for dear life. I might as well have slapped her. "What?"

"On my way back from looking at an apartment." The one that wasn't actually available. "Someone hit me, and—" I won't get into Troy and Adam with her. "—a couple of other guys from behind in the employee lot."

"Oh my God. Are you okay?"

"Is that a real question? I got fucking kidnapped." You wouldn't believe it, but I used to walk on eggshells around her. I really did.

She shakes her head. "Max didn't say. He, uh, mostly wanted to know when you'd be back at work."

I breathe out hard through my nostrils, as if I can expel all the weariness and confusion in one forceful breath. "Look, I don't have the energy to argue with you, but in case you weren't aware, your boyfriend is kind of a dick. I feel like a truck hit me. I don't even know where I'm going to be living in a few days. I need some time, Gina. Away from work, and no offense, but away from you."

She bites her lip, tears threatening to spill over. I don't know if I've still got drugs in my system or I'm just at my wit's end, but why is she crying when she's not the one who could have died?

"Right. I guess I deserve that. Just, uhm... Will you let me know if there's anything I can do?"

"Probably not." No, I did not mean to say that aloud. For someone whose job it is to speak diplomatically to all manner of entitled assholes, I'm doing a real shit job of it right now.

Dammit. Pretty soon I need this woman to sign off on our divorce agreement. Pissing her off won't work in my favor.

Still. Funny how after everything that's happened, the wrath of my angry ex doesn't hold the weight that it used to.

All at once, the mental roller coaster starts again. First, it's anticipation. Climbing high, remembering how oddly arousing it was to have Adam and Troy touch me in that charged environment. The tingle and buzz of the pills in my system. The wonder and newness of it all. The free fall of coming harder than I have in my entire life. The horror of Adam collapsing and needing to go to the hospital.

"Gina."

She's still staring at me. Oddly, curiously, as if I'm a stranger. Maybe I am. I can't say I've wanted to look at myself in the mirror much since we were rescued. When I do, I feel like I can see every moment of the past few days on my skin. Every lick, every mark, every bruise.

The person looking back at me isn't someone I've met before.

"Yeah. Sorry. You're right." She turns to go but then stops again with her hand on the doorknob. "It's weird, isn't it? We spent so many years looking after each other..."

A tension in my chest I hadn't been fully aware of seems to loosen. "I know. But I'm not your responsibility anymore."

"Still. I am around if you need a friend."

I nod, but reaching out to her is the last thing I intend to do. Gina's sad smile as she leaves tells me she already knows.

Once she's gone, I head to the bathroom for a glass of water, again studiously ignoring my reflection. I'll have to face it eventually. Just...not now.

I've barely filled my water glass when there's another knock at the door. "I told you I'm fine," I say as I pull it open.

But it isn't Gina on the other side of the door. It's Troy.

"Expecting someone else?" He wiggles his eyebrows playfully, in spite of his obvious exhaustion.

The sight of him standing in front of me makes my breath catch. "I really need to start checking the peephole."

The truth is, I'm glad he's here. Even though nothing about us makes sense and the smart thing would be to close the door.

Instead, I lean against the doorframe. Fatigue covers me like a weighted blanket, as if my body finally feels ready to wind down. "What brings you by?"

He rubs his forehead. "Adam's perky nurse kicked me out. He needs his rest. I went home, but it's weird being there by myself."

"Perhaps if you'd explained to them that you're

medically unable to be farther than ten feet apart without losing oxygen, they'd have let you stay."

He shakes a finger at me. "You joke, but it's kind of pathetically fucking true. We've been looking out for each other for so long I don't really know who I am when I'm flying solo."

There are a lot of things I could be feeling right now. Sympathy. Maybe disgust at that level of codependency. But that burning sensation in my sternum? If I didn't know better, I'd think it was jealousy. Or envy.

Troy leans to the side, mirroring my lean against the doorframe. "Also, it seemed like we should talk. Without a bunch of our nosy friends around. What you did when you stood up and volunteered, that was..." He trails off with a shake of his head.

"Stupid."

His expression is naked and raw when he says, "Stupidly fucking brave."

That's... Wow.

There's something I don't think I've ever been called. A warm sensation washes over me, and I find myself stepping backward into the room.

"You want to come in?"

He considers me for a moment, as if he's not sure if the invitation is sincere. To be honest, I'm not sure what I'm doing here. All I know is that I've been pacing the floor in this room until I'm dizzy, unable to make sense of the jumble of thoughts in my head.

The list of people I can relate to right now is extremely short, and one of them happens to be standing right in front of me. The slight swelling on his jaw and the shadowy bruising around his eye do nothing to diminish how glad I am to see him.

Troy steps inside. Closes the door. Leans back against it with his arms crossed over his chest. I'm waiting, quiet and still, except for the thunder booming in my chest.

Then, with a blur of movement, everything's in fast-forward.

It's me who moves first, I think, rushing blindly until I realize I'm in the middle of my hotel room with my arms wrapped around an off-the-clock sex worker, a man who fucked me so hard I've felt empty ever since, and I'm clinging to him with the desperation of a man dangling over a chasm.

I've been slipping since I walked back into this hotel. He's my rope.

His kiss is bruising, almost punishing. If it hurts him, I can't tell. "I could fucking kill you," he murmurs between kisses. "You could have gotten yourself killed. That guy could have wanted one of his goons to fuck you, and not us."

"I know. I know." All those possible disastrous outcomes have passed through my head. "I couldn't let Nadia—"

Troy's shaking hands come to either side of my face. "I know, Kitten."

God, that name. That stupid goddamn pet name made me want to punch him in the face the first time I heard it, but now its tenderness is making my eyes burn.

Troy's teeth sink into my bottom lip. The tang of blood hits me, but then his tongue is sliding into my mouth to sweep it away.

"Sorry," he whispers.

"I'm not. I'm not sorry about any of it." It must be true,

because I haven't been able to speak a single word of bullshit since I got back.

"What can I do? What do you want?" he asks.

"I don't know. I'm too tired to even think right now."

To my surprise, Troy steps back, still with his hands on either side of my face. For the first time, he gives me a smile that looks genuine. "There's my answer, then."

Next thing I know, he's pushing me toward the bed. He's grasping greedily at my belt buckle, tugging at the button of my slacks, and I'm surprised to find myself doing the same with him. We flop together in a heap on the mattress, with our hands still grabbing and clothes flying everywhere.

It's not the same buzzy fever dream as before, but I'm caught in this strange place between awake and asleep where everything feels floaty and surreal.

"Lay back, babe. Let me make you feel good."

While he kisses his way down my body, I sink into the mattress. I moan when he wraps his hand around my cock. The usual embarrassment hits, but it's dimmer and duller than before.

Mostly, it's fascination. This hand with rough, sure fingers and large knuckles. Troy's bright eyes and wicked smile. How good it all feels.

"Lemme ask you something, Kitten. What's with you seeming so embarrassed about your own dick?"

My face burns. Slapping my hand over my own eyes doesn't help. "Ugh. It's stupid. Toward the end, things between my ex and me got pretty toxic. We both felt trapped. She, uh, made it pretty clear I'd let her down. In every way possible."

Understanding dawns. "Kitten." He's studying me, his gaze sliding back and forth between my face and my erection in his hands, with lust in his hooded eyes. "Let me tell you a story."

"Right now?" I look pointedly at his hand on my cock.

"No better time." He stills his hand and looks me in the eye. It's a little awkward, lying here like this, but the longer we do it the less strange it feels.

"Fine. Tell me your story."

"So, shortly after Adam and I landed in Belle Argo, we got hooked up with Brennan, who in turn hooked us up with a client who was in town for a week on business. Aussie guy. Big. Taller than you. The man had a battering ram where his dick belonged."

"Why are you telling me this while we're naked?"

"Even taking him nice and slow, I could hardly sit down for a week. My point, Kitten, is that bigger isn't always better. Your dick is just fine. Trust me, if I didn't like it, I wouldn't be here. Aside from Adam, you're the one person I don't have to pretend with. I'm here because I choose to be. Because I want you."

In this moment, the reminder of what he does for a living isn't the bucket of cold water I'd have thought it would be. Right now, it's so good to simply feel connected again. Why does touching him feel more meaningful than anything I experienced with my wife?

It's a problem for later.

Shoving away the doubts and insecurities, I reach down to grasp him as well. He's longer than me, but thinner, with a strange swath of scar tissue on the side. Curious, I slide my thumb over the spot.

"Circumcision went a little sideways," he murmurs.

Nodding my understanding, I resist the urge to ask how he can be so confident in his nudity in spite of it.

Do I mind it? Does it change the way he made me feel? The way he's making me feel now?

I'm here because I choose to be.

No. I feel right for the first time in days. Months. Ages. So maybe he's right. Maybe a dick's appearance doesn't matter.

He captures my mouth with his again, and I'm done for. I'm whining into him, gasping for breath as I fuck into his hand. Our hands and mouths on each other are fast and dirty, every kiss and lick and rough swipe stirring my blood. Troy has this magic way of finding the exact spots that make me moan, and I can't even care about why.

Lightning shoots through my veins when his fingers find my hole, pressing gently. In spite of the ache, I'm suddenly buzzing, right on the verge, and unable to hold back.

My back bows with the force of my release. My mouth stretches open so wide there's a twinge in my still-bruised jaw. When he spills into my hand moments later, I relish the sticky heat on my fingers.

It's tangible proof that I've pleased him. When I grab a tissue to clean off, I almost regret wiping him away.

Troy collapses on the bed, facing me, looking heavy-lidded and wrung out. I did this to him. Me.

I'm here because I choose to be.

His glassy, tired gaze and the shallow breaths puffing from between his lips must match my own. I run my hand over his chest as it rises and falls.

"Holy shit, Kitten. Not bad for your first time doing hand stuff."

"You really mean that?" I regret the vulnerability in the question as soon as I ask.

For a rare moment, Troy's face softens. "I'm getting the

sense that you haven't had a whole lot of people say nice things to you."

"Says the man who accused me of being a homophobe and then insisted on jerking me off to prove I wasn't."

"No." He kisses the center of my chest, and I find my fingers tangling in his hair. "I jerked you off when you said you had a problem with PJ being controlling with Fallon. I was challenging your assumptions."

"Ah. Makes total sense now." Sort of. I don't know. I'm too damn tired. There are so many other things I want to say, but my eyelids weigh a ton, and my brain is slowly grinding to a halt.

"I think we both need some rest, Kitten."

"Mmm."

I'm half aware of Troy pulling tissues from the bedside dispenser to clean off. He reaches for the soft blanket I stole from the linen closet at what used to be my house and throws it over us both.

He doesn't ask if he can stay, and I don't offer. It's just something that happens. After all the recent upheaval, this man wrapping himself around me is the only thing that makes sense.

I'm here because I choose to be.

As his breathing evens out, I realize I'm choosing him too. For maybe the first time in my life, I'm choosing someone for myself. Both of them, since I know they're a package deal.

I barely register my fingers curling into the hair at his nape as I drift off.

CHAPTER TWENTY

TROY

I WAKE up in a cozy cocoon, but I'm alone. Weirdly, I'm on my left side, spooning a pillow, the way I usually wake up when I sleep in Adam's bed. Except the pillow is still warm, and it smells spicy, like Wes.

The night before floats back to me. Then the day before that. And the night before that, when I wasn't sure if we were going to survive. Fuck, now I'm definitely awake.

Not that it was the first time Adam and I had been in a precarious situation, but Wes being there added a whole other level.

Speaking of Wes and other levels...

"Huh."

I scan the room with bleary, sleep-crusted eyes, stretching to see if I can hear water running in the bathroom, but there's nothing. Strange, right? Did he really leave me in here on my own? I wouldn't have. Does he actually trust me that much?

Then again, the pressure-cooker shit we all went through together seems to cause a fucked-up sort of bonding. I'm sure it's got to do with why Adam and I are so close. Over the years we went from confiding about our bastard fathers to literally saving each other's lives.

One thing I did do yesterday after Adam was settled at the hospital was to run out and get new phones. I check mine to see if there's anything from Adam. Nothing yet, which hopefully means he got a decent night's rest.

Apparently the group chat's been group chatting while I slept, though.

Christian: So, there was this police detective lurking around my new apartment. You guys think I should be worried?

Simon: Just stay away from him

Michael: Brennan mentioned someone new in town slinging drugs, right? Maybe he's looking into that. Your place isn't exactly on the up and up.

Christian: That's the truth. I don't know anything about that though. My ex might.

Adam: Then you should definitely stay away from him. Your ex is a POS and informing on him won't do you any good.

Fucker.

Troy: Oh good you're up Adam thanks for letting me know

Adam: Literally grabbed my phone just now and answered an existing text before messaging you I'll never do it again I swear

Simon: Oh reeeealy?

Prince: Thought it was unethical to separate a bonded pair

Ravi: Yeah I have some questions

Troy: I'm sure you do. Adam, I'll see you soon.

That's enough of that for now.

As I'm returning my phone to the nightstand, a beep sounds and the door pushes open.

"Hey, you're awake." Wes comes in slowly, carefully balancing a to-go tray with coffees and a couple of pastry bags.

"Kitten, did you bring me breakfast?" I'm making light to cover the gooey warmth in my chest. Nobody's brought me breakfast since my mother died. Adam would, I'm sure, but he sleeps later than I do.

Wes's cheeks turn red as he sets the coffees down on the little table next to my phone.

"It's nothing much. Chef Lorraine down in the kitchen is one of the few people who doesn't give a shit that Max has told the entire hotel to stop helping me. Probably because she could go literally anywhere in the world and get paid as much as she does now. Maybe more. And I'm the one who told her about the opening here."

He pauses, looking uncertain. "Her sister and I were in a cancer support group together. Chef moved here to help take care of her."

"Oh, shit." Is it fucked up that I'm sort of thrilled about this? Not that he had cancer, thank you very much. I'm not that kind of dick.

But him telling me? That he's sharing his life with me like a regular person and not someone he wants but can't stand? I like that part.

I slap the mattress next to me. "Come have a seat, Kitten."

He hesitates before slipping off his shoes and sliding in next to me. He's fully clothed still.

He hands over one of the bags, containing a toasted bagel. "I wasn't sure about how you take your coffee."

"Hell, I'll take it any way I can get it," I say as I grab one of the cups.

Wes chuckles, but then he gets serious. "I'm such an asshole. I didn't ask last night how Adam's doing."

"Don't do that." I take a grateful gulp from my to-go cup. "You were dead on your feet last night. We both were."

"Yeah." He shakes his head, huffing a breath. "I can't believe I finally got some sleep. I was so messed up after we got back. Exhausted, but also..."

"Wired?"

"Wired. Exactly."

"Me too."

The expression on his face looks a lot like gratitude. Maybe he's not used to being understood. Which I also get. It sucks. A lot.

"Part of that is probably the drugs," I explain. "That shit they gave us, I don't know what all's in it, but it's been circulating around the area for a few months now. Even Brennan, who's got his hands in all sorts of dirty shit, is trying to get it off the street. Probably a mix of Molly and something that gets you horny and hard. Maybe boner boosters or coke, or all three. I know it shoots your blood pressure sky high. It's been tied to a lot of deaths in town."

"Jesus." Wes looks a little shell-shocked.

"Yeah. I'll be honest, I've taken it a couple of times before. After the last time I didn't want to do it again. Thought my heart would blast its way out of my chest. So for that alone we're lucky we all got out alive." I nudge him with my elbow. "Especially you, old man."

"Hey, fuck you." He laughs a little, in spite of the worry on his face.

"You know I wouldn't be able to joke about it if you weren't so self-conscious about it, but I love seeing you blush. So, you're older. What's the big deal?"

I'm being real with him here.

"Car insurance premiums? I don't know." Wes shakes his head. "I'm not self-conscious about my age. I'm self-conscious that my age minus your age equals a two-digit number."

"You know it doesn't bother me. It doesn't bother Adam. We like you. We think you're hot. And you're not nearly as big a dick as we originally thought."

Wes bends up one leg, hooking an arm around it. "Nice to know I've got that going for me. Seriously, though, I've changed quite a bit since I was your age. I've finished college, gotten married, and helped my wife through multiple miscarriages. I've had cancer. Those things change you. *Life* changes you."

"What about your first time getting kidnapped and pounded by a much younger man?"

He groans. "The way you phrase that, it sounds as if the man who fucked me is the one who kidnapped me."

A grin spreads across my face. "Babe, if you'd continued to be difficult with us, we probably would have. We're morally ambiguous like that."

"Morally amb—of course you are." He runs a hand through his hair. "You know, the thing with you guys... You're right, I was surprised I liked it. It fucked me up that I couldn't stop thinking about you, and especially that I couldn't stop thinking about *that.*"

"Kitten..."

He squirms, hugging his knee tighter. "It's not normal to be glad that someone is holding you down and fucking you because it takes the decision out of your hands. Right? I even liked that it hurt. You're not supposed to get off on someone hurting you."

Hell. For Adam and me, it wasn't the worst thing we've experienced. For Wes though?

"Babe. It's not something to be ashamed of. I've seen kinks you wouldn't believe. Adam and I used to have a regular who wanted us to fuck in front of him while we made fun of how useless his dick was."

For the time being I'll leave out how we all know what Wes's brother's into. Nobody in our friend group has been marked safe from accidentally walking in on Fallon and PJ's shenanigans. There's usually some spanking or breath play involved. Not to mention the fact that getting caught is clearly one of their kinks.

"For the record, I'm not into you making fun of my dick."

As if we didn't already know. "Understood. But you get my point, right? It's fine if what we did together felt good. Regardless of the circumstances. Human contact is meant to feel good. Even if you weren't 'supposed' to like it. Maybe you need time to come to terms with it, but if that's what you're worried about, don't be."

"I appreciate that. It's not the only reason I've been hesitant, though."

"Because you're still married? Because we're escorts? Because we're friends with your brother's 'gold-digging' boyfriend."

"Dammit, I'm never going to live it down that I called him that, am I? I was really in a bad place when all of that happened. My whole life felt like it was dangling over a paper shredder. Hell, it still does. I don't even have a new place to live. There's nothing in town I can afford." He sighs. "At this point I may have to leave town. Or sleep in my car for a little while."

"Fuck no." No to every bit of that. "You are not leaving, and you're sure as fuck not sleeping in your car. I won't allow that. It's a fantastic way to get jacked and stabbed and left by the side of the road. And if you leave town, we'll have to come after you."

This might be one of those times when I've gone too far. He's looking at me like I just announced I'm a vampire.

"You could stay with us, you know." I take a breath, wishing Adam were here. He'd agree, but it's weird making decisions without him. I'll head to the hospital as soon as Wes and I wrap things up here.

Doesn't matter, though, since Wes squashes the idea fast. Too fast. "No, I absolutely could not."

Are those nerves I hear? After what we've gone through, is crashing at our place really so scary?

"Why the hell not? It's not the classiest place but we keep it clean. Well, Adam does, mostly. Still. You were looking for a place in our building."

"It's not the address, Troy. Whatever's going on with the three of us... I don't even know what to call it. For a little while longer I'm legally still married, as you pointed out. I've never been in a relationship with a man, let alone two. Even if we were exclusive it would be jumping the gun to move in together, and the two of you *are* actively fucking other people." He flinches like even he's offended by what he just said, but it's too late.

"Never fucked anybody raw except you and Adam, Kitten."

I like how he's stopped giving a shit when I call him that. Progress.

Something in his demeanor shifts, though, and not in a good way. He slugs some coffee and then rubs his eyes.

"I'm not sure that's as meaningful as you think it is, Cupcake." Everything from his expression to his body language slams shut.

Well, fuck me. And not in the fun way this time. In the middle of rubbing at the sudden ache in my chest, I force my hand back to the mattress.

See, when I call him Kitten, it sounds like a term of endearment, but that cupcake sounded an awful lot like he wanted to spit fire. It sounded judgy, and if that's the way he's going to be, then I'm definitely going to leave and see Adam.

I throw off the blanket and get out of bed stark naked, hunting around for my clothes. "You know what? Fuck you, Wes. Adam and I take our health and safety seriously. When you do what we do, safe sex matters. We weren't on the street too long because we couldn't afford to be, but we met plenty of guys who were willing to go bare if the client paid extra. You know how risky that is when you don't have decent medical care?"

Wes looks wary. "You're right. Sorry."

I pull on my pants and thrust my arms into my shirt. "It is what it is, right? One of the risks of living the life we live."

"One of, but not the only," Wes counters. "It's dangerous, what you do. You could get arrested. You could get killed."

"Is that what bothers you, or do you think we're cheap gold diggers like you accused PJ of being?"

Not too many things shake me these days. The cost of pride is sky high in this world, especially when you do what we do. But trying to give this guy something meaningful and having it thrown in my face?

I don't expose my belly like that for just anyone.

Fuck me for thinking Wes would be different. That maybe after what we went through, he saw past what we are to *who* we are.

He runs a hand through his hair. I'm vaguely satisfied to notice it shaking, glad I've rattled him the way he's rattled me. "For fuck's sake. I've admitted I was wrong. How long are you going to keep beating that horse?"

"Here's the thing, Kitten. PJ quit escorting when he got together with Fallon. Opened a little ice cream stand with his best friend. So adorable and domestic. Adam and I, we don't have any other plans. We ran away from home when he was sixteen and I was seventeen. We didn't finish high school, didn't go to college. Our marketable skills are mostly limited to all the different fuck positions we know and how well we can suck a dick. If you can't handle what we do then you can't, but I won't stick around and be judged."

What I don't tell him is Adam and I have been working on a plan for years to quit. Almost since the day we started. That plan isn't close to fully formed yet, though, and I'm too raw to share right now.

If Wes can't handle the worst of us, he can't have the rest. The shitty part is, I thought we were already over that hurdle. He's known about us since the beginning and it hasn't seemed like a deal-breaker before now.

Wes jumps to his feet. "Hey. Look. I don't know *how* I feel about it, okay? It's not exactly the only reservation I have about whatever it is we're doing here. I'm not sure it's even in the top ten. In the last few weeks I've gone from the two of you fucking around with me for giggles to not knowing—*again*—if I was going to die. Forgive me if I'm not ready to pack up a moving van and play house yet. Give me a damn minute here."

To be fair, what he's saying makes sense for a regular person who lives in the real world. Adam and I aren't exactly normal.

As I button my wrinkled shirt, I struggle to bring my breathing under control. "You're right, Wes. Where Adam and I come from, there's usually not time to think things over. The night we ran away, I had all of ten minutes advanced notice. If time's what you need, fine." I check my phone. Visiting hours are open, so I can go see Adam now. "Meanwhile, I've got shit to do."

I take my coffee and the rest of my bagel and get ready to storm out. Except when I fling open the door, there's that pretty blonde who was dumb enough to cheat on our kitten.

"Oh." She pauses with her hand raised to knock. She's shocked, but she recovers quickly. Then, in a super classy move, she looks around me as if I'm nothing more than the door still blocking her view. "Wes? Can I speak with you?"

He looks at me, angry but also questioning. He's glancing back and forth between us with his mouth hanging open and panic in his eyes.

Fuck it. I'm not going to linger where I'm not wanted.

But I'm not above embarrassing the shit out of him on my way out.

So I blow him a kiss and give a little finger wave. "Thanks for the breakfast in bed, Kitten. We'll talk soon."

"Wha..." The shock on her face is precious.

I only wish I could stick around to watch Wes's face turn red.

CHAPTER TWENTY-ONE

WES

I'M ABOUT to do something I didn't do nearly enough in all the years Gina and I were together. Suck it up and apologize.

My inner asshole is protesting. Old me wouldn't have done this.

It's the vulnerability of sorries I hate most, but this feels important. And maybe, I can admit, I want to see Adam again. He seems to be more level-headed. More thoughtful. Maybe he'll let me explain where Troy didn't.

When I arrive at Adam's hospital room I expect Troy, if not a room full of sex workers. I brace myself when I push open the door. To my surprise, it's only him. Sitting up in bed, reading one of my brother's mystery novels.

"Hey, Westy. You read these books?" He holds up the novel. Book two or three in the series—I'm not entirely sure.

"I read the first one. It was good. I'm not as much of a reader as my brother, though."

It's not that I don't want to support my brother and the books he writes, but sitting down to read fiction has always been guilt-inducing. There are so many other things I need to do and worry about; how can I spend time reading a story for fun?

Our mother would have called it lazy. She called twice on my way over, by the way, and I sent them both to voicemail. How do I explain that I'm not in the mood to talk because I'm too busy questioning my entire existence to help her decide which option she should choose for her new air conditioning system or talk her through setting up her smart TV, or whatever crisis she's having this week?

"I should pick the series up again," I add.

Adam smiles and sets the book aside. "Hey, get over here." I walk to the bed, but then it hits me what he really meant when he pats the mattress beside him the same way Troy did.

"I don't know if you've noticed, but I'm kind of a big guy, and hospital beds aren't made for two." Hell, hospital beds were the bane of my existence when I was going through treatment. Not all of them were made to comfortably accommodate a person my size. Some barely gave me room to roll over.

"Shut up and get in here," Adam says. "Between the beeping and the smells it's been impossible to sleep in here by myself. I could use a nap."

"Hmm. I guess it's good to know you and Troy are both equally codependent." Even as I snark at him, I'm lowering one of the handrails and sliding in beside him. He scoots over to make room, setting the book down and curling toward me.

"Yeah, I heard Troy crashed with you last night." He

situates himself so we're almost nose to nose. "He stopped by earlier."

Interesting. I wasn't sure. "I'm surprised he's not here right now."

Adam's eyes sparkle with amusement. And now I can officially mark down the first time I ever noticed another man's eyes sparkling. I don't even know what to do with that information.

He brushes his hand along the side of my face. "So, here's the secret. I love Troy. With a capital L. He also is the absolute worst when he's scared."

Scared? I think back to the night before. "He didn't seem scared. Exhausted, angry, and kind of dickish..."

Adam laughs. "Trust me, he's fucking terrified. Considering all the shit we've seen, he doesn't handle death well. Not that anyone died, but things got risky. He'd never admit it, but he's not handling this well. He never does. And yes, part of that is not being allowed to stay with me." When he looks at me again, it's full of meaning. "Glad the two of you were able to lean on each other, though."

Since I'm not sure what exactly Troy's told Adam, I'm hesitant about my reply. Also, I'm trying this new thing where I don't lie to people. "Not sure I'd call what we did leaning on one another."

"Why not? Orgasms can be very healing."

"So he told you."

Adam shrugs. "We tell each other most things. Not everything. Almost everything. The stuff we don't tell, we usually know anyway."

There's a scratching sensation against my cheek. Adam resting his stubbled face against mine. I don't hate it.

"The thing is, we might not be here if we hadn't relied

on each other. You can call it codependent if you want. It's probably the truth. Still, it's the way it is because it's how we needed to be. I wouldn't know who I was without him. I wouldn't want to."

Even without Troy in the room, I feel the intimacy in Adam's words. "Where do I fit into all of this?"

"You didn't like my previous answer?"

"I'm not convinced I understood your previous answer. Telling me I'm fun to fuck with makes it sound like I'm a video game you both want to play. Something you'll wander away from when you get bored."

"Kitten," Adam breathes. "That's not it at all."

But how can he be sure? There's no denying the fear that slices through my center when I think of them getting tired of me. It doesn't take a professional to know it's not healthy to be clinging to these two men. I'm sure it'll pass. These knots twisting in my gut will go away when I'm on firmer footing, but not yet.

Not right now.

Adam nudges his nose against mine. "I also said you were real, and that was the honest truth. We like that you're a little damaged and fucked up, because so are we. Someone who hasn't been a little broken wouldn't get us. And Troy and I have done everything together for so long, if we're going to date someone it makes sense we'd do that together, too." He wrinkles his nose. "I've sort of had a girlfriend on and off, but it was never going work long-term because she and Troy don't really like each other. That's a deal-breaker, even if she does leave her fiancé."

"I don't even know how to unpack that statement." The fiancé part gets lost in my knee jerk reaction to the word "girlfriend," and the way everything inside me gets hot and tight.

I think I'm jealous again, and I sure as hell don't like it.

"She's not someone you need to worry about, Wes."

I move to sit up. "Who said I was worried?"

His hand lands on my arm. "Don't. Don't go yet."

"Fine." I settle back in, surprised by how much I like having someone to cuddle. Gina and I hadn't done that in years, even when we did sleep in the same bed. "I came here to apologize, actually. Troy and I somehow got into a fight. I got defensive. I don't entirely remember what I said, but I weirdly got the impression I hurt his feelings."

"Tell me what happened."

"We..." It feels strange talking about this so openly. "Well, you already know about the orgasms. We fell asleep, which I think we both really needed. The next morning we're having coffee, and it comes up that I don't have a place to live in a few days. Troy offered to let me stay with you guys. Which... It's not that I don't appreciate the offer, but it's not a good idea. And I made a shitty comment when he pointed out that he hasn't fucked anybody bare except us two. It didn't come out the way I intended, but it pushed a button, getting reminded right then about what you guys do for a living."

Adam nods, serious. "Sure. Yeah. He burst your bubble. I see where you're coming from. And also why Troy got pissed."

"Care to share with the class?"

He narrows his eyes. "Not sure if it'll help or scare you away."

"Now you have to tell me, or I'll start imagining things that are probably worse."

"Fine. Troy thinks he's going to die."

There's a moment when time feels frozen. Even my heart seems to stop beating. Somewhere in my head, a needle scratches across a record.

"What the hell?" I don't know what I thought he was going to say, but it wasn't dying.

Adam sighs. "His mother had some pretty severe mental health issues. In the interest of time I'll leave it at that. Troy's dad was a real piece of shit, deep in some not-so-legal import and export stuff, and wasn't home a lot. The year he and I met, she killed herself. Since people in our parents' circles didn't do things like therapy, he had nobody to help him make sense of it."

My heart squeezes at the thought of a confused teenager trying to figure out why his mother left him behind. I had the same thoughts when my father passed, even though his illness wasn't the same.

"What about you?"

"Oh, sure." Adam nods enthusiastically, scraping his stubble against my face. "He had me. I was raised by the prominent leader of a South Florida gang whose idea of toughening up his 'pussy' kid was to put a gun in my hand and force me to shoot someone who had betrayed him. Ended up shooting him instead." He pulls back, looking me in the eye. "You'd be surprised, but I'm not exactly the poster child for healthy myself."

Maybe I should freak out over what he just said. But I heard it before, in that building. And if what he said about his father is true, I almost understand.

Dammit, his eyelashes are so long. "That's...that's terrible. I'm sorry." I'm aching right now. For both of them. For myself.

"I'm not asking you to be sorry. I'm hoping you'll try and understand. We came from a fucked-up world and ran away so we could live in one that was only slightly less fucked up. We did impossible things to make it to tomorrow. What happened in that building? If you hadn't been there with us, it would have been just another Tuesday. Through everything, when it came down to it, Troy and I only had each other."

There's a lump in my throat when I swallow. They've only ever had each other, and they both want me. Maybe I don't feel ready, but it means something that they want me to be a part of what they have.

Since Adam's giving me something important, I try to give something in return. "My dad died when I was twelve. I had my mom and my brother, but I was the one who had to take care of them. Never felt as if I had anyone to rely on but myself. People helped a little, but the kind ladies who brought casseroles and my dad's coworkers who came by to help us repair the dishwasher eventually disappeared. I think it would have been everything to have a friendship like yours."

Adam makes a noise of understanding. "So, if something had happened while people were relying on you, that would've sucked, right? Well, Troy seems convinced that someday whatever mysterious force pushed his mother to sit in her car with the garage door closed and the engine running is going to come for him, too. Like one day some sort of curse will be triggered."

"That's..." Morbid. Chilling. Relatable. "My dad died of leukemia," I tell him. "Years later, when I got it too, I was sure I wasn't going to survive. Because he hadn't. So, I think I can understand."

"You're okay now?" Adam's forehead creases with worry.

"I've been in remission for a long time. I see my oncologist every year. I take my meds, get blood work. So far, so good. But, Adam, I don't understand how Troy's anxiety relates to me."

Adam's arm curls around my waist. "I think... He won't talk about it, but I feel like he's been on this quest to find someone for me. In case he's ever gone, you know?"

That doesn't even make sense. And he wants that person to be me? That's not something I could live up to, even if I tried.

"He knows you can't replace a person that way, right? Besides, I told you I had cancer. Statistically, there's a halfway decent chance I'll get it again. A woman I was in treatment with was on her fourth round. I'm not anyone's best bet."

"And I have diabetes, which, as you've seen, comes with its own complications. We've all got shit to deal with, Wes. Here's the thing. Troy pleaded with one of the nurses to stay the last time I was in the hospital. This time, he went to you."

"I'm sor—"

"Don't be. I'm not. Like I said, I'm glad you two could lean on each other. If he'd stayed, he would have been up all night, with his pacing and worrying. If he'd actually slept his snoring would've driven me nuts. It worked out."

I'm surprised to find myself smiling. "We were both so worn out. I didn't even notice he snores."

"It's not so bad if you roll him onto his side."

There's a sudden warm feeling as I recall Troy and me wrapping around each other before falling asleep. Not too different from the way Adam and I are wrapped around each other now.

It doesn't make sense, the way they both feel so much like home. I'm sure a therapist would have a field day. They'd probably also tell me this level of need is unhealthy, but I can't bring myself to care about that right now.

"We're all three pretty fucked up, Wes. But Troy likes you. That day when he started messing with you at the gym, it was a rough day. His mom's birthday. He was already in a bad mood and looking for someone to take it out on. Maybe I shouldn't have gone along with it, but..."

But Adam goes along with everything Troy wants. That much is clear.

"Anyway. I hope you'll reconsider," he says quietly. "About crashing at our place. If it feels too much like playing house, you could sleep on the sofa. Or in Troy's room. He usually sleeps with me anyway."

How do I say that I don't like that idea either? Is it possible to stay with them while not sharing the same bed? That doesn't feel right.

Everything is happening too fast. At the same time, the idea of losing my connection to the only two people in the world who make sense to me makes my insides shake.

"I don't know. I can always sleep in my car."

"Oh, fuck no. Don't do that." Adam shakes his head.

"Troy said the same thing. Actually, he said I wasn't allowed. Maybe he forgot I've been making my own decisions longer than you've been alive."

"He didn't forget. Like I said—he's scared. Florida law prohibits sleeping in public places. You sleep in that car on the nice side of Belle Argo, you risk getting arrested. If you do it on the not-so-nice side of town, you risk getting hurt or killed. No way in hell you'll get a comfortable night's sleep. Not with that big body of yours. I know you care about your health. Sleep matters. Don't make us have to drag your ass by your hair back to our cave, okay?"

Adam's right. They both are. "I'll think of something."

"Of course you will. Hey, could you do me a favor, though?" He points across the room. "There's a bag in there with all my stuff. Grab it for me."

Reluctantly, I slide off the bed and bring it over.

"Here." He hands a key over. "They're probably going to let me out of here sometime later today, and the clothes I came in with are pretty destroyed. You think you can go to our place and grab me something?"

The key is on a plain ring by itself. For something so small, it weighs heavily in my hand. Taking it would be a bad idea. A commitment I'm not sure I can make. But it also feels precious and rare. I can't bring myself to say no.

"I guess I could." Something doesn't make sense, though. "Why are you asking me? I bet Troy would jump at the chance."

"The fastest route to our place goes directly past that little hardware store on fifth, and you could swing by and get the key copied. In case you change your mind at any point about staying with us. No obligation."

Ignoring the voices telling me how completely irresponsible this is, I fold my fingers over the key.

"Kitten?"

Later, I'll probably need to think long and hard about the way I automatically turn to face him.

"It's okay to accept help, even if it's not coming from where you think it should. If Troy and I hadn't done that, we wouldn't be here now."

"Right. I'll give that some thought." After I'm done spinning out over answering to "Kitten."

"I'll tell Troy you stopped by." He picks up the book again, dismissing me.

Well.

I guess I've got things to do, then.

CHAPTER TWENTY-TWO

WES

I TEST my newly copied key in the lock, surprised it actually works. Everything's been so surreal lately, I've begun to question my perception of reality. So, really, I think the situation could have gone either way.

Speaking of surreal... When I swing open the door, there's a gun in my face. On the other end of it is Troy.

"Jesus fuck, Kitten." He lowers it to his side. "What are you doing here?"

I grip the key in my fist. "Why are you pointing a gun at me?"

"Because someone was coming into my fucking apartment."

"Well. Thanks for not shooting me." Exhaustion pulls at my body. A few days ago this would have been terrifying. Now it's more of a "been there, done that" situation. I'm already over it.

I don't know what that says.

"Don't worry, it's not loaded." He lays it down on a battered and scarred coffee table. One like my mother had ages ago, with a piece of glass in the center. In this case, someone has used to the glass the way someone would a whiteboard, including a reminder to pay the rent and what I guess is a very mature and adult shopping list of nuts, nog, and "those fruity things I like."

"Great. Fantastic. I feel so safe now." Without any invitation, I enter and sink onto the lumpy sofa. One solid night's sleep apparently doesn't wipe away a deficit like the one I'm carrying.

Troy narrows his eyes at me. "What are you doing here, Wes? Where did you get a key?"

Realizing I've closed my eyes, I manage to pry them open. "Are there a ton of people running around Belle Argo with keys to this place? Where do you think I got it? I stopped by the hospital to see how Adam was doing. He asked me to get him some clothes."

For some reason, Troy laughs. "Did he? That little fucker."

"I don't understand."

Instead of explaining a damn thing, Troy assumes a defensive stance and rolls his neck until it cracks. "Why bother stopping to see Adam? You made it pretty fucking clear you didn't want a relationship with us."

"I didn't..." Fuck, I'm not alert enough for this. I run my hands through my hair and lean forward, propping my elbows on my thighs. "That's not what I said. I said I didn't know what the hell we were doing, and moving in together seemed premature. But..." Oh, this is painful to say. "Adam pointed out that I'm pretty short of options at the moment. Until I find something else it's sleeping in my car—"

"Which I already told you, you are not fucking doing." He firms his jaw.

"—which I can admit probably isn't safe. Or that shitty roadside motel in Beacon Hill—"

"Which is full of dealers and whores. Not the classy kind like me and Adam, either."

"—or there's begging my brother to let me use his guest room—"

"You'll have to put up with him and PJ fucking all the time."

"—which would put a strain on our already strained relationship. So, if you don't mind me crashing on the sofa temporarily—"

"Fuck that. Adam's got a king bed. Plenty of room."

I drop my head back, expecting to meet the cushion of the sofa. Once again I'm too tall, and I thwack my head into the wall instead.

"Ow. Listen. If your plan is to interrupt everything I say and steamroll over every one of my ideas, then maybe I need to reconsider."

"Shoot me some good ideas and I won't." He rounds the coffee table and straddles my legs, sinking into my lap.

"Troy," I groan tiredly. I'm pretty sure my intention is to tell him we can't do this, whatever it is, right now. I need rest. I need space to think. I need—

This. Exactly this. Letting him sink against me, I give up and release a tired groan.

His nose runs along my jaw. "I don't know what it is, but you smell so fucking good, Kitten."

"Probably my deodorant." I stocked up during a buy-one-get-one-free sale. "I'm out of aftershave and I don't wear cologne."

"Spicy." He kisses my jaw. "Manly." Then my throat. "Sexy as fuck."

Okay, I don't know who can stay stoic in the face of being kissed this way and, oh hell, being licked and called sexy, but I'm not that person.

"Troy," I breathe. "We probably shouldn't..."

We shouldn't confuse things. If I'm going to stay here, it should be a roommate thing, shouldn't it? Clear boundaries so nobody's confused. Except I'm already well past confused, lost in a haze of arousal and starved for affection.

I'm drowning in him, in both of them. If I'm honest with myself, I don't really want to be rescued.

When Troy yanks my shirt free of my slacks, I wind up helping him. Somehow, I'm the one who takes care of the button and zipper on my pants. When he stands up, I'm the one who pushes them down to my ankles.

"Turn over." He slaps my hip. "Face in the cushions, ass up in the air."

You'd think my first concern would be, do I really want to do this? Does he want to fuck me? Am I ready again so soon? I'm still sore.

Any one of those things.

Instead I blurt, "When were these cushions last cleaned?"

As protests go, it's got all the strength of a wet paper bag. That I ask even as I'm getting into position destroys all my credibility.

"Just do it." Troy slaps my hip again. And I can't seem to say no to him.

Sure fingers pry my cheeks apart. His hair brushes my lower back.

"What are you—"

Then something wet touches my hole. "Ohmy-fuckinggod."

Behind me, Troy makes a noise that's half moan and half laughter. "First time getting rimmed, Kitten?"

"Everything's a first with you two." The confession slips out before I can call it back. But it's true. When did I last enjoy sex? Long ago, I decided I could pleasure myself more easily with fewer complications.

Or so I thought.

"Speaking of firsts," he murmurs. "When Adam gets out, we're going to have a do-over. The two of us fucking you, without all the bullshit from before. Just the three of us."

"Is it—" My breath puffs out, short and labored. "It's fucked up, but it was so hot. Being watched. Th-the danger. I've never come harder in my life. Do you think that was the drugs?"

"Hmm." Troy plays with my balls, pulling and rolling gently at first, and then squeezing a little.

"Ow!" In spite of my protest, blood surges to my cock. "Fuck, why do I like that?"

The pain grounds me somehow, both bumping my pulse and relaxing my muscles. It's excitement and anticipation, like the part of a roller coaster ride when you're cresting the first hill. I know I like it, even if I don't understand why.

When he returns to working his tongue in maddening patterns around, but rarely quite touching, my asshole, I'm too busy whining and begging to ask more questions.

A trilling noise comes from my pocket.

"Oh, let's see what we have here." There's a rustling

sound as Troy pulls my phone out. It lands with a soft thud on the cushion next to me.

"Answer it," he demands as he prods my still sore ring with a wet finger.

The caller ID says it's my brother. "Are you fucking serious?"

The pointed tip of Troy's tongue spears into me. As soon as I'm sinking into it, he pulls away with a slap to my ass.

"Troy, come on."

"Answer it or I'll stop. Put it on speaker."

"He'll hear." For God's sake, did more blood just surge to my cock?

Look at you, Wes. Get kidnapped once and you've turned into a fucking pervert.

"Three rings, Wes. Better hurry."

Goddammit, my common sense must have given up the ghost back at that industrial building in Beacon Hill. I hit the speaker button with a clumsy finger. "Yeah?"

The second I answer the call, Troy's tongue returns to its previous ministrations. I have to bite my lips together to keep the desperate noises stuck in my throat from coming out. Burying my face against my braced arm only does so much to muffle my heavy breathing.

"Wes. Hey. There you are. You haven't been answering your phone. Mom called, worried because you haven't answered her calls either."

A finger slides inside of me. I have got to stop this before—

Troy pulls out again. Thank God.

"I didn't hear it ring," I manage. "Is this an emergency?"

It comes out sounding short and rude, but it's all I've got right now.

"Uh, well, I mean, you tell me. Gina called. She seemed to think you'd had a male escort in your room at the Premiere. Which doesn't sound at all like something you'd do, except..."

Troy slides what feels like two fingers into me at a maddeningly slow pace. When he brushes my prostate, I'm shoving my face into the cushion.

"...and then PJ said you were at the hospital when he went to visit Adam, so I felt like I should ask—"

"Fallon." I sound like I'm choking on something. That something is my own tongue.

"Look, I'm not trying to pry. I've asked you to stay out of my personal life and I owe you the same in return, but you went through something really traumatic recently, so it felt important to ask—"

Another finger glances over my prostate.

"God. Damn. Fucking. Fuck." There's no covering the way my breath stutters or the way my voice cracks.

A few weeks ago nothing was more important than my brother wanting to talk to me. Now? I can feel myself slipping, my body choosing Troy with every stroke.

"Wes? Are you okay?"

My molars grind together. "Look, I'm fine, okay? I just need..." *Oh, God, he's stretching me.* "I have to go."

I hang up the phone, throwing it somewhere across the room. If I'm lucky, maybe I broke it for good.

"What the fuck is wrong with you?" I all but scream the words straight into the sofa cushions.

All I get out of Troy is a strangled laugh. "Damn, Kitten. Watching you try to keep your shit together while I played with your ass? Really turned my crank."

I shake my head, trying to dislodge something I can't

shake. It turned my crank too, but in a way that was twisted and honestly infuriating.

"You can't...do things like that." When I press my face against my arm again, my skin is tight. Hot. Burning.

"Is this a hard limit? A definite no?" His teeth sink into the flesh on my hip. The pain makes me howl and then push my ass backward for more.

God, I don't even know. "Are you going to finish, or not?" I demand. After all that, I deserve for him to finish. I demand it.

"You want my tongue or my fingers, babe?" He pauses. "Or do you want me to fuck you again?"

I release a heavy breath. I'm so hard I could pass out. This time I can't blame it on any drugs in my system.

"Fuck me."

He goes still behind me. For once, I may have thrown him off. "It's going to hurt, Kitten."

"I know."

Something strange buzzes in my belly. Excitement. Anticipation. The rollercoaster ready to barrel down the hill.

There's the click of a lube bottle getting popped open, and my anticipation builds. Slippery fingers push at my entrance. "You sure, Kitten?"

"I'm sure," I whisper. "Hurt me."

My head drops as I brace myself, waiting for Troy to make me fly.

If I thought things would be less intense this time, I was wrong. A minute later I'm shouting into the sofa cushions. Troy's body presses against mine.

"You good, Kitten?"

"I'm good. Promise. Just fuck me."

"Not trying to hurt you again." The way his voice shakes. Oh God. What do I do with that?

"I asked you to." Tears sting my eyes. Not because it hurts. Because I can't ignore the way he's asking with so much tenderness.

His fingers dig into my hips. Still, he seems to hesitate. "Babe—"

"Stop asking. Stop asking and fuck me." Nothing makes sense right now. I'm angry, frustrated, my throat clogged with emotion. There's this kernel of sweetness threatening to unfurl in my chest thanks to the concern he's showing me, but at the same time all I want is for him to stop asking me.

Stop making me choose.

"Like before," I insist. "Fast. Hard."

Troy's lips brush my shoulder. "If that's what you want."

He pulls back and adjusts his grip, thrusting into me with intent. It's not so brutal as before, though it's hard to tell for sure since before every sensation was heightened by those pills we were given. He's steady with his rhythm, testing the angle until he finds the one that makes me shiver and cry out.

"There it is, babe. There you go. You're so good for me, aren't you, Kitten? Is this what you need? You need for it to hurt? You need to be reminded you're alive, don't you?"

"God, yes." The words slip out on a gasp. I'm clearly past caring that I'm getting sofa fuzz into my mouth. "That's how I feel when you touch me. Alive."

Low laughter, and he thrusts harder. "Listen to you. Gonna blow up my ego with that kind of talk."

Should I care? Do I? No, no, I don't. "It's you. And him." Him. Adam. "The way you make me feel—I didn't think that was possible. I didn't know I was like this. Did you make me this way? When you jerked me so hard my skin burned and then pinched me while Adam sucked me and then..."

And then.

And *then.*

As the words tumble, I'm both terrified and euphoric. Maybe this is how you become someone new—by saying the scary part out loud and owning it.

I've never been this honest. Not even with myself.

Troy groans, low and loud. One hand leaves my hip, sliding over my stomach and across my nipples. His grasping fingers make my cock surge. "Babe, I'm no expert, but maybe your freak just matches ours."

"Mmmph." I'm getting close. Every push and pull pinches and burns and brings me higher at the same time. I'm at the end of a race, my lungs burning and my heart threatening to burst out of me as I sprint for the finish line.

"Harder," I beg. "Please, Troy."

"As you wish, you dirty slut," he says in a way that sounds fond and teasing.

"Aaaargh." The worst of the pain hits right as I come. As he slams home, my body jerks and shudders and my mouth stretches wide on a silent scream as I unload all over the sofa cushions.

Fiery aftershocks hit me as I tighten around him. His cock jerks inside me as he fills me. Another first.

If the way he mumbles "Oh, Kitten" against my back does warm and fuzzy things to my insides, I don't acknowledge it for now.

Later. Everything will happen later. Whenever that is.

And what if my nervous system calms as Troy lays himself against my back and we both float down to earth? If the act of getting fucked until I'm aching is what makes the world feel right side up again? What if I'm starting to realize what's happening here means a whole lot more than just sex?

Yes. Also later.

So much later.

CHAPTER TWENTY-THREE

TROY

"I TOLD YOU GUYS, I'm fine." Adam is in the passenger seat of the Mustang, looking a hell of a lot better than when Brennan got us out of that warehouse.

Wes is crammed in the back, also looking worn out but much better. The rear seats of two-door cars weren't made for guys his size, though.

Adam and I have dealt with hospital homecomings before. Whenever my best friend ends up getting admitted, though, I'm a mess.

Trees and fences and farmland whiz past us on the rural road that leads from Beacon Hill, where Adam was hospitalized, back to where we live in Belle Argo. It's a scenic but otherwise uneventful drive.

At least, it better be.

Part of me is bracing for Adam to tell me he still feels like shit or to pass out on us, and then we'll need to go right back. It's happened before.

"Right." I pat his leg. "I'll be the judge of that."

"Fuck you," he mutters.

"Not until you get your energy back."

He grumbles and leans his head against the window, mumbling something I can't hear. Meanwhile, a glance in the rearview tells me Wes is pretty much the same as he's been this entire time.

After we fucked earlier, he withdrew into himself. Since then it's been a lot of deep sighs and staring into space. Which doesn't in the least bit make me nervous.

Even though Adam and I have touched and explored every inch of Wes's body, we still can't tell what's going on in his head. He could be second-guessing this thing we've started. Maybe it's too much, or he's over it now.

Adam glances my way and then toward the back seat as well, as if to ask me what's going on. The truth is, I don't know.

Then, out of nowhere, Wes asks, "Hey, can we stop the car?"

"What?" I hit the brakes without thinking, not really knowing why. Good thing the road is empty right now, save for the carcass of an armadillo that met an untimely end. "Kitten, you okay?"

Wes answers by tapping Adam's seat so he can get out of the car. Which doesn't tell me what I want to know.

Until he makes a sharp left and starts heading down an overgrown gravel driveway, I'm not at all clear on where he's going. There's a shoddy fence across it that looks as if it's been damaged for a long time. A couple of signs have been nailed to the posts. One says Private Property, and the other says, For Sale. Price reduced.

Adam ducks back into the passenger seat. “Might as well see what’s up, right?”

“You sure you’re still feeling okay?”

He narrows his eyes. “If you don’t stop asking, I’m going to tie a knot in your nutsack.”

“That’s not really my kink, babe.”

“I know.” He shoots me another look before following Wes down the drive at a more leisurely pace. Since I’m apparently the only one who hasn’t been called home by the mother ship, I pull into the driveway and stop with the car nosed up against the busted gate so I can join them.

“What is this place?” I ask when I reach them. Wes has stopped about halfway down the drive, facing a large house that’s got the sort of vibe you see in horror movies. You know, the kind where it used to have a prosperous family living there but one night the father went off the rails and murdered everyone with a broken wine bottle?

The faded siding looks like it used to be a cheery yellow, and the pillars on the rocking chair porch are faded. The front steps are definitely a safety hazard.

Wes shoves his hands into his pockets. “The Beacon Lake Bed and Breakfast.”

“I think I’ve heard about this place.” Adam lifts an eyebrow. “Didn’t someone die here, forever ago?”

Seriously? “I fucking knew it.”

“The original owner.” Wes nods. “Local legends say she was a witch, and a spell went wrong. Burned the whole place to the ground. After they rebuilt, it kept changing ownership. There are rumors that it’s haunted. Guests used to report seeing the woman’s ghost standing at the foot of their bed.”

For as creepy as that fucking story is, I think it’s the first time I've seen Wes look truly alive. He hardly ever even smiles. I'm talking genuine smiles, not the customer service, ass-kissing bullshit he does while working.

"Didn't know you were so into all that horror shit." I nudge him with my shoulder.

Wes does seem to love his scary movies, but this is another level. I enjoy a good animal documentary. Doesn't mean I wanna go see the polar bears in person.

"Watched a lot of movies during chemo. Horror was my favorite. I'd get tired, but not tired enough to sleep. Watched all sorts of things. Except romantic comedies. Those always pissed me off."

I can guess why. "So, you wanna go ghost hunting, or what? What are we doing here?"

I'm not trying to sound impatient, but I know I do. I'm antsy about getting Adam home.

Adam shoots me a look and mouths *I'm fine* at me again.

Wes does a three-sixty turn, looking around the property. It's objectively a gorgeous place, with a lake sparkling in the distance and massive trees that look older than the town. "I've been following the history of this place for a while. It last closed in the early two thousands, and it's been empty ever since. The elements haven't completely taken over, so someone must be maintaining it." He gestures toward the grass. "Someone's been mowing. But it's never gone up for sale until recently. They keep dropping the price, so they must be motivated. It's two and a half acres of land here. Some developer will probably grab it soon."

His smile fades on the last sentence.

Adam nods toward the building. "You ever been inside to look around?"

Wes shakes his head. "Unless they've dropped the price to whatever my car is worth, there's no point."

Adam's expression tells me he doesn't like that defeated look Wes is wearing any more than I do. "What's the harm in looking around?"

Wes shrugs his shoulders and turns back for the car. "It's probably a safety hazard inside, anyway."

The group chat buzzes from my back pocket.

Simon: Everyone making it to brunch this weekend?

Christian: Sorry, I know I've been MIA. I'll be there, though.

Troy: Glad to see you back, buddy

Christian ran into some trouble when an abusive ex gave him a head injury or something. It's nice to know he's coming back to the land of the living. Been worried we weren't going to see him again.

Michael: Probably.

Dean: Probably?

Michael: I think I can make it. Not 100%. Probably.

Michael: Hey, Troy, Brennan said there were drugs wherever you guys were taken. Was this another dealer moving in, or what?

Troy: Not sure. Probably or what

When I glance over at Adam and Wes, a shiver runs through me. I'm not ready to talk about what happened to us, not to anyone else.

Considering the whole situation with Wes, trying to explain what happened when we were taken would only cause an explosion of questions we're not ready to answer.

That ball is in Wes's court, so I return my phone to my pocket.

There's a meow from the tall grass. Looking down, I find

a white cat with orange and black patches staring at me expectantly. Wes crouches down, giving her a finger scratch under her chin. "What are you doing here, huh? Do you belong to someone?"

His smile is wide open. Sweet and awestruck. Am I jealous of the way he's looking at that four-legged creature, or do I just want to make him smile that way more?

"She must." Adam gestures to her. "Looks well fed."

Downright fluffy, if you ask me. "Definitely too friendly to be feral."

"You sure? You're friendly and also feral." Adam laughs.

I give him the finger. "Probably a barn cat for one of the nearby farms or something."

Wes shakes his head and stands, appearing even more dejected than before. "You're probably right. Maybe I can come back and check on her sometime, to make sure."

I follow behind him, still confused. "Not to be a dick here, but why would you want this old house anyway? If there's a ghost, or people think there is, and it keeps scaring folks away, that doesn't make a whole lot of sense."

"See, that's the thing though." Wes stops again, turning to look back at the place. He waves his arms toward the big house. "Look at the place. It's gorgeous."

"Bet if we got a little closer, you could hear the paint peel."

Ignoring Adam's slap to the back of my head, I raise my eyebrows at Wes. I'm asking legit questions here.

"It needs someone to give a shit," Wes counters. "The direction the property's facing, you know the light sparkling on the lake in the morning has got to be fantastic. According to the listing there's an owner's cottage out back and four en suite bedrooms in the main house. If it were marketed as a haunted hotel rather than a regular B&B, people would pay to stay here. High-end B&Bs in this area rent for as much as four hundred a night, which would allow the right buyer to recoup investment costs in as little as—"

He stops and his hands drop to his sides. "Never mind. This is probably boring for you guys." With sluggish steps, he turns to head back toward the car.

Adam looks at me and I look back at him. "What just happened?" he asks.

"I'm not sure."

But I think I know. I think Wes showed us a piece of himself, something he maybe hasn't shown anyone before, or maybe something nobody else has cared about. It feels important. Something we should handle with care.

Wes is already climbing back into the car. Nothing else to do but follow him.

He's silent the rest of the way home. The sun is setting, remind me none of us have had dinner.

"We need to get you food," I tell Adam.

"Let's order something when we get back."

"There's a lasagna in the fridge," Wes says. Which, I'm honestly glad to know he's still with us.

Except... "When did we get lasagna?"

"I made one earlier. While you were in the shower. You didn't notice the smell of it baking?"

"Figured it was one of the neighbors cooking." I laugh, hoping Wes will too, but he's back to looking out the window again.

When we get home, he trudges up the stairs to our place, letting himself in with his key and heading straight for Adam's bedroom, where we've both been sleeping.

Adam takes a deep breath. "It's good to be home. Smells like sex in here, though."

"Yeah, sorry you missed the fun. Wes says they've got some enzyme cleaner at work that should—"

The bedroom door slams shut. Adam looks as confused as I feel. Is this still about some busted hotel?

"Kitten? Aren't you going to have dinner with us?"

He calls through the door, "Not hungry. You guys go ahead."

Adam rummages in the cabinets. "Go see what that's about. I'll join you two when I'm done out here."

Nodding, I head to the bedroom, where I find Wes sprawled face down on top of the blankets, still wearing all of his clothes.

"Not sure what you've got planned," I say, "but whatever it is, you're wearing too many clothes."

"Have you heard anything else about the people who took us? Do they know anything?"

"I talked to Ravi, who talked to Liam. Sounds like they've been working with local law enforcement, but it also sounds like the boys in blue aren't putting in a ton of effort. According to Liam, the cops showed up, came up with a story about what happened, and all but put the case to bed. I did get a text from Brennan that he'd like to meet with us at some point, but I don't know if he's actually heard anything else or if he's being a nosy asshole."

Wes frowns. "Why would he care?"

"Brennan's an old southern lady trapped in the body of a forty-one-year-old criminal. Or, I don't know, a cat or something. Whatever's going on in his territory, he needs to be in the loop even if it's got nothing at all to do with him. Could also be about the drugs. He's been trying to get those pills off the street."

"Wait. Brennan's my age?"

"That's what you took away from all of that?"

"He looks a lot younger than me. Fuck."

"Hey." I crawl over to him. "Stop. We don't give a shit."

He gives me a flat stare. "Wait until you turn forty. I promise you'll start caring."

"As long as you still think I'm hot, it's all good. Wipe that ugly-ass scowl off your face."

He flips onto his side, propping his head on one arm to look at me. "How can you talk about us being together in twenty years? We barely know each other, and this is a highly unusual situation."

"A three-way relationship? I promise it's not."

"Don't play dumb." He flaps his free arm in the air, sort of jerky and exasperated. "Everything. All of it. The two of you and your creepy, dubious mating ritual of constantly cornering me in semi-public places. Getting kidnapped, drugged, and fucked while they fucking filmed us. I'm still technically married. I'm not even gay."

"Kitten." Reaching out, I trail my fingertips over his stubble. "None of us are gay."

"It's not about being gay. Or whatever I am. Bisexual, pansexual, heteroflexible... I don't know."

"Someone's been busy searching things up on the interwebs. There's no pressure to pick a label, you know."

Wes sighs. "It's feeling like I've gone way too far in life without knowing myself." He flips onto his back and starts kneading at his own forehead with both hands like his brain is a lump of dough that needs pounding into submission.

"Every time I try to wrap my head around this, I feel like I'm losing my mind."

"That why you've been staring off into the distance like you're seeking the answers to the mysteries of the universe?"

"What we did earlier," he says quietly. "When I begged you to hurt me again—"

"There's nothing wrong with it, you know."

"I know."

Hmm. "Do you?"

A frustrated groan comes out of his throat. "Yes. No. I don't know. I don't even know why I liked it."

"Does it matter?"

He shakes his head. "Maybe not. I don't know. I'm not even sure I recognize myself when I look in the mirror anymore. When Gina and I got together, I was a virgin. I'd been the awkward, nerdy kid girls didn't even want to be friends with lest I get the wrong idea. The second time we have sex, she gets pregnant. Her parents insist we get married, and thus begins a decade and a half of slogging through a life I never chose."

"That sounds fucking miserable." My fingers walk themselves down his throat. Down to his chest.

"People always said marriage was hard. I figured that was what they meant. I kept trying to make things work, but at some point she had already given up. Now, suddenly, I've got two men who are so hot people pay more money than I can afford to fuck them, and I'm discovering a whole new side to my sexuality. It's confusing. It's weird. It's—"

"Better late than never?" We both look up at the sound of Adam's voice. "Maybe you just hadn't met us yet. And if you were with the same person for all that time, you just never considered any other options."

Wes looks thoughtful. "Maybe."

Adam crawls into bed on the opposite side of Wes. "Tell us about the house."

"I already did."

"Tell us more," I say. "Why are you so into it?"

Wes opens his mouth. Closes it. Shakes his head and mumbles something about being dumb.

Adam comes in with his softer touch, lifting Wes's chin and murmuring a quiet "Please" that anyone would have trouble denying.

"Fine. It's this pipe dream I've always had. Something more personal and intimate than the Premiere. A place where I can foster a genuine connection with guests. I don't know if you've noticed, but I like serving people." Color rises to his cheeks. "Gina seemed into the idea at first, but over time, things unraveled. I couldn't give her the dream she wanted, and she was no longer interested in mine. Which, I suppose, is fair."

"It's bullshit, is what it is." Adam's fist is clenched, and I get why. The resignation in every line in Wes's body is a lot to take.

"Forget it," Wes says on a yawn. "There's no point in wasting energy wishing for something I can't afford. I really am exhausted. And I know Adam needs the rest."

As he closes his eyes and drifts off, my best friend and I look at each other.

"He seems awfully fucking sad." Adam's forehead crumples. "What are we going to do?"

"We'll figure something out." I hope.

CHAPTER TWENTY-FOUR

TROY

I'M DRAGGING a suitcase down a fancy patterned hotel hallway that weighs as much as I do. The wheels keep sinking into the carpet. "Kitten, what the fuck do you have in here?"

"Mostly cookbooks. I know they're heavy, but one of these days I'll have a real kitchen again, and I didn't want to leave them with Gina. Do you want some help? I didn't ask you to drag my baggage down the hallway."

I turn to where Adam and Wes are trailing behind. Adam's only carrying Wes's laptop bag because neither of us wanted to give him anything heavier. He may be out of the hospital, but he's still seeming awfully tired. We all have been, honestly.

"I do not need help. Unless you wanna help me take my pants off." I make my eyebrows bounce, hoping he'll laugh.

Wes frowns but otherwise doesn't acknowledge the

joke. It's making me kind of crazy that we can't seem to chase the defeat out of his eyes. Am I being too much? Or not enough? He's moving in with us, so something must be working.

We're starting to wear him down, I think.

As much as I've been dying to stir up a little something between all three of us, most of what we've been doing together has been sleeping. There's been some team masturbation in the shower, but primarily we've all been resting or watching movies. Adam needs to heal, and so does Wes, even if he says otherwise.

It's awfully fucking domestic.

"Are you sure you don't need help?" Adam's raising his eyebrows at me. He's annoyed that we're being protective, but how can he blame us?

We all cluster together in the elevator. I'm satisfied by the way Wes watches Adam while I'm watching him.

Wes cuts his gaze over to me. "What?"

I sort of smile, while biting my lips together so I don't say what I'm thinking. He's still pretty squirrelly about the idea of all three of us being in a relationship, even though we basically are. If I told him it filled some long-empty spot deep inside of me to have a third as part of our "us," he might never come back to our apartment.

And we want him there. It'll be easier to talk him into staying if he's already moved in. I haven't even thought much lately about the other reason I wanted Wes and Adam together so much.

Which is...good. I hope.

Lately, everything's been nice. Normal. Even if it didn't start out that way. Am I delusional for thinking maybe this could all really work? Worse, I need it to work. I need this thing between the three of us, because now I don't know if any of us would be the same without it.

"I don't get it," Adam says. "You said most of your stuff is either in your trunk or still at the house you shared with your ex. Why bother packing up an entire suitcase full of cookbooks?"

Wes lifts one shoulder. "I knew whatever I left behind I'd risk losing. That suitcase also has all the mystery books my brother wrote that I haven't had time to read. I tried to make sure I wouldn't leave behind anything important. And you can't keep books in a car; the humidity would be terrible."

There's pain on his face. He won't say so, but it's obvious he's still feeling shitty about the rift he created between him and Fallon.

"I've gotten the impression Fallon's not exactly hurting for cash," I tell him. "If you lost them, he could probably give you new copies."

"They're not replaceable." Damn, the stubborn set to his jaw is fucking sexy. Kind of arrogant—I can see why PJ thinks of him that way—but it's making my jeans tight. Then he hits me with "The publisher changed the covers a few years ago. I like the originals" and the swelling in my chest stuns me silent.

Whatever's happened between them, Wes loves his brother. It shows even when he doesn't want it to. In spite of all the hissing and the claws, our kitten's all fluffy on the inside.

Within seconds of stepping off the elevator, I hear a familiar voice. One I'd rather avoid.

"Troy. Adam." Joseph Rigby approaches dressed in his standard uniform of beige cashmere, his flat-bottomed dress shoes making an annoying, echoey *tap-tap-tap* on the hotel's polished floors.

At first I consider speeding up a little. We could pretend we didn't hear him. Except Wes is the one who stops first, and I can almost hear him wondering who this person is. Or maybe he knows, since Rigby spends a lot of time on the VIP floor. Maybe he's wondering if Rigby is one of our customers.

Which, unfortunately, he is.

Awkward.

I stop short. "Mr. Rigby. Hello."

"Joseph, please. How many times do I have to tell you, Troy?" He grasps my shoulder in a way that's obvious and familiar. Next to me, Wes goes rigid.

"I'm so glad to see the two of you," Rigby continues, oblivious to the tension. "Adam. I heard you were ill. I'm relieved to see you're all right."

His grabby hand moves from my shoulder to Adam's. He pats my best friend's cheek before sliding that same entitled palm along the side of Adam's neck.

Okay, no. We don't let clients touch when we're not on the clock. "Adam, we need to go." I grab his arm. Next to me, Wes releases an audible breath. "Sorry, Mr. Rigby. Appointments to keep."

"Of course." Rigby nods, but he looks pissed. The guy's a little tight-lipped about how he makes his money, but I'm sure he's in the sort of position where he doesn't often hear the word no. Lots of our clients suffer from the same affliction.

I call it "Entitled Asshole Syndrome." Tough condition to live with, I'm sure.

"I was concerned after I heard what happened," he

murmurs. "I only wanted to be sure the two of you were all right."

That fast, Wes is tense again.

Rigby heard about what happened because he's the client we were supposed to be spending a second night with at the Premiere when we all got slugged, drugged, and tossed into a van. Brennan must have called him. The guy's a little annoying, but he's our highest-paying customer and we wouldn't have wanted him thinking we ghosted. His statement leaves things wide open for interpretation, and I can practically see Wes drawing conclusions.

"We'll, uh, see about rescheduling as soon as we can," I assure him. Which won't be for a long while if we can help it. Maybe never.

I'm thinking the three of us need to establish what we can all handle as far as Adam and me working in this business before going forward. Doesn't feel right going on with things as usual.

I glance at Wes and then at Adam, trying to let them both know. Adam nods, but Wes looks like he's about to shoot smoke from his nostrils.

"Oh. My apologies." Rigby holds his hand out. "Mr. Monroe. We haven't officially been introduced. I hardly recognized you out of your traditional work attire."

Wes hasn't moved his clothes to our place yet, so he's been borrowing stuff from Adam. Wes and Adam are about the same height, but Wes has more muscle, so even when wearing Adam's baggiest sweats and loosest T-shirt, everything fits tightly on him.

His blush tells me he's still feeling self-conscious. Personally, I think he looks hot as hell.

Ever the professional, Wes shakes Rigby's smarmy-ass hand. Even though the dick seems like he's trying to put Wes in his place by saying he knows he's an employee here.

"Hello, sir. I hope you're enjoying your stay."

Guess you can't take the hotel out of the boy...

"Oh, I definitely am. One of my favorite places to stay. An excellent full-service establishment." He gives Wes a wink, which...come on. Gross. He makes it worse by adding, "I believe you dropped by my room the last time these two were visiting me."

"I thought your name sounded familiar. That must be why," Wes murmurs.

Oh. *Shit.* Adam told me about that. I hadn't noticed Wes was there. Didn't think Rigby had, either. We must not have blindfolded him well enough.

Wes is clearly used to dealing with people like this, though. In spite of him being dressed like an activewear model, he straightens his spine and raises his chin, smiling politely. "Anyway. We aim to please here at the Belle Argo Premiere." Then his face turns hard in a way I've never seen it. "If you'll excuse us. We should go."

Funny how he made "we should go" sound an awful lot like "Go fuck yourself."

Honestly? I fucking love it.

Rigby chuckles, finally stepping away. "Of course. I've got meetings anyway, but I do hope the two of you will be in touch about rescheduling soon."

Adam nods his acknowledgment without saying anything more. We wait until he's turned his attention away from us before we head for the door. Wes is practically vibrating, but doesn't say another word.

"Wes."

Unfortunately, he's got the longest legs of all three of us, so he pretty easily pulls ahead in the parking lot. While trying to figure out how to discuss this with him, I'm scanning the area for any signs of movement. After all, this is where we got jumped.

It's clearly on Adam's mind too. "Has there been any word about the guys who took us?"

Up ahead, Wes's shoulders stiffen. He doesn't turn around, though, until we reach his car.

When he finally looks at us, his body shudders. "That Liam guy called me. Not much information we hadn't figured out, though. Illegal porn, people being taken, and it turns out a few bodies were found behind the facility where we were kept. He said most showed signs of overdose. The rest are nowhere to be found. He's thinking they were transported overseas. They're looking into it, but there's a chance those people are gone for good."

"Jesus." Adam scrubs his hand over his stubble. "We got lucky."

"Really fucking lucky." I nod my agreement.

"He did say—" Wes's voice trembles. "—that the guy who seemed to be calling the shots there had a burner phone that had only ever made calls to a few numbers. Two were the guys we, uh, killed." He looks around before saying the last part quietly. "But the last one was to a number they haven't been able to trace. Possibly a buyer, but he thinks more likely whoever was pulling the strings."

"Wouldn't surprise me," I say. "Some of these rich fucks we trick for—you know, the ones with fuck-you money? Get-away-with-murder money? They see everyone else as another product they can buy. If they can't find someone to dance the way they want, they pay somebody. And if they can't pay someone to do it willingly, they'll pay someone to do it unwillingly."

"Yeah." Wes looks down at his shoes. "As someone whose job it is to kiss their asses and smile while doing it, it feels especially gross."

His fists clench tight enough to whiten his knuckles.

"Hey. What's important is we're all okay." Adam, ever the peacemaker, reaches over and loosens Wes's hands, threading their fingers together. Adam's got this sweetness that makes it easy for him to get what he wants. I think it's the real reason his dad hated him so much. Still, even I'm sort of surprised when Wes relaxes and takes his hand.

"We may be okay, but how many other people weren't?" Wes's face is etched with pain.

Right there in the parking lot, his knees buckle. That suitcase and Adam's hand are the only things keeping him from hitting the ground. "Jesus, we almost *died.* How many other people did? I should've spoken up about my suspicions sooner. Should've made peace with Fallon in case something happened. I should've contacted Liam sooner, or—"

"Hey. Cut that shit out," I growl. "You tried, remember? You said that Max guy blew you off every time you brought it up."

"I could have pushed harder, though. I could have escalated things when Max dismissed me—"

"Stop." Adam grips his chin, forcing Wes to meet his gaze. "We don't want to hear you talk shit about yourself. Don't make us punish you."

"Kitten." He lifts his gaze to mine. Even in the middle of this serious moment, I have to admit, I'm loving this. I called him Kitten. And he fucking *looked at me*. Adam said he did it back at the hospital, too.

Wes may think he's holding out on us, but he's already on board. We've hooked him and tossed him on the deck.

He's all ours now.

I bump my forehead against Wes's big shoulder. "We can't go back in time. All we can do is make new choices."

For a second he looks like he might be gearing up to argue more, but then he stops.

"That's actually kind of wise," he says.

I give him the finger. "I have my moments. Blame my mom. She was into that self-discovery stuff." Not that it helped her in the end.

He and Adam exchange a look. Probably because I haven't mentioned my mom around Wes before. Well. Whatever. There are a lot of conversations to be had. It's one more on the list.

First, though: "You know what? It's kind of been a day and we've all been tired as hell. I say we go home and watch something awful." I glance at Wes. "We can order from that ramen place you like."

Wes's eyes widen. "Really?"

Jesus, the fucking hope and surprise in that single word. Maybe his ex and his parents weren't all that bad, but everything I've seen from Wes since the beginning is that the poor guy is starved for touch, for love, for approval. And yes, for ramen. Nobody fed our kitten where it counted.

Every time one of us does the smallest thing, like throwing his favorite beer in the cart at the grocery store or bringing him coffee before his shift, or if we praise him in any way, you'd think the heavens had opened up.

What the hell made this guy think he didn't have any value?

In the dark of night I privately wonder if it wasn't the real reason he volunteered himself when we were all taken. Even more privately, I wonder how big of a piece of shit it makes me that I'm glad it all worked in our favor.

In the end, I just hope we're enough to keep him.

CHAPTER TWENTY-FIVE

WES

"THIS IS A BAD IDEA."

It's Sunday morning. Troy, Adam, and I are sitting in my idling car in one of the parking garages for Belle Argo's downtown area. Their merry band of sex workers likes to meet up over brunch. Which I know, because I crashed once before. To hassle my brother's boyfriend.

Which is also why I don't want to go back.

"It'll be fine," Troy says. With his brows crouched low like they want to escape the conversation, he sounds more confident than he looks.

Since Troy usually seems so sure of himself, this isn't inspiring confidence.

"My brother will probably be in there." Which is another reason I think this adventure is ill-advised. Showing up to what is essentially a family event with Adam and Troy? He'll have questions.

Troy shrugs. "Only one way to find out." He slaps his

hand on my leg. "Anyway, let's get in there and rip off the bandage, or whatever. This won't be nearly as weird as when we all found out PJ was fucking his teacher."

I wince. "I'd rather not think about my brother with PJ any more than I have to."

"Or the time Simon showed up so covered in bruises he looked like he'd been jumped in an alley," Adam adds helpfully.

With a resigned sigh, I rest my forehead on the steering wheel. "My gut tells me this will be a mess."

Troy slides possessive fingers along my stomach. "You'll feel better after some pancakes, Kitten."

I doubt it, but his touch is enough to get me to agree. "Fine. Let's go."

We head across the street and push into the cozy but upscale establishment. I have to admit, once we get inside and the smells of coffee and maple syrup make their way to me, my stomach is growling. For the first time in days, I have a real appetite.

If the sudden appearance of my hunger has anything to do with the fact that I'm finally getting decent sleep and gratifying sex, well, that's a rabbit hole to explore another time.

"Relax," Troy murmurs in my ear as we enter the back room.

"How exactly do you expect me to do that?"

Adam answers by putting his hand against my back, which I'm pained to admit actually does help me relax. A little.

The back room of Gil's restaurant is already full. A long table, covered with coffee carafes and stemmed glasses of mimosa, seats a crowd of people I've mostly only met in passing before. Sex workers, all dressed down and chattering like it's a polite orgy.

Or one of those murder dinners.

When every person in the room trains their wide, curious eyes on me, I'm back to my original assessment. This was a catastrophic idea.

Ravi sends me a friendly wave. I get the impression he's like that with everyone. Liam isn't here, but my brother is. And so is PJ.

My brother's face is the most curious looking of them all. And PJ looks the most like he wants to murder me. Then again, it's his default setting.

Great. This'll be fun.

Clearly nobody updated Adam and Troy's RSVP, because there are only two chairs at the table. Troy confidently drops himself into one and then slaps his own leg. "Come here, Kitten, you can sit on my lap."

There is no chance in hell he didn't say that at the top of his lungs on purpose.

Ignoring him and my flaming hot face, I grab a chair from the corner of the room and drag it over, pushing my way in between Troy and my brother.

To Troy's pouting face, I say, "Unless you want me to stab you with a fork, you'll scoot over."

He bats his eyelashes. "Kitten." He leans in to whisper in my ear. "It's not fair to tease us when we're in public and we can't do anything about it. We'll have to come up with a way to make you sorry later."

The heat on my skin could set every reclaimed wood table in this place on fire. He's behaving this way deliberately, and what pisses me off is that it's working. I don't know how much of my response is my own embarrassment and how much is the weight of my brother's stare, but either way I'll be lucky to make it through this meal with my sanity intact.

When a waitress appears to take our order, I ask for water and juice, and a fruit and quinoa parfait. I manage to ignore how the conversations around us have all died down until after I'm done placing my order.

"I told you this was a bad idea," I murmur to Troy.

Adam reaches behind Troy to pat my shoulder, which doesn't exactly make anyone less interested in the situation.

My nerves hit me hard. I've dealt with angry senators at the Premiere wanting everything to be just so for their daughter's beachfront wedding, and a visiting rock star and his entourage who insisted on having every member of the staff being at their beck and call. I've survived getting kidnapped.

Sitting here at this brunch table with my pulse thrumming in my ears, I can't even look my own brother in the eyes. Or anyone else.

"All right," Troy says as he leans back in his chair. "Let's get this out of the way. Wes here is crashing at our place for now. If you have questions, ask them. We reserve the right not to answer. Anyone who has a problem with that or anything else is welcome to shut the hell up."

Chatter starts up again. A gorgeous Black woman with a head full of braids at the end of the table stands, gesturing for everyone to settle down. Eve, I think.

"Okay. Okay. Everybody hang on." Eve shuts everyone up again with the efficiency of a preschool teacher overseeing a school assembly. "We're talking dating, right?"

Are we dating? I really feel as if I should've been given some talking points before coming in here. I look to Adam and Troy, who both cross their arms over their chests and answer with "Yes" and "Damn right."

Michael, who I remember meeting at the hotel with Dean and his daughter, leans forward. "Can you please tell us when this started?"

Again, I look at Adam and Troy. Both of their faces are disturbingly blank.

Troy gives me a nod. "Kitten?"

What's happening here? What do I even say? Did it start with that aggressive hand job in the locker room? The closet? The kidnapping? The day I had breakfast in bed with Troy and then climbed in next to Adam in his hospital room?

"It's recent."

A guy with a lot of facial piercings leans forward. "Would you say this all kicked off in the month of December?"

"Uh." I've never been good with dates, but I'm pretty sure the locker room thing was the only thing that didn't happen this month, and I feel like that counted more as a hasty hookup than anything else. "Sure. I mean, yeah. Guess so."

Michael punches his fist into his hand. "That's right. Time to pay up."

"Hang on." Now Simon is standing. "What about Adam's girlfriend?"

Why does this seem like it's turning into some sort of bizarre game show?

A waitress brings food for me, Adam, and Troy, and if I didn't know better I'd say she was taking her time on purpose. I leave my parfait untouched, because for the first time someone has asked a question that I, too, would love to have answered. Also, Troy was right. I should've ordered pancakes.

"We're not seeing each other anymore." Quieter, Adam says, "I texted her from the hospital after Troy brought my new phone." I assume that was meant for me, or me and Troy.

Well. Okay.

I'm surprised when Ravi holds up his hand, as if he's waiting to be called on in class. More surprised when Troy slides his pancakes my way, telling Ravi, "Go ahead, buddy."

Ravi pushes up his glasses. "Well, you know, not to be rude, but is it, like, all three of you? Together? Like boyfriends, together?"

"Wait. Hang on." Eve again. "I just realized none of this matters, because the deal was when they admit it, not when it started. Am I right?"

A guy at the far corner from me, fairly average height, lean, brown hair—I think I heard someone call him Christian?—snaps his fingers and points to her. "You're right. It was when do they admit it."

"When they admit they're a *couple*," Michael states. "Does this even count?"

Everyone's talking amongst themselves again.

Eyes wide, I lean over to Troy and Adam. "I understand the words everyone is saying, but what exactly is happening right now?"

"There's a pool," Adam explains. "These guys have been trying to get us to admit we're a couple for forever."

"We never confirmed or denied," Troy adds. "Now that you're ours, I figured we'd better get it out of the way so they don't keep picking at you for answers. Figured you'd prefer it that way."

Oh. He's right. I would. Still, it's weird.

Troy nudges me. "You should do the honors, Kitten."

"I really don't want to."

"It'll be good," Adam says.

You know what? They're right. I've gotten too used to avoiding conflict. If I can manage a classroom of bored freshmen or a hotel full of entitled millionaires and billionaires, I can handle a brunch full of sex workers.

"All right, here's the deal." I reach down, searching for the authoritative volume I use when I'm teaching. "I'm aware I didn't make the best first impression with any of you. I apologize. Not going to make excuses. All I can tell you right now is that I'm, uh, living with these two for the time being. We're exploring things. So, you could say we're together. In a relationship. Yes."

Then I pick up my water glass and drink as if I've been wandering the desert, because my throat is raw and I need to pretend everyone isn't staring at me. It helps to ignore the sudden swell of murmuring and the money changing hands.

In the end Eve seems to be the winner. I try to not to wonder what her bet was.

Fallon leans over to me. "Hey. Are you all right?"

For the first time in a while, I manage to look at my brother. Really look.

He looks good. Better than I do, probably. But considering his wife passed a little over a year ago and he'd been miserable for most of the time since, it's nice to see him without a downcast expression and bags under his eyes. As painful as it is to admit, PJ's been good for him.

"I'm fine." At his doubtful expression, I add, "Really. All things considered. I won't say I'm not shaken up, but we're all dealing with it."

Fallon's expression softens. "Okay. Good. But I'm talking about the fact that you just came out to a room full of strangers."

Right. "Honestly? That was easier than dealing with Gina when she showed up at my hotel room while Troy was doing the world's most obvious walk of shame out the door."

Fallon laughs. "That was real, huh? Sounds exactly like something he'd do." He sobers quickly. "Seriously, though? I know things have been tense between us lately, but you're my brother. I want to know you're okay. Last couple of times we've talked, you haven't sounded like yourself."

Well, the last time we talked I was on all fours and Troy was fingering my asshole, so...

Even as the memory makes my blood surge, I wince. Not a conversation I want to have with my brother. Or anyone.

"I've been a controlling dickhead," I say instead. "Maybe it's a good thing that I'm different lately."

"Thank fuck someone finally said it," PJ puts in.

Fallon turns to glare at his boyfriend, who only grins.

My brother turns back to me. "I'm serious, Wes. What happens when everything the three of you went through comes to a head and you need to get away from each other?"

"Watch yourself, Fallon." Troy's warning is clear.

"Don't threaten my brother." To Fallon I say, "Look, I can't see that far into the future. I'm trying to get my feet underneath me again. Honestly, if you want to help me, you could go visit Mom. She's been nagging me about when I'll come see her, and I can't handle that right now."

It's hard to take the sympathy in my brother's eyes. "You shouldered a lot, dealing with Mom when she couldn't get out of bed after Dad died, and then making sure I got to school and soccer practice. I didn't understand for a long time, and I'm not excusing the shit you pulled with me and PJ, but I can see how you felt like it was still your job to look out for me. Your actions were fucked up, but your intentions were good."

"Thanks. I think." I give my brother a tired smile.

"Sure." He slaps my shoulder. "I'll be honest, I'm not sure whether this is the new you or something you're trying on, but I'm happy if you are. And I'll see if PJ and I can get up there to see Mom soon."

PJ pipes up. "She's gonna fucking love me."

I try not to laugh at that, but I do anyway. She's always been overly concerned about Fallon and me having a partner, so maybe she will.

And thank God. I should want to see my mom, shouldn't I? But I've been the adult in our relationship for so long. What I need right now is a little time and space. Space to figure out my own shit, space to process every mind-fuck discovery I've made about myself lately, without having to parent my mother alongside everything else.

While Troy is turned in his seat to talk to Prince, his hand slips under the table to squeeze my upper thigh. Adam moves to wedge his chair sort of in between and behind us both, threading his fingers into my hair. I still can't make sense of how simply having them both touch me like this calms me the way it does.

"You know, you could come and stay with us if you need to," my brother says quietly. "We've got plenty of room."

How do I politely tell my brother that I never once wanted that?

"I appreciate the offer, but I've accidentally walked in on

PJ fucking you enough times that I need to soak my brain in bleach."

Really, I'm usually better at diplomacy than this.

"We can..." Fallon clears his throat. "We can keep it to the bedroom. It's not a big deal. I'm worried about you, Wes. I want to help."

All the times I wished my brother would worry about me —that *someone* would—this isn't one of them. "I'm serious, Fallon. Maybe this is my karma for not believing you when you tried to tell me your relationships with Marina and PJ were consensual, but I'm, uh..." My hand finds Troy's under the table. "I'm good right now. Really."

"Will you at least let me help out a little bit? I know money's been tight—"

"No." I spit the word out, sharper and louder than intended. "No," I say again more quietly. "Thank you. But I'm fine."

The last thing in the world I want to do is mooch off my little brother. Especially after the number of times I accused PJ of being a gold digger.

I'm given a break from the questioning when the waitress comes around to refill our drinks. "Thanks, Bethanne," I say after checking her name tag. After we all assure her we don't need anything else, she smiles at me and disappears.

I've managed a couple of bites of Troy's pancakes when Fallon starts again. "If you don't want to stay with us, I understand, but I don't want you to think you aren't welcome—"

"Baby." PJ lovingly slaps his hand over my brother's mouth. Who knew such a thing was possible? "Leave it alone."

Let's call this event the first time in history that my

brother's boyfriend has come to my aid in any way. I silently thank him for intervening.

Until he adds, "He doesn't want to stay with us because he's clearly all about that A-plus double dicking, and you can't blame him for not wanting to give that up."

I stand corrected. *Fuck you, PJ.*

I've never had to work so hard not to squirm in my seat like a kid who got caught stealing.

"Hey, Wes." Ravi gets my attention from across the table even as my face melts.

Grateful for the distraction, I lean forward. "What's up?"

"So, Liam mentioned wanting to follow up with you about, uh, what happened. I think they've got a lead on whoever was responsible. Is it okay if I tell him where you're staying?"

I glance at Adam and then Troy, who both nod. "Sure."

"Oh, shit." I flinch at the sound of PJ's voice. "This is delicious. He's asking his daddies for permission."

Jesus. "I'm staying at their place. It's called being polite."

PJ stands, jamming his hands into his pockets. "Look, it's cool you've turned over a new leaf or whatever, but your new leaf is pretty damn funny considering how you used to give Fallon shit about how our relationship worked."

"I've already apologized. What else do you want, a body part?"

"That's enough." Troy pushes out of his seat.

Adam follows. "Yeah, PJ, you're the one being a dick right now."

The guy with a lot of metal in his face asks "What the hell is going on now?" and the next thing I know, everyone is talking again. *Arguing.* Troy and PJ are getting in each other's faces.

When the pushing and shoving starts, I grab hold of Troy's shoulder and spin him toward me. "Hey. Stop. Eyes on me."

Troy surges forward again. "He doesn't get to talk to you that way."

"Can't hate on me for speaking the truth, asshole." PJ's hand goes deeper into his pocket. I'm pretty sure he keeps a knife in there.

Stepping between them, I nudge Troy backward while Adam tugs him from behind.

"Stop," I repeat. Firmer. Louder. In spite of how I know it's going to look, I lean in to put my lips against his ear. "Thank you for defending me. I don't want to fight with my brother, and I don't want to cause drama. Let's just get some to-go boxes and get out of here."

"You're right. We're going to go." Adam takes a drink of his coffee and slams it on the table, towing me out toward the cash register in the main room.

Well, we tried. I give everyone an apologetic wave, avoiding my brother's concerned gaze.

I'm sure he's looking for an explanation. How do I give him something I don't have?

CHAPTER TWENTY-SIX

WES

MY MARRIAGE WAS ROLLING DOWNHILL LONG before it finally ended. I don't even remember when Gina and I last slept in the same bed. Which is why it surprises me how quickly I've gotten used to sleeping in a bed with not one but two someones. How quickly I've come to enjoy waking up, overheated but secure, sandwiched between two muscular young men.

Which is probably why I jolt upright when I wake up alone. Or maybe it's the whisper-yelling coming from the direction of the kitchen.

"...it's a stupid fucking idea and..." That sounds like Troy, but I can't tell for sure. I can barely hear them.

I stumble into the living room to find Troy and Adam facing off. Lots of animated gestures and hair pulling as they stare each other down. The way the two seem to be so in tune most of the time, it's strange and worrying to see them argue.

"What's going on, guys?"

They both stop short, looking a bit guilty.

"Kitten," Troy murmurs with his gaze still trained on Adam. "You're up."

"Yes, I am." They're in the kitchen, near the refrigerator. I step up to the breakfast bar that separates the kitchen from the living room and lean over, sliding my gaze from Adam to Troy and back again.

They're both tense. Troy seems angry. Adam mostly looks tired.

"Someone want to fill me in on what's going on?"

Adam's jaw firms. "It's nothing."

"It's the polar opposite of nothing," Troy snaps.

"Okay." I brace my hands on the Formica in front of me. "Here's the thing. I've got a list longer than Troy's dick of why this entire relationship is shakier than the rope bridge I tried to build in seventh grade. I've got an appointment in —" I lift my gaze to the microwave clock display. "—a little over six hours to sign divorce paperwork with a woman who spent the latter half of our relationship lying to me, so what I will not tolerate is the two of you keeping secrets. The minute that starts, I'm gone. Do you understand?"

A banging noise from the apartment above tells me at least someone was listening. Troy seems to flinch. Adam only stares, wide-eyed and silent.

Adam cracks first. "Tell him."

"You tell him."

"Fine." Adam leans his back against the refrigerator door. "Rigby. The guy you met the other day at the hotel."

"The one the two of you were supposed to be fucking the day we got kidnapped," I say through clenched teeth. I've been trying to ignore how that encounter left me seething.

One thing's for sure—I don't like it. But is it a deal-breaker? Not yet. Which, after my relationship with Gina, makes me question my own sanity.

Truthfully, what Adam and Troy do for a living has spun my brain until I'm dizzy.

I want them. I care for them. The sex is good. Better than good. Amazing. Life-changing, literally.

No, I don't want them fucking other people. But I knew who they were when this started. It wouldn't be fair to change the terms. Even if I wish I could.

Still, I feel like I need to set some limits here. I cannot, will not, tolerate secrets. "Well?"

"That's the guy," Adam reluctantly agrees. "As you say, he had booked us for another overnight when we all got taken. He's wanting us to reschedule soon. We don't have a lot of wiggle room, since he already paid Brennan—"

"Your pimp." When I set up Fallon's "blind date" with PJ, Brennan was the one I called. I want to hate the man on principle, except he did help rescue us and get Adam to a hospital after the kidnapping incident.

"Right. If he doesn't kill us for not delivering on the job, Rigby might. He seems decent, but the rumor is he's got friends in dangerous places. Guy doesn't respond well to the word no. Troy is pissed—"

"I'm not pissed. I'm saying you're not going."

"—that I think we should do it and get it over with when he thinks I should be taking it easy."

"Also, because if the three of us are together, then this has to be something you're on board with," Troy adds.

"And you assumed I wouldn't be." It's not a question. The answer is obvious.

"Are you?" Troy's expectant, certain that he already knows my answer.

He doesn't seem happy when I say, "I'm not sure."

Both of them answer with a bewildered "What?"

I hold up a hand. "Don't get me wrong. I hate the idea of you guys leaving to go fuck someone else. But as a guy who's still paying his ex's mortgage and drowning in debt, it's not my place to make demands on how you pay rent. Especially not while I'm freeloading here."

"You're not freeloading. We invited you," Adam insists.

"The outcome is the same." I close my eyes against the emotion clogging my throat. It means something that they're thinking of me in all of this. They could easily have told me to suck it up or get out, and what choice would I have had?

Troy scoffs. "We can afford to lose the job. Hell, we can even pay the guy back."

"Are you sure we're ready to make that call?" Adam asks as he worries his thumbnail against his lip.

I've got a bigger worry. "What about Brennan? You said he'd kill you. Are we talking literally?"

The man I spoke to, the man who came to retrieve us at that place, seemed okay enough for someone who had a raging bull tattooed on his neck and a semi-automatic in a belt holster, but what do I know?

Adam looks uncomfortable. "Maybe? The thing is, we've worked for him for a while. He's taken good care of us. But my dad probably seemed like an okay guy too, until you crossed him. And..." He looks at Troy.

He turns to face Troy, who returns the glance. "Brennan's only cool to a point. He has a hit man on his payroll. And owns property on Lake Jessup."

Shit. "Isn't that the one with, like, thirteen thousand alligators?"

"Closer to, like, twelve thousand, I think," Troy says.

Adam shakes his head. "Nah, thirteen thousand sounds right."

"For fuck's sake." I put my hands up. "Twelve thousand, thirteen thousand. Once you get over a number that amounts to many thousands of alligators, does it really fucking matter?" My own voice rings in my ears. "Is there *any* chance Brennan just likes to fish? Maybe he's going there for the largemouth bass?"

Another bang on the ceiling.

"Sorry, Jalen." The two call up.

"Oh, yeah, that's the hit man," Adam says, pointing upward.

What. The. Fuck? "You're telling me the guy I've been pissing off upstairs kills people for fun and profit?"

Troy shrugs. "He's never really mentioned whether he enjoys it."

"Seems like kind of a serious guy, actually." Adam nods.

I run my fingers through my hair. "Jesus Christ. This is a punishment, isn't it? This is what I get for deciding to have my midlife crisis in the form of two much younger men who happen to consort with pimps and hit men. I'm either going to hell, or I'm already there."

I pinch myself and it hurts, so I guess I'm awake. Or in hell.

TBD.

Troy reaches across the counter, grabbing my hand and forcing me to make eye contact. "Here's the thing, Kitten. We like it with a third. We always have. But we never really considered the possibility of someone who didn't come from our world. Or didn't at least understand it. If it's too much, we get it."

"I call bullshit," Adam murmurs. "He doesn't want to scare you off, but he's already in. And when Troy is in, he's like a barnacle. Good luck getting him off your ass."

"Seems to have worked out okay for you," Troy fires back.

Adam's eyes soften, and his lips curve into a slight smile. "Guess it did."

Ignoring the way my heart does a little flip, I step back and put my hands on my hips, taking a moment to observe the two of them. Adam keeps insisting he's fine. He's been resting and watching his blood sugar. I'm inclined to believe him.

But... "Adam, I don't know much about having diabetes, but I've had cancer. Focusing on recovery is the most important thing. Sometimes it takes longer to bounce back than you think. If you believe you're up for this, then I can't say otherwise, but I'd rather you stayed home to rest." Turning to Troy, I ask, "Would Rigby accept a substitute?"

"Maybe. It's short notice, but we could see if one of the guys is free."

It's possible that I'm completely out of my mind or this is some sort of stress-induced psychosis, because the next words out of my mouth are "I could go."

At least I'd know what was happening, right? Would that make it easier to take?

"No, you could not." Troy puts his hands on his hips.

"Why couldn't he?" Adam asks.

"Yeah, Troy, why couldn't I?" I'm resisting the urge to cross my arms over my chest, but I'm definitely feeling oddly defensive.

"Because..." He glares at Adam, clearly willing him to agree. "You don't have any experience. You'd hate being treated like a piece of meat. We don't want you to have to touch a random old guy's dick."

"You could do the dick-touching, so he doesn't have to," Adam helpfully suggests.

Jesus.

Troy fires back with "Yeah? What if Rigby wants to fuck him or choke him with his dick? Put him in his place somehow. You're cool with that? Because I'm not."

Would now be an appropriate time to laugh or cry? This is officially the most ridiculous conversation I've ever had in my life.

I'm setting aside Troy's possessive comment for now. I like it a little too much.

I drop my chin to my chest. "Okay, look. I'm not saying I'm thrilled about the idea, but I'd never been fucked or forced to swallow another man's dick until we all got kidnapped, and I managed, didn't I?" Realizing I've gotten a little too loud again, I try to soften my voice. "Right?"

The two of them exchange worried looks.

"Say you do this." Troy's clenches his fists. "Say you do it, and you hate it. It freaks you out, it makes how we earn our money a little too real, or whatever the hell else might go wrong. Are you going to leave us when that happens?"

Oh. I get it now. "Is that what it's really about?"

Neither of them answer, which feels an awful lot like a yes.

Exhaustion weighs me down, and by the looks of it Adam's having the same trouble. It's too late for all of this.

For a moment I cradle the back of my head in my hands, staring up at the popcorn ceiling. "Think this conversation is draining all the cells from my brain. It's a lot, and in spite of my recent switch to working the night shift, I'd actually like to sleep some more. Why don't we all get back in bed and finish this later?"

A reluctant smile spreads across Troy's face. "Sure thing, Kitten. You going to let us fuck you again before we all go to sleep?"

I glance at Adam. "You up for that?"

Adam perks up. "How about you grab onto that countertop? You'll find out exactly what I'm up for."

My pulse jumps. They want to test how well I can handle both of them?

Good. Let them try.

CHAPTER TWENTY-SEVEN

TROY

WELL, this night sure has taken a turn.

Of all the things I thought Wes might say about us having to schedule a do-over with Rigby, it wasn't an offer to tag in as a pinch hitter. Relief fucker?

Anyway. Not happening.

Here under harsh kitchen lighting with the too-loud hum of our refrigerator is not the place to keep hashing this out. Maybe he thinks he'd survive it, but I don't. Or maybe I wouldn't. Our ugly world has tainted Wes enough.

Since we're tabling the entire discussion for later, and since Adam's currently pulling down Wes's sleep shorts, I may as well enjoy.

My best friend glances at me with his eyebrows raised.

"Let me see you kiss him," I tell Adam.

Wes and I kiss pretty regularly. Adam and I were each other's first kiss, but we don't do it much. Adam isn't as into kissing in general, but I want to see them that way. I need to.

"Stay put, babe," Adam says as he circles Wes. Apparently he's sticking with his demand that Wes keep his hands on the countertop, and I fucking love it.

To think most years we don't even exchange gifts. Who thought we'd get to have our very own extra-large submissive for Christmas?

I'm already getting hard, but when Adam guides Wes's head around so he can press their mouths together? Fuck, that's perfect.

I don't know if Adam sees it, how good the two of them are. Wes either. Maybe he's thinking he'll fly his freak flag for a little while and move on. Maybe this is all experimentation for him.

For me, though? It's like I told Wes already. I licked him, so he's mine. Since everything that's mine is also Adam's, well...

And someday, if I'm not here anymore, they'll have each other. That'll be good.

Wes gasps as their tongues tangle. There's a sliver of air between each of their lips, and for some reason that makes it even hotter than if they had their faces mashed together. Wes is hard, his hips bucking and his body seeking Adam's even with the way he has his arms pressed flat on the countertop, gripping the far side. He'll have some marks from the hard surface later, no doubt.

It shows how much they're into each other, though. I like that. It's perfect.

Grabbing a bottle of lube from the drawer next to the sofa, I squeeze some into my own hand and then toss it to Adam. "He likes it when it hurts."

Not that Adam doesn't know. My statement makes Wes

blush, though—something he does pretty easily. More, please.

"What do you think, babe?" Adam murmurs as he drizzles lube into his hand. "Should I use my dick, or use my fingers?"

Wes's needy whine is a thing of beauty.

Mmm. "Both. I want to see you fuck him." We haven't done that yet. So far I've topped Wes every time. For his part, Wes has shown surprisingly little interest. Fine with us.

Adam gives Wes's dick a few strokes before moving around to explore his hole. When he slides a finger inside, Wes makes all these cute noises, gasping and hissing. A couple of high-pitched squeals. Like a kitten.

Damn, I'm good at picking nicknames.

"Mark him," I tell Adam.

Wes groans long and loud, moving his grip to the edge of the counter. Adam leans down, pressing a kiss to Wes's shoulder, then one at the base of his neck. When it looks like he's about to lay a kiss on the other shoulder, instead he digs in with his teeth.

"Argh!" Wes's knees wobble. His cock jerks. He drops his forehead to the counter, pushing his ass out more.

Adam smooths his hand over the bite. It didn't break the skin, but it's angry-looking and red.

Running my hand over Wes's arm, I say, "Tell him what you want, babe."

Wes's breath puffs against the counter. "Do it again. Please."

The way he shakes off a full-body shiver, makes my cock throb.

Adam slides his finger out, turning to me with a grin. "Did we create a monster?"

"You heard him," I say. "Do it."

Adam pushes his front against Wes's back. With his hard dick riding the cleft of Wes's ass, he digs his fingers into each of Wes's hips and then leans down to bite his flank.

Wes makes a strained noise in the back of his throat. I get to work stroking myself, wishing a little I'd gotten my phone out to record this. I'd love to make that sound my new ringtone.

"Two fingers, Adam."

"No. No," Wes insists. "Fuck me."

"Gotta get you ready," Adam counters.

"No," our kitten practically whines. "I want it like before."

Hmm. "Which before, Kitten?"

"The time—the—*you know*."

I slide around into the kitchen so I can lean over the counter and whisper to Wes. "You want Adam to fuck you so hard it hurts, like when we got kidnapped and that bad man told us to make you scream?"

Wes lifts his head, pupils blown wide and glowing in the dimly lit kitchen. "Yes. That's what I want."

Adam meets my gaze. Holy fucking hell. I'm not sure whether either of us realized our kitten was this feral.

"You heard him."

Adam nods. "If that's what he wants."

The moment Adam slams home plays across Wes's face. It's in the jerk of his body. The sharp intake of breath. The parting of his lips. The full-body shudder.

"You heard him, babe," I say. "Make him scream."

"W-what about Jalen," Wes gasps as Adam slides out and in again.

"He'll understand." I move around to put my hands on Wes's where he's gripping the counter. "You think I should take a picture? Send him a video? Should I invite him down to watch?"

Just trying to define the parameters we're working with here. For science.

"I don't..." He laces his fingers with mine and pulls me forward.

We're locked in some weird push-pull where we're staring each other down while Wes grimaces and grunts and grips my fingers like a vise every time Adam thrusts into his tight hole.

"You don't what, Kitten?"

"I don't kno—aaah!" He bites his lips together, but he's already getting too loud. Another thump comes from upstairs.

"Hang on, Kitten." I let go long enough to grab my phone. With one hand I stroke myself over my sleep pants; with the other I thumb through the prompts to record a video. It isn't long, and you can't see Wes's face from the angle I choose. Still, it's enough to give anyone a clear idea of what's going on down here.

Then I return to my previous location, and I show it to him. With my best friend fucking his ass, I hold up the video of the two of them.

"You see that, Kitten? Look at that big, built, gorgeous fucking body of yours, taking Adam's dick like a champ. You want me to send that upstairs, so the nasty hit man won't get angry about your fuck noises?"

"Y-ye—oh, God!"

Another bang.

"Send it," Wes breathes.

For good measure, I add a quick message.

Troy: We'll be done soon

Jalen: Fuck, man. Go about your business

That's pretty much what I thought he'd say. Jalen likes his quiet, but he'd never begrudge someone getting laid.

Wes reaches for my hands again, so I drop the phone and grab on. I can tell he's close when he loses control of his volume again, and these cute little high-pitched noises come streaming out of his throat.

"God, he's so fucking tight," Adam moans. "You feel so fucking good, babe."

"And you look sexy as fuck," I say.

Wes's eyes open wider. Like he isn't sure if we're being serious.

My hands tighten around his. "He's right, Kitten. I've been inside that ass. Fucking heaven."

Whether it's coincidence or that's the thing that pushes him over, I don't know, but he shudders and grips me tighter, letting out every sound his lungs will allow.

Adam lets loose a long, pained groan as he finishes inside Wes's ass. Not wanting to let go of our kitten's hand, I end up pulling myself out and shooting on the kitchen floor. I'm so worked up, it doesn't take long.

Annoying, since I'll have to clean it up, but whatever.

Wes collapses across the counter with a weary sigh. "I'm so mad it's taken me this long to realize how good that feels."

"You were waiting for us, that's all." I lean in for a quick kiss before grabbing paper towels to clean up the floor.

I get a fuzzy feeling when Wes reminds me to watch my head as I stand back up. He's a sweet guy, after all, our Wes.

"Can we—" Wes hesitates as he's pushing himself away from the counter with shaky arms. "That was good. Really good. I never thought I'd say something like this, but I like it when you guys take control. I'd like it if we could do it sometimes as if..." He coughs.

"Babe?"

"Kitten?"

Wes finishes, "As if I don't have a choice."

Adam raises his eyebrows. "We'll need a safe word."

Wes shakes his head, and for a moment he won't make eye contact with either of us. "We didn't have one before. That's the whole point. I want you guys to be in control."

My stomach tightens. "Kitten, we can't play that way without a safe word."

"He's right." Adam suppress a yawn. "Or a hand gesture, at least. I've heard of girls at the strip club putting up their middle finger if a customer gets too handsy in the private rooms. We need some way to know if we go too far or accidentally hurt you in a bad way."

Wes sags against the counter. "You're right. Fine."

"Good Kitten."

Adam yawns again. "I need a shower before bed. You guys coming?"

"We don't all fit at once," I remind him. Not easily. We've done it, but Wes is a big guy and Adam and I aren't small.

"Something to keep in my mind whenever we move," Adam says.

He gives me a significant look. I think maybe, possibly, he's onto me. Maybe I'm projecting, but it feels like he's letting me know he expects there to be three of us in the future.

I want that too.

"Who's moving?" Wes is mumbling and barely picking up his feet. Maybe Adam really did fuck his brains out.

"Conversation for another day, Kitten."

He seems to accept that as an explanation. Even though it isn't one.

I give myself a speedy wipe down as I watch them go.

It's always been a thing in the back of my head that someday I'd find someone to look after Adam when I'm gone, and the good news is, I definitely found him.

I'm just not as okay as I used to be with the idea that I might not be there too.

Logically, I know it's not a given that I'll turn out like my mom. Right now, I've got two really good reasons to stick around. But backup plans are a good thing, right? If Adam and I hadn't had one all those years ago, we might not be here now.

I turn off the kitchen light, letting the darkness fall over me before I follow them to bed.

CHAPTER TWENTY-EIGHT

WES

Adam: Troy wants to know if you want to get food after this.

Troy: Brennan wants to know if he can meet with one of us. Something he wants to talk about.

I may be jiggling my knees in a conference room chair that makes my ass hurt, but I also can't hold back my smile.

Wes: Why are you both texting me separately? Aren't you right next to each other in the car?

Adam: We decided to get out of the car. It's a nice crisp day.

Troy: Yeah, love it when Florida winter sets in.

Wes: I don't see how you think that's different.

Adam: We were sitting. Now we're standing.

Troy: And we're outside.

A year ago, maybe even a month ago, I don't think I'd have had the patience for their level of silliness. Now, I feel like I need it to breathe.

They make me forget all the serious shit I used to make myself miserable over.

It's not as if I can control them, so why worry? Turns out I like it fine when they're the ones controlling me.

"Wes." Gina stares me down from across the table. It's a look I've seen plenty of times over the years. Frustration and disappointment, with a heavy dose of "Do you see what I have to deal with?"

"Sorry." I put my phone to sleep and place it face down on the table. Both of our lawyers are due here any minute. As soon as they arrive, we can sign the papers and be done with this entire thing.

Her nose scrunches up. "Are you sure you're okay? You've seemed really strange later. Especially since..."

"The word you're looking for is kidnap. I was kidnapped, Gina. And yes, under the circumstances, I'm fine."

"You forget I know you, Wes. And I don't think you are. You've been missing work—"

"Because I was kidnapped."

"—and is that a bite mark on your wrist?"

I tug the cuff of my shirt down. This morning Adam and Troy wanted to reenact a scene from some vampire TV show they like. They thought it would be hot.

It was.

"Gina. It's none of your business."

"Wes. You're not yourself. Just because we're not together anymore doesn't mean I can't still care about you."

Right now what I am is wishing I could go back to this morning in Adam's bed with him and Troy sandwiched on either side of me. Or even a little later when Troy brought me coffee and overnight oats while I got dressed. The warm domesticity of it all still glows in my chest.

What my ex sees as cause for concern, I see as me finally waking up.

My temples throb. "Maybe not, but it does mean my personal life doesn't have anything to do with you."

It doesn't escape my notice that everything coming out of my mouth right now sounds a lot like what my brother spent months saying to me before I finally agreed to butt out of his life.

Karma's a real motherfucker, isn't it? If I could afford it, I'd send a massive apology bouquet.

Gina's lawyer walks in and drops his briefcase on the table. "Mr. Monroe, your attorney is, uh, parking his scooter. He'll be up momentarily, and then we can get started."

Fantastic. When money's tight and you need to get a divorce, sometimes you're forced to call on a recent law school grad who's still living with his parents and is offering representation in exchange for gift cards to his favorite video game vendor.

Scooter and living accommodations aside, he's a nice enough guy. And whenever I go to his house, his mother has brownies.

"Thanks," I say.

I've barely managed to relax back in my seat when Gina bursts out with, "Sorry, Archie, can you actually give us a minute?"

"No. We don't need—" But he's already leaving. What does he care? He's getting paid by the hour. I'll probably end up owing mine another gift card.

"What are you doing?" I turn on my ex. "We're this close to being rid of each other, and you want to—what?—interrogate me about my personal life?"

She sits back in her chair. "Your mother called me last

night. She said you haven't been answering when she calls. You haven't even sent a text to check in."

"I've been busy."

"Fallon says he's barely heard from you."

"Again, busy. And stop talking to my family. They're not yours anymore." As soon as I say it I feel like an asshole. She legitimately looks hurt.

"Last few times I've tried to call you, it's gone straight to voicemail."

Still. "How is it that I'm the one with a recent head injury and you're the one who doesn't seem to remember what 'busy' means? Do you need me to get you a dictionary?"

"Do you even hear yourself right now? Do you realize how utterly bizarre you're acting, Wes? You had a male escort in your hotel room. The same one, I believe, who I saw waiting outside the building on my way in here. You keep telling me you can't afford to keep covering the mortgage—"

Troy kissing the back of my neck as we woke up this morning. Adam sliding to his knees in front of me in the shower.

"Is that what this is really about? Because no, Gina, I'm not paying sex workers. And I never could swing the damn mortgage, but here I've been working two jobs to make it happen because that house made my wife happy." I lean heavily on the word wife. "In a few minutes, you're not going to be that anymore. I don't even care to dig into your implication that a person who gets paid for sex wouldn't spend time with me otherwise, but I promise you I'm not paying th—him."

Now that I think of it, I haven't paid for much lately. Since I moved in with the guys, somehow one of them always ends up ordering dinner, bringing me a smoothie, or grabbing us all coffee. Every time I try to return the favor, they brush me off.

That's... Huh.

Gina's staring at me as if she's seeing a stranger. "Wes, I'm serious. This isn't you."

If we didn't have papers to sign, I'd walk out right now. "You're right. It isn't me because I've spent the better part of fifteen years either trying to make up for getting you pregnant or trying to make up for the fact that I couldn't actually give you a baby. And I'm sorry, but I'm tired. I don't have it in me to give a shit anymore. I will always care about you, but you're the one who made the decision to go elsewhere."

The way she rears back, you'd think I'd slapped her. "I only strayed after you had completely checked out, Wes."

I open my mouth to fire back, then snap it closed before I let anything come out. No good will come of revisiting the same old argument.

Finally, I say, "You're right. I did. I'm sorry. What is this really about?"

She presses her fingertips against her forehead. "I don't know. Now that we're here, it all feels so final."

"We've both moved on. Isn't this what you wanted?"

She toys with the zipper tassel on her purse before finally admitting, "You were right, you know. Max is kind of a dick."

I raise an eyebrow. "Trouble in paradise?"

"I think...I thought being with him would fix something. Lately I've realized how unfairly I treated you for things that weren't your fault, and once we sign these papers there's no fixing any of it, is there?"

There's this theory I have, that we all carry around an

invisible bucket of emotional shit. Mine's chock full of old hurts, guilt about not wanting to talk to my mother, wondering who the real me is, and the fact that I can't seem to sleep at night anymore unless I'm between two muscular young men.

This bomb Gina's just dropped on the table? It's one giant question too many.

"Maybe someday we can be friends again. But right now? No." I shake my head. "You know it's for the best. You deserve to be with someone who wants the same things you do. So do I."

"And are they?" Her concern looks genuine, and that's the part that hits the hardest. "Those two young men waiting for you downstairs? Do they want what you want? Are they what you want?"

Are they? I don't know what the future holds, but I can close my eyes and smell them around me. Feel their tongues and their fingers on my skin. See Troy's grin as he offers to order ramen for me and Adam stretching like a pleased cat when I run my fingers through his hair.

Right now? "Yes, they're what I want. I didn't expect it, but it's the truth."

"Okay. Good. That's good." She presses her lips together. I'm surprised to see the quick swipe of her hand as she dashes a tear from her cheek.

"Mr. Monroe?" My attorney pokes his head into the room. He's got a bike helmet clutched under one arm. Jesus.

"I think we're good here," I tell him. I look to Gina to confirm. Thank goodness, she nods her agreement.

In the end, it's a surprisingly efficient process to unravel fifteen years of life with another person, but after a review of our brief divorce agreement where Gina gets almost everything because I simply wanted to be done, we're saying goodbye.

On our way out of the building, she puts her arms out for hug. "I'm happy for you."

"Are you really?" I half laugh as I pull her against me.

She's familiar and comfortable against me, but the hug feels strange. We don't exactly fit anymore.

"I think...eventually I will be."

Over her shoulder, both Adam and Troy look exceptionally put out by our amicable parting.

I try to give them a look that says, *It's fine. Stop looking at me like that.*

Adam looks expectant. Troy scowls.

Finally we part ways, and I approach these two young men who have somehow pulled me into their spiderweb. Not that I want to escape them anymore.

"Everything okay?" Adam asks.

Troy, always a little more over the top, adds, "That didn't look like a divorce hug. A little too much lingering, if you ask me."

"It was a goodbye hug." Surprising myself, I put one hand on each of their shoulders. I lean in to kiss Troy first, and then Adam.

When Gina and I were first dating I was uncomfortable even so much as holding hands in front of others. I didn't want the curiosity or the judgment I could feel coming from other people when it came to public displays.

In light of recent events, I've decided life's too short. I've chosen to control the controllables, and I can't control what others think.

What I *can* do is choose to ignore them.

“You never did answer,” Adam points out. “About going to get food?”

“You’re the one who needs to eat regularly. What do you want?”

“Don’t worry about me. We grabbed a snack while you were in there signing the paperwork.”

“What about you?” I look at Troy.

“We’re straightforward, you know that.”

I laugh. They are, aren’t they? It’s one of the things I love about them. I don’t know what the hell I’m doing in any other part of my life, but with them things feel simpler. Easier. Like I can figure it all out, and when I do I won’t be alone.

For a second, I freeze. The first time I ever used the L word with Gina, we’d already been married for months. And here it is flitting through my head as easy as breathing.

My gaze swings between the two of them. Adam’s got his hair pulled back today, a few escaped strands blowing into those dark eyes I’ve learned I can easily get lost in. Troy’s jaw is set, and he’s still casting uncomfortable glances across the parking lot as Gina gets into her car.

Knowing they’re both here for me causes something in my chest to flutter. “You know what? Just take me home.”

CHAPTER TWENTY-NINE

WES

IF I THOUGHT RETURNING to work would give me a sense of normalcy, I was sorely mistaken. Nice as it is to get the well-wishes from folks who haven't seen me recently, I'm sleep-walking through my day.

Teaching has been easy enough. My intro-level hospitality course is populated with apathetic teenagers who are more concerned with their social media feeds. If I placed a life-sized cutout of me at the front of the room and played a recording, I'm not sure they'd notice the difference.

At the Premiere, however? As remembered echoes of student chatter follow me through the brightly lit hotel lobby, I can barely remember where I am.

"Mr. Monroe. Mr. Monroe?"

Oh. Right. That's me, I suppose. "Yes, Murray?"

The hotel housekeeping manager chuckles awkwardly. "Everything okay? Seems like you zoned out there."

Oh. Yeah. Fantastic. I'd rather be at home in between two

men, but barring that, I'd rather do literally anything other than be here. Wrestle a skunk. Dunk my head in boiling water. Paint a snake's toenails.

"Sure. Fine. Getting used to being back, that's all."

"Right. Of course. I heard what happened." He pushes his glasses up his nose with one finger. "And, well, on that note. I wanted to let you know Nadia quit. She stopped in yesterday with her daughter and said she would 'clean sewers or start an OnlyFans' before she came back here." He looks saddened by the news, but personally I can't blame her.

When I let myself remember, I can feel her shaking against me when those two men approached, ready to shove pills down her throat.

"She has to do whatever is right for her."

"Sure. Sure. Was it really awful, then?" He scoffs, most likely at himself. "What am I asking? Of course it was."

As it so often does these days, everything from that night plays in fast-forward behind my eyes. The drugs, the confusion...the continuous grappling with how Adam and Troy made me feel good even though they weren't supposed to. I can only be grateful they were there with me instead of someone else.

Underneath it all is the mixed blessing that it brought the three of us together. Things could have been much worse, and I'm grateful they weren't.

"We survived," I manage.

"Well. I truly am sorry." He takes a step back. "I'm here if you need a friend, eh?"

"Sure. Thanks."

We both know he's only being polite. Besides, I can't fathom talking to anyone about this who didn't experience what we did that day. Fallon has made more attempts, and it's not that I don't trust him, I just don't know how to confide in him.

Not about this.

I'm shuffling mail at the front desk when a hand lands on my ass. "Who was that guy? You think he was involved in all this?"

A startled yelp escapes me, and I turn to find Adam at my side. Since he's got both hands behind his back, the hand on my ass must belong to... "Troy. You can't do that here. In fact." I give both of them a look. "You can't be behind this desk. And why would Murray be involved?"

"Adam is convinced that someone who works at the hotel set you up. Maybe that Max douche."

"What?" They're right that Max is a douche, but I can't picture him going that far.

"Someone who worked here would know the employee lot has no cameras," Adam argues.

"So would anyone who's scoped the place. Relax, Kitten." Troy gives my ass another squeeze before moving himself to the far side of the desk. "We wanted to come by and see how you're doing. Your response to the text we sent you earlier seemed pretty bleak."

I blink at them both. "You asked if I wanted to see a movie on my night off and I said, 'sure.' How is that bleak?"

Troy rolls his eyes. "Because usually you send us a cute GIF with a guy giving a thumbs-up, or something snarky like 'only if I get to have popcorn.' By comparison, your one-word answer did, in fact, seem bleak."

"Okay. Well. I don't know what to tell you. You asked if I wanted to watch a movie, I agreed that I did."

They glance at each other in that way they do, which I'll

admit I don't love. They've got years of being together and their own silent communication, but it leaves me feeling like a third wheel in my own relationship.

Is there a problem here? Are they getting tired of me?

Stop assuming the worst-case scenario. That's how you got into trouble with Fallon, remember?

So I suck it up and ask. "Okay, what's going on?"

"Nothing," Troy insists.

"It's all good," Adam adds.

"Great. Fantastic." It's too early in my shift to be this tired. "Remember when we agreed that this situation didn't work if we weren't honest? If I need to keep reminding you both—"

"Hey. Chill." Troy's hand lands on the desk in front of me. It reminds me of the night we fucked while he held on to my hands and stared into my eyes. My body's response is dizzying.

A tight breath rushes out. "Sorry. It's been harder than I thought settling back into a routine here. Everything feels off."

"We get it. We're not too happy about getting back to normal either." Troy glances at Adam again. "But we never exactly nailed down what we wanted to do about Rigby. We weren't trying to lie, but it didn't seem like the right moment to get into it."

"You guys aren't on your way there now, are you?" I glance up above my head as if I could possibly see who's on the VIP floor from here.

"No. No way. But Brennan needs an answer." Troy leans in. "We tried offering to refund him for the booking, but Rigby's insisting on getting what he paid for. Brennan's not wanting to piss off one of his best customers. Adam insists he's feeling up to it, but—"

"I already said I'd do it." Will I really? The idea fills me with dread, but I would.

No fucking wonder everyone's worried about me. First I volunteer for shady illegal porn, and now I'm offering to whore myself out?

Come to think of it, I'm a little worried about myself right now. Except, why should I be too good for it if they're not?

Because it's not the sort of thing you do.

And yet. And *yet*...getting on my knees before work so I could swallow a twenty-three-year-old's cock wasn't something I did either, until it was.

The two men in front of me seem equally shocked. "We, uh, didn't think you were serious about that," Adam says.

"You two do it all the time." I glance down the desk, where Dima, the night clerk on duty, is dealing with an older woman cradling a fluffy Pomeranian. The dog, for his or her part, is growling in Dima's face. Handling guests who bring their pets is such a crapshoot. Better him than me.

When I'm convinced nobody's close enough to overhear, I ask quietly, "We'd use condoms, right?"

"Fuck yes," they both say at the same time.

"We're both on PrEP, and we'd never fuck a client raw," Troy adds. "Nobody but us three, remember?"

Nobody but us three. Something in my chest loosens. "Right. I know."

"It's okay if you need us to say it again," Adam says, as if he senses my unease.

"Thanks. I looked into that stuff, but..."

"It can be pricey," Troy agrees. "There's a free clinic on the East End, though. We can all go together if you want."

I nod. All at once there's a burning pressure behind my eyes that I can't quite explain.

"I still don't think it's a good idea." Adam toys with his lower lip. "It's not you, babe; it's not wanting to expose you to all that."

"To Rigby," Troy clarifies. "Bad enough how he acts like he's above you. We don't want you subjected to that part of our world." His phone buzzes in his hand. "Shit. Rigby wants to do it on Saturday."

My casual shrug is all bullshit and bravado. "Saturday's good. I'm not working that day."

"Oh yes you are." Max comes around the corner.

"No." I turn to look him in the eye. "I never work Saturdays."

Max took me off the schedule for weekends after he started sleeping with Gina. At the time, I was pissed. Tips are better on the weekends, and some of the VIPs hand them out freely.

"After you missed all that work, I retooled the schedule," he says while he rifles through a drawer, not looking at me or anyone else. He really ought to, though. I'm not sure what *my* face looks like, but Adam and Troy are all but cracking their knuckles.

Wrong as it is, I remember that guy Adam beat to death, and picture him destroying my boss's face.

"I took sick leave, Max. I'm a salaried employee. You can't force me to make up sick leave."

He gives me a smarmy grin. "Are you sure about that?"

"Is this because Gina suddenly realized she can have a

more meaningful relationship with her vibrator than with you? That's not my fault."

His hand shoots out and grabs my wrist. "You need to watch yourself, Monroe. I'm still your boss."

"Hey." Adam's face appears over Max's left shoulder. I didn't notice when they moved back behind the desk, but as I'm wondering about it, Troy's hand clamps down on Max's right arm.

Max's face reddens. He's clearly in pain and trying not to let it show. "I don't know who the fuck you think you are, but you'd better let me go before I call security and have you banned from the premises." With a wince, he glances over his shoulder. "I know the two of you do a lot of...business here."

He manages to make the word "business" sound as disgusting as possible.

"Don't you fucking talk down to them," I growl. "Threaten me all you want, but you leave them out of it unless you want your balls shoved into your throat."

Where did that come from? Wes of a few months ago would be appalled at all of this. Discussing sex work. Watching someone I'm sleeping with threaten my boss.

Hearing *myself* threaten my boss. I don't know who this new Wes is, but it's funny how little I care.

"You don't fucking mess with Wes again," Troy adds. He's still got his hand on Max. From the looks of things he's digging his thumb in, pressing on sensitive tendons. "Try to ban us from this hotel and find out what happens. It'll hurt you more than us. And if you hurt Wes? Then you'll definitely be hurting more than us."

This is completely ridiculous, juvenile, chest-thumping behavior. Why does it make me want to jump them both?

Adam looks at me over Max's shoulder. "You want us to take you home, Kitten?"

Dima, who's crossed in front of the desk on his way to the concierge stand, looks over and mouths, *Kitten?*

My face flames as I shrug and turn back to Adam. With one last glance at my shithead boss, I nod. "Yeah. Take me home."

"You can't walk out." Max moves to block my exit. "You've barely started your shift."

"Right. Well. Fire me, then." I drop the stack of mail I was shuffling and grab Troy's free hand. "Let him go. Take me home."

Apparently those are the magic words, because Troy reluctantly complies. "Fine, Kitten. Let's go."

"Monroe," Max calls behind me. "I know the GM of nearly every hotel in a two-hour radius. It's no problem at all to give you the boot and see you blacklisted from the entire business."

I'll be honest, I almost stop. He's probably bluffing. But if Max really has those kinds of connections? I'm nauseated at the thought. What the hell am I doing?

But then Adam tugs on my hand. And Troy says, "Don't worry, Kitten. We'll figure something out."

Fuck it. I'm choosing Troy and Adam. Let Max come for me. I'll hit him myself.

After showing Max my middle finger, I walk with each of my hands in one of theirs.

CHAPTER THIRTY

WES

I'M STILL GETTING the hang of navigating Adam and Tory's apartment at night. I keep the lights off because I don't want to wake them, but I've learned the hard way that if I don't proceed carefully, feeling along the wall as I go, I'll stub my toe on the bed frame. Or run straight into the nightstand.

My knees have taken a lot of abuse lately, and I can't even blame it on the boys forcing me to the floor to suck them off. I *wish*. It's only my lack of direction.

If I use my fingers to trace the bathroom doorframe until I find the edge of the light switch, that puts me in line with the side of the bed. From there if I take a few steps, I'll find myself next to—

A hand clamps down over my mouth. "I'm only going to say this once. If you tap out, everything stops."

Troy. He's trying to sound different. Lower and raspier, but of course it's him.

I'm still catching up when he asks, "So. What do we have

here?" His breath puffs against the base of my neck, making my cock jerk.

"What are you doing? What do you want?" I whisper when he pulls his hand away. The breathiness in my voice is embarrassingly real.

"You, baby." His lips brush my ear. "All we want is you." Something hard and cold scrapes along my jaw. A knife, maybe? Wasn't expecting that.

The unknown spikes a bit of fear in my bloodstream. At the same time, my cock gets heavy and full.

"W-we?" They lied. When they said Adam wouldn't be home tonight, they *lied.*

For me.

How fucked up am I that I find it kind of sweet?

"Are you scared, Kitten?"

"A little," I admit. Even though we discussed this whole scenario at length, I don't really know how it's going to go. Anticipation has my heart trying to drill its way out of my chest.

"Good." His teeth clamp down on my ear.

Wait. Where's Adam, though? Oh, shit, I hope someone else isn't here. I'm not sure I'm ready for a stranger. I'm barely ready for the two of them.

Definitely more nervous now. He's doing this on purpose. My body hums with anticipation.

Then Troy says, "Let's see what we can do to turn that little bit into a lot."

Before I can react, he shoves me forward.

I fly through the dark, landing on the bed. Hands grab me, rolling me until I'm on my back.

"Adam, hold him down."

The first thing I think is, *Thank fuck. Adam's here.*

The second thing is that Troy said something very similar to this the first time they touched me. When Adam held my shoulders in that locker room while Troy jerked me off.

"Oh God," I groan when Adam—I think it's Adam this time—pulls my shirt off. Cool air hits my nipples. It only gets worse when someone closes their teeth around one. A second mouth does the same on the other side.

Oh hell.

My body jerks as sensation zings to my hard cock. My breathing turns frantic and choppy. Excitement rides the knife edge of fear. The sharp drop of that theme park ride where you're trapped in a broken elevator and then plummeting thirteen stories.

"Please. Yessss," I hiss when my sleep pants get yanked off. My boxer briefs go next, both so quick the scrape of fabric on skin burns a little.

"You should stay quiet." Troy's between my legs, I think. "Unless you want us to hurt you, you understand?"

So if I want it to hurt, I make noise. Got it. Good. "Yes. Yes, I understand."

Which is why I let out a clear and filthy moan when his mouth closes around my balls.

There's a hard pull on my nipples. "Quiet." I think that's Adam.

Never before in my life have I whimpered in bed like such a needy slut, but here we are. Didn't even know I could make these kinds of noises.

A mouth envelops my cock. "Oh, thank fuck. That feels so good."

Then Troy bites my hip. Adam presses his nose to mine and murmurs, "You're going to get it now, sweetheart."

That's not something they usually call me. Is that part of this whole thing?

Like a jungle cat, Troy's shadow slinks above me. He hovers, letting our cocks brush the barest amount.

"Please..."

"Please what?" Adam. His stubble scrapes my face.

My muscles clench. My hips jerk. I swear this is more thrilling than the personal best I got when I ran my last race.

"Please. I need more. I need—aaaah!"

Teeth sink into my flesh. Both of them at once. They work in tandem, biting my shoulders. Near my collarbones. My pecs. My biceps. All the way down to my wrists.

I'm squirming and whining. The more I whine, the more they bite. Not hard enough to break the skin, but enough to make it burn and tingle. Enough to make my body shiver. Without asking, I've figured out Troy doesn't like making me bleed.

"Please, please," I keep saying, over and over.

For every three or four touches elsewhere, I get one or two on my cock or my nipples. They're toying with me. They've got to know they're driving me crazy.

It's what they do.

"God, touch me. I need it." The begging feels shameful. Humiliating. Especially knowing it does no good. They've got their plan, and it won't matter what I say.

But there's always a chance. And doesn't desperation turn us all into fools?

My frantic begging is cut off by lips on mine. Adam. His stubble is softer, and his long hair brushes my face. He's coming from the side, his mouth slanted at an awkward angle. I don't care. Needing to taste him, I push my tongue against his.

"More," I moan into his mouth as Troy rubs a slippery finger around my hole.

"I can't take this," I whine again.

They're going too slowly. Too much teasing. I'm amped up times a million, and I need one of them to fuck me.

"Don't you think it's up to us to decide what you can take?" Adam asks.

Then he straddles my chest. The pressure and heat of his skin on mine is oddly calming. Hands encircle my wrists, pinning my arms over my head. The smooth head of his cock pushes between my lips.

At the same time, Troy presses two fingers into me. Even though he's being gentler than he has to be, the pressure feels intense. Not nearly as intense, though, as the anticipation. When his fingers brush my prostate, I clench desperately against him. The moans coming out of me sound like they belong to someone else.

A voice in my head tells me I'm losing my mind.

But then his fingers withdraw and the head of his cock presses against my hole. *This is it. Here we go.*

When Troy shoves past my resistant muscles to slide inside, my shout must reverberate around Adam's cock. He moans too, pushing himself in farther. He's at the back of my throat, but he's being careful.

"That's so fucking good, babe. You're our good little cocksucker, aren't you?" Adam murmurs as he fucks my face with shallow thrusts. "I bet you need this. I bet you would let us strip you down and tie you up and use you for our pleasure, over and over again. We'd milk you dry, wouldn't we, Troy?"

"We'd milk ourselves dry." Troy's tone is sinister as he fucks me. He's slower this time, and I'm impatient. There's this simmering heat in my belly, and I want to bring it up to a full boil.

I moan, since it's all I can do with my mouth full.

"That's right, Kitten," Troy continues. "We'd cover you in our cum. We'd mark you as ours. Our slutty, straight daddy. Bet you'd love that."

Oh God. I so would.

It's like I've had this alter ego living inside me, and something about these two men brought him to life. It wants them to own me.

I want them to own me.

Fuck. They already do.

They fucking own me.

Troy thrusts into me with quick, purposeful strokes. Each one makes my pleasure build.

It's not long before Adam's cock swells in my mouth. I'm drooling and uncoordinated while trying to keep the suction going. This is still new as well. My jaw hurts.

Practice. I'll get there. After finishing cancer treatment, I trained to run an ultramarathon. A hundred miles in the heat through Dade City. If I can train to do that, I can train to suck a dick.

"Should I come in his mouth?" Adam asks. He's not asking me.

"Not this time." Troy's breathless as he pounds me without mercy. He's going to bruise my ass with those hip bones. "We're going to mark this little slut. Let him know he's ours. Force him to look in the mirror later and see what we did to him."

They're talking about me like I'm not even here. Like I'm an object. My orgasm is so close I can taste it.

"Good idea." Then Adam pulls out and blasts me in the face.

In spite of their discussion, it takes me by surprise when his cum splashes across the side of my cheek, my nose, and into my open mouth.

While I'm coughing and sputtering. Troy slows his pace. He doesn't ask, but I know he's waiting to make sure I'm okay.

"Don't. Don't stop," I beg. To let him know I'm all right. Except my tongue runs away from me. "I'll be good. I'll show you how good I can be. You'll keep me, right? If I'm good for you?"

Jesus, what am I saying?

Tears spring to my eyes as I realize that I mean it. I've never been enough for anyone. I want to be good enough for them. I'm not sure what it would do to me if they decided I'm not.

I'm not able to think about it for long. Troy's hitting my prostate like the expert he is, and I couldn't hold back if I tried.

"Oh God, fuck me. So hard. Come inside me. Own me. Fucking make me yours. I need it. Harder. Harder. *Please.*"

Who even am I right now?

My release comes on a guttural yell. I'm grateful for the dark so they can't see my tears mixing with Adam's cum on my face.

Troy's hips, bony and lean, strike me hard with each thrust. I'm *definitely* going to be so sore tomorrow.

Good. I'd rather the pain not fade too soon. Their pain comes with pleasure. I chose it. It's mine.

When he comes inside me with a yell, when the banging

comes on the ceiling again and Troy yells "Fuck off, Jalen!" I'm too lost to care.

In the wake of my orgasm, I feel as if I'm floating on an ocean, getting rocked by the waves. Nothing but peace. Pleasure. Belonging.

Adam keeps his hands around my one wrist even as Troy pulls out and lies down beside me.

"Should we clean him up?" he asks Troy. Why does he sound far away?

"In a minute." Troy throws one leg over mine, brushing my hair from my forehead with gentle fingers.

"Was that a knife at the beginning?" Why is my skin tingling all over? The cool rush is intoxicating.

Adam chuckles. "A butter knife. Did it work?"

"It worked," I murmur.

"Good." He lets go and takes up what's become his usual place on the far side of the bed.

Gently, Troy kisses my temple. "Is that what you wanted, Kitten?"

I nod against his mouth, too wrung out to really parse what I'm feeling. Humiliated, lying here covered in their fluids. But also deeply satisfied. My chest swells with something that feels a little too tender. Too attached.

Yes, it was exactly what I wanted. They're exactly what I wanted. I'm too broken open to say what I really feel.

They did this for me. And I love them so fucking much.

CHAPTER THIRTY-ONE

TROY

"ARE you thinking what I'm thinking?" I ask Adam while we both stake out the employee entrance to the Premiere hotel.

We've turned into fucking movie villains, stalking our own boyfriend. Not that I give a single fuck.

Adam purses his lips. "That the fancy bakery downtown with the good bagels will be open soon, and Wes likes the blueberry ones, so we should stop on the way home?"

In spite of the threats Wes's boss made, he went back for his next shift with surprisingly little trouble. I'd like to think we put the fear in the skeezy dick bastard. Either that or his threats were just plain empty. Most likely the fear, though.

"Is that really what you've been thinking the whole time we've been sitting here? Bagels?"

Adam hums while pulling his hair back with a black band. "Well, you and I both really like the bagels, but a dozen split between us is too many. With Wes it comes out to four bagels each instead of six, so yeah. Why not?"

"Figures." I laugh and squeeze his leg. "That's not what I was thinking."

He turns in his seat, looking more serious. "You were wondering if we need to be worried about whoever kidnapped us trying something again."

Lately it's all I can think about. Remembering the blood running from Adam's temple, the way Wes could've gotten himself hurt or killed, it all makes me go cold.

"It's not likely, right? Liam and Brennan said they took care of everyone they could find. And Ravi said Liam has a lead on whoever was pulling the strings."

Adam hums. "But they haven't confirmed it yet, which means someone could still be out there planning more of that shit. Yes, it worries me."

"You don't think it could've had anything to do with your brother, do you?" Ever since the night Adam shot his father and we both ran, we've wondered if his brother might come after us somehow.

"If Santi was going to kill me, there are easier places to find me than the employee parking lot of a hotel. Besides, I basically handed him the business on a platter. That woman, Nora—"

"Nadia."

"Yeah. I think she said there had been someone else from the hotel there. Those guys clearly had camped out here. Maybe they were picking people off. Hotel staff going missing gets dismissed. We saw that when Wes tried to sound an alarm. For all we know it has nothing to do with us. This is a tourist town. They could even be doing the same thing at other places."

I draw a sharp breath. "Shit, I didn't think of that." I shake my head. "Hopefully Liam finds that fucker soon."

Adam turns in his seat. "There's something else I've been thinking about."

"Rigby?"

Adam's mouth twists. "I've never really liked the guy."

"Me neither. But he's our biggest paycheck."

My best friend's fingers tap the console. "Right, but I was talking to Michael a little about our portfolio numbers. We haven't made a firm plan for quitting yet, but...we could afford it, I think. We'd have plenty of time to figure something else out. Wes has tried to be cool about it, but it bothers him. And maybe it makes me a hypocrite, but the more I think of it, the less I like the idea of Rigby touching him."

I shake my head. "If you're a hypocrite, then so am I. I don't like the idea of anyone else touching him."

"Well, yeah. Exactly."

"Okay. Only way to resolve this." Before either of us can second-guess anything, I pull out my phone and hit the button for a video call. A few seconds later, our pimp's face appears on the phone. He's up and dressed, even so early in the morning. I can make out the collar of a shirt and the knot of his tie. But his sandy hair is sticking up on end, and the circles under his eyes look dark.

Where the hell is he? It's not his office. Some falling-apart building. The East End, maybe? There are a lot of those over there.

"This better be good. It's six in the morning. What do you fuckers want?"

Maybe he hasn't been to bed yet?

"We need a favor." I lean toward Adam so we can both get into the frame.

"You know how I feel about favors."

"Don't ask unless you want to risk getting your dick chopped off," Adam parrots.

His tone may be casual, but he reaches across the console to grab my hand. This is a risky ask we're making, so I grab back.

"You've helped some of the others," I point out. "Remember when you saved Simon's life and gave him a loan so he could go to nursing school?"

"Remember when he spent five years on his back paying off the debt he racked up?"

Adam and I glance at each other. "Fair point," I say. "But this is important."

"We want out," Adam blurts.

My eyes pop wide open so fast they almost hit the windshield. "What the fuck, man? I was going to ease him into it."

Adam bites his lip. "I couldn't keep it in."

Brennan makes a loud throat clear over the phone. "What the fuck are you idiots talking about?"

"We're seeing someone, and we don't wanna fuck other people anymore." Adam slaps his hand over his mouth.

"Are you serious right now?" I give him a light slap on the back of the head. Giving someone like Brennan Doyle too much personal information is like handing him a loaded gun and then standing still so he has a clear shot.

"I didn't mean to." He bites his lips together, but it's too late. He's already said too much.

"Guys," Brennan says again, "shut the fuck up. You've got three upcoming jobs on the books, including the boyfriend experience with Mr. Rigby. You get those done, and I won't schedule you for anything else. Easy."

"Okay. Great," I say. "There's one little thing, though."

"We need to cancel them," Adam says.

Brennan drops his chin to his chest. "Fuck you. Adam, listen to Troy. You really need to stop talking."

"My bad," he murmurs.

"We can pay you back," I tell Brennan. "Or we can find someone to take over the jobs."

"I can probably get Dean to take the other jobs. They're first-timers, and he's always looking to earn more. But Rigby? No. He specifically wants the two of you, and I'm not trying to piss off a customer who has a quarterly golf outing in West Palm Beach with two US senators and a known felon."

Ugh. "Right. That's trickier."

"We could try talking to him," Adam suggests.

"Don't." Brennan sighs, adjusting his tie a little. "God forbid something unplanned comes flying out of your mouth again. You could accidentally start a trade war."

"I'm not going to—" Adam frowns. "Wait, what does Rigby do for a living?"

Huh. Come to think of it, I'm not quite sure. "He owns a couple of companies or something. Something to do with real estate or land development?"

"That's not the point." Brennan sighs. "Okay, here's the deal. I texted you about my friend Nate wanting to meet with you. I owe him a favor. You do the meeting, and I'll consider it a favor to me."

Shit. Shit, really? My spine straightens. "So, you do your fiend a favor by getting us to do you a favor, and in exchange?"

We need him to spell this out. No misunderstandings.

"Meet with Nate and I'll smooth things over with Rigby."

Adam pummels my thigh with his nervous fingers. "You're serious?"

"So long as you manage not to piss me off between now and then. And don't ever ask me for another motherfucking thing unless you're ready to owe me a kidney."

Adam opens his mouth to say something again. I slap my hand over it before he does, indeed, piss Brennan off.

"Got it. Thank you." So fucking much. Jesus Christ. I could kiss our pimp through the phone right now.

Adam mumbles something similar from behind my hand.

There's a jarring knock at the window. I look over to find Wes's ex peering into the car. What the hell does she want?

"Thanks again, Brennan. Gotta go."

I hang up and roll the window down. She gives us a little wave. "Hi, guys. Got a minute?"

For the woman who made Wes afraid to let us touch his dick? I doubt it. "Not to be rude, but we're from Miami and Florida winter is too cold for us this far north. Whatever this is about, say it fast. We're letting the heat out of the car."

She glances around. "You can't loiter out here, you know. Max doesn't want to upset the VIPs, but this is getting ridiculous. You're here all the time lately."

We're here all the time because of Wes. Not whatever she's thinking. I should give her the same speech I gave Max.

"We're picking up Wes." I check the time. "He should be out any minute. Then we'll leave."

"I don't know what's going on with the three of you, but don't you think it's beyond inappropriate for him to be seen with two known sex workers?" She whispers the end of the sentence, like if she utters the phrase too loud, more of us will appear.

"Lady, the only way someone knows is if they've hired us. In which case they're not going to say anything."

"I know, and I've never hired you."

"Only because you work here and you've seen us before. Also because you're overly invested in the life of someone you recently divorced." I gesture across the parking lot to where Wes is trudging toward us. "There he is now. Better scurry inside."

Wes gives her a questioning look as she walks away but doesn't say anything until he climbs in behind Adam. "Why was Gina talking to you?"

"She doesn't like us being here."

"Well, officially, the hotel has a policy against—"

"Please. You know this has dick to do with hotel policy and everything to do with her not wanting us around you."

He settles back in the seat. "Right. Well. That's not my problem, and it's not yours. What I do with my personal life stopped being any of her business when I walked in on Max bending her over our newly updated bathroom vanity."

"Ouch."

Wes gives a short shake of his head. "It's in the past. Let's go."

"So," I say as I pull out of the parking lot, "one of us is going to have a meeting with a friend of Brennan's next week."

"About?"

"Not sure. He said if we do it, though, he'll smooth things over with Rigby so we don't have to do the job."

"Didn't you say that could cause problems?"

I glance in the rearview. "We know you don't like it."

"I don't feel like it's my place to ask you—"

"Fuck that. We're all in this together, Kitten. Of course you can ask."

"I can't tell you to quit earning money. The only reason I'm getting by right now is because the two of you aren't charging me rent." He swings his gaze back and forth between us. "Which you really should be, by the way."

My long sigh ought to tell him how tired we are of discussing this.

Adam twists in his seat. "No, we shouldn't. We don't need the money, and you do. It wouldn't be fair."

"Which is also why we feel good about quitting," I add. "We've got enough in savings to float for a while until we figure out something else to do."

When I check in the rearview, the hope on Wes's face is unbearable. So is the gentle touch of his hand on my shoulder. I want to pull over and fuck him right on that cramped back seat.

"You're sure?"

"As sure as we can be without getting a definite yes or no from Brennan," Adam says.

"I understand. If you have to do it, then you have to. I'm still willing to, uh, you know. Sub in. If needed." Wes sounds about as enthusiastic about the idea as we are.

The way his halting suggestion makes my skin crawl? Right there is reason enough to find a new line of work.

"No need, Kitten. It's gonna be fine." I reach up to my shoulder, putting my hand over his. It feels good, the way he's trusting us. The way he's letting us take care of him.

For whatever fucked-up reason, I get my jollies from taking care of people. Going all the way back to when I was a kid and I was the only person who could make my mom smile.

"I'm going to wait and try not to get too excited," Wes says. "Until we know what Brennan's friend wants. Should I maybe go with you?"

Adam frowns. "I can go. He only said it needed to be one of us."

"But the two of you hardly ever go anywhere apart."

Agam and I exchange a knowing look. "We don't want to leave you alone right now," I tell him. "Just in case."

"In case whoever kidnapped us tries again? I've been thinking about that, but what are the odds of it happening twice?" Not that he exactly sounds relaxed about it.

"You've been thinking about it too?" Adam asks.

"Can't stop thinking about it. *But.* I also can't live my life looking over my shoulder. You two should go to the meeting. It's silly to sit around and wait for me in the parking lot while I'm working."

"We don't sit here the entire time," Adam protests.

"I'm not sure that makes it a whole lot better."

"Whatever. Kitten, give Adam your phone."

"What? Why?"

"If you let us put a tracking app on your phone, then maybe we'll stop sitting out here while you work."

Wes hesitates. "How's that going to help? Those guys took our phones before."

"Yeah, and they were dumb enough to take them to where they were holding us before they crushed and tossed them. They didn't even break yours all the way. It would make us feel better if we had a way to find you. Just in case."

Adam turns and bats his eyelashes. "Please?"

"Fine. Frankly, I'm surprised you didn't do it when you bought me a new phone." Wes sighs and pulls out his phone, handing it over to Adam. "I must be absolutely out of my mind, but here."

"You're with us, Kitten, so you definitely are."

And maybe we are too. But it's okay, because we have each other.

CHAPTER THIRTY-TWO

WES

"YOU DON'T NEED to walk me inside," I tell Troy on the way into work the next week. "Wasn't the point of you putting the tracking app on my phone so that you wouldn't need to be glued to me all the time?"

It's been a few weeks now since we were kidnapped. Aside from Gina continuing to give us worried looks, everything's been surprisingly good. Even Max seems to have backed off of his micromanaging and threats.

Yes, I'm still questioning my sanity. But every day it's a little less. When I leave work exhausted at six in the morning and go home to crawl in between two men who give me the best orgasms of my life, it's difficult to care.

When Troy gives me a flirty grin and says "You know you love it" I can't help but smile. I don't argue. I've been feeling an awful lot of strong feelings for the both of them lately. Love feelings.

Still, I have lingering doubts. Is this really falling in love, or are we trauma bonded? Both?

Even considering the question makes my chest tight. Whatever this is, it feels too important and too real to pass it off as something other than love.

"I think you've got better things to do with your time, that's all," I say instead.

Sure, I'm the one who insisted on total honesty. Really, though, if I'm going to come out with something as intense as telling them I'm falling in love with them, shouldn't I wait until I'm one hundred percent sure before I say it out loud?

Lately I've questioned a lot of things, especially whether I ever loved Gina the way I should have. Unfortunately, I think the answer might be no. Did I care for her? Absolutely. Part of me still does. Mostly, though, it was obligation.

None of that is what I feel when Adam makes me a to-go cup of coffee to bring to work, or when Troy's hoarse whisper in my ear asks me how much I want him to destroy me while he fucks my ass.

It is overwhelming to comprehend when I have an entire night shift looming ahead. Or anytime. I'm constantly thinking about it and also trying not to.

Troy squeezes my hand. "Nothing more important than making sure you're safe, Kitten."

Last night he and Adam fucked me in front of their open living room window. Even two floors up, someone could've seen. I came so hard I almost collapsed and chipped my tooth on the windowsill.

It's a good fucking thing I'm a runner. I'm conditioned for endurance. Otherwise, the two of them might be the death of me.

The thing is, I never thought I could feel this cared for, even if the way they go about it is slightly unhinged. They make me feel wanted, and not simply for what I can give to them.

I think they might actually want me for me. Just as I am.

As we reach the door, I turn to say goodbye. "I'll see you when I get off."

"You better not be getting off without us there."

"Walked into that, didn't I?" But I laugh anyway. Only a little, because there's a question I've been dying to ask. "Are the two of you really thinking about quitting the business?"

"We basically already have." Troy's hand twitches and his gaze cuts away. I'm coming to realize he has trouble with eye contact when he's feeling vulnerable. "Brennan said he'd handle the gig with Rigby, and the other two we had scheduled, he's already reassigned to other guys."

"What about, you know, income?"

"Told you, Kitten. We've got savings. We've got time. Christmas is around the corner. New Year's. We'll all be able to spend time together for real and see if this thing will last when we're not all swimming in drama." Then he takes me off guard by breaking into laughter. "What am I talking about? Of course it will."

"How can you be so sure?" It's one of my worries. What happens when there's no hate-fucking and no kidnappings to fuel the fire between us?

Then he reaches for my tie to pull me forward, kissing me right there in the parking lot. He presses his cheek against mine to whisper, "How can we get bored when we've got you asking us to jump scare you and fuck you in the middle of the night?"

Okay, it's forty-five degrees out here, but I'm absolutely

boiling right now. It still makes me squirmy when he kisses me in public, but I let him anyway. Ignoring the click of heels passing on their way out of the building, I kiss him back.

Softly. Sweetly. It's not the frenzied hunger we kiss each other with when we're in bed, but it's satisfying.

"Go," I tell him when I pull away. "I've got work, and you said you wanted to call Adam to make sure he got to his meeting okay."

Adam's meeting with this friend of Brennan's who wanted to talk to one of them for some reason. We don't know what about, but it hasn't stopped me from manufacturing a long list of what-ifs in my head.

At the top of that list: What if this person wants to hire them? What if they want a boyfriend experience? A long one?

My stomach hurts.

The address Brennan gave is at a beach house on the far end of Belle Argo. Not a "modest" beach house like where my brother and PJ live, but one of the big ones that cost tens of millions of dollars and have more square footage than a big box store.

It means a lot to me that they're willing to put the escorting on pause while we work out the ins and outs of being together. It also makes me nervous. It's a lot of pressure. Am I enough to justify the change to their lucrative income stream?

I'm afraid they'll come to resent me. Like Gina did. Like I came to resent my mother. What if one day they look at me and regret that they stayed?

It's too much to discuss for now, so I say goodbye and head inside.

After I make my way down the carpeted hall of the employee wing and out to the shiny marble lobby, I stop at the concierge stand. Roy, who's been with the hotel forever, is holding himself stiffly as he packs for home. "Evening, buddy. How are you feeling?"

"Oh, not awful. Still swollen. A little sore." Roy took a spill off a curb and did a number on himself recently.

"You know, there used to be a stool up here. Would it help if you could sit during your shift?"

"Oh, absolutely. I thought of that, actually, but I haven't had time to look for one."

"Let me put my stuff down, and I'll go see what I can find."

"Oh, no, I don't want you to go to any trouble—"

"It's no trouble. Let me go now, so I don't get pulled into something and forget."

He looks relieved. "Thank you, Mr. Monroe. That's kind of you."

"My pleasure."

Speaking of pleasure, I take note of the tender ache in my ass as I deposit my things in the management office. It's been a challenge getting Troy and Adam to be willing to fuck me as much as I want them to. We all like it when they get rough, when they hold me down and "make" me take them both, but they seem unwilling to risk really hurting me, no matter how much I beg.

And believe me, I've begged.

I smile to myself as I make my way back down to the service wing, where the storage area is. The hotel bar was redone a few years ago, and I'm pretty sure some of the old bar stools are still here.

At least, I hope so. Gina asked me to bring a few home

for our kitchen, now her kitchen. Some other employees probably nabbed some too.

As I search, I experience yet another strange feeling—would it be dissociation? That thing where you feel like you're standing outside your own body?

It's surreal how much change I've seen in the last year. My marriage ending, getting too involved in my brother's shit and fighting with him. Getting kidnapped. Strangest of all, having that last experience result in somehow being both happier and more out of control than I've ever been.

All the way in the back of the storage room, partially hidden behind some rolled-up area rugs, are a couple of the last remaining stools from the old bar. I give myself a mental high five and drag one out and down the hall to the main lobby.

This will be good. It'll allow Roy to take the weight off his feet without bending his injured knee too much. When I arrive at the stand Roy's already gone for the day, but I place the stool there for when he returns.

"Mr. Monroe. Nice to see you." I look up, and to my horror, Mr. Rigby is standing in front of me, smiling.

Usually I'm great at putting on a game face with the VIPs, but it's different coming face-to-face with the man who's fucked your... Wait.

Are they my boyfriends?

Whatever they are, they've got a history with him. I trust what Adam said to me about it being transactional. I still don't like it. I don't like picturing him with his hands all over them. Or knowing he's probably helped pay for the apartment I'm currently living in.

"Good evening, sir. How may I help you?"

His face is neutral. Pleasant. "Oh, I don't know that I need anything really. Thought I'd swing by and say hello."

"Oh. Well, hello." Something tells me this man doesn't simply stop by for pleasantries, and I'm unnerved by what he might say next. I take a step back, ready to take myself literally anywhere else. Maybe someone needs help with a toilet clog or changing some bloody sheets.

"It's interesting, Mr. Monroe."

Dammit. His voice stops me in my tracks. "Interesting, sir?"

"I've been a regular of your two young men—" I don't like the way he puts emphasis on the word "young," especially when I'd possibly put this guy in his early-fifties. "—for a couple of years. Now, seemingly out of nowhere, I find they've decided to quit escorting entirely. Since I haven't seen them around here lately, perhaps you can let them know how much they'll be missed."

"Mr. Rigby. I don't discuss my personal life with guests—"

"Oh, of course not. I understand." He nudges my shoulder as if we're buddies. "I'm not simply a guest, though. I'm the new owner. Technically, I'm your boss."

Fuck. This guy can't be serious.

For one thing, I thought I'd met the owner, and this isn't him. For another... "Why are you staying here all the time if you're not a guest?"

"Perk of the job." He laces his fingers behind his back. "Max keeps a suite open for me. I can see you trying to do the mental math. The previous owner ran into some legal trouble, you see."

"Right. He sold to his business partner. I've met them both."

"Well." Rigby leans in and gives me a wink. I'm about to risk my job again by telling the guy we are not buddies. "Between you and me, the business partner stretched himself too thin when he took on this property. Truly, it was an excellent opportunity. Great profit margins on luxury hotels." He laughs and slaps my shoulder with the back of his hand. "What am I saying? Of course you know. Don't you teach an entire course on this stuff?"

"How do you—"

"You know, there might be money involved, but I genuinely care about those boys. And this...situation... between the three of you seemed to come out of nowhere. Felt like a good idea to look into you. My condolences on your divorce, by the way. I hope you're not too overextended financially to be a good partner to them. They're good boys, and they deserve the best. They work *very hard.*"

Let me add how much I hate the way he puts emphasis on the words "very" and "hard." Don't get me started on him calling them good boys. Bile rises in my throat.

There are plenty of things I want to say. I've got enough experience dealing with men like Rigby to restrain myself. I'm tired of it, though. I'm tired as hell of men who look down on people who don't have the kind of money they do.

"Kind of you to be concerned, sir. If you'll excuse me, I'm needed elsewhere. Please don't hesitate to let one of the staff know if we can do anything to make your stay a pleasant one."

I've nearly managed a graceful exit when he wraps his hand around my wrist. Rigby's surprisingly strong.

"Actually, there is one thing you can do, Mr. Monroe. Those two owe me a night, and I've been informed by their —" He clears his throat. "coordinator—"

"Their pimp. Might as well speak plainly, shouldn't we, sir?"

He glances around but his smile only widens. "At any rate, I've been informed that they are no longer open for business. They still owe a night."

"They're willing to pay the money back."

"I don't want the money back. I want the service I paid for."

The service he paid for. Acid burns my throat.

"Mr. Rigby." I pull myself out of his grasp. "I'm sorry to disappoint you, but this isn't my decision to make. It's theirs."

When I walk away, I don't look back. For a change I spend the majority of my shift in my office, uninterested in socializing or helping customers.

The strange, possessive way Rigby talked about Troy and Adam has left me with a pit of snakes writhing in my belly. I've never wanted to pummel somebody's face more.

I hope you're not too overextended financially to be a good partner to them.

Worse, I'm wondering if he's right.

CHAPTER THIRTY-THREE

ADAM

THERE'S a dark cloud over Troy when I get up in the morning. He'd already gone to bed when I got back last night.

Now he's at the stove pushing hash browns around a pan, but he's curled in on himself the way he used to be when his father got drunk and beat him for existing.

"What's wrong?" I look around. "Where's Wes?"

"Shower." He gestures with his spatula. "He's in a bad mood. Wouldn't tell me why."

"Is that why you look like some shit went down?"

"Some shit definitely went down, I just don't know the details. He came out of work this morning looking like he was trying to solve a math equation and that equation had punched him in the face."

"Shit." I drop myself into a kitchen chair. "I need to talk to you guys about something, too."

"The meeting?" He turns the burner off and faces me, leaning back against the oven door.

"Yeah. Brennan's friend wants—"

The bedroom door opens and Wes comes out. He's larger than both of us. Older, and presumably wiser. But the hopeless slump of his shoulders makes me want to go over and comfort him. To hold him and promise everything will be okay.

Even though I don't know. How can I promise anything when I don't know what's wrong?

"Kitten?" Troy's struggling. His face shows a mix of frustration and hope, and I know him well enough to know he doesn't let himself hope with almost anybody.

"What's wrong, Wes?" I ask.

His dark hair is wet, combed hastily with his fingers. He's freshly shaven, and under different circumstances I'd want to go to him and slide my fingers over the smooth skin on his jaw. Breathe in the clean scent of him.

He's got that same look on his face Troy mentioned, though. And the real problem? Even though he's normally heading to bed around this time, he's dressed in daytime clothes. And holding a black travel bag.

Troy lifts his chin. "Going somewhere?"

Wes goes still. Belatedly, he looks down at the bag in his hand. Almost like he forgot he was carrying it at all. "I was thinking I might go and stay at Fallon's for a bit. He and I really haven't gotten a chance to talk, and I'm feeling like I should."

Troy must have been squeezing one of the oven knobs behind his back. There's a loud clang as one pops off and bounces off the metal door, landing on the kitchen tile.

"That's all?" I ask. "You want to talk to your brother?"

I should eat soon. Maybe that's the reason for the sour sensation in my stomach. Somehow, I don't think so.

“I guess...” Wes seems to be avoiding making eye contact with both of us. “The three of us have all been in each other’s pockets for weeks now. Figured I could use some time to think. We all could.”

“Time to think about what, Wes?” The steel in Troy’s tone tries to cover what he’s really feeling.

Desperate. Afraid. Out of control.

Wes shakes his head as he blows out a heavy breath. “It’s nothing. This is a lot, that’s all. The two of you, everything we’ve been doing... It’s a lot.”

“Did your ex say something to you again?” Something must have happened. When I left yesterday, everything was fine.

“It wasn’t—” Wes runs a hand through his wet hair. “I don’t feel like I have any business asking, but are you two aware that Rigby has a thing for you?”

Troy and I both laugh. Not to dismiss Wes’s concerns, but: “Rigby’s married,” Troy says. “He doesn’t have a thing for us. He’s like any other guy in this town who’s richer than sin. He’s used to getting what he wants. He’s probably taking it as a slight that we canceled on him, that’s all.”

“No.” Wes gives his head a single, decisive shake. “You didn’t hear him. You didn’t hear the way he talked about you like he owned you.”

“That’s how all those rich fucks are. You’re either a business associate, competition, or property,” Troy insists. “The guy paid us well to do a job. That’s all it was. Eventually, he’ll move on to someone else.”

The flare of Wes’s nostrils jangles my nerves. “You don’t believe us, do you?”

He shakes his head, looking sad. “I don’t. I’m sorry. I’m not even saying you’re lying. I’m saying the way he spoke about you, it was creepy and possessive and gross. Maybe he's better at hiding it in front of you, but he feels some kind of ownership over you."

Troy walks up to him, running a palm over the center of his chest. "Some people might describe our feelings for you as creepy, possessive, and gross."

Which only gets a hint of a laugh out of Wes. He gets serious again pretty fast. "Look. This is none of my business, so tell me to fuck off, but..." He struggles for a moment. "How much does that guy pay you?"

"A lot," Troy says.

I nod. We've come a long way from fifty-dollar blow jobs so we could cover our sleazy motel room for the night. Which is a good thing. Usually.

"H-how much are we talking here?"

Uh-oh. This feels like a test, and I'm not sure what we're supposed to say. Troy's uncertain as well. It's no good if we lie, but if we tell him the truth?

"Ten grand a night," I blurt before I can second-guess.

Fuck. There I go again blurting shit out when I need to keep my mouth shut.

"It wasn't always that much," Troy hurries to add. "Inflation and stuff. You know."

"You've got to be kidding me." Wes backs up into the couch, sinking down heavily. He props his elbows on his thighs, dropping his head into his hands. "All those times I gave PJ shit about being after my brother's money, and here you two make more in a night than I do in a month."

"Hang on." Troy starts toward him, but whatever he sees on Wes's face stops him.

I try, "PJ's situation is different. He didn't make as much because he wasn't, you know, full service with the clients."

Not that it justifies the things Wes said about PJ, but I get why he thought he needed to look out for his brother.

I'm pretty sure the only reason I'm still alive is that my brother doesn't want to kill his only living relative. Or because me killing our father worked out in his favor. Mostly though, I like to think it's because we're brothers. Brothers are special, or at least they're supposed to be.

Wes looks back and forth between us, eyes a little wild. "You two know I'm broke, right? Things were tight before Gina and I decided to divorce, and even a fairly friendly one like ours costs money. I've got credit card bills and student loans I'll be paying off until I die. I'm forty-fucking-two years old, and I'm so far in the hole I can't even see my way out. What the—" He kicks one leg out, knocking the glass from the coffee table. "What are you even doing with me?"

It's not the money Wes is mad about, I don't think. It's how the money makes him feel. Still, his judgment stings. "Do you honestly think that matters to us? Relationships aren't about one thing. Definitely not money."

"It may not be the only thing, but you can't tell me it's not important. I spent fifteen years with someone I could never please. Plenty of them were spent arguing about the things we couldn't afford. You two are too young to understand yet, but believe me, it matters."

Troy crosses his arms over his chest. "Hold on a fucking minute there, Kitten. You think it's a walk in the park running away from home when you're underage and one of you has a chronic health condition?" Troy shoots me an apologetic look. "I took care of my mother every day until she killed herself. Adam shot his own fucking father in the face to get free of the hell he was living in. You think we haven't lived? What were you doing at that age?"

Troy's kind of yelling, and all I can think is thank God our upstairs neighbor is a hit man, and everyone else in this place makes a habit of minding their own business.

When he turns to look at me though, my heart clenches. My best friend's eyes are wet, and they mirror the same thing I'm feeling.

How do we fix this? Wes may be sitting in front of us, but it's clear he's already out the door.

Wes grits his teeth. "When I was that age, my father was dead, and I had been dealing for years with a mother who wouldn't get out of bed. I was raising my little brother. It wasn't an option to run away. I couldn't date, or party, or go fucking anywhere."

"See? We're not all that different," I argue, still not quite understanding what it is he's so mad about.

"I got Gina pregnant on our second fucking date. The sex was so awkward that if it hadn't happened there probably wouldn't have been a third. And the three of us—" He gestures with one hand between me and him. The other between him and Troy. "—do you really think we'd be here now if we hadn't had an intensely life-changing experience together, or would the two of you have gotten distracted and moved on by now?"

"No." Troy curls his hand into a fist. "Don't start with that shit."

"We're not together because of that," I argue. Wes's anger is infectious, and I can feel my own rising to a boil. "We're together because Troy thought he was going to unalive himself one day and I'd need a replacement soulmate. Except I don't give a single shit about any of that and neither of you are going anywhere."

Which, okay. Probably just went a little too far. I'm

standing here getting more furious by the second over Wes's assumptions, which only help to remind me how much I hate Troy's assumptions.

Troy turns to me with wide eyes. "What are you saying?"

I shove my finger into his chest. "Come on. You honestly thought I didn't know? Ever since your mom died, you've been afraid one of these days you were going to, I don't know, lose your tether to humanity or something. Well, news flash, you can't replace one person with another. It's fucked that you thought you could try. I love you both, idiot. Nobody is allowed to leave."

It's the way Troy's eyes flare wide that makes me realize what I've said.

Oh. Fuck.

Wes presses his lips together. "See, this is part of the problem. Now the two of you are fighting because of me." The way he shakes his head, I don't know if he didn't hear the L-bomb I let slip, or if he's pretending he didn't.

With jerky movements, he reaches for his travel bag.

"Wait," I say. "Brennan's friend. The guy I met with last night. He does adult films. Legit ones. More legit than what happened in that place we were taken to, I guess. Brennan told him about that video of us, and he's willing to pay us for the publishing rights. He's even interested in paying us to do more like them. It's a lot of money, Wes."

He slows on his way to the front door. "What does that have to do with anything?"

"You're standing there telling us you don't feel equal because of financial reasons. You keep talking about your mortgage and your credit card bills. This is a way for you to get a lot of money without fucking some stranger."

Rather than helping, every word out of my mouth pushes his shoulders closer to his ears.

"I don't know, Adam. Before I thought maybe I could, but... I'm not like you guys."

"You're saying you're too good for it? It's okay for us, but not the guy who slept here for free and ate our food?" Great. Troy's raging, and his filter's switched off.

"Troy." I put my arm across his chest, warning him to back off. His words aim for the jugular when he's hurt. That's the last thing we need.

He shuts up, but he's pushing against my arm like he thinks he can bully Wes into staying.

"Are you breaking up with us?" It's hard to ask, but someone needs to.

How did this even happen? When I left here yesterday they both kissed me goodbye. The corner of Wes's eyes crinkled when he smiled and told me to hurry back. Now we're at each other's throats?

Wes is quiet. Too quiet, and for too long.

"Sounds like a yes to me," Troy murmurs.

Wes shakes his head. "I haven't even said anything. The truth is, I don't know. I need...time. I need to think. I need to apologize to my brother for calling his boyfriend a gold digger when one of your fucking clients accused me of the exact same thing last night. I just—I need to go."

Hugging the duffel bag to his chest, he turns and walks out the door. Even though every line in his body is tight with anger, he closes it pretty quietly. Always considerate, our Wes.

It takes a second for me to make my feet move. When I do, I'm shoving my feet back into my shoes and sprinting to the front door.

"Don't." Troy grabs me by the arm as I'm pulling it open. "Let him go."

What? "We need to do something, Troy. Are you telling me you don't want to fix this? After you're the one who planted a flag in him and declared he was ours?"

Troy stumbles back, collapsing on the same spot Wes vacated. The coffee table sits there in front of him, still with the glass piece in the middle off kilter. "He said he needs to think, so we need to let him. Let him talk to his brother. Let him do whatever he needs to do. We all need to calm down. Fuck knows I do. We'll figure this out."

I'm not thrilled with this plan. There's an invisible gash in my gut, and I'm standing here doing nothing. Both of us are. For all he's trying to sound confident that things will work out, Troy's crumpled like a piece of discarded scrap paper.

And me? In a short period of time I went from hating that Troy had Wes in his sights to needing them both to stay. If Wes doesn't come back, Troy and I will survive, but it won't be the same.

From the look on his face, he knows.

"What if doing whatever he needs to do includes leaving us behind?"

Troy's smile is grim. "I don't know. Maybe we'll have to hunt him down and kidnap him again."

CHAPTER THIRTY-FOUR

WES

SOMETHING KEEPS HITTING me in my face. I slap it away, too exhausted and too numb inside to do anything but return to sleep. Whatever it is though, the assault only gets more aggressive.

Followed by an unamused "Wake up, fucker."

Pulling a pillow over my head, I mumble, "I can't deal with you right now, PJ. Go find someone else to torment."

"Are you kidding me? Fallon said he's tired of your mopey ass sitting around here and not talking about what happened, so I came to get a front-row seat to the drama."

A crunching noise has me rolling onto my back and cracking open one bleary eye. "Are you actually eating popcorn?"

The door to my bedroom swings open. "PJ, what did I tell you about the popcorn?"

My brother stands there giving his dominant boy toy a look that's half exasperation and half affection. For once,

I'm fucking jealous. Three days ago I left two dominant boy toys of my own in their apartment. I've been hating life ever since.

I can't bring myself to discuss it. And even though every day feels like I'm dying inside, I can't bring myself to go back. Can't shake the feeling they'd be better off with someone who can give them the world, like that dickbag Rigby can.

So the guy's married. So what? I was too, until recently. Sure hasn't stopped the man from sleeping with them anyway.

"Fuck." I slam my head back into my pillow and try to cover my face again with the other one. I'm thwarted by my brother, who grabs it and forces me to look at him.

"This feels like backwards day," he says. "You're the one wallowing in bed as if someone died, and I'm the one being a responsible adult."

Except in my brother's case, last year his wife *actually* died, and what I thought was being a responsible adult was actually me being a controlling asshole.

I force myself to sit up. "Fine. I'm up. Okay?"

Several pieces of popcorn cascade down my front. I glare at PJ. "You were throwing popcorn at me?"

A stray thought reminds me that I could totally see Troy and Adam doing something like this, and the empty ache in my center sharpens.

PJ, the little shit, looks too gleeful. "Fallon said I wasn't allowed to laugh at your misfortune on account of you looking like someone kicked your puppy, but that doesn't mean I can't have a little fun."

"I suppose that's fair." I gather up the popcorn and toss it into a nearby trashcan. "Seriously, PJ, I owe you an apology. Well." I turn to my brother. "Both of you. I was trying to protect you, but instead I tried to shove you into a version of happiness you didn't want. I shouldn't have set you up with a male escort to get you laid, and I shouldn't have tried to break you two up. That was tacky. And wrong. I'm sorry."

"And clearly a case of transferring your own desires onto someone else." PJ throws a handful of popcorn into his mouth, waggling his eyebrows.

"You enjoying that popcorn, asshole?" What happened to not laughing at my misfortune?

"Mmm. It's white chocolate and marshmallow flavored."

"PJ." Fallon's tone is sharp. I assume he's trying to send a message, but PJ only looks more and more delighted.

"Oooh, it's the teacher voice." PJ points his finger at me. "Wes, I accept your apology. Now get the hell out so your brother can rail me without him feeling like we have to be 'considerate of your feelings.'"

I stand. "Why did you use air quotes?"

"Because I don't actually care that much about your feelings, bro."

"PJ," my brother bites out again.

"Fine. Fine." PJ puts his hands up. He stands, gathering the bag of popcorn. "I'm gonna let you two talk. Congrats on the divorce, by the way." He shoves a fist in my face, which I bump listlessly.

Once he's gone, my brother's stern expression softens. "Talk to me," he says.

So I tell him. Most of it, anyway. The confrontation in the locker room that started it all gets glossed over. Most of the sex parts, really. Especially the kidnapping. I admit to it happening, I even admit it bonded us, but I don't give details.

Some things I'll never want to discuss in detail with my baby brother. Ever.

"It's weird. Ever since it happened, I don't feel right when I'm away from them. We were each other's lifeline that night."

"Okay." My brother sits in the chair vacated by PJ, crossing an ankle over his knee. "I'm still not entirely sure I understand the three of you together."

"Join the club." Even as I say it, I feel like I swallowed glass.

My brother holds up a hand. "But. If you're happy, then what's the problem? You said they're quitting sex work."

I shake my head. "It isn't even that. I don't really like them fucking other men, but I understand it. It's how they survived."

"Then what's got you crashing here when you could be with them?"

I close my eyes against the pain that hits my chest whenever I miss them. Which is way too often.

"This Rigby guy took it personally that I was getting in the way of his access to them. Not that I asked them to refuse the date. But he made it clear he was pissed, and he also made it clear he thought I was taking advantage of them the way I accused PJ of doing with you. I keep thinking, what if this is my karma? Maybe I don't deserve to be happy with them. Especially not after the way I treated you two."

"Wes. Quit." Fallon looks disappointed. "You didn't understand then. You said it yourself, you'd only been with one person, and for a lot of your marriage sex more purpose-driven than pleasurable. It makes sense you didn't know what you really liked."

"Right." I'm listening, I swear. Also, my hand is creeping toward my phone like it has a mind of its own. The number of times I've written some lame-ass apology text only to delete it before sending could win me a prize.

My brother clears his throat. "Okay. I'm not exactly cool about the judgment, but I also understand where you were coming from. You didn't get my relationship with PJ because you couldn't see how someone would enjoy our dynamic. From where I'm sitting, you've got bruises around your wrists and what look like bite marks on your collarbones. Are Adam and Troy abusing you?"

At first I think he's mocking me. Or judging. But no. The question is sincere.

I close my eyes, remembering the last time all three of us fucked. I'd gone into the bedroom to get ready for work. Before I could make it to the shower, I was flanked by both of them. One held me down while the other peppered bites and kisses all over my body, refusing to touch my cock until I begged. When Troy finally sucked me into his hot mouth while Adam held my wrists behind my back, I came so loudly it made the hit man upstairs bang on the ceiling again.

At the time I decided if pissing off a hit man mid-orgasm was how I went, it was a perfect way to die.

"They're not abusing me," I insist. "I didn't know before —" God. There's so much I don't know how to say.

My voice shakes when I say, "I didn't realize how unhappy I was with Gina. Or I did, but... I figured feeling alone and unfulfilled must mean I needed to try harder. I didn't know I could feel the way I do now. About anyone, including another man. Or *men*. I didn't know what I needed until they showed me."

"Neither did I," Fallon says quietly. "Not until I met Marina."

I nod. At least we finally understand each other.

"But, Wes, this shit with their client or whatever? Don't you think if they wanted more with him than a pay-for-play situation, they would have done it before now?"

"I don't know. They said he's married, but you and I both know that doesn't always mean much. Mom used to say shit about how men don't commit unless you make them." I'm glad there's not a mirror around, because I know my face right now is twisted and ugly.

That man tried to claim ownership of *my* men, and he had no fucking right.

"We both know Mom has her own issues," Fallon says quietly. "And while we're on the subject, I know you took on a lot with both of us when Dad died. I never really said thank you."

"You were too young to worry about it."

"At first, sure. Then later, I let you handle things with Mom because it was easier to let you. I should've offered to help."

I rub my forehead. "She's getting older. She's going to need more in the future. I'm... I don't feel like I can handle it on my own anymore. I don't know what to do."

"Simon, one of the guys PJ used to escort with, works in a pretty nice assisted living facility. When PJ and I fly up for Christmas, I'll discuss it with her."

"Fuck, I forgot all about Christmas."

"I already told her you can't make it."

"It'll hurt her feelings if I don't come."

"She'll live. It's not your job to keep looking out for everyone. It sounds like those guys are finally giving you what you need. You deserve to take some time to enjoy that. You deserve to be happy, whatever that means for you."

My lips stretch into a smile. "Thanks. That's really great of you."

"Just ignore PJ when he starts in on how you owe him one for going in your place. I love him, but he can be an asshole."

"PJ? An asshole? You don't say."

Fallon laughs. "Hey. He's my asshole. And in spite of what he said, you're welcome to stay here as long as you need."

Heat and moisture spring to my eyes. "That's... Thanks. Really. You're right, though, I haven't been happy since I walked away from them. Obviously, we all need to talk. Actually, uh, I've decided I need to quit my job. It's toxic, having to deal with Gina and Max in my face every day. Not that I'm jealous or anything, but he's a dick, and she keeps giving me her two cents about my personal life."

Fallon gives me a dry look. "Yeah, it's a real pain in the ass when people do that."

I'm tempted to try and smother myself with the pillow again. "See? Karma. I need a clean slate. There's got to be a way to make money that doesn't suck out my soul. After I go in and give Max my letter of resignation, I'll go home and work things out with Adam and Troy."

"Good. Glad to hear it." Fallon gets up and heads for the door. "I'll let you get ready to go, then. And remember, I'm here anytime if you need me. Just..."

"Don't come by unannounced. I know." Learned that lesson the hard way. More than once.

Fallon's face turns the color of strawberries as he lets himself out of the room.

Meanwhile, I pull myself out of bed feeling more human than I have in days. I whistle off-key while I get ready for work, looking forward to going in for the first time in ages.

So I can quit. So I can be better. So I can be happy.

With both of them.

CHAPTER THIRTY-FIVE

WES

IT FIGURES. The night I march into work with my head held high, ready to tell Max he can cram this job up his uptight ass, he's already gone home for the day.

Still. Simply for having made the decision, I'm lighter and less stressed than I've been in forever. Nobody's screwing with my good mood tonight. Not Max, not the yappy Pomeranian on the tenth floor, not the "eccentric" visiting CEO from California who keeps insisting we only bring him green food.

Nobody.

I slip into Max's office to leave the letter on his desk, taking the time to tape it to his computer keyboard for good measure. It'll be the first thing he sees when he sits his ass down in the morning.

"What are you doing in here?" Gina's voice breaks into my focus.

"Shit." I nearly make myself dizzy by lifting my head too quickly. "You startled me."

"Sorry." A crease mars her forehead. "I saw the light on. Max already left for the day, so I was going to turn it off. What is this?"

Not sure whether she's referring to the roll of tape in my hand or that I'm behind our boss's desk, but either way it's the same answer.

"Came to drop off my letter of resignation. I'm leaving."

"Are you serious?" She leans her hip against the doorframe. "All those times I suggested we leave and go somewhere for a fresh start. Now you're quitting?" Sadness crosses her features.

Gina and I have fought so much over the years; I think I made her the villain in my head. Really, I need to own up to the role I played in our problems. "You're right. And I'm sorry. We moved here to be near my brother and it's the same reason I never wanted to go anywhere else. I should have been more flexible. Or maybe we should have split up earlier. Either way, you deserved better."

She straightens her shoulder. "Thank you for saying so. For the record, so did you. I let my misery turn ugly and I tried to punish you for it. That wasn't fair."

Gina's never really been one to apologize, so this is a lot. "I forgive you."

"I appreciate that. But, Wes, do you really want to leave? I thought you liked this job. Is this about...them?"

Them. Adam and Troy. Certainly it has to do with them, but not exactly.

"It's about me. I'll be healthier and happier not having to run into you and Max every day. Not walking through the same employee parking lot I was kidnapped from. Not seeing—" The customers who have fucked Adam and Troy "—the VIPs I don't like and whose asses I have to kiss anyway. Ideally, not working nights."

She wrinkles her nose. "That was unfair of Max to do to you. I should've said something."

"Don't worry about me, Gina. I'm not your problem anymore. And I'll be fine."

"You know, I'm not sure things are going to work out with Max anyway."

Color me surprised. "It's none of my business what you do with your personal life, Gina."

She seems to take the hint, straightening and backing away from the door. "Right. Well. Good luck, Wes. I'll see you around."

I return the roll of tape to its location on Max's desk and leave a minute after she does. I'm about to go to retrieve my two-way radio when I spot Emmy from house-keeping pushing her cart down the hall. Her limp looks even worse.

"Hey." I turn to follow her. "Thought you were going to get that thing checked out."

Her smile looks tired. Strained. "Oh, I will. Took your advice and put in the request for time off. I'm waiting for Max's approval."

"Tell you what—" I relieve her of the heavy trash bag she's trying to keep from toppling off the cart. "—let me take this. Go home. Tomorrow, get in to see your doctor. I'll make certain the time off gets approved."

Worry creases her forehead. "You're sure? Boss man's not your biggest fan."

"Absolutely. There's no reason for him not to approve it, I'll talk to him about it when he gets in tomorrow. Besides, I put in my two-weeks' notice this evening, so what's the worst he can do to me?"

Unexpectedly, she lurches forward and throws her arms around me. "Thank you, Mr. Monroe. We'll all hate to see you go."

Well. I didn't expect that response. Or the lump of emotion in my throat.

Emmy disengages, quickly heading off down the hall. Probably decided to leave me with the cart before I change my mind. Which makes me chuckle.

I'll miss everyone here too, but the more I think about it the more I'm excited about the idea of leaving. The way I left things with Troy and Adam has me nervous, but I'm hoping we can talk it out.

In fact...I decide to finally go ahead and shoot them a text.

Wes: I'm sorry about the way I left things before. Can we please talk when I come home after work?

I'm hoping my use of the word home will clue them in to what I'm thinking.

We'll get it all worked out. We get each other. I believe that.

Smiling, I hoist the top bag of garbage from Emmy's cart and head out to the walled-off enclosure where the hotel hides several large dumpsters from view.

Chilly air seeps through my clothing. There's a cold front coming. Belle Argo usually averages temps in the sixties to eighties this time of year, but my weather app warned me we could see high wind and lows in the twenties and thirties tonight.

When I left my brother's place earlier this afternoon, it was sixty-five out. Now, the chill on my skin tells me that's been dropping steadily. Chafing my arms for warmth doesn't work too well when I'm carrying a huge bag of trash.

God, I can't wait to finish my shift and go home. It's been hell not having Adam and Troy on either side of me. The stinging night air has me missing their warmth even more.

Maybe that's why it takes me a minute to notice that the flood lights that illuminate the dumpsters don't seem to be working. Or why I don't immediately register the footsteps behind me.

Until a voice says, "Mr. Monroe. I have a request."

I freeze in the midst of swinging the garbage bag into the bin opening. It swings back and hits me in the face. Gross.

A second later, when I hear the now-familiar click of a gun being cocked, I drop the bag. Turning, I find Rigby, of all people. In the moonlight I can see he's wearing his usual uniform of high-end loafers and a cashmere sweater. Pressed khakis that are probably worth more than my car.

He's also pointing a weapon at me.

Even as my pulse spikes, my mind is surprisingly focused. "If you're unhappy with the turndown service, I can look into that for you."

"I'm unhappy with Adam calling to let me know that I should leave you alone. That he and his 'best friend' are 'for sure' quitting the business."

"That has nothing to do with me, you know. They'd talked about doing it anyway."

"Oh, I know. They'd mentioned it to me. Several times. Each time they did, I'd offer them more money and they'd change their minds. Which was a win-win for everyone."

Until I came along. I see. Okay. "Here's a novel idea. If

you wanted them, why didn't you simply ask them out on a date?"

Rigby gives me an impatient look. "My marriage provides me with money and connections I'm not anxious to relinquish. Beyond that, the whole mating song and dance isn't what it's cracked up to be. You should know that as well as anyone. When you pay someone to perform a service, they're expected to perform it to a certain standard. Especially when you pay as well as I do."

A shiver hits me that has nothing to do with the weather. "You want to have power over them."

"Sounds awful when you put it that way." Which isn't a denial.

Gross. I shove my hands into my pockets, feeling for the button on my key fob that allows me to send an emergency signal from my car. It's out there in the parking lot beyond us, but I don't know if I've got the range to make it work.

"I'm curious. Would you be this angry if I'd taken away your chef or your gardener?"

"You're damn right I'd be angry. Callum and Elana are extremely valuable to me. Would I go to this kind of trouble? Probably not. For you though, it's not simply about Adam and Troy. It's about your disturbing tendency to get involved in the lives of your very temporary employees."

"You're aiming a gun at me because I try to be a good boss?"

"Son, *I'm* a good boss. I own three companies. Everyone loves me. But if an employee fails to show up for work without explanation, they're fired. End of story. It's not your place to follow up."

Wait. "This is about Nadia and the other missing staff?" If that's true, then... "Did you have something to do with all the other people who were taken? Me? You were responsible for me and Adam and Troy, your precious, favored 'service performers,' getting kidnapped?"

He clicks his tongue in a way that makes me want to rip it the fuck out. "That part was an accident. They weren't supposed to be with you." It's hard to tell, but he almost sounds regretful. "The point was to get you out of the way, which would keep you from dating them and from nosing around about the missing employees. Win-win."

Something tells me the words win-win are going to trigger murderous rage for a long time to come. If I survive.

"You are stupidly fucked up, you know that?" I'm saying this as a guy who got off on having my ass destroyed while our kidnappers caught us on film. At this point, I'm an expert on fucked up.

"I prefer the term eccentric. Less 'I need outpatient services' and more 'lovably quirky rich uncle.' My nieces and nephews adore me."

Because they don't know you're a psychopath. "Whatever helps you sleep at night, Rigby."

As we talk, I make a point of stepping a few inches to the right, and then a few more, hoping he'll be too focused on his delusions of—I don't know, romantic servitude?—to notice I'm edging toward the enclosure opening. The employee parking lot has horrible lighting, so if I can make it out there, I might be able to hide. Call for help, or even make it to my car.

Rigby takes a breath and re-focuses his aim on me. "I know you think I'm being unfair, but I'm looking out for the two of them like you are."

Unfair is not the first word I'd use. "By killing me?" Another sideways step.

"You're not suited to take care of them like I can. I tried to tell you."

"You're right. I'm not. They're the ones who take care of me."

Now I'm hating myself for arguing with them when we last saw each other. Why couldn't I have said thank you instead? Thank you for feeding me my favorite foods and teaching me who I really am and for making me feel seen.

Thank you for making me feel *loved*.

Rigby scoffs. "Of course they would. They're good boys, but they're young. They don't know yet what's best for them. Maybe you wouldn't understand, but I've raised two children. Sometimes what they want and what's good for them isn't the same thing."

"They're adults." What's worse here? That he's talking about Adam and Troy as if they're children for him to "raise"? That he's buying his own PR?

Or that I almost bought it too?

And... "I love them. They make me happy. I want to make them happy. Isn't that all that matters?"

"You'd think—"

Footsteps on pavement draw his attention. Out of nowhere, something hits me from the side. Somone.

"Troy?"

He shoves me out of the way, inserting himself between me and Rigby's gun. "Wes, get the hell out of here."

"I'm not leaving you here with him. What if—"

"Wes, go."

Rigby actually fucking smiles. "Since we're all here, let's use this an opportunity to have a talk. Where's Adam?"

"Visiting his brother in Miami."

"What?" I'm about to ask why I didn't know they were

even back in touch, but then I remember I walked out a few days ago and haven't talked to them since. Of course they wouldn't loop me in.

"Don't worry about it." Troy jerks his chin at the quirky billionaire with the gun. "You're going to let Wes go. If you do, then you win. I'll go with you. Adam and I will do whatever you want."

I'm going to be sick. "Troy, don't—"

"If you hurt Wes though, you don't get us. You don't get anything."

"Troy, no. Don't let him win."

I reach back for his hand, but he slaps it away.

"Come on, Wes. You said it yourself, our relationship doesn't make sense. We were always on borrowed time. Now, I swear to fucking God, if you don't run I will murder you myself."

My heart sinks. "I'm not leaving you here."

"Wes. *Please.*" Troy keeps his gaze trained on Rigby. "This man's got more money than God, a steady hand, and a shiny Colt 1911. What exactly do you think is going to happen right now?" He takes a deep breath. His stance is loose, his expression stoic, but there's an edge in his voice.

Terror.

"I'd listen to him if I were you, Mr. Monroe."

Right now I'd give almost anything to punch Rigby in his smug asshole face.

This is worse than my first marathon attempt. Twenty-four miles into the race, my legs turned to noodles. Dehydrated and completely out of fuel under the hot Florida sun, I fought so hard to get to the finish line, but in the end I ate pavement.

Right now all I want is to fight for Troy. To fight for us.

But there's a man with a gun pointed at him and Troy is begging me. Not even when we got kidnapped did I see Troy looking so terrified.

"Wes. I'm choosing. I don't want you here. Go, before you get shot for someone who doesn't even want you."

He's lying. He's got to be. It doesn't stop the words from stinging.

Troy's entire demeanor has gone icy and cold. As much as I want to stay and argue, there's still a man with a gun waiting not so patiently, and if he gets mad enough, he could shoot us both.

So I give Troy one last pleading look, and then I do what he asked me to.

I run.

CHAPTER THIRTY-SIX

TROY

I'M silent as Wes disappears.

Regret chokes me as I stand there, focused on Rigby's gun. When Wes's footsteps fade, I'm able to relax some, more as Rigby drops his hand to his side. Not that I'm completely convinced Rigby still won't shoot me.

At least Wes is safe.

Adam was picking up dinner when I texted him that I was here. From the ramen place Wes likes. Rigby doesn't need to know Adam is on his way. With luck, Adam will find Wes in the parking lot and get him out of here. Rigby never needs to know.

"For someone who claims to love you, he certainly didn't take much coaxing to leave."

Lightning cracks across my chest. "Did he tell you that?"

Rigby doesn't answer me. The way he looks as if he ate something nasty makes me believe it's true.

Which is fucking amazing. Especially considering Adam

and I worried the whole "we need to talk" text was a breakup thing.

Extra especially after Wes went and stayed with his brother for three days. We were planning to track him down if he stayed gone much longer, but every day has been torture.

But this? Showing up and finding Rigby pointing a gun at Wes? Almost killed me.

"You don't know him," I tell Rigby. "You have no room to judge."

Wes is the guy who took care of his mother when she couldn't get out of bed. He's the person who tried, in his own misguided way, to get his brother back on the road to happiness even while his own marriage was falling apart. Who offered himself up to protect a coworker he didn't know that well.

Honestly? "He's a hundred times the man you are. I'm fucking glad he ran."

Rigby lets out an impatient sigh. "You and Adam struggled to stay afloat for too long. You deserve someone who can take care of you. He can't do that the way I can."

There's no way to explain it to a man who's used to getting anything he wants if he only pays enough money. Wanting Wes was never had anything to do with dollars.

"It doesn't matter," I tell him. "I said I'd go with you if you let him go. Let's get out of here."

The longer we stay, the more likely it is that someone else could come by. Some innocent employee could get caught in the crossfire. Wes could decide to come back.

If I have to choose between Wes gone and Wes dead, I'll choose the one that keeps him alive.

"Where's Adam, really?" Rigby doesn't move, holding his ground in the entrance to this weird dumpster enclosure.

I'm trying to run through my options without being obvious. If I make a break for it, maybe I can get past him and get to the employee entrance or get lost in the expansive parking lot before he shoots me.

I could run toward the guest lot, which has cameras. But what if someone else gets shot? I could wait him out until hopefully he puts the gun away, then I could attack. Rigby's fit for a guy his age, bulkier than I am, but I think I could take him.

It's funny. I've spent so much of my life certain my mental health would lead me down a dark road I couldn't return from, and now here I am desperate to live so I can go home and eat ramen with the two men I love.

Clarity comes in the strangest moments, doesn't it?

From standing here alone, my muscles are so knotted I'm aching. Never mind how my nipples could cut glass. It's cold as penguin testicles.

"Rigby, I already told you where Adam is."

"You mentioned some time ago that Adam hasn't spoken to his family in years. You honestly expect me to believe there was a sudden reconciliation?" He steps closer, stopping a couple of feet away. From here I can see the look on his face, which I'm betting is the same look he gets when the hotel restaurant brings him the wrong order.

Choosing my words carefully, I try, "You know how it is with family."

"That's not an answer. Even if it were true, there's no way Adam would go back to Miami without you. You see? I know you both. Years of conversation and sensual lovemaking—"

Ew. *Ew.* It was definitely not that. Every time the man put his mouth on me I fought to not cringe.

"—are far more important than a few weeks with a man who's likely using you as an experiment."

Fuck. Rigby may as well have slid a knife between my ribs and twisted. I can see it now, how Wes came home after one conversation with Rigby questioning everything. Asshole's sure got a knack for warping reality and making it sound true.

Probably a big help when making business deals to screw over homeowners or whatever it is he actually does. I've never really paid close attention.

Rigby takes a step closer. "You know I'm right."

"I'm sure you're used to being right." It would be easier to agree with him. All I really want is to leave, but that's not happening now. I made a bargain for Wes's safety, and what's keeping me in place is not knowing what might happen I don't comply.

One of the things I wanted to tell Wes was that I talked to Ravi earlier. His boyfriend has Rigby on his hit list. Someone tried to traffic Ravi a while back, and Liam's pretty sure Rigby was involved.

If I can distract him, maybe I can get a message to Liam.

If I can do it carefully. Brennan made it clear we needed to proceed with caution around this guy, and if someone makes Brennan cautious? That's not something I should ignore.

"Well." I edge toward the parking lot, giving Rigby the same impatient look I give Adam when he's not ready to go somewhere on time. "Time to go, right? Wes left. I stayed. Let's go back inside. Up to your room or something."

If we can get inside the hotel, it should be easier to get

away from him. He can't shoot me in there. Too many people.

Rigby glances around. "We're waiting for Adam."

"I already told you he's not coming."

"And I already told you I know you both too well. The two of you barely shower by yourselves. Since you aren't with him, he must be on his way."

Fucking dog with a bone, this guy. His accuracy makes my skin crawl.

He closes the gap between us, close enough to run his manicured fingers over the lingering tender spots on my jaw. It's not swollen anymore. The bruises have faded. But the guys who took us got me pretty good. Chewing still hurts sometimes.

My instinct is to recoil. For all the times I've had sex with men I didn't know and didn't even like. For all the times I've had sex with *this* particular man I didn't really like. It was something Adam and I got used to, because we had no choice.

Now? Now, we've chosen Wes. And Rigby doesn't get to touch me anymore. I take a step back. And then another.

"Don't. Still hurts."

"I'm sorry about that," Rigby says. I'd swear he means it, too. "They weren't supposed to take you. I wasn't aware how serious things were between the three of you before then."

I'm sorry, but did he say what I think he said? I'm tempted to check my ear for wax. "Are you telling me you were behind us getting fucking kidnapped?"

Rigby holds up his hands. That pricey beige sweater he's wearing seems all wrong when we're standing next to dumpsters and he's holding a weapon. Would he shoot me if

I shoved him into one of them to get his off-white wardrobe all dirty? "It was an accident. They were only supposed to take Wes. I sincerely do apologize."

Holy fuck. How did we not realize this guy is maximum-strength psychotic? A chilly breeze blows, and I can't stop shivering.

"You're saying you're the one running some freaky illegal porn-on-demand business?"

"I prefer to use the term 'bespoke.'"

"Your guys almost killed Adam. Aimed a gun at me. Told me to make Wes scream w—" I cut myself off. Fuck this guy. He doesn't get to see how much doing what I did to Wes wrecked me, even after knowing he didn't hate it.

Anyway, it's not effective to threaten a guy who has a gun if you don't have one yourself. If he didn't look so comfortable holding the damn thing, maybe, but that's an if for another lifetime.

"Trust me, I'd like to have a word with my men about that." Rigby pulls a face. "Especially since the three of you only seemed to get closer afterward. But something tells me that since the three of you got away and I haven't been able to reach any of my employees since, you've already taken care of making sure that mistake won't be made again."

"You're fucking right it won't." In spite of the pure horror of this shit, my chest swells. We protected Wes.

My phone buzzes frantically in my pocket. Ordinarily I'd say it's bad form to check your messages in front of a megalomaniac holding an expensive, engraved Colt, but I'm starting to think Rigby won't kill me. Not if he wants me. I hope.

Besides, it's probably Adam. I need to try and tell him to

stay the hell away from here until I can convince Rigby we should leave.

"Something wrong with Adam?" Rigby asks when I unlock the phone. But the steady buzz of messages isn't from Adam at all.

Wes: Back up

Wes: Back up

Wes: Back up

Wes: Back up

Wes: Back up

Wes: Back up

Wes: Back up

Wes: NOW

Out in the parking lot there's a squeal of tires. Headlights.

It isn't until I take several healthy steps backward and Rigby looks like he's still trying to figure out why there are high-beams barreling toward us that I fully grasp what's happening.

"Wes, don't." Not that he'll hear my horrified whisper.

But he keeps coming. I can't stop him.

It's a blurry mess when Wes's bumper plows into Rigby, bouncing off one of the massive dumpsters. The next thing I know, Rigby's pinned and sightless, half of him sprawled across the hood of Wes's car.

Blood all over those pretentious fucking clothes of his.

"Holy shit," I breathe. Then I realize Wes is half slumped over his steering wheel. "Wes."

He groans when I throw open the door. His airbag deployed and his face is a mess. There's blood coming from his nose, but he's moving. Still wearing his seat belt.

"Did I get him?" Wes is groggy and uncoordinated. Can't seem to figure out how to undo his buckle.

"Did you—are you fucking kidding me? What were you thinking? You could've killed yourself."

"S'okay." He reaches up through the open car door, caressing my cheek with his palm. "You're okay. I...thought he might kill you." Then he passes out again.

"Fuck." I shoot a text to Brennan.

Troy: SOS

Troy: Going to need a doctor. And your lake house.

Who fucking cares if this means owing Brennan a lifetime of favors. That's a problem for later.

Then I call Adam.

"There you are," he says when he answers. "I've been waiting by the employee exit."

"Get over to the dumpsters. Fast."

I reach into Wes's car to turn off the ignition.

"Pull the car around," I tell Adam when he runs up. "You need to get Wes to Brennan's doctor. I'll take care of the body."

Adam's eyes widen when he takes in the scene. "What the hell happened?"

I nod to Rigby's body, then to the gun, which I snatch and stuff into the back of my pants. "He was trying to keep Wes away from us. Liam thinks he was in business with whoever tried to take Ravi awhile back. He's the one who had us kidnapped. I told Wes to get out of here and instead he ran Rigby the fuck over."

Adam's mouth drops open. "I can't believe he did that."

"Rigby, he said Wes loves us." My eyes burn. Maybe that shouldn't be relevant right now, but it is to me. It just fucking is.

Adam smiles slightly. "Then maybe I can."

He runs for the parking lot, pulling the Mustang up a few minutes later. "Not exactly the best car to transport an injured person, but it's what we've got," he says when he jumps out.

At that moment, Wes groans. We extract him from the car as gently as we can and move him to the Mustang's passenger seat.

"Careful," I tell Adam. Even though I know he will be.

"It would be better if we could call an ambulance." Adam shakes his head. "We're not supposed to move him."

"If we don't move literally all of this as fast as possible, we're fucked. Wes especially for being behind the wheel."

"I know." Adam nods. "Don't worry. I'll take care of him."

It hurts to swallow. "I know. Help me get the body into Wes's trunk. I'll take care of the rest." I gesture to the bloody scene.

After we handle Rigby, I give a quick kiss to Adam and place a gentle one on Wes's forehead. "Be careful."

There's blood on my shirt, so I strip it off and stuff it into the trunk with Rigby's body. "Fuck, it's too cold for this," I mutter. Then I sprint for the hotel. I need some of that fucking enzyme cleaner Wes is always talking about. Or some bleach. Anything to wash away the blood on the ground or at least make it so a crime lab can't tell who it came from.

Thanks to us following Wes around like lost puppies these past few weeks, I know there's a room close by where they keep linens and cleaning stuff.

My lungs burn as I approach the building. I need to get in and out fast, before anyone notices what's going on back here. Before anyone sees me. I've never tried to clean up a crime scene before, but then again, Wes never killed someone before.

Jesus. The reality almost stops me cold.

Wes *killed* someone for us. Wes loves us. So I'm going to do this for him.

Then I'm going to pin his ass down and make sure he knows we love him back, and that he's never allowed to leave again.

CHAPTER THIRTY-SEVEN

TROY

My feet slip on the frozen grass a handful of times. By the time I've got Wes's car all the way in the lake, I've face-planted against the bumper at least seven times.

At least the body's in the water. Hopefully being dragged to the bottom by gators as we speak.

Never dumped a body before. The reality of it chills me more than the cold front. At least I found another shirt to wear in the gym bag on Wes's passenger seat.

The sound of running footsteps has me raising the gun I took from Rigby. I drop it to my side as fast as I can when I realize the person running toward me is Wes.

"Fuck me." Then I'm running too.

We crash together in a tangle of limbs, Adam pulling up the rear.

Wes presses his lips to mine. "You're okay. Thank God you're okay."

I pull back, scanning him for damage under the moonlight. “Me? Kitten, you’re the one who smashed your car and then passed the fuck out.”

“The doctor said it was something called syncope,” Adam says.

Wes nods. “Too much adrenaline. I’m fine. Sorry I scared you.”

“No sorries.” My fingers tangle in Adam’s hair. My other arm wraps around Wes’s waist. I’m freezing, and I can’t get close enough to them.

I pull back. “So fucking glad you guys are okay. You are, right? You’re both okay?”

“We’re okay.” Wes shivers against me, pulling us close. Then he straightens, eyes wide. “What did you do with Rigby?”

I hook my thumb toward the lake. “Let’s say all those gators in there will eat well tonight.”

Adam doesn’t look at all surprised. Wes, though, takes a second.

“Oh. God.” His body crumples to the grass. “Jesus, you shouldn’t have had to do that.”

“You saved us, Kitten; least I could do was handle cleanup.”

“Like when one of us cooks dinner, the other cleans up,” Adam offers.

“That’s not at all the same,” Wes almost whines.

“Hey.” I get on my knees in front of him. Give his cheek a playful, gentle slap. “He deserved it. I’d destroy anyone who tried to hurt either of you. Like Adam did when his father threatened to keep us apart. Like you did tonight, by killing Rigby. That was fucking brutal, by the way.”

“He thought he owned you. Both of you. Whatever he was planning to do with you, I couldn’t let him. The two of you own me; that's how it works. You own me, and I own you. Nobody's allowed to take you away."

Fuck, our kitten is so fucking fierce. A collective shiver passes through all of us. The weather, Wes's declaration, everything.

"Let's get inside," I tell them. "There's a fireplace we can use to warm up."

We all stumble in on tired legs. Me, I'm in the middle of an adrenaline crash. The other two don't look much better.

Which reminds me. "Really sorry about your car, Kitten."

The look on his face when he told us it was all he had? Wrecked me.

"I'm not." Wes's fingers find the hair at my nape for a moment before collapsing onto the lumpy old sofa. "Between you and the car, it was never a question. Things can be replaced. People can't." He scrunches his forehead in thought. "Not that I'm exactly sure how I'll do that yet. I kind of quit my job this evening."

Adam looks at me with his eyebrow raised. *Should we tell him?*

We definitely should.

My oldest friend goes over to where Wes is sprawled with his head back, climbing into his lap. "We had an idea about that, actually."

Wes blinks his eyes open. "Oh yeah?"

Brennan's fireplace looks poorly maintained, but I'm able to get a fire going. As soon as I've got heat circulating, I collapse on the sofa next to both of them. "Less of an idea, more of a deal."

"Like a contract," Adam adds.

Wes looks back and forth between us. "I'm not following."

I reach over to squeeze his upper thigh, getting a little of Adam's ass in the process. "After you left the other night, Adam and I talked. We decided we weren't going to let you go. We figured we'd start with offering you something we knew you'd want in exchange for sticking around and giving us access to your tight ass."

"You're saying you wanted me to whore myself out to you?" His tired laugh soothes my soul.

"That's right." I squeeze Wes's leg. "If that didn't work, we figured we'd have to kidnap you again. Take you out to that abandoned bed and breakfast, chain you up, and leave you with the ghosts until you agreed to never leave us again."

For a guy we've just threatened with kidnapping, Wes hardly seems fazed. "You know, I didn't actually leave you guys. I went to visit my brother. To patch things up with him, to clear my head, and yes, to maybe consider whether or not all of us being together was the right thing, but I hadn't decided yet."

"Too risky," Adam says.

"Never hurts to be proactive," I agree.

"Well." Wes threads his fingers into my hair again. "I can't see falling in love with someone else I trust enough to do the things I like you both to do to me. You're stuck with me at this point."

Adam perks up. "You really love us?"

Something inside me settles. Hearing it from Rigby was one thing. Hearing it from Wes? I didn't realize how much I needed it from him. "We love you too, you know."

"Surprise." Adam's all sarcasm.

Fine. I suppose it's been obvious for a while, at least on our end.

"Well, it took me by surprise." Wes's free arm pulls Adam in for a kiss, his tongue licking against Adam's lip.

"You two are so fucking hot," I moan. When Adam begins grinding himself against Wes, I add, "Probably better if we don't fuck you tonight though, Kitten. You've been through a lot. You need rest."

Adam groans and pulls away. "Please, not another lecture on the importance of sleep." He regards Wes seriously. "You'll have to get used to those."

"I'm not lecturing about anything. Wes fucking killed someone tonight. He's not from our world, and if he's not reeling yet, he might be later. He already got so overwhelmed he passed out. Besides, his asshole's probably still wrecked from last time. All I'm saying is we should take a beat, right?"

Adam signs. "Not that I'm happy about it, but Troy's got a point."

But Wes has a gleam in his eye. "I haven't gotten to watch the two of you together yet."

"You could have if you'd stuck around that time you brought food up to Rigby's hotel room."

"No, I fucking couldn't have," Wes grits out. "Even then I didn't like the idea of seeing you two with someone else. I just wasn't ready to admit it yet. Honestly, Rigby's lucky I didn't kill him sooner."

"Aww. Kitten's got claws, Adam."

"Spicy." My friend nods. "I love it."

Wes sits up, looking more alert. "Look, I'm serious. Rigby wanted to take you away from me, and if I'm stuck with you, then it's like I said. You're stuck with me too."

"We're all stuck with each other," Adam agrees. "It's good that we love you back."

"In a fucked-up, kinky way," I murmur.

"I don't care how you love me as long as you do." Wes glances at me and then at Adam. "Now, let me see you fuck him."

I slide off the sofa and pull myself up to standing. "Let's see. We didn't exactly come prepared. Wonder if there's any lube out here."

"It's Brennan's place," Adam points out.

"True, that pervert's paraded every twink from here to the Georgia state line through here."

"Your pimp seems like a real piece of work," Wes says.

"Ex-pimp." Adam nuzzles Wes's neck. "We quit."

"Yeah, that was the deal Adam mentioned. The B&B you took us to? We made an offer on it yesterday. We can all live there together, help you run the place. Help you with repairs."

Wes's eyes go wide. "What? You can't do that."

"Try and fight us. You'll lose," Adam puts in. "Anyway, Troy and I worked construction a little after we left home. I'm handy with a circular saw."

I clear my throat. "He's lying. Don't let Adam near any sharp shit. He's excellent at pounding things, though." I laugh. "Bonus, there's that lake out back in case we ever need to dispose of any more bodies."

"I'd really like to have that be a thing we never do again," Wes insists.

"Oh. Also, Brennan bought this farm nearby that used to have a cult living there, so we'll practically be neighbors with him." Adam looks excited, but Wes does not.

Honestly, poor guy looks like he's got heartburn. Maybe

it's all the stress. "That's not the selling point you might think it is. Anyway, you should withdraw the offer. Even at a reduced price, that property is way out of my price range. And it's going to need repairs we can't do ourselves. No way I can even begin to handle that."

"But we can," Adam insists.

"Right." I lean in to claim Wes's lips for a second. "You can't stop us. It's already in the works."

"Jesus, Rigby wasn't kidding when he said I was the gold digger." Poor Wes looks devastated.

"You're not digging anything when we're practically throwing it at you. Listen, our buddy Michael talked us into investing most of our earnings. We've got plenty of money. We hadn't quit yet because we didn't know what else to do, but now we know."

"Yeah. We're going to buy a house for you, and you're going to be our whore." Adam's getting too much amusement from this.

Wes sighs. "You're going to make me regret calling you that forever, aren't you?"

"Without question." I put my hand on Wes's shoulder. "Now. Let me go see about that lube."

The bathroom cabinet provides what I'm looking for, and when I return, Wes and Adam are kissing again on the couch.

"Starting without me?"

"Trying to keep him awake until you got back."

"Hey. I'm fully awake here." Wes yawns as soon as the words are out of his mouth.

"That's sad, Kitten. I was only gone for about thirty seconds."

Adam chuckles and climbs out of Wes's lap, settling on a

thick area rug in front of the fire. "Hurry, then. Get over here so you can fuck me, babe." He turns to Wes. "Unless you want me to fuck him?"

Wes licks his lips, considering. "I want you to ride him," he tells Adam.

And here I am rubbing my hands together like a wicked movie villain. "This'll be fun."

I slick myself up, and Adam climbs on top. "You want to stretch him out, Kitten?"

"Not sure I know how."

"Grab the lube and finger me a little. Easy peasy," Adam says.

The look of concentration on Wes's face is adorable as he prods carefully between Adam's cheeks.

Who turns to say, "Babe, Troy plowed into you with hardly any prep at all. I promise, I can handle more than that."

"Do you like it though?" Wes swallows. "I like it when you guys make it hurt. I don't want to do that to you if it's not your thing."

Aww. Wes's cheeks look extra rosy in the glow of the firelight.

Adam reaches down, sliding his hand along Wes's arm. "Whatever you want to do to me, I'll like it because it's you."

"As long as you're not performing with me. I never want that."

"Never," I promise, and Adam nods his agreement. "Now climb up here and ride me, Adam."

We haven't done this in a while. For whatever reason, Rigby liked it when Adam fucked me, and he was our most regular client. A lot of the guys who hired us liked to be double-teamed. Occasionally, I'd fuck Adam while he fucked his ex, but that didn't happen often.

"Oh hell." It's more of a groan as Adam's heat wraps around me. "Just remembered Ruby. You did break up with her, right?"

Adam lets out a low moan. "Told you. I sent a text."

"I'll send her a fucking text. Make sure she gets the message." Wes is pulling off his clothes. There's want in his eyes. And determination. He straddles my legs, taking up a position pressed right against Adam's back. He snakes one arm around Adam's waist, the other wraps around Adam's shoulder, with a hand resting on Adam's pec. He captures Adam's earlobe between his teeth. "That day I saw you outside the hotel with her? I fucking hated it."

Adam whines. "We still thought you hated us."

"Maybe I did. Didn't stop me from wanting you."

Can't help but laugh at Wes's possessiveness. "Be sure to let her down easy, Kitten."

Wes makes a noise in his throat. Sort of a rumble of satisfaction, maybe also one of ownership, given the way he's pawing at Adam. The hand on Adam's waist slides lower, taking hold of his cock.

"Oh, damn, that's good," Adam moans.

"That's it, Kitten. Jerk him off. Help him come. After the night we've had, I won't take long."

It's a good thing I'm on my back. The subtle, tired shaking in my muscles that's followed me since the hotel has gotten worse. It's difficult to simply keep my hands on Adam's waist, to keep moving with him as he rises and falls on my cock.

I'm wrecked and strung out, needing release. I could blow at any second. All I'm waiting for is Adam.

"Harder, babe."

Not sure which of us Adam is talking to, I lift my hips as best I can, fucking up into him. Wes shuttles his hand faster over Adam's cock. Soon enough we've got him shaking and spilling all over us both. The second he's spent, I let loose, shouting my release so loud it echoes around the little cabin.

At first I'm thinking Wes hasn't come yet, but then I realize he's been rubbing off on Adam's ass. His breath stutters as he shoots all over Adam's backside.

We all collapse together, too worn out to get up and shower yet.

Wes lifts his head to look at me. "You guys don't really want to buy me a house, do you?"

"Nope." I press my lips against his. "We want to buy all of us a house. Oh, also, when we went back with a realtor, that chubby cat was there, only less chubby and she had a litter of four kittens. Not sure if she was dumped or what, but she's ours now, like you are. Promised the realtor a massive bonus to make sure they're all taken care of until we move in."

Maybe it's the fire, but Wes's eyes look downright misty. "That... Wow. I've always wanted a pet. Gina had allergies."

"Well, you've got five of them now. And you've got us. And you're never allowed to leave," Adam reminds him tiredly. "We'll tie you up in that little cottage out back if we have to."

"If that's what you want." Wes gives me a tired smile. "You know that place is on acres of land. Lots of room for the two of you to chase me down. Or whatever."

Fuck. Yes. This is going to be so good.

EPILOGUE

MICHAEL

DEAN'S HAVING A NIGHTMARE. Again.

I've seen it so many times, I've almost got it broken down beat by beat.

"No," he whispers. "Please, somebody help."

A mournful whine leaves his throat.

"Where—where are you taking her?"

This is usually when the tears start.

"No. No. No," he whispers again.

My phone buzzes in my hand.

Troy: Party next weekend! It's a holiday party and a we got a new house party and a we're quitting the business party.

Adam: And a moving party so wear sturdy clothes.

Wes: Why did I get added to this group chat?

Troy: Because you're a whore now too, Kitten. Our whore.

Ravi: Wes! Hi!! Liam wants to talk to you. To thank

you for taking care of something I think? Something about trash removal

Fallon: Guys I'm begging you. Do not talk to my brother that way where I can see or hear it.

Wes: Karma, brother. For all those times I walked in on you and PJ fucking.

PJ: Won't happen if you don't visit, Wes. Problem solved!

Idiots.

I silence my notifications and return the phone to my back pocket. Just in time for—

"No!" Dean shoots up into a sitting position, his eyes flying open in the middle of the scream.

At first he doesn't notice me standing here by his bed. His gaze is unfocused. Sightless. His breath saws in and out, ragged and loud.

He runs his hands through his blond curls before falling back to the mattress. His head hits the pillow with a quiet thump. One hand presses against his chest, as if he can keep his heart from flying out. Right now I know it's going a mile a minute, and he's willing it to calm down. He's got his eyes squeezed shut, as if he can make what he just saw disappear by hoping hard enough.

"Bad dream?"

"Fuck." His eyes fly open again. Tears cling to his lashes as he studies me in the glow of the little cat night-light his daughter picked out for him. "Mike."

He stares at me.

I stare at him.

For a minute he holds out on me, even though we both know he'll crack first. We both know what he's going to do.

Sure enough, he slides over to the far side of the double

bed, pulling the sheets back as he goes. He's wearing a loose pair of basketball shorts and nothing else. Orange. I hate the color orange.

"Those shorts are ugly."

"School colors," he murmurs. "You know that."

"Take them off."

He hesitates. Why does he even bother?

"Dean. You want me to make it better, don't you?"

A long, tired sigh. "You know I do."

"Then take the shorts off."

They snag on his erection as he pushes them down and kicks them to the floor. I love that he's already hard.

I love that when he wakes up in tears, he reaches for me like I'm the one who can save him. Or ruin him.

Most days I'm not sure which I want to do more.

Maybe I just want to ruin myself. For hating him. For wanting him. Not that I'll ever give in to that want. Neither of us deserve it.

"You need to earn it."

His Adam's apple bobs with a thick swallow. "I know."

"But you still want it."

"Yes."

"You need it." Not a question. We both know.

"Yes."

"Beg me."

"Please, Michael."

"You don't deserve it."

"I know I don't deserve it."

"Tell me how much you owe me."

"I owe you everything."

"That's right."

When he reaches for me again, I pull away, moving

around to stand by the foot of the bed. He's too tall, so his feet hang off the end. His daughter sleeps on a queen mattress with her favorite princess blanket down the hall. In the primary bedroom.

Dean will sacrifice anything for her. As he should. As if it absolves him of anything.

"Hands and knees," I tell him.

Long legs tangle in mismatched thrift shop sheets in his rush to comply. He slides to the floor, balls his hands into fists, bracing. Head bowed. Waiting.

He's not an athlete anymore, not the way he used to be, but he still keeps in shape. So it takes a while before his arms start to shake with the effort of holding himself up. Until the muscles in his back and shoulders start to bunch. Until he's whining for a reason that has nothing to do with his nightmare.

"Mike. Please." He whines again.

But you know what he's not doing? He's not thinking about the dream. He's not thinking about *her*.

Neither of us is.

When the tremors in his arms get stronger, when he looks like he can barely hold on, is when I finally let him move.

"Good boy," I say. "Now crawl."

THANK YOU FOR READING DUBIOUS!! I hope you loved this dark MMM romance. Find out what happens next with Michael and Dean in Payback.

Dean

Everything I do is for my daughter. Everything.

Including working as a male escort to support us both.

I may be a dumb college dropout with zero marketable skills, but as a former athlete I can make good money from my body, and I can give my little girl the life I didn't have.

There's one big problem, and that problem is my daughter's uncle. Michael hates me. He has every reason to. It's my fault his sister, my kid's mom, is dead.

But I can't raise her alone. Ella needs her uncle. We both do.

So, I'll do anything it takes to keep him around.

Anything.

Michael

Dean was supposed to be mine.

But he ended up with my sister, and now she's gone.

He's my connection to my niece, but there's so much toxicity between us now.

Around other people, we get along for the greater good. When it's only the two of us though?

Well, I'm enjoying making him pay.

If only I could ignore the part of me that never stopped wanting him.

THANK YOU FOR READING DUBIOUS!! I hope you loved this dark MMM romance. Find out what happens next with Michael and Dean's enemies to lovers romance in Payback. Find it at https://books2read.com/u/3nd7o6

. . .

Want a bonus epilogue, where Wes, Adam, and Troy do porn, but this time the legit kind? Go to https://dl.bookfunnel.com/kle5qdx8u9

Want early access to future releases? Go to https://www.patreon.com/cw/BethChristopherRomance

ACKNOWLEDGMENTS

Huge thanks to all my readers, most of all my street team and those of you who have made it your mission to get the word out about these books. You have my deepest gratitude.

Thank you to Elizabeth Babski at Babski Creative Studios for working hard to come up with an awesome cover design and for bravely putting up her hand to be one of my first beta readers. Thank you to Sydney Feron @editivepublishing for seeing exactly what these guys needed. Many thanks to Lea Vickery and Kate Wood for proofreading and advocating for these characters!

Most of all, thanks always to my husband and kids for your unwavering support. Well. Mostly unwavering. To my youngest who said, “My friends think you’re cool but I don’t get why,” I will remember what you said when your birthday rolls around.

ABOUT BETH CHRISTOPHER

Beth Christopher is not part of the cool kids club. She's part of the "went to bed early with her dog and a book" club, the "said something awkward in public again" club, and founding member of the "got distracted thinking about ramen again" club (the meetings involve sitting lost in thought while her cats judge her). She writes down the stories in her head when she remembers to, and when she's not writing she's likely doing unusual kitchen things (like making cheese out of cashews) or watching Ted Lasso (the Christmas episode is the best episode and she will die on that hill). She lives with her family and her fur babies in Belle Argo, Florida.

ALSO BY BETH CHRISTOPHER

The Belle Argo Escorts

1. Blackmail (enemies to lovers, hurt/comfort, brat/a-hole)
2. Switch (age gap, teacher student, Dom awakening)
3. Guardian (age gap, guardian, power dynamics, vigilante)
4. Dubious (throuple, age gap, late bi awakening)
5. Payback (enemies to lovers, taboo adjacent)

Related Standalone: Dark Romance AU (hitman and male escort, in the Belle Argo Universe, originally written as part of the multi-author series, Because Cannon Sucks!

www.ingramcontent.com/pod-product-compliance
Lightning Source LLC
LaVergne TN
LVHW041101080826
845145LV00007B/1645
9781969810213